In Death We Trust

Books by the same author

What's Truth Got To Do With It?
ISBN: 979-1904440802

The Molecule Man
ISBN: 978-19044440963

In Death We Trust

by

David Crigman

Librario

FT Pbk

Published by

Librario Publishing Ltd.

ISBN 13: 978-1906775117

Copies can be ordered via the Internet
www.librario.com

or from:

Brough House, Milton Brodie, Kinloss
Moray IV36 2UA
Tel/Fax No 00 44 (0)1343 850 617

Printed and bound in the UK
By Cpod, a division of The Cromwell Press Group

Typeset by 3btype.com

Cover design by Melissa Thomas-Anderson

Prologue

Bright red angels' trumpets plants in terracotta pots were strategically located about the enclosed courtyard so as to provide some shade from the relentless sun, while untrained bougainvillea spilled carelessly over the top of the white stucco walls. In the centre of the area stood a circular stone table with a tiled surface and four lime green wicker chairs crowded around it. Although the late afternoon sun was still fierce, the air felt good to her after the grotesque experience she had just endured.

Only one of the chairs was occupied. So engrossed was the heavy-set man in two small booklets he was poring over that he did not even lift his eyes as she lowered herself silently into the chair opposite.

"You're dead," she finally announced.

"Feels good" he answered after a pause, leaning back in the chair and tossing the plum-coloured booklets on the table in her direction. "And it didn't even hurt."

"I've just spoken to the mortician. He's coming for your body immediately. You'll be cremated tomorrow," she continued, now able to see clearly that the booklets were British Passports. The pickpocket must have found his prey and now the local forger could get to work.

"Did the quack ask any awkward questions?" he enquired.

"He was only interested in his eighty bucks. Mind you, he did say you looked older than forty-one," she laughed.

It was her laugh that had first caught his attention in the Casino at Cabo San Lucas four years ago. Despite the massive injustice that had blighted his life, or perhaps because of it, beautiful women were often attracted to him. His square face and brooding eyes somehow exuded mystery, holding the promise that here was a man with a story to tell. But Jenna wasn't beautiful. Her skin was too pale in contrast to her jet black hair. Her face was too small for the powerful athleticism of her body and three years working as a craps dealer in Las Vegas had made her as tough as nails and it showed in the sharpness of her features. And that laugh was as feminine as a tumbler of Jack Daniels. It began deep within the flat belly and exploded from her chest like a runaway truck.

Chapter 1

"Alibi. Tell me, Senora, what is this word?" demanded the hard-faced man in his thick accent, swiftly tossing back yet another shot of cheap tequila whilst drawing in breath through his yellow teeth as the harsh liquor hit the back of his throat. The scar tissue across both eyebrows, coupled with the high cheekbones characteristic of the Sonoran Mexican, rendered the eyes almost invisible, just narrow slits lost in a raw, sallow face, brutally re-shaped by the countless fists that had landed on it in and out of the ring.

His question had been addressed to the raven-haired American woman with the prominent beauty spot on her upper lip sitting opposite him in the run-down Tamazula cantina but, as he spoke, her attention was distracted by the ringing of a cell phone, which had been lying dormant on the plastic table amidst yesterday's salsa droppings and alongside her untouched Cuba Libra.

"I'm with him now," she breathed quietly into the silver phone. "You've waited this long, so learn to be a bit more patient" she continued, before sliding her scarlet thumbnail abruptly across the cut-off button and turning her gaze back to the desperado opposite.

"It's a Latin word. It means I was somewhere else and I can prove it. So it wasn't me who did it. You get the picture?" came her reply.

Jesus Olivares nodded his understanding in her direction whilst holding the smeared, empty glass up in the air which signalled his need to the disinterested bartender who eventually aimed his bulk at their table, armed with the bottle that bore no label and a dirty saucer bearing a couple of tired-looking lime wedges.

"Ola. Alibi. "*Coartada*" en Espanol. Where the guilty hide," he grunted, squeezing a piece of lime in his gnarled fist so that a few drops of juice and half a dozen pips fell into the re-filled glass. "So why does that make you look for a cadaver?"

"There's no need for you to know," she replied sharply, finding herself fascinated by the misshapen knuckles that made the back of his hand look like a chunk of dark brown volcanic rock. "Just give me a price. It's got to be white. Male. Unembalmed. Middle-aged. Natural death. And fresh. I've checked the Law. In this part of Mexico an unembalmed body must be buried within 24 hours. It should be easy to find one"

The old fighter's upper lip curled in distaste as he privately acknowledged that the Americana had done her homework. Forty bucks could buy the whole shooting match. An empty prayer from the priest over the untreated corpse in a plywood box and the final drop into a common grave before the body was even properly cold.

Olivares slowly reached for the packet of Delicados and the orange two-bit lighter that sat on top of it. In his fighting days he'd never smoked, but he'd been surrounded by the agents and hangers-on who did. As the hard dealing over the prize money reached its critical point, he'd always observed that was when they reached for their cigarettes. Silence was a powerful bargaining tool and he let the grey-blue smoke linger in the air and the pungent Delicado aroma fill his nostrils while the sharp-featured face opposite watched him and waited.

"Where you from, lady?" he eventually asked.

"Worked Vegas for a while, but New York raised," came the quick reply. "Why do you ask?

"I fought at The Garden once, Senora," he said gently. "Towards the end of my days. Fodder, they called me. New word to me. Strange word. You know that word?"

"How much?" she snapped back, growing tired of his crude bartering technique. "It's a price I want, not a review of a has-been career"

"Fodder for the new boy. Give him the viejo who's hit the canvas too many times," the boxer continued, ignoring her jibe and moving at his own chosen speed. "I teach him a lesson but the ref give the New York boy the decision. Ten thousand bucks they paid me. And that's what I want for a cadaver" he suddenly announced in answer to her question. "If I'm caught stealing it from the grave, I lose my job and probably end up inside. So it's ten grand, Senora."

"I don't think so" she observed cruelly. "You dig holes in the Tamazula cemetery. You don't make ten grand in a year. Once the mourners leave, if there are any, all you've got to do is pull the body out of the box and put it in the trunk of my car. Then fill the hole. You get two grand."

His fists tightened instinctively at her arrogance, but experience reminded him of the fighter's trusted adage. Feint with the left and then bring over the right, and that's exactly what he did. "Two grand for the stiff, lady. OK, by me. But you're buying a *coartada*. So it's another eight grand to keep my mouth shut." It was the blow that won the contest.

Almost three weeks had passed before Olivares rang the Senora's silver phone and breathed the words that she and her lover had been awaiting with increasing anxiety. The excuse for a funeral took place at three o'clock the same afternoon and was attended only by the gentle priest and the Panamanian crackhead who shared the shanty house with the recently deceased American alcoholic.

Within the hour the body was stretched out on the weeping woman's bed, a stranger's death mask and the aura of the grave permeating the poorly furnished room and frightening her, as the already discolouring body was subjected to a perfunctory examination by the old Tamazulan medico, Doctor Hidalgo, whose unsteady hand quickly scratched out the death certificate, identifying cardiac arrest as the cause of death.

"I'd been away for a couple of days" she sobbed to the doctor from the corner of the room where she lay back, slumped in the brocade armchair and beginning to heave as the smell of death and decay hit her stomach. "I told him it was the liquor or me. He was like that when I came back. Cold as ice".

"Been dead at least twenty four hours, maybe a lot longer" muttered the old man. "Still, no doubt it's a natural death. Corazon. His heart. You can have an autopsy to confirm, if you like. Costs a lot extra."

"No. No autopsy. He'd had trouble with his heart and he wouldn't lay off the booze. No need for an autopsy."

"OK. Your decision. I need his name and place and date of birth."

"Inglese," she replied, wiping her dry eyes with a white linen handkerchief. "Birmingham. Inglaterra. He was forty-one but I don't know his exact date of birth."

"Forty-one. Looks older than that. Drink. This town. It does that, you know. And his name?"

"Paul. Paul Arthur Locke. With an 'e' on the end. Everybody called him Pal," she replied, thinking to herself that the old quack should know a good deal about the effects of booze, looking at his tremulous hands and smelling the liquor on his breath.

"There's the certificate, then," he declared, swiftly completing the information with his cheap ballpoint pen. "You'll need it for the funeral. You want help with arranging that?" he asked, stuffing his copy of the papers into the worn black leather bag which sat on the bed alongside the body. The woman was silent for a few seconds, as she watched him screw the disposable gloves up into a tight ball which he dropped into the waste bin at the foot of the bed, along with the wooden spatula with which he'd poked and prodded about in the dead man's mouth.

"No. I've decided on that already," she eventually replied, shaking her head and letting the long black hair fall across her face as she got out of her seat, deftly avoiding the Doctor's proffered hand. "He's to be cremated. I know that's what he'd have preferred."

"Your choice" he grunted. "Cheaper. Then, that just leaves my fee. Eighty dollars."

As soon as he'd departed with four twenty dollar bills folded into his pigskin wallet, the woman closed the unlined yellow curtains in the bedroom and, averting her eyes from the exhumed corpse, made her way along a flag-stoned passageway towards the walled courtyard at the rear of the building, already talking on her phone to the mortician that Olivares had suggested, so as to ensure that she did not instruct the same firm that had carried out the first funeral.

Bright red angels' trumpets plants in terracotta pots were strategically located about the enclosed courtyard so as to provide some shade from the relentless sun, while untrained bougainvillea spilled carelessly over the top of the white stucco walls. In the centre of the area stood a circular stone table with a tiled surface and four lime green wicker chairs crowded around it. Although the late afternoon sun was still fierce, the air felt good to her after the grotesque experience she had just endured.

Only one of the chairs was occupied. So engrossed was the heavy-set man in two small booklets he was poring over that he did not even lift his eyes as she lowered herself silently into the chair opposite.

"You're dead," she finally announced.

"Feels good" he answered after a pause, leaning back in the chair and tossing the plum-coloured booklets on the table in her direction. "And it didn't even hurt."

"I've just spoken to the mortician. He's coming for your body immediately. You'll be cremated tomorrow," she continued, now able to see clearly that the booklets were British Passports. The pickpocket must have found his prey and now the local forger could get to work.

"Did the quack ask any awkward questions?" he enquired.

"He was only interested in his eighty bucks. Mind you, he did say you looked older than forty-one," she laughed.

It was her laugh that had first caught his attention in the Casino at Cabo San Lucas four years ago. Despite the massive injustice that had blighted his life, or perhaps because of it, beautiful women were often attracted to him. His square face and brooding eyes somehow exuded mystery, holding the promise that here was a man with a story to tell. But Jenna wasn't beautiful. Her skin was too pale in contrast to her jet black hair. Her face was too small for the powerful athleticism of her body and three years working as a craps dealer in Las Vegas had made her as tough as nails and it showed in the sharpness of her features. And that laugh was as feminine as a tumbler of Jack Daniels. It began deep within the flat belly and exploded from her chest like a runaway truck.

After six rigorous months amongst the small-time gold miners fifty miles north of Cabo he'd been in need of some female company and the loud American voice and raucous laughter had made him turn in her direction. Her green eyes had instinctively locked on to his and, although he was considerably older than she was, his rugged looks and sense of intrigue had captivated her. She gave him her CV soon enough. The daughter of a wealthy New York architect, long since ostracized by the family because she had refused to go to college or follow the pre-ordained path. She had chosen the open road and adventure. In return she had become the black sheep. They had been together for over two years before he trusted her enough to tell her the whole of his story, explaining how, after his release, he had just wanted to get the hell out of England.

Drifting around South America, firstly riding with the gauchos in Argentina, before spending time as an *esmeraldero* in the Muzo Valley in Columbia buying emeralds from the *quaqueros*, the treasure poachers, who scavenged along the bed of the Rio Itoco and tunneled into the hillsides at night, forever seeking the elusive green fire from deep within the mines. His perilous weekly journey from the Valley to Bogota involved avoiding the clutches of the National Police and dodging the bullets of rival gangs of *quaqueros*. The rewards garnered from the illicit haul were substantial and he'd built up a considerable sum by the time he moved on, crossing the Darian Gap and eventually settling in Mexico where he'd first seen those green eyes which glinted just like the emeralds the *quaqueros* pulled out of the hillside. By the time he had recounted the full and bitter history of what had driven him to such an emotionally meaningless, peripatetic life she had found herself thirsting for revenge as much as he did.

Chapter 2

Without giving any signal the metallic blue-black Cadillac Escalade turned sharply off the main road and headed recklessly up the hill towards the small village. The road quickly narrowed, but the driver made no allowance for the fact that Berkshire by-ways had not been constructed for American urban tanks which were even more imposing than the heaviest Range-Rover, and the odd vehicle that he encountered coming towards him was bullied off the thin tarmac and on to the muddy grass verge. All of the glass panels had been custom tinted so as to render the occupant invisible, but the locals knew only too well the identity of Raymond Leon Millard and his team of enforcers. Just beyond the fifteenth century church, the Escalade swung to its left and then abruptly halted at the two enormous wrought iron gates which guarded the end of the long drive to the Keeling Estate that lay hidden behind the perimeter of tall conifers. Razor wire ran along the stone wall that extended around the full perimeter of the estate.

The driver's electric window glided down noiselessly and an arm, swathed in the bulky sleeve of an Armani leather jacket, emerged to punch the code into the keypad angled off the iron stanchion alongside the right hand gate. The manicured index finger struck the four digits in quick succession. 1604. Millard never had any difficulty in remembering the code. His birthday was on the sixteenth of the month and four was the total of men that he had killed to date.

Too impatient to wait for the gates to open fully, Millard nosed the Escalade in their immediate path, the bonnet almost touching the iron RLM monogram and the powerful engine straining to take off. Until three years ago the property had been the private retreat of a publisher and had possessed a sense of serenity. Since Millard had acquired it, its elegance had been replaced by tasteless high-tech and its tranquility destroyed by loud juke box music and Estuary English.

The tree-lined drive ran for three quarters of a mile before it opened up into a large circular expanse featuring a lily covered koi pond with a stone statue of Jupiter as its centerpiece. The choice of the Supreme God of the Roman Pantheon, the Grand Protector of all Laws, was Millard's idea of irony.

Two Rottweillers sat impassively on the flagstones surrounding the pond, trained not to react to Millard's arrival when he shouted their names through the driver's window. Any intruder would have had his throat ripped out before he ever reached the main house.

On each side of the imposing set of stone steps which led up to the double front doors of the massive Tudor-style establishment stood a life size statue constructed in reconstituted Carrara white marble. Bacchus on the left and Hebe on the right.

To the side of the main house stood a coach house, now converted to a garage with its own air-conditioning system so that the cars were never subject to the vagaries of the English climate. The automatic doors hinged upwards to admit the Escalade which he eased in between the Bentley Arnage R and the brand new crimson Ferrari, the other stalls being occupied by the Mercedes 500, the black Mini Cooper S and the E-Type Jaguar. Hurrying along the covered passageway which connected with the side of the main house, he headed straight for the recreation room where a young black girl, dressed in a scarlet tank-top exposing plenty of cleavage and a bare midriff, with a real diamond in her navel above blue jean cut-off shorts, was stretched out on the white leather sofa staring at a plasma television screen which extended across the full length of the side wall. Her bare legs rested across the arm of the sofa and the blackness of her skin contrasted erotically with the whiteness of the leather. So absorbed was she in Jerry Springer's latest foul-mouthed female guest that she scarcely troubled to acknowledge Millard's entrance into the room.

"Can't you turn that crap off?" he barked at her in his ugly, clipped Essex accent, marching swiftly past the Wurlitzer and pouring himself a generous measure of Glenfiddich in the cut glass tumbler from behind the mahogany bar which he had shipped in from New Orleans.

"You had a call from LA", she announced flatly, not even lifting her head to look in his direction, nor making any attempt to comply with his demand.

"Yeh, so spit it out", he replied, walking behind her and sinking into one of the deep armchairs alongside a ceiling to floor glass partition which provided a complete view of the indoor pool and Jacuzzi which were situated on a lower level of the house.

"It was Tommy Langham" she continued, still staring with fixed eyes at the screen on which the studio guest was now baring her breasts defiantly at the camera while the audience hooted and whistled in delight. "He said he'd seen some good news in an American newspaper report. . . ," her voice tailing away in laughter as Springer's Security Guards tried to cover the woman's upper body with a blanket.

"Get to the point, Alicia, before I put my boot through that screen," Millard snarled.

Raising one long shapely leg up from the sofa so that Millard got a clear view, Alicia Daley ran her hand provocatively down its full length, making him wait before she eventually spoke. "Pal's dead. They found him collapsed in some dump in Mexico. Booze. Tommy said you're too late to send flowers. They burnt him last week."

Not a flicker of expression passed across Millard's face but a pulse on the right side of his neck started to beat visibly beneath the skin. It was an involuntary physical response of which he was well aware and his right hand went instinctively to cover it, so that the girl could not see any sign of reaction from him to the news. The narrowed eyes betrayed nothing. The iris was of almost the same blackness as the pupil, giving him what Pal had referred to in the trial as "the aspect of the Devil". As a young man his hair had been jet black and, whilst it was now thinner and tinged with grey, the impact of his darkness remained. In one look at a man's face an immediate impression is made in the mind of the observer. Some faces projected kindness or sorrow, fun or morbidity. Millard's face conveyed darkness. Devil darkness.

For several minutes he sat motionless while the crude laughter from the TV show erupted periodically from the screen, waiting for the pulse to quieten and reflecting on the enormity of the news that Alicia had just relayed. Suddenly, in one move, he threw the contents of the tumbler down his throat, unfurled his six foot three rangy frame from the chair and strode purposefully towards the double doors.

"Where you going, Ray?" piped the girl, this time half-turning her head towards him, "you've only just come in and you said we might drive up to town tonight".

"You ain't travelling nowhere tonight," he snapped. "Me? I've got a meeting later with Ecklund. He's pushing hard for his money. But first, I'm going celebrating. Enjoying a death." As he slammed the door behind him, she could hear his special sound as he disappeared down the hall. Somewhere between the noise of cruel laughter and the baying of an animal savaging its prey. It was exactly the same sound that he'd made when he'd slowly broken her forearm across his knee on the only occasion she'd tried to stand up to him. No-one stood up to Ray. That's what really excited her about him.

'Always take out the insurance.' Millard had learned that essential lesson the first time they had sent him down. Two hard years in Parkhurst. His organization had already removed a dozen Mercedes saloons from South London forecourts and spirited them into

Eastern Europe before an underling's loose tongue had blown the scheme apart. The coppers could only prove the last shipment of a couple of 500SL's and so he'd drawn a two stretch. That's when the old hands had started to talk to him about insurance. At first he'd paid scant regard to them on the basis that if they were so clever how come they were rotting inside Parkhurst Gaol. Then he began to see the differences between talking a good strategy and actually putting one into practice. By the time he came out he had built himself a reputation for being the man not to cross. The new look, high-tech master rogue. Not only had he delivered a sharpened spoon into the liver of Liverpool's prize villain, Ronnie Kelton, who was serving life for a double murder and had been bullying his way around the system for over a decade, but he'd also demonstrated that he had the brains to control the rackets yet never got caught. As Kelton had gone down he had pulled the weapon out of his own innards, thrust it straight through Millard's right calf and then bled to death on the concrete floor of his cell. No prisoner or guard had hurried to help him and no-one chose to say anything that might point the finger of guilt in any particular direction. Kelton was Millard's first successful death.

Cruising along in the outside lane of the M25 heading for the old Peckham haunts, Millard pressed the button on the walnut veneer that triggered the CD in full quadraphonic. The vehicle was in pristine condition just like he had always kept all of his cars. Jimmy Van Heusen and Sammy Cahn eased their gentle way into the privacy of the Escalade, courtesy of Frank the Maestro. Thrown casually on the front passenger seat was a bulky briefcase containing the hundred thousand he'd just taken out of his home safe before leaving the house. Smiling to himself, his thoughts wandered to the insurance policy that had saved him from a fourteen year sentence or worse. The policy in which Pal had been the premium and Millard had performed his second killing. His special sound filled the interior of the vehicle, momentarily drowning out Frank's "The September of My Years" as he re-lived the ecstasy of that death. Sweeter than the first, for this time the victim had been a copper.

Half an hour later, as he pulled into Hanover Street on the edge of Peckham where the old terrace houses still survived, he glanced at his watch. Bruce Tisdale would be in the dingy back room of "The Plume of Feathers" by now, like he was every night of his life, except when he was inside, which was fairly often. The gleaming Escalade stood out like a sore thumb in the squalid backstreet but everyone in the area knew it was his vehicle and it was as safe as if it had been under armed guard. All of South London knew that you didn't mess with Ray Millard. Pushing the battered street door open he strolled casually into the front bar where a silence immediately descended across the entire room as the regulars recognised the tall, brooding figure with the eyes of black. Nodding in the direction of the odd sycophantic greeting, he walked through the bar and into the back room where, in his customary position in the far corner, Bruce Tisdale was huddled over a pint of black and tan while he studied form for tomorrow's meeting at Kempton Park. All the other tables were deserted. This back bar was for the loners; for the hard men.

Bruce was old muscle. Crowbars, blackjacks, lead pipes and knuckledusters. Blunt instrument handiwork. Grievous bodily harm with intent. Always with a purpose. Always for money. Bruce had stood alongside Millard on that night all those years ago when Millard had shot the copper. They were still comrades in arms but nowadays they operated on different levels. Street level and penthouse. All because they were different in one major respect. Bruce was short in the brains department. Dark secrets were safe enough with him, but he had got caught too often and he wore the gaol years on his face and in the lines of his body. His head was square, too large for even his substantial body and he seemed to have occasional trouble in controlling its movements, causing Ray to suspect that the crowbar that put him down a couple of years back had done lasting neurological damage. Millard never used him now. The new enforcers were more subtle and more effective. Designer clothes, shaved heads, clean fingernails and a Beretta 92FS tucked into the armpit.

"How you doing, mate?" Bruce mumbled, the great head lurching upwards as Ray slid into the seat opposite him, placing the briefcase he had brought in from the car on the floor at his feet.

"Earning a crust," came the light response as the publican appeared with a fresh pint for Tisdale and a large Irish whisky for Millard which he placed carefully on the time-scarred table.

"On the house," he said quietly as he moved away and back towards the main bar. "Good to see you in here, Ray" he added emptily.

"Busy, are ya Bruce?" Millard asked.

"Yea, got a nice little job lined up. Keeping my hand in," came the reply.

"Glad to hear it. I got a meeting with Ecklund later. That bastard always wants his money yesterday. But I wanted to see you first mate. Rather than let you pick the news up on the grapevine."

"What news?" Tisdale enquired apprehensively.

"It's Pal, mate. He's dead. Drank himself into an early grave somewhere in Mexico. Tommy Langham phoned."

Tisdale looked across the table and stared into the eyes of the man opposite. Although it was almost impossible to distinguish between the iris and the pupil, Bruce Tisdale saw behind the blackness and recognised what lay in the deepness beyond. Triumph. The look of triumph. It was exactly the same sensation as when Bruce had watched from the Public Gallery in the Old Bailey as Ray and Pal had stood together in the dock over twenty years ago and the jury had returned their verdicts.

Slowly picking up his fresh drink, Tisdale took a long draught of the beer and put the straight-sided glass carefully back on its grubby, stiff cardboard mat before eventually offering any response. "Losers die early" he grunted. "And Pal was a loser. Big time." There was little expression in the voice, but Tisdale was not comfortable. Even blunt instrument merchants had certain basic standards. There was little satisfaction in crushing someone who had done nothing and had never represented a threat. Over the long years he had avoided thinking about Pal and news of his death was a painful reminder of what he preferred to forget.

Meanwhile, Millard was leaning back in his chair, sipping his whisky and chatting easily about the case and how he'd beaten the rap at Pal's expense. Chipping in with the odd comment for appearance's sake and readily accepting the chasers that the publican steadily brought at Millard's behest, Tisdale quickly realized that his drinking companion had sought him out for only one reason. He was celebrating Pal's death. Relishing it. And, on the subject of Pal, Tisdale was the only man with whom Millard could speak freely. By recounting the sordid details of the wrong they had done him, Millard was satisfying himself like a vulture picking at the red carcass flattened on the highway. What made it worse was that Tisdale knew that he could not risk offending the most feared criminal in London and, with a growing sense of self-loathing, he heard himself joining in the contemptible exercise of picking over the bones.

"You always got to have the insurance in place," Millard repeated yet again. "And we had the best Lloyds could offer," he laughed. At least it was meant to be a laugh, but it sent a shudder down Tisdale's spine, for it was the same sound he'd heard when Millard pulled the trigger and the copper had slumped into the corner of the garage, his limbs twitching in the final throes of a brutal death.

The garage had belonged to Pal who was building up a business importing old truck engines from the Far East, re-conditioning them and installing them in European models. Ray had paid him to import two Dodge engines from Burma and Pal had telephoned that afternoon to inform Ray that they had just arrived, still in their crates, but he'd have them opened up and ready for Ray's inspection the next morning.

The summons for Tisdale's assistance had come in this very pub that same evening. Ray wanted to break in to Pal's garage with some muscle and uncrate the engines and empty them of the heroin which was crammed into every valve and chamber in those hulks of metal and about which Pal had been kept in complete ignorance. Pal's commercial premises were situated on the edge of a run-down industrial estate, safe from any prying eyes. The security on the doors was weak and, within two or three powerful twists of the crowbar, they were inside and tearing open the two wooden crates. Ray had insisted that they both wore gloves throughout the entirety of the operation and had known exactly what he was doing, for in less than half an hour the engines had disgorged their dozens of polythene packages, stuffed with white powder gold.

"There's over half a million quid here. This is going to be my first Ferrari" Ray had panted, the sweat pouring off him as he started to carry the packages towards the stolen car he had parked out in the back. Ray was forever telling Bruce, Pal and anyone else who would listen that he would be driving a Ferrari. As he had reached the small wicket door that led to the yard, the copper had appeared out of nowhere, switching his flashlight on at the very second that Ray had pushed open the door. Dropping his load to the garage floor, Ray had backed into the garage whilst the uniformed bobby, spotting the light switch on the brick wall, had clicked it on, illuminating the whole interior of the garage in a harsh, unforgiving light.

Under the helmet the face was young, hardly old enough to shave and obviously nervous as he realized that he had two men to deal with. Tisdale, a fearsome sight at the best of times, was still clutching his crowbar and the officer reached for his truncheon and his radio at the same time. "It's only a burglary of a garage" he began in a thin, piping voice, "don't make it worse by resisting arrest."

They were the worst words he could possibly have uttered because, in that one sentence, he told Ray that this was not a drugs bust. No-one had shopped him or blown the deal. This was a young rookie, on his own, on night time patrol, who'd stumbled across what he thought was a minor break-in at an empty garage. He hadn't even cottoned on to what was in the polythene packages that lay on the oily floor. Before the officer could even press the button on his radio, Ray had drawn the gun from his inside pocket and pulled the trigger. There was less than a dozen feet between the barrel of the gun and the smooth face of the young man just starting out on his career when Ray provided him with a third eye, courtesy of a parabellum.

"No teenage cop was going to catch me with half a million quid's worth of horse, Bruce" Ray had spat out callously before the body was even still. "The powder's down to Pal. It's in his yard, in his name. We've just got to stick him with the gun."

Without a backward glance at the body on the floor, Ray had grabbed a black denim jacket which was hanging on a nail in the far corner of the garage where a dented kettle, an empty milk bottle and a dirty cup sat on a wooden bench. Bruce had often noticed Pal wearing that jacket and was puzzled to see Ray grab it before turning off the light and heading for the car. "Got to put it on, fire the gun and get some firearms residue on it, before we slip it into Pal's garden shed later tonight. The gun goes under his spare tyre in the boot of his car. We've got a busy night ahead. The coppers'll find the gun and jacket soon enough. Insurance, mate. You've got to have insurance."

As these tortured recollections forced their way back into Tisdale's half-functioning brain, he was aware of the arrival in the back bar of a tall, muscular black man in a full length Crombie overcoat and trilby with a velvet band. Around the neck was a heavy chain which hung outside the coat, so that the gold medallion, as big as an Olympic medal, could clearly be seen. The man simply stood in silence alongside their table, waiting for Millard to issue the orders. No introductions were necessary. One of the new generation of Enforcers. Ray would take Honey Hogan along whenever necessary and, clearly, he was required for the meeting with Ecklund.

Leaving Hogan standing there for a good five minutes while he finished his drink, Millard eventually bade his farewell and left "The Plume" with the Enforcer in tow. Just like he'd walked out of the dock at the Old Bailey as a free man all those years ago. The Police had found the body, the heroin on the garage floor, Pal's jacket in the shed and the gun under the spare tyre. Pal had been charged with heroin importation and murder. But Ray had miscalculated. Unknown to him, Pal had put some of the paperwork on the engines in Ray's name and given the Police at least the basis of a case against Ray on the heroin charge, but no evidence at all which would enable them to charge him with murder.

Of course, Pal had claimed at trial that he was innocent of both charges and that Ray was behind the drug importation and no doubt the murder as well. The jury acquitted Pal of the murder as it seemed too simple for the Police to have found the gun and the jacket so crudely hidden, but they convicted him on the drugs charge and he was sentenced to fourteen years. For a crime he hadn't committed. Ray had walked. Tisdale swallowed down the last chaser and pushed his chair back. Ray had called it insurance. Tisdale called it savagery. It was more savage than any GBH he'd ever done. And, as the one witness who could have cleared Pal and put Ray away for life, he'd remained silent. Those were the rules.

Honey Hogan took the wheel of the Escalade for the short journey to Ecklund's office while Millard silently reflected on how he was going to deal with the meeting. Millard had laundered most of the drugs money of the major operators in London and Manchester for the last decade, but since September 11th, the British Government had been making life very difficult and the latest Anti Money-Laundering Legislation was threatening to undermine the foundations of his business. The four million loan he'd raised to finance the purchase of the Keeling Estate was producing crippling repayments. Last month Rick Salerno, one of his most profitable coke distributors had been convicted at Snaresbrook and he was under heavy financial pressure from other deals. The last thing he'd wanted at this particular time was Don Ecklund calling in his mark. At the last count the debt stood at just under two million for three deals in which Millard had cross-traded massive quantities of high grade cocaine through Ecklund's connections.

Don Ecklund's office never closed. It was based on the old Chicago speakeasy principle. Located off Wandsworth High St, its frontage was an ordinary office supply shop with an open plan lay-out and a counter running along the back end, always manned by ever-changing shifts of hard-faced young men with unsmiling eyes and charcoal suits. They didn't seem to know much about selling office equipment but they were very familiar with the faces and names of those who were allowed admission into the twilight world that lay beyond the innocuous looking grey door in the far corner of the shop.

Inside there were forty-eight telephone operators, staring at their ever-changing computer screens, punching the keyboards in short bursts, each wearing a headset, shouting into their microphones, placing and taking bets on races, sports events and private wagers all over the world. You could bet live on the 3.30 two mile chase in Hong Kong, the outcome of one hand of poker in a Vegas Casino, or the winner of the middleweight fight taking place in Rio. All at the same time. If it moved you could bet on it and Ecklund's punters from all over the world placed their bets through this one call centre. The business was officially registered with the appropriate Government Agencies but it was about as legitimate as a bacon sandwich in a Rabbi's kitchen. To be accepted by Ecklund a punter had to show access to the sterling equivalent of a minimum of one million in cash. Once he'd seen you'd got it, Ecklund's purpose was to relieve you of it faster than Mike Tyson ever threw a left hook.

At the far end of this Trading Floor there was a sound-proof glass window and door which guarded Ecklund's inner sanctum, where he conducted all face to face business and from where he had an over-view of all the activity. As Ecklund beckoned Millard to come through to the office, Hogan was discreetly intercepted by a front desk clone and shown to a small sofa. Millard knew the protocol. Enforcers were allowed to attend, even if armed, but they never got beyond the door to Ecklund's office. That was for principals only. Once Hogan was seated, now entrusted with the briefcase that had accompanied Millard, the heavy glass door opened and Millard stepped inside, passing immediately through a screening device which would activate if he was carrying or wearing any metal. His cufflinks and keys had already been deposited at the front counter.

Don Ecklund came round from behind his desk to shake hands. The two men were not dissimilar in age and appearance. Dark, lean and topping out at around six feet three, both had arrived at the same destination in life. Big money and dirty money made by stamping on anyone who got in their way. However, whilst it had been an upwardly mobile journey for Millard, Ecklund's passage had been socially downhill. His father had qualified as an accountant and sent Don to Rugby School and King's College to read economics. Almost as soon as he had arrived in London, Don had run riot. Drugs, fights, scams and expulsion from the University before the end of his first year. Then, discarded by the family, he had put his considerable mathematical brain and his newly-acquired street toughness to work and started to build his Empire, naturally gravitating towards the high-grade villains like iron filings to a magnet. Single and still treated as an outcast by his family he marched hedonistically through life, trampling on those who might threaten his progress and caring only about himself.

"Have a seat. Good of you to call in, Ray" he declared, oozing insincerity in that upper-class accent which grated on Millard's nerves.

"I got your message. You're getting anxious about your cash," Millard replied coming directly to the point, watching Ecklund walk back round his enormous kidney-shaped desk to resume his seat in the high-backed executive chair.

"You know how it is. I got investors in three different countries pressing for their cut on those deals. We agreed you'd settle by the end of last month. Just wanted an update"

"I brought you a hundred grand in tonight" Millard answered, gesturing with his head in the direction of his Enforcer sitting quietly on the sofa outside. "Honey's got it in the briefcase"

Ecklund remained silent, staring through the glass at the perpetual motion of his minions beyond. Despite the fact that it was chilly in the office, as Ecklund insisted on keeping the air-conditioning up high at all times, Millard felt beads of perspiration breaking out across his upper lip and his right hand moved involuntarily to his neck when that damned tic started pulsating again. Whilst Ray was confident that he remained King of the Heap in their subterranean world and that his organization carried more muscle than Ecklund would be able to handle, nevertheless this situation could prove to be extremely damaging. That was why he'd agreed to come to Ecklund's office which, in itself, was a show of weakness. Normally, he would have made Ecklund come to see him but he hoped that the concession to the other man's ego might buy some more time. The debt to Ecklund was developing into a serious problem.

In the long silence Millard took a good look around the large, dimly-lit office. In the far corner there was a titanium eight foot high fridge. Set within the right hand door there was a 14 inch television screen along with a radio and a touchpad tuner and in its counterpart on the left there was another LCD display screen showing a computerized list of all the contents of the fridge. Caffeine-free diet drinks, health foods, fruit, yoghurt, vitamin preparations. In the opposite corner, and of similar dimensions, was a safe which was as formidable as any to be found in the vaults of the Bank of England.

To the side of the safe, on a hard, straight-backed chair sat a man. Ecklund never introduced him, but Millard knew exactly who he was. Shrader Miskin, Ecklund's last line of defence. Brought up in a small Russian community near Calgary, of Ukranian parentage, Miskin possessed extraordinary strength. Standing a good couple of inches shy of six feet, he consisted of fifteen stone of honed muscle. He had been a bullrider for four seasons, had competed in The Iron Man Triatholon five times, the Alaskan Iditarod twice and then become a prizefighter. Not in the boxing ring. But in a cage. Behind locked doors out of sight of the Police. Two men, bare-fisted and barefoot would punch, kick, gouge and throttle until one was unconscious. Winner take all. Ecklund had seen him destroying a Syrian brute in the Bangkok cage and offered him a job. Miskin nodded in Millard's direction, remaining seated and silent.

But, even more striking than Miskin was the glass tank which ran along the entirety of the wall immediately to the left of Ecklund's chair. Fitted with its own lighting, micro rain forest eco-system, lush green foliage and small pools of water, it dominated the room, although its live inhabitants were, for the moment, still and quite invisible.

Ecklund levered his rangy form up from the desk and wandered slowly to the far end of the tank where, on a small side table, sat, three white cylindrical plastic containers. Picking one of them up he prised off the lid which had holes pierced through it, put in his hand and extracted four or five black insects whose waving legs Millard could see sticking out between his fingers. Leaning over the tank he dropped the writhing insects inside, replaced the lid on the plastic container and watched intently as the foliage began to stir. Half a dozen small, blue frogs came scurrying out from their secret places beneath the large leaves. Millard noticed that the blue on their legs and underside was a darker hue than that of the head and back which were covered with an array of black spots.

"Come on, my little devil beauties" Ecklund whispered softly as he watched them swiftly track down and attack the handful of live crickets he had thrown into the tank. "Know what these are, Ray?" he asked gently without waiting for an answer. "They're poison dart frogs. All the way from Columbia. They release poison from their skin. So toxic that the Indians would gather it from them and use it on the tips of their blowgun darts. "Would certainly kill a monkey. Can kill a man," he added.

Millard watched in fascination as the small creatures began to devour the crickets with remarkable speed. "I thought numbers was your game, not biology," he remarked.

Looking back over his shoulder towards Millard, Ecklund's face was lit up in a grotesque reflection by the tank's internal lighting in such a way that his face appeared as if it was detached from his body, accentuating the thin lips and the thread veins running across the cheeks.

"No, Ray" he replied. "Survival is my game. These frogs have only one defence. Their poison. They can't move very quickly and they can hardly swim. See. . . " he pointed towards the feet of one of the creatures that had cornered its prey right up against the glass. ". . . they don't have any toe webbing. Very unusual for frogs. All they have is their poison. But the source of that poison is their diet. Termites, ants, beetles. Whatever it can find in the wild. Deny them that diet and their ability to produce poison disappears. Giving them crickets satisfies their hunger, but unless we can provide them with their natural diet they'll lose their poison and it's a struggle for us to keep finding the right stuff"

"So out in the wild these frogs wouldn't survive?" Millard responded

"Exactly" Ecklund declared, as he walked back to his seat and looked across the desk. "Like I said. Survival. I also need to keep my poison level up to survive, if you follow my meaning. Else I lose my credibility out in the wild. I need to retain my ability to defend and impose sanctions"

Ray Millard had not been on the wrong end of a serious threat since the gold bullion job at the airport many years ago. Joining forces with Frank Fitzgerrel in the days when the IRA still had some clout, they'd cleared five million a team and not one arrest. It was six months later when, through a chance remark from one of Fitzgerrel's minions, Millard had learned that the total take had been fourteen million and not the ten million Fitzgerrel had claimed. He and his team had been cheated of two million and the Paddies had been laughing behind his back ever since. When he made the phone call to Fitzgerrel he'd received the last threat anyone had ever made against him. "Shut the fuck up, Ray. Or else it's two bullets through the back of each knee. Splintered kneecaps will plaster the walls."

It had taken five long months before Ray had struck. Fitzgerrel had a night meeting in Swansea Docks. Just one minder with him. After the business was done, they had walked across the deserted docks to where they had hidden their car inside a cargo warehouse.

From deep within the shadows, Millard had put one slug in the back of the minder's head and four in Frank's legs. His magazine still held another six bullets when he leant over the screaming figure writhing on the filthy floor.

"It's your brains that going's to plaster the walls, Frankie, not my knees," he whispered as he pushed the muzzle of the semi-automatic tight under the man's fleshy chin. "Then you're going out on that old tin can you saw anchored on Pier 24. They've promised they'll drop you in the Irish Sea, so you'll feel at home" he added in that exquisite second when such minimal physical effort takes the top off a man's head." His special sound echoed around the empty ware-house but, he was in such a state of ecstasy that he never even knew he was making it. That had been his third and fourth killings and now, albeit far more subtly, this educated piece of shit opposite him was on the edge of issuing him with an ultimatum.

"Sanctions. That's a big word, Don. Sanctions. A very big word. I know you're an educated geezer and all that but are you sure you fully understand what that word means?" Millard asked, speaking very quietly. There was a menace in the voice that Ecklund had not heard before and he recognized immediately that he had come perilously close to crossing the rubicon. Millard's reputation was not built on fiction. It was time to back off. It was all well and good to make veiled threats when Miskin was sitting in the room but Millard had the capacity to strike when the Ukranian was not at his side.

"The hundred grand's welcome. But I need to know when the rest's coming through," he replied in a more subdued tone."

"Two months. I'm as keen to settle as you. The interest's a killer on what I owe you. That's the best I can offer unless I swing early payment on my Turkmenistan deal. But don't start talking sanctions to me, Don. I'll put that down to you getting carried away by the poison dart frogs," Millard declared with a note of finality.

"I can handle two months if necessary. Glad you dropped by. We know where we are now."

"I'll tell Honey to leave the briefcase with your man," Millard replied, nodding in Miskin's direction while getting to his feet and turning towards the door. "You can return the case when you get the rest of the money. You'll be coming to my place then, you see. You can meet my pets when you do."

"What pets would those be, Ray?" asked Ecklund

"Rottweillers, Don. Rottweillers. Natural diet is important to them. Just like your fucking frogs. Except it ain't beetles they need. It's flesh. Preferably of the two-legged variety."

"It can't be me coming to the house," Ecklund replied nervously. "We're opening up a branch down in Oz. Sydney. Big future down there and I'm off any day to set it up. Probably be gone for a few months, so one of the boys here will have to come to your place to collect. Unless you get a sudden injection of the readies in the next week or so, in which case I'll still be here to pick it up personally."

"Funny how you never mentioned Down Under 'til I told you about my pets."

"Makes it no less true though. I've no woman or kids here. And Oz is seriously good news for my kind of business. Got the contacts. Bought the premises. The boys can handle this place easily enough without me, it runs like clockwork. I should be down there in a week or two. Earn the cash in the morning. Lunch at The Rocks. Surfing off Bondi in the afternoon. That's my agenda for the next few months."

"Let's hope the sharks don't get you, then, Don. Wouldn't like to think of you being devoured by your own kind," Millard responded as he walked slowly away, leaving the glass door open behind him, reflecting on Ecklund's blue frogs, Miskin and sanctions.

Chapter 3

Alderney. Better known to Devon fishermen as Bacardi Rock. When those stinging storms whipped up the English Channel a line of light blue crabbing boats could be seen moored in the harbour while the crews caroused in the bars, downing tax free Bacardi until the wind dropped and the seas let them venture out again. When Bob Atwell had started in the business as a boy some twenty years ago, the waters were teeming with crabs and lobsters. Working in a three man crew out of Dartmouth on forty hour trips they could shoot half a dozen lines of a couple of hundred pots a line and start hauling in the first catch almost as soon as they'd laid the sixth. Returning into the estuary the tanks would be overflowing with the catch and the decks would be awash with a red-blue seething mass of primitive crustaceans that would turn into two hundred pounds a man by the time they'd loaded the Billingsgate lorries waiting on the Kingswear side of the river. Three trips a week, weather permitting, and money beyond the singing of it.

Then along came the Soviet block factory ships hoovering up the contents of the ocean like some monster anteater wiping out colonies of insects in a few obscene intakes of breath. Hot on their heels were the French and Spanish trawlers, with nets weighing over two tons and extending up to a hundred yards in length, intent not only on fishing out the waters, but also keen to put the Devon crabbers out of business by deliberately cutting through their lines and leaving thousands of pounds worth of financially irreplaceable gear on the ocean floor. The crabbers were being dealt a fatal blow and the British Government, tied helplessly to the apron strings of Europe, were, in typically craven fashion, prepared to let them perish. Decent, hard working men like Bob Atwell were forced to cut corners and take risks in a last ditch attempt to survive.

"Three more of the same," Atwell called out loudly to the young barmaid in the crowded Alderney pub, staring hard at the two faces opposite him in the corner booth they had now been occupying for over an hour, already having consumed the best part of a bottle of Bacardi. It was perfectly obvious to the crabber that the strange couple were not Colin and Helen Hargreaves as they were claiming to be and it was equally plain that, once they had established he was the skipper of a working boat and intending to catch the next tide for Dartmouth, they were going to proposition him for a discreet passage across the Channel and into the English port without announcing his extra two passengers to the Customs and the Harbour Master. Atwell found himself intrigued by the raven-haired woman who was dominating the conversation in her loud American accent and his eyes kept wandering back to the beauty spot on her upper lip which seemed to add to her mystique. Much younger than her English husband, she had provided the shallow cover story that they had sailed to the island from Torquay on the yacht of some rich London associates and, after a drunken night ashore, a row had broken out, culminating in the others abandoning them.

As soon as the barmaid had safely deposited the next round of drinks, the man asked the question that they had been building up to ever since they'd picked him out in the pub and moved in at his table.

"Any chance of a ride home, Skipper?" he ventured cautiously. "We'd pay our way."

"Got your passports with you, have you?" was the reply Atwell had kept ready for the moment when the question was eventually asked.

"We've got them, but we'd rather not get involved in all the formal stuff," the heavy-set man replied. "Gets complicated, you know, given how we came out on the yacht and got dumped and all that."

"The catch was poor this trip and I've got the room for you alright. But as Captain I have to see your passports and raise the flag on entering harbour which will bring Customs aboard," Atwell responded in his deep Devon drawl, aware that the woman's green eyes were watching him intently, weighing up his every word and gesture as the conversation moved inexorably towards the subject of money.

When she had worked the craps tables at The Imperial Palace the woman had learned the hard lessons. Punishing eight hour shifts on the tables. Every move watched by a Pit Boss standing behind her and a myriad of unseen eyes observing through the overhead cameras. The oblong table surrounded by a shouting, heaving throng of players and spectators. Thousands of dollars in bets riding on each throw of the dice. A split second to calculate the complex odds on a variety of bets. That is how she had lived for three years, dealing with tough, demanding men on a daily basis. Negotiating with an unworldly fisherman from rural Devon on the topic of money was like playing the kids at Snap in comparison.

"We know the crabs aren't biting too well, Bob," she began forcefully. "We don't want any gold braid climbing aboard. You moor mid-river and use a dinghy to come ashore, by which time it will be dark so no-one will see us. Spell it out. How much?"

"I'd lose my ticket if it got out and I've got a couple of crew who'd put a price on their silence," he replied, shocking himself at the ease with which he was prepared to sacrifice his integrity, just like the Government had sacrificed him and all the other fishermen.

Her most recent haggling with a man over money had involved buying a corpse from a grisly Mexican grave-digger who'd once boxed at The Garden. He'd also started beating about the bush and had to be brought starkly to the point, she reflected to herself.

"Let's get to it. How much?" she repeated, fixing him with those green eyes, while a smile played around the corners of her mouth, seemingly further accentuating the beguiling beauty spot.

"Two and a half grand for the whole shooting match," he declared. "The boys'd get a cut and the rest is mine. I'm the one taking the risks here."

"That's a hell of a lot of crabs, Bob. Our offer is fifteen hundred. Cash. Half now. The balance when we're standing safely on Dartmouth quay. Take it or leave it," she responded immediately.

"I won't go below two grand," he announced after a few seconds hesitation. "Fifteen hundred now. Five hundred on Dartmouth quay."

"You've got yourself a deal," she smiled without even looking at the man she claimed was her husband, whose mind was now elsewhere. After the flights on false passports from Guadalajara to Mexico City and onward to Paris, followed by a surreptitious sailing from the French coast to Alderney, their passage to England was now secured. His thoughts were moving onwards. To the End Game.

Sitting in the window seat of the chocolate and cream liveried coach, Jenna was captivated by the picturesque wooded slopes that lined the Dart Estuary along which the old steam locomotive was pulling them, puffs of smoke and steam trailing in its wake. Although she'd had no sleep lying down below on the fishermen's bunks whilst the great diesel engines had thumped relentlessly through the night, filling her clothes and hair with the smell of oil mixed with fish, the sight of the gleaming green paintwork and brass fittings of the pannier tank steam engine had lifted her spirits beyond measure. Pal seemed to know everything about the old Great Western railway that would carry them from Kingswear to Paignton and, in the clear morning air, he had pointed out Portland Bill which she could see across Lyme Bay. The anxieties of being rowed ashore in the early dawn light with their one holdall had now evaporated and Pal's animation and enthusiasm at the spectacular scenery was proving to be contagious.

"That's the Greenway Estate," he announced, pointing to a large house on the outskirts of Churston. "Where Agatha Christie lived. You've read some of her books, haven't you?"

"Hercule Poirot," Jenna replied. "The ABC Murders."

"And Dead Man's Folly," Pal added with a grin. "Set right here. Appropriate we should pass this way with a name like that, don't you think."

Despite the lack of sleep her big laugh filled the carriage which, apart from an elderly couple at the far end of the coach, was empty. After walking the deserted streets of Dartmouth until the first ferry had taken them across the river to Kingswear, they had caught the early train out of Kingswear, intending to connect with the Paignton-Birmingham Express. Pal was going back to his roots, albeit temporarily.

"What if we can't find the bastard?" she asked softly as her laughter subsided. "He's hardly likely to have his name in the phone book and you can't go sniffing round the old haunts. That really would be a Dead Man's Folly."

"He's territorial. Like a wolf. He only operates in The Smoke and only south of the river. No doubt with all his bent millions he'll have some grand drum out in the Stockbroker Belt, but he'll only do business in South East London. At a guess I reckon there'll only be three or four authorized Ferrari dealers supplying that whole area and he'll have at least one Ferrari tucked away in his garage as sure as a skunk stinks. It's a trophy. The ultimate flash."

"How can you be sure he'll get it serviced at an authorized dealer? He may have a local garage or a particular mechanic he uses," she enquired.

"You need to understand the mentality, Jenna. Whilst the core is rotten, the exterior has to shine. Clothes from the finest stores. Houses set amidst the latest glitterati. Alongside the footballers, the dot com merchants, the new money. Best restaurants, best hotels, best garages. The froth is what counts. You want the Ferrari serviced then it goes back to the pukka dealer. We'll find him alright. All we have to do is to follow the money."

Jenna looked through the window to observe that the track had now turned slightly inland and she had momentarily lost sight of the coastline. The magnificence of the Dart Valley and the soft woodlands had now given way to roads, cars, houses and people as the steam train elegantly pulled them into Paignton Railway Station, its whistle blowing repeatedly to announce its joyful arrival. As the train let out a final contented belch of steam, the American woman with the emerald eyes felt the harsh bite of reality as she reflected on the true nature of the mission which had brought her to Pal's homeland.

A small fire in the metal dustbin outside the back door of the rented service flat in Birmingham had consumed the stolen passports in the names of Colin and Helen Hargreaves, but Pal realized that it would need much bolder action to complete the execution of the overall plan now that he had completed the reconnaissance phase.

Once they had left picturesque Devon behind them and been thrust into the heart of urban Britain, the full impact of the hideous changes that had overwhelmed the country in the years of his absence had shocked him. Checking into a service flat as Philip and Susan Vance in one of the maze of side streets running off Broad Street on the edge of Birmingham City Centre had given Jenna and Pal the opportunity to wander amongst the people. Ethnic minorities seemed to have become ethnic majorities and the whole population, white, brown, yellow and black appeared to have been stripped of all charm. Abruptness abounded. Litter infested every pavement, every street corner and shop doorway. Snatches of conversation that floated across the ether as people passed were peppered with obscenities. In the new-look trendy shopping malls, gangs of scruffily dressed youths of all hues hung around in the doorways and at the bottom of escalators. Menace was permanently in the air. The entire population, male and female, seemed to have been tattooed and the women sported their tasteless inked logos on over-exposed cleavage or blubbered midriffs which stuck out from their cut-off tops. Clusters of gypsy-looking peasants speaking in harsh Eastern European tongues eyed the handbags and pockets of passers-by, forever looking to strike. The generosity of spirit that had enriched the British people over centuries seemed to have been knocked out of them in the blink of an eye.

Pal recognized the irony of these observations, for his own revenge mission here was as ugly an example of human weakness and sin as might be found but, even in his renegade soul, the appalling decline of his own people had saddened him. In Columbia and Mexico there had been no rules. Thieves loitered everywhere and violence was never more than an inch below the service. But they were a people who endured misery and poverty, where hunger, disease and infant mortality were rife. Apart from the narrow band of the social elite, the only objective of the common populace was survival. Britain had not faced those extremes and, as Pal saw it, their descent into the cultural gutter was unforgivable.

Yellow Pages in the Reference Library had contained the details of five Ferrari dealers in the South-East London catchment area and he'd struck lucky on the fourth telephone call.

"Your record and invoice for your last service were given to you when you collected the vehicle, Mr Millard but we'll gladly send you a copy in the post. You've already paid so no money is owing," the young receptionist pleasantly announced after making the appropriate enquiry and turning the history up on her computer screen.

"Do your records show that you have my home or my business address?"

"Keeling House, Radford, Berkshire," the girl read off the screen. "Yes, home. That's fine. Thanks for your help."

Obtaining a set of wheels had proved almost as simple. A short bus ride had taken him to a super-sized Texaco Service Station alongside a mini-market. Dressed so as to render the CCTV cameras worthless, he'd ambled along the aisles of sliced bread and canned soup watching the forecourt through the window. Within five minutes, the middle-aged female driver of a dark green Ford Fiesta LX was at the rear of the check-out queue while her keys sat obligingly in the ignition of the unlocked vehicle alongside Pump 6. Before she had even opened her purse, her well-kept Fiesta was chugging its way back towards the massive car park over the central Railway Station. Locating the exact counterpart of the model and colour for cloning purposes had proved child's play and a set of copy plates of the legitimate Fiesta, paid for in cash, had finished the morning's work.

By-passing Oxford that same night had taken him on to the narrow lanes of the Royal County of Berkshire. Jenna had helped him study the map that afternoon, although they had already decided that she should not accompany him on the first journey. Her turn would come. Mrs. Jane Buxton's little hatchback handled very nicely. He'd found her name and address inside the lid of her glasses case in the glove box when he'd consigned every personal item in the car to the bin at the Service Station on the M40. Smooth stick-shift, nippy through the gears and good on petrol although, he reflected wryly to himself, her taste in music wasn't quite up his street as he checked out her pre-programmed radio selections.

After an hour he spotted the white arm of the signpost to Radford and soon the lane climbed upwards towards the village he'd crossed the world to find. Noting with interest the large barn set back in the open fields on the left a mile or so before the village centre, he dropped the car into third and made the final approach at a crawl. It was now nearly two in the morning and the place was entirely deserted.

At the top of the hill, the road swung suddenly left to expose a magnificent old church and he pulled over to the side where a few other vehicles had been parked. After all this time, all the planning, all the hatred, he had surprised himself at the sense of calmness within. In his woollen hat, donkey jacket, black trousers and desert rubber-soled boots, he was unidentifiable. Swinging the backpack on to the front passenger seat he carried out a final equipment check. Long range Nighthawk 7 x 70 night vision binoculars. Good up to 1000 yards or more under the clear, starlight conditions that prevailed that night. The push-button flick knife with the narrow eight inch blade was tucked securely into his pocket. Heavy duty wire cutters. Pliers. Flask of hot coffee and two blocks of Cadbury's chocolate as this vigil may take until light. The large-scale Ordinance Survey map in case he had to cut and run across the countryside. The shooting stick. Thick industrial gloves. And finally, the Beretta 92FS 9 millimetre semi-automatic. This version had a delayed blow-back double action and was built on a combat-style alloy frame with a matte black Bruniton finish and room for fifteen rounds in the magazine.

Slipping silently along in the shadows, he had only travelled a couple of hundred yards from the church when he suddenly came across what he was satisfied had to be the gates to Keeling House. The two imposing wrought iron gates bore no address plate, but hammered into their structure, Pal's keen eyes picked out the three letters that told him all that he needed to know. RLM. Moving away into the blackness created by the hedgerows he quickly absorbed the information. Gates unscaleable. Whole perimeter walled and topped with razor wire. Long straight drive, tree-lined but minimal cover. Moving swiftly off to his left, always staying in the shadows, he began skirting the perimeter wall seeking out the weak spot. There always was a weak spot, it was just a matter of recognizing it when you saw it. He might be forty-one but Pal was a bull of a man and had kept himself in top shape. Prison, the emerald mines, weights, running, a naturally rugged body and living with a young, tough female had all contributed. He moved quickly, silently and without effort until he reached a small hillock which ran up to the foot of the wall on the west side of the house.

Jabbing the pointed end of the shooting stick into the soft earth right against the wall, he opened up the hinged flaps and stepped up onto the seat until he was able to see clearly into the grounds. Keeping his head back from the razor wire, the Nighthawk provided the clearest of views. Beyond a large terrace at the rear of the house he could make out a cluster of outbuildings consisting of old animal pens and stalls. No cars were visible by the house and everything appeared to be in darkness. He could wind the pieces of cut wire together afterwards ensuring that his incursion would almost certainly go unnoticed.

Extracting the cutters from the bag, he gripped the razor wire firmly in the re-enforced gloves and cut half a dozen strips so he could pull himself up on to the top of the wall. The wire tore at his heavy clothing as he turned and, leaning downwards, grabbed the shooting stick that would be needed for the return journey. Now breathing much more heavily, he dropped the eight feet on to the other side. The calmness he had experienced up to this point had suddenly evaporated. With that push over the wall he had moved significantly closer to the reality of the dreadful act he believed he would perform. His heart was beating too fast, he was sweating and a piece of the vicious wire had caught his cheek as he dropped, opening a cut which was stinging and which bled on to the back of the glove as he wiped his hand across it.

Crouching at the foot of the wall, he obeyed Jenna's training instructions to the letter. Fifteen deep breathes. In through the nose, out through the mouth. Oxygen dragged to the base of the lungs. Take control of your own heartbeat. Now coming back under control. Calmer. Focus. Ready.

Re-positioning the shooting stick in the ground, right under the narrow gap in the wire, ready for emergency escape, he moved cautiously forward. After forty yards the ground fell away and the trees thinned, leaving an expanse where there was absolutely no cover. Pal dropped to one knee, bringing the Nighthawk up to his eyes in the same movement and training them on the open expanse and beyond to the house. As his eyes adjusted to the artificial amber light of the precision equipment, he suddenly felt his blood run cold and the effect of Jenna's exercises was vanquished in but a second.

They were right at the edge of the Nighthawk's range, two of them, side by side, moving together in long, loping strides like grotesque creatures of death from Greek legend, eating up the ground with effortless ease. In a flash, Pal jumped up and raced for the wall, the Nighthawk banging hard against his chest as he desperately fled, while his panicked mind raced through the options. If he got on to the top of the wall he would be safe, but if they reached him first then they would tear him apart. Their instinct was to rip out the throat. He'd seen the arm of a burglar in prison that had been savaged by just one bite from a Rottweiller, leaving the emaciated limb shorn of the entirety of its bicep. The only choice then would be to shoot them both. If he did, then his revenge plan would be finished, as Millard would maintain a heightened state of alert for months to come. He had to make the wall.

Despite his state of fitness, the terror that the dogs provoked had robbed him of his wind within a dozen paces. His breathing was ragged and his legs became heavy. In the darkness it was imperative that he managed to run directly to the shooting stick and, although he was now less than forty yards from the wall, it was impossible to be precise as to where the stick was. In the next second he heard them. The sound of their movement was reverberating in the night air and then he actually heard a terrifying noise from deep within their throats. They were not barking, nor growling, it was a primeval rasping and baying as they sensed and smelt the terror of their prey.

Although it slowed him down, Pal was unable to resist the involuntary turning of his head over his shoulder as he fled. He probably had five or six seconds left. This was his last possible chance to go for the gun or else they'd be on him before he could release the safety catch and pull the double-action trigger. But then he saw the stick. Within another six paces his right foot was on the wing and his right arm was hooked over the top of the wall, oblivious to the wire now slashing through his upper clothing. Bringing one knee on to the top of the wall he was up and, in one movement he swung round so that he could reach down for the stick. As he looked down, he saw their gaping mouths. Slobbering spittle hung from their lower jaws, their wicked teeth bared and, within their frenzy, that hideous rasping sound scattering the saliva through the air. As his fingers closed around the seat of the stick and he pulled his body backwards he felt their slobber spray across his face as, in one final frantic leap, they hurled themselves at their prey, their lethal teeth closing upon fresh air as he fell in a heap, stick in hand, on the outer side of the wall.

Back in the sanctity of the car it had taken him the best part of an hour to recover from the ordeal, reflecting all the while on the oddity that they had never barked. The hot coffee had made him feel sick and, despite the warmth of the night and the weight of his clothing, he was shivering with cold.

All the time he knew that he must return to the wall and repair the wire so that his tampering was obscured. Just as importantly, he had to devise an alternative plan. Entry to the house was plainly an impossibility.

Forcing himself back to the wall he plaited the severed ends around each other with the pliers and, as he completed the job, he became aware of the noise of an approaching vehicle. The topography of the land was such that the noise of the engine coming up the hill reverberated across the valley in the stillness of the night. Pal could judge by the sound that the engine was powerful and that the vehicle was being driven fast. For a moment it stopped and Pal put the Nighthawk to his eyes and strained his ears. Within half a minute the noise began again, louder and closer than before and then, suddenly, a large dark vehicle loomed into the Nighthawk's vision racing up the drive towards the house and, in an instant, he knew what it was. A metallic black Cadillac Escalade. Three hundred and forty-five horsepower. Vortec 6000 V8 engine. As powerful as a space rocket with retro burners. He'd seen them in Guadalajara. Exactly the sort of over-the-top, macho flash that he would expect Millard to have as his runabout. You could bet your bottom dollar that there would only be one of those in this neck of the woods. After a moment the engine died and the stillness returned. Pal could no longer see the vehicle, nor had he heard a car door slamming, so it was likely that Millard had driven directly into a garage which connected internally with the house.

Hurrying back to the car the alterations to the original plan were already forming in his mind as he slid into the driver's seat and drove back out of the village, stopping at a point which gave him a view out across the valley. The earliest hints of the new day were showing on the horizon, lending an eerie aspect to the panorama, but allowing him to identify the excellence of this vantage point. In his mirror he could see most of the road which led up to the village and, ahead to the right, the outline of the old barn that he'd observed earlier.

Knocking the gear stick into neutral he let the car meander downhill with just the odd touch on the brake until he came to the gate that led to the barn. A hop over the shaky wooden gate and a ten minute inspection of the unlocked barn told him all he needed to know before he set off back towards the M40 and the big City.

Chapter 4

Thin early rays of sunshine danced their way easily through the cheap, unlined curtains of his small bedroom along the South West edge of Clapham Common and, in those first few seconds before full consciousness returned, he thought he was back in the apartment in Henry Street in the heart of Brooklyn Heights. Lying perfectly still beneath the heavy duvet, which he'd learned would remain necessary for the full duration of a normal English summer, he gradually turned his head to see that the hair spread across the adjacent pillow did not consist of tight, red curls but was long and blonde. In that second he came fully awake, with the realization now accompanying every such awakening that he would never see those red curls again. Nothing could prepare you for a loss of that enormity. Firstly, the massive impact of the Doctor's news, coldly delivered, offering no hope, merely reciting the pharmacist's potions which might ease the mechanics of death. Then, the four months of hell, watching helplessly, as, despite her steel and courage, she finally succumbed. At the end, he had wished death for her, only to find himself standing in the grim cemetery overlooking the concrete of the nearby freeway, gripped by a sense of guilt that he could ever have denied her one day of life. Abandoning her to an eternity of the pounding and frenzy of the ceaseless traffic he had walked away, taking his guilt with him. The punishment of a guilt where there should be none had proved to be a destructive process.

Lost in his thoughts he suddenly became aware that the owner of the blonde hair had opened her sleepy blue eyes and was watching him, knowing without asking what thoughts possessed his mind in those first moments of a new day.

"Where is he today?" Jake asked.

"Stockholm. A meeting of all the European Directors. No wives. Back tomorrow night," the woman answered softly, pressing her naked, lithe body close against him, seeking to remind him that life must move on.

For a few moments she managed to carry him away to a world where sadness had no place and, afterwards, as she lay draped across him, his thoughts drifted back to their first meeting on the hard streets of the West Side of New York during those awful September days of 2001. By then he had been alone for nearly four years, throwing himself into his work to fill the void. And then the Towers had gone down. For three weeks he had been one of the countless number who had driven themselves back into the wreckage time after time, tearing at the rubble, wrenching the metal aside, choking on the dust, gagging on the smell, sweltering in the heat, desperate to find life, but invariably unearthing death in all of its hideous ugliness. Occasionally, amidst the severed limbs or dust-whitened corpses, he had stumbled across a memory of life. The key ring with a small photograph of a lover attached, the pen with a name engraved and a child's toy watch.

Like all the others, he had worked six hours on and six hours off, around the clock, sleeping on the street beds erected along the pavements of the West Side and eating at the Field Kitchens. Occasionally, he'd march the twenty blocks to the Emergency Quarters where his crew could take a shower and hand over their filthy clothes for washing and then walk back, ready for another six hours. The whole area teemed with uniforms of every kind as gangs of exhausted men made their way back to the street beds to collapse in a state of hopelessness. Army and Police vehicles lined the streets as far as the eye could see. Tanks on the roads. Armoured vehicles, ambulances, NYPD vehicles. New York had become a War Zone. It had lost its innate self-confidence. The abrasive humour had been smashed.

Whilst the noise of the heavy machinery droned and screamed the people had become silent.

One evening, under an exquisite clear blue sky, he had slumped in a chair at the Field Kitchen alongside one of the freighter piers with his hamburger and coffee when an English voice had asked him if he'd like a refill. That was the first time he had seen her. Hair tied back under a scarf. No make-up. Clear, fair complexion. Big blue eyes. Generous mouth. Stonewashed jeans and a Yankees T-shirt. One of the thousands of volunteer women running the kitchens while the men fought their way in and out of Ground Zero. An actress in a British production on Broadway for the summer, she had come in on the QE2 and she'd seen the magnificent downtown skyline with the two pinnacles standing at its heart as the great liner sailed up the Hudson River and moored at its mid-town pier. The cast had returned to London when the production was cancelled but she had decided to stay on to help when the terrorists had struck.

Over many cups of coffee in the ensuing days she learned that, although he was a detective in the NYPD, he was in fact British. His parents had moved to New Jersey when he was a boy but he had retained dual citizenship. Gradually, she had told him of her empty marriage to James Albright, industrialist, socialite, power-broker and tyrant. At the end of that week he'd gone back to his apartment, cleaned up, pulled his best suit out of the wardrobe and taken her to dinner at his favourite Trattoria on 46th Street. With his dark hair, sad brown eyes and broad shoulders he had already won her heart and, when he saw her for the first time in make-up and all her finery, he had felt the stirrings of a new beginning and the possibility that there was a life beyond the memory of those beautiful red curls. On that same night they had become lovers and secrets had been revealed.

It had proved to be a big move. Six months later he had resigned from the NYPD and passed the transfer admission tests into the Metropolitan Police Force in London. Relinquishing his lease on the Brooklyn apartment he had located a very modest flat in Clapham and found himself working South London at Detective Sergeant level. Lauren Albright, under her stage name of Lauren Callaway, continued to get the auditions and frequently win the roles and would regularly meet him for lunch and dinner, spend two or three nights a week in his bed without making any attempt to keep the fact of their relationship from her husband.

Over many months, in every way that he could think of, Jake had tried to persuade her to leave the dreadful man, but in vain. A luxurious Chelsea town house, credit cards without a maximum and his support of her stage career were the prizes. The odd business dinner party and social function on his arm were the cost. Incapable of bearing him children, sexual relations between them had ceased long ago. Jake had come to accept that either he recognized that this was her compromise or he ended their relationship. She would never leave Albright. To a degree it worked. His tough New York policing methods proved effective in London and he was quickly promoted to Detective Inspector with responsibility for organized crime in the South East London Division and he was still able to spend a good deal of time with Lauren.

Occasionally he saw Albright on the television, puffed up with his own importance, giving a business interview or commenting on some Government fiscal measure. When Lauren was there she would immediately turn the television off and his name was no longer mentioned by either of them. It had therefore come as something of a surprise when, a couple of months ago, Albright seemed to have decided that the time for a confrontation had arrived and had telephoned Jake at work, demanding that they meet for what he called "a civilized discussion."

Jake had suggested meeting in one of the many pubs around

Canary Wharf, where Albright's corporation owned an entire office block, but he had declined, insisting that they meet in St James' Park.

In addition to having seen him on the television, Lauren's description of him had made recognition easy. Slightly shorter than her, thinning hair, rimless glasses, soft round the gills from all of the corporate dining and an air of haughtiness and disdain. Sitting on the bench in the autumn evening sunshine, Albright had immediately opened the discussions.

"I'm ordering you to stop sleeping with my wife. I've grown weary of her adultery. Is that clear enough for you, Kempner?" he barked.

"Why don't you just let her go? You've no affection for her. She means no more to you than one of the companies you acquire," Jake replied calmly.

"In a sense you're right," Albright acknowledged. "But a man in my position is judged by his acquisitions. She attends the functions where I need to display her. She wears clothes from the top fashion houses. That's how it is and you're getting in the way of that arrangement."

Jake turned his face away from the odious man and stared at the trees. He could see glimpses of the Palace through the foliage as the first leaves had already begun to fall. Whilst the man exuded a certain aura of power, he represented no threat to Jake beyond his influence over Lauren. Turning back towards him, Jake spelt it out in plain New York English.

"Your money cuts no ice with me. We both view you with loathing. You're a greedy and arrogant bastard. I want her to leave you and she would, if you'd just let her get on with her own life."

"I'll never divorce her," Albright replied forcibly. "In fact she does have the choice to leave me. Not even I can manacle her to the walls. But you'll have noticed that she doesn't choose to go."

"That's only because you'll stop her getting any part in the theatre again. That's a serious threat. She has no marriage and can't have children. Acting is her life."

"Precisely. Live theatre depends on the money that the producers will put up. I know the producers. They'll never go against my wishes. Besides, in case you haven't noticed, she's rather partial to the Rolls and the accounts at Harrods," Albright snapped sarcastically.

Jake decided that he'd had enough of this charade. "This conversation has absolutely no purpose," he said with a note of finality in his voice. "I'll continue to see her for as long as she chooses, whether you ever let her go or not."

"You fail to understand me, Kempner. I'm not asking you to do anything. I'm ordering you. Otherwise I give Commander Macpherson a call and you'll find yourself out of the Force," came the threat which Albright had been choosing his moment to deliver.

"That's bullshit, Albright, and I'm not kicked around quite so easily as Lauren. Half of the Met is having affairs," retorted Jake. "Try bullying me and I'll call your bluff. My affair with your wife will be plastered all across the tabloid press. If that's what you want, fire away. Otherwise, we continue as we are. Unsatisfactory as it is. She sees me as and when she wants."

"Well, don't say you weren't given the chance," Albright spat out. "You make an enemy of me and, sooner or later, you'll pay the price."

Without warning Jake suddenly moved along the bench, grabbed Albright's expensive jacket lapels and shirt front in his large fist, thrusting his face so close to Albright's that he could smell the whisky on his breath.

"Listen very closely," he snarled. "If you ever make one move against me I'll come after you and give you the kind of beating the NYPD trained me to hand out. For now, you're getting just one little taster," he added, putting a short, sharp left jab straight into the face. Albright's glasses fell to the floor while blood spurted from his nose and dripped on to the hand-stitched suit and white cotton shirt. Jake stood up and threw the couple of shirt buttons that had become detached into the cringing man's lap as he pressed his handkerchief against his nose in an attempt to staunch the flow of blood.

"One lesson I learned early," he called back as he set off down the path away from the deflated executive. "Most bullies are cowards at heart and you're no exception."

Jake had not told Lauren of the meeting and he doubted that Albright would have raised it with her, finding some other explanation for his bloodied nose. Since then the two men had kept their distance and the off-beat relationship with Lauren had continued.

"Where are you today?" she asked, snapping him abruptly out of his reverie.

"Snaresbrook Crown Court. Rick Salerno bites the dust this afternoon. I've arranged with the prison to get him there early this morning. Before his lawyers arrive. I'm going to see him down in the cells to offer him a deal in exchange for some information."

"I didn't think you were supposed to do that," said Lauren.

"You supposed right," he replied. "But Salerno is only medium grade. Distributes coke to the dealers in the Night Clubs. I'm interested in the information he's got on someone at the top of the tree. Either he'll talk to me or refuse to see me. It's his choice, but he knows that it's Judge Mary Trott who is sentencing him."

"Is that significant then? Lauren enquired.

"Very significant. You know what the crooks call her? 'Give'em a lot, Trott," that's her nickname," he laughed, pushing back the duvet and heading for the shower. "Salerno is looking at double figures. A sealed brown envelope from me delivered to the Judge behind closed doors saying he's given us useful info could save him four years. I don't care about Salerno. I'm after his boss. The Big Boy with the

Berkshire Estate and the brand spanking new Ferrari. Sooner or later I'm going to nail that bastard."

"Make sure he doesn't nail you first," she replied ominously. "From what I've heard you say about him he's high octane."

"In New York we'd have shot him by now. Over here you're too restrained."

"And who has got it right? New York or London?" she shouted as he closed the bathroom door behind him and the noise of the water cascading out of the power shower began.

His answer to her question could be heard loud and clear over the sound of the gushing water as he belted out the opening lines of his favourite song.

"Start spreading the news. New York, New York. . . ."

Jake put on the plain grey suit which he always wore for Court and took the Tube to Snaresbrook which was located in the premises once occupied by the Royal Wanstead Boys School. Whilst the mischief of schoolboys may have remained constant over the years, London East End villainy had changed dramatically. The days of the armed robbery gangs like the Krays and the Richardsons had been consigned to history. Bank hold-ups had become almost obsolete. Wages snatches were virtually unknown. None of this owed anything to a decreasing crime-rate nor some successful Government initiative, despite the repeated deceitful claims by the Home Office to that effect. The explanation was that the career criminals had come to realize that the risks of armed confrontation could be avoided, whilst the rewards could be infinitely greater, if they turned to the new speciality. Narcotics. Forget cannabis, amphetamines and ecstasy. The money was in Class A. Cocaine and heroin. And so sawn-off shotguns had been replaced by semi-automatics. Knuckledusters had been replaced by mobile phones. Any risks were run by the street salesmen not by the chief executives who set up the deals by telephone to Amsterdam, Karachi, Bogota and all places beyond. Snaresbrook's Court List was now little more than a narcotics dealers processing plant. But almost always the smaller fry. The street corner dealer, the pub handler, the Night Club supplier, but seldom, if ever, the importer or wholesaler or orchestrator.

"Is it down to you that I've been shipped out to Belmarsh since my trial, Kempner?" Salerno grunted, as he slouched on the wooden bench with his back against the graffiti-littered cell wall.

"You asked the Judge for a Report, Rick. You could've been sentenced immediately after the jury potted you and gone back to Brixton with the ten-stretch we all know you're going to collect," Jake responded, closing the cell door behind him and wiping the grimy slats of the bench with his hand before sitting down.

Alvaro and Anita Salerno had arrived in London from Naples, opened a greengrocery in East Ham, worked hard, reared two boys and tried to travel through life with a smile. Nico had done them proud. Athletic and enthusiastic, he had been signed by Brentford as a schoolboy, played five seasons for them as a midfielder, when West Ham, tottering on the edge of relegation, had bought him in a state of panic. The Hammers had failed to avoid the drop, Nico had been released on a free transfer to Brighton where he saw out his career before opening a restaurant in the Lanes.

Outshone by his brother at sports and naturally lazy, Ricardo had gone the other way. Taken on as a bouncer at the local night club, not because he was particularly skilled with his fists, but because he was so overweight that he looked the part, he'd eased his way into dealing, eventually becoming attached to one of the many tentacles of the Millard Organisation, drifting along in a purposeless existence. Prison time was making him look him even more vacuous.

"What you want with me?" Salerno asked abruptly. "I told the screws I didn't want you near me."

"I got your property from when we arrested you. CD's. Stereo equipment. Some files. We've got to return it to you. Where do you want it taken? Your folks? Nico? Wherever you say."

"Bullshit. That ain't why you're here. My solicitor deals with all that stuff. Say what you want or just piss off, I don't want to be seen with no copper."

"That's why I've come to your cell and not to a conference room. No-one can see you talking to me," Jake assured him.

"You think the screws'll keep their gobs shut, do you, Kempner?

"As far as they're concerned I'm here for you to sign some papers about your property. It's not a problem. But you're right, I do have another agenda."

Salerno brought his feet up on to the bench and swung round to look directly at Kempner for the first time since his entry into the cell. His face had got even fatter in prison, his chins had increased in number, he hadn't shaved and he had a bad case of body odour, but, at the back of the small, reddened eyes, Kempner could see the glint of interest.

"OK, like I said, what you want with me?" he repeated.

"You're going to draw ten, Rick. We caught you with thirty grand's worth of coke. The kids that use that Club are babies. Under twenty-one. You were corrupting them. This Judge is tough. I know that's why you went for a Report. You hoped you'd avoid her for sentence but she reserved the case to herself. Let me tell you something, Rick. She had a nephew. Read Greek at Cambridge. Overdosed on coke. Dead. She's on a mission. You might get twelve," Kempner declared, repeating the line that he'd dreamt up on the Tube journey and watching the sweat breaking out across the upper lip of the fat man opposite.

"For Christ's sake, Kempner. Spare me the shit. What you got for me?"

"You know who I want. He supplies Dunning, the Head of Security at your place. Dunning doles it out to you. I want to know the places he meets up with Dunning so we can be waiting for him. You tell me and I send this letter into the Judge," he answered, pulling a brown envelope out of his inside jacket pocket and thrusting it into the podgy fingers with the bitten-down nails. "Go on, open it. It's not sealed. It describes your co-operation".

There was a long silence while Salerno read the typed lines to himself, before folding the paper, putting it back in the envelope and returning it to Kempner.

"Do you know what Millard would do to me if ever it got out?" asked Salerno.

"But it won't get out. I'm not asking you to give evidence against him. I want the rendezvous places. He'll never know it came from you. I'll know. The Judge'll know. The wigs'll know. That's it. And I promise it will save you at least four years. Ten will become six."

"And do you think Millard is some kind of dummy? You think he won't know that thirty grand's worth of coke, sold to kids, plus a plea of not guilty is worth ten? And I draw six. And then, a few months later, with a suitcase of coke, he and Dunning are surrounded by armed cops at a meeting place only the select few know about. I come out earlier, but I never walk again. Go fuck yourself, Kempner. I'll do my ten."

"There's another way of looking at this, Salerno" Jake replied, abruptly switching to the last name and hardening his tone. "You say you don't like Belmarsh. And yes, I did get you shipped out there. And if you don't co-operate I can make it far worse. You've never been on Category A, have you? No visitors. Restricted phone calls. Searched every time you go in or out of your cell. Moved without warning in the middle of the night. Wood Hill. Hull. Wakefield. The hardest wings of the hardest gaols. You want some of that, do you?"

The smell in the confined cell was getting worse as Salerno's sweating increased and there was a significant hesitation before he came to his decision.

"I can't do it," he finally declared. "You don't know just how powerful he is. A brewery wants to open a new Club? They need his permission. With contracts for his bouncers who'll then set up the dealing. Anyone resists, he burns 'em, he pops 'em. Say anything he doesn't like and it's a wheelchair or worse. I just can't do it."

Kempner got to his feet, looking down with a mixture of contempt and pity at the broken figure on the bench, whose head was now down on his chest, and reluctantly recognizing that the man's reasoning was absolutely accurate.

"OK, Rick. I got your message. And don't worry about Cat A. It was a try-on. I see the strength."

The large head came up and offered a nod of gratitude as Kempner began to open the cell door.

"One last thing, Jake," he said. "Close the door." He waited while the Inspector pushed the steel door closed, before continuing. "I know where you're coming from and I'm grateful about the Cat A stuff. So I'm giving you this. There's a geezer out there offering ten grand to give you a serious going-over. It ain't Millard. It's posh money, if you get my meaning. And it's personal not business. So watch your step."

"Who is it?" Kempner demanded.

"I ain't got a name. It just got mentioned amongst a couple of the hard men in Belmarsh. Some toff wants a copper done over. Your name come up. To do with a woman. So you owe me, don't ya?"

"I only owe you if you give me a face," came the retort.

"The only face I can give you ain't worth nowt. He stamped on a screw's head last week. They've sent him to the glass cell."

"Which glass cell?" demanded Kempner. "As far as I know there's only two in the whole country."

"So you won't have much trouble in finding out who it is, will ya? But in the glass cell they ain't very likely to talk to a cop, are they? If you try, then my name don't come out, right?"

"I'll promise you that, Rick. Your name won't feature. And I'll see if we can swing you back into Brixton. Handy for the folks visiting and all that," he replied softly as he left the cell, thinking of one man in a hand-stitched suit sitting on a park bench and another man languishing in a glass cell.

Chapter 5

After carefully re-evaluating the details of the plan, Pal and Jenna had slept by day and kept their vigil on the road up to Radford at night, waiting out the first two nights until first light, with no sign of the Escalade. He'd stood silently inside the barn, accustoming himself to its unusual light conditions that made it permanently hover on the edge of twilight and full darkness.

Measuring about forty feet by thirty, the building had just one level. A hard-earth path that must have been worn over the centuries worked its way from the roadway gate, around the barn, until it reached a pair of substantial, hinged wagon doors on the far side. There was no lock on these doors and entry was gained by simply lifting a restraining plank of wood. On the road side of the barn were counterpart doors, seemingly less frequently used because they scraped heavily against the ground when he tested them. No doubt these would have been the wagon's exit and with both sets of doors open, the wind would have blown straight through to help winnow the wheat from the chaff. Within the barn three bays were positioned between the massive supporting buttresses which ran from the concreted floor to the roof. In the right hand bay were old animal stalls and pens, whilst to the left there lay a coiled up hosepipe attached to a tap and an array of saws and felling axes leaning against the wall alongside piles of bagged fertilizer.

On the third night there was heavy cloud and a light drizzle was falling, lending a slick to the road surface as they pulled the Fiesta on to the side of the tarmac just beyond the gate entrance. Pal got out to lift the bonnet while Jenna slipped across into the driver's seat, turning the engine off, but leaving the sidelights on. Wearing a white blouse, tailored trousers and low heels, her clothing was in stark contrast to Pal's black combat jacket, trousers and full face balaclava, rolled up on the forehead above the eyes. As the engine cut off, the stillness to which they had grown accustomed over the last two nights again invaded the valley.

While sipping their third cup of coffee from the flask the noise began. Starting as a distant drone from below, it quickly gained strength as the eight cylinders drove the tank up the hill, bouncing its roar off the hillside. Throwing open the passenger door, Pal tipped the remnants of his coffee on to the verge, tossed the plastic cup into the footwell and took a long look into the pale and anxious face at his side.

"Do we go, girl?" he breathed.

"We've come too far from Tamazula to turn back now," she replied assertively, prompting him to roll athletically out of his seat and force himself underneath the chassis of the Fiesta.

As she levered herself out of the driver's door and picked her way cautiously twenty yards up the road, the rain started to come down harder but the three hundred and forty-five horsepower machine was burning its way up the hill, filling the night air with the sound of its power and making her oblivious to the rain soaking through her shirt. Suddenly, she could see the lights flashing through the trees below and hear the tyres cutting through the surface water on the road, racing ever closer towards her like a raging buffalo on the plains.

The big wipers were on half speed and Sinatra had just moved into the second chorus of "Summer Wind" when he came round the tight bend ahead of Nolan's Barn. The high beams picked out a small hatchback on the left hand side of the road, bonnet raised, and just beyond it, the figure of a woman, startling in her contrasts, black hair, pale face, white shirt, dark trousers, frantically waving him down in the rain, chest thrust forward so as to accentuate her shape.

Odd phrases of the assurances that Pal had given her flashed through her mind. "He'll stop, Jenna. I know how he thinks. You need to understand the ego of the man. He's the genuine article; a bastard of the highest order. But he doesn't play at being macho; he is macho. And that will make him stop. His own self-image will make the decision for him."

Just as Pal had predicted, the Florentine leather shoe jammed on the power brakes and he slowed alongside her, eyes darting hither and thither, ensuring that this was not a set up. She could feel the heat from the throbbing machine, but the tinted windows and the height of the vehicle made it impossible for her to see the driver. Activating the electric passenger window so that it opened only a few inches, all she heard was the crooning of 'Old Blue Eyes' before a disembodied voice called from the distant driver's side.

"What's your problem, lady?" the voice barked warily.

Although she had rehearsed her lines a thousand times, harsh reality froze her in her tracks. This was the most dangerous man she had ever encountered. He had stolen a decade of life from someone she had come to love. Destroying others for his own purposes, trampling underfoot anyone who got in his way was second nature to him, and she knew that he was prepared to discard lives with the ease that she would swat a fly.

"It's a rental car. Just died on the hill," she shouted, struggling to be heard across the engine, the rain and the music, deliberately emphasising her American accent in the hope that it would more readily convince him that she was just a stupid tourist.

"I'm over from the States. Visiting my sister. I don't have an English cell phone to call her. She lives the other side of Radford. I just need a ride to a call box. . . ." she continued, still shouting into the void. All she could see of him through the few inches of the passenger window, was the top of his head, thinning dark hair, slicked back with streaks of grey.

Suddenly, the engine cut out and the music stopped. The window came down the full distance and he leant across the passenger seat so that his head loomed into view, still high above her, but enabling her to see the face as he interrupted her.

"Use my phone," he announced, passing a small, Ericson through the window. It's switched on. But make it snappy, love, I've a home to go to."

As he was leaning across she got a clearer view of him. Long head. Small, uneven teeth exposed in what was supposed to be a half-smile, but the immediate aura he presented was one of menace. His wariness seemed to have lessened, but she could sense him weighing her up as his eyes constantly flicked from her to his mirrors, checking the area around the vehicle. When he had passed her the phone she could see that his right hand had come off the steering wheel and was hovering at his side, leaving Jenna in no doubt that he was armed.

Fumbling with the buttons she put it to her ear and, after a few seconds, started shaking her head. Pal had explained that he would not be able to pull the driver's door open from outside unless and until Millard unlocked the passenger door and triggered the central locking system. They had not bargained for him passing his phone out of the window. Somehow she had to make him unlock the passenger door.

"I'm sorry. This phone is different from mine. I can't see the buttons in the dark," she mumbled helplessly.

"Work it out, lady," he snapped. Punch in your number. Press the green button."

Jenna took a step back so that he could see her clearly. The rain had soaked her blouse, making her bra and the shape of her breasts stand out through the wet transparency of the sheer material. Her hair was now beginning to stick to the side of her face as she seemingly struggled to operate his phone, aware of his eyes ranging over her upper body.

"For Christ's sake, give it here. I'll do it for you. Park your self inside," he snapped, pressing the unlock button and pushing open the heavy passenger door in one movement, simultaneously activating the interior light.

White leather seats, a dashboard of illuminated dials and LCD displays, that unique new car smell. All these things registered in her mind as, phone in hand, she put her right foot inside the Escalade, like a Trojan soldier climbing aboard the Wooden Horse.

Then, with the lightening speed of a rattlesnake attack, Pal struck. Having emerged from underneath the Fiesta on his belly, using his elbows to propel himself across the rough, wet tarmac he had dragged himself like some predatory reptile towards the Escalade, always keeping below the viewing range of the mirrors, then, in one fluid movement, flinging the driver's open and screaming at Millard so loudly that Jenna saw Millard instinctively recoil in alarm.

"Both hands on the fucking steering wheel," he screamed through the balaclava which was now pulled down. "Else you get a bullet straight in your neck." The muzzle of the Beretta's silencer was cold and wet as he thrust it under the angle of Millard's right mandible, with such force that his head jolted violently backwards and, despite himself, he cried out in pain.

"If it's money. . ." he grunted hoarsely, his voice half-strangled by the Beretta's pressure on his larynx.

Pal had deliberately held the Beretta in his left hand so as to leave the right free to swing the sap that he'd bought off some mindless deadbeat with a shaved head in a sleazy Birmingham pub. The vicious swing travelled no more than twelve inches but he could both hear and feel the right cheekbone crack as Millard's scream pierced the air. He had warned Jenna that she was bound to witness this but it still made her feel sick to see such raw violence perpetrated by a man for whom she felt such deep affection.

"Now I want your piece" demanded the voice, muffled from within the mask. "Where is it?"

"Inside pocket of my leather jacket" croaked Millard, slumped in his seat and feeling the blood running down his throat from the internal damage caused by the blow. "What the fuck do you want. . . ?"

"Just shut it," growled Pal, tucking the blackjack into his belt. "The gun's under your jaw. My hand's going in your pocket. One move and I'll take your fucking brains out."

It was a Hechler and Koch, .45 caliber, top of the range, just as you'd expect from Millard thought Pal, as he put it into his combat jacket pocket.

"I'm stepping back. Get out of the car. Hands where I can see them and head for the barn," demanded Pal. There was no sound of any approaching traffic, but the sooner he had the gangster out of view the better. As Millard was led at gunpoint towards the barn, Pal heard Jenna fire up the Escalade and set off down the hill.

Now, in the stillness of the night, they were alone. Following close behind him, Pal was reminded of the latent power of the man. At six feet three he was probably five or six inches taller than Pal but, even shocked and injured, he walked with a feline lightness of foot.

Millard had not spoken since leaving his vehicle. Inside the barn Pal forced him to kneel in his immaculate trousers on the filthy floor before pulling the wagon door closed. The torch cast bizarre shapes across the floor and walls and, within its beam, Pal could see that the right side of Millard's face had come up like a grapefruit, completely closing the right eye and giving him the appearance of some macabre, medieval gargoyle.

"I've got cash," Millard whispered. "I live up the hill. I've got cash in the safe."

"I ain't interested in your drugs loot, Ray," Pal growled.

"You know my name. Your voice, it's muffled but it sounds

familiar. Do I owe you money?" Millard asked, his own voice distorted by the fractured cheekbone and the pain of talking.

"It's time you owe me, not money," declared Pal, pulling the balaclava up so that his face was revealed. "I always said you had the aspect of the Devil. You look even more like him with your cheekbone re-organised."

Millard would not be able to see anything with his head down and the glare of the flashlight blinding him and Pal deliberately let the deathly silence linger as the full impact of his words registered in his prisoner's mind. The phrase stolen from Shakespeare would reveal to Millard the identity of his assaillant and his brain would be working out all the angles as the logic of the attack on him found its context.

"This barn's probably two or three hundred years old, Ray. Must have seen a lot of things in its time. But I doubt it's ever seen an execution, 'cos that's what's going to happen here tonight."

Keeping the Beretta trained on Millard's head, Pal slowly walked a few feet to his right so that he was now head on to his prisoner and leant against one of the mighty wooden pillars.

"This ain't the Bailey, but I'm the Judge and the jury. I find you guilty of murdering that young copper. And I find you guilty of stealing my best years. My wife dumped me and I've never seen my kid from that day to this. All down to you, mate."

For many years Pal had dreamed of having this man at his mercy. His principles had now been hopelessly corrupted by prison and the scum with whom he'd had to share cells, lavatories, meal times and talk. Since his release he'd led a tough life of little purpose beyond survival. Yet, underneath, in the depths of his soul, he knew he was not a wicked man. There was, ironically, a sensitivity within him, that had helped him retain some sense of decency. The notion of taking another man's life offended all his natural instincts and it had disturbed him that during the planning he had never once stopped to ask himself if this was right or wrong. Nor had he ever entertained a moment's doubt that when, eventually, he had Millard at his mercy, he would pull the trigger. His loathing and suppressed anger ran so deep that he saw this act of murder as the extermination of some foul vermin.

Extending his arm so that the muzzle was within twenty feet of his prisoner's head, he prepared to fire but, at the point of squeezing the trigger, he stopped for he saw that the man's shoulders were shaking and a noise was emerging from his mouth which Pal had not heard for many years. It was a cold, disembodied sound, like a wolf which has just brought down its quarry and is now salivating at the prospect of flesh.

"Returned from the dead, have you, Pal?" the distorted voice observed, prompting Pal to hold off a moment longer. "Nice little move, that is. I like it."

"Where do you hear that?" he snapped.

"Reckon the coppers won't go looking in your Mexican grave?" Millard continued, ignoring Pal's question. "Listen, why don't you get smart? You're right, I do owe you. I saved my skin at your expense. It's the name of the game. Now it's your turn. I'm talking a million here. Cash. By the end of the week. . . ."

"Damn you, Millard," didn't you listen to what I said. "This is an execution site not a market place," Pal interrupted in anger and frustration.

Millard had lived his life under the constant threat of violence and had learned to ride through any crisis until some chance of a counter-strike arose. The early, intense pain had given way to a numbness running from temple to chin, the swelling now eliminating all vision from the one eye, but the other eye had slowly grown accustomed to the strange barn light. Inch by inch he had slid his left hand backwards towards his sock as Pal continued to give vent to the years of hatred.

Like he'd always said. Carry the insurance. This particular policy nestled in a sheath of heavy duty black nylon webbing with riveted corners and lashing holes to fasten it around his leg. The six inch blade was tempered high carbon steel with a shaving sharp edge. It was the Rolls Royce of throwing knives with a point sharper than a harridan's tongue.

His fingers closed on the Paracord handle and his thumb slipped into the shallow guide ready for the throw that he recognised was his last stand between life and death. Moreover, he would have to throw left handed, for there would be neither time nor opportunity for any attempted transfer to the right. And, it would be a blind throw, aiming for his target only by the sound of the voice which continued to pour out its venom.

As Millard's hand flashed in an arc, wrenching the blade from its sheath and launching it at the sound of the voice, Pal was aware of the sudden movement, the glint of steel and, in an instant, he pulled the trigger. Even with the silencer, the noise of the gunshot still filled the barn, bird wings flapped in panic in the rafters as they fled from their roosts and Millard screamed, but Pal heard almost none of it as the cold steel passed under his clavicle.

The force of the blow had driven him backwards against the wooden pillar and, putting his hand to the back of his shoulder, he could actually feel the spear point which had penetrated through the soft tissue and combat jacket but just missed the bone and was protruding through the other side. Blood was flowing freely at both point of entry and point of exit and Pal grabbed the pillar to keep himself upright until the immediate shock subsided. There was no sound from Millard and, in severe pain, Pal slowly bent down, retrieved the flashlight which had fallen from his hand and swung its beam to the spot where Millard had knelt to reveal the long body spreadeagled on its back, the head at an unnatural angle and the right side of the face a morass of ripped-open bleeding flesh. There was no sign of breathing or movement as Pal gathered up the Beretta and the used shell case. Tipping the fertiliser out of a half-empty plastic bag, he dropped the gun and shell into the bag and, fighting the pain, spent the next few minutes taking the necessary steps to ensure that he left no clues. Then, quickly emptying Millard's pockets and removing all of the evidence, he staggered towards the wagon doors and out into the cold, night air.

Cursing himself for not contemplating that Millard might have a reserve weapon, he stumbled his way back to the Fiesta, dropped the bonnet and inched his way into the driver's seat, chucking the fertiliser bag with the evidence on the front seat while feeling the point of the protruding knife catching on the car upholstery. Changing gear with his left hand was going to be a nightmare but he dared not pull the blade from his shoulder until he had made the rendezvous with Jenna at the rear of the Fox and Rabbit on the north side of Banbury.

Just before he joined the Motorway he had pulled into a lay-by as the pain threatened to overwhelm him, but a moment's rest revived him. Taking advantage of the stop, he pulled Millard's gun from his pocket and slipped it with the Beretta and bloodstained surgical gloves into the fertiliser bag. Forcing himself out of the car, badly hampered by the injury, he picked up several heavy half-bricks from a pile of rubble at the edge of the lay-by and dropped them into the bag, before struggling to tie the bag tightly with some twine from the car. Twenty minutes later he swung on to the large pub car park of the Fox and Rabbit and the Escalade sprang into life as Jenna spotted his arrival. With a flash of the lights, she followed him out of the car park, into the country lane and then down the dirt track which led to the river. The hatchback bounced on the stones and in the potholes of the track, sending stabs of pain shooting down his body and causing the five gallons of petrol in its green can in the rear compartment to slosh about.

After a mile of isolated countryside they came right alongside the river which was full and racing as the rain continued to fall. Once he had come to a halt underneath the spread arms of the old elm tree, he killed the engine and lights, put on the interior light and leant back in his seat with his eyes closed, while Jenna pulled alongside, ran round to the hatchback and slipped into the passenger seat.

Immediately shocked at the spectacle of his deathly white face it was a second before her eyes focused upon the brown Paracord handle protruding from the front of his shoulder.

"What the hell is it?" she gasped in horror.

"It's done," he breathed. "The job's done."

"But what's he done to you?" she cried.

"Don't panic," he replied weakly. "With your help it's not going to kill me. The bastard must have had it laced to his leg. But you'll deal with it.

"How on earth am I supposed to deal with it?" Jenna demanded, staring at him in disbelief.

Forcing himself up in the seat inch by inch, he cautiously turned towards her. "We're getting out of the car and you're going to pull it out," he announced, his voice suddenly getting firmer as he began to see the way forward.

"I can't do it," she whispered, tears now falling down her cheeks. "I can't do it, Pal. We've got to get you to a hospital."

The car windscreen was beginning to mist up and the air inside the car was heavy with the sweat born of his fear and pain. He knew that he had to act quickly and decisively.

"We can't risk going to a hospital. We don't know when Millard will be found. With this kind of injury hospitals call the cops. I don't know how much strength I've got left, so toughen up and just do what I tell you," he barked at her, opening his door and gradually easing his way out of the vehicle.

Jenna followed suit and ran round to support him the few yards to the elm tree whose branches offered some protection from the unyielding rain. Pal leant his back against the trunk and slowly lowered himself to the ground, the noise of the rushing river providing an eerie background to his involuntary grunts of pain.

"What do I have to do?" Jenna asked, her voice shaking with fear, but knowing that Pal was right. Hospital meant the Police and the whole plan would end in catastrophe. "Tell me exactly what to do."

Pals' eyes had adjusted to the darkness and he could see Jenna clearly and could feel the uneven ridges of the bark against the back of his head while the dampness of the ground was seeping through his trousers. The wet was making him cold and the cold was sapping his deeper reserves.

"Kneel. Get both hands round the handle. Pull it straight out. The edges are like a razor. Any vertical movement will extend the wound. Pull firmly in one continuing action and don't stop until it's out, even though I may scream or pass out. Have you got that, Jenna?" he asked, the voice thin and hoarse, but the directions precise.

"Got it," she said.

"When it's out, get my upper clothing off me any way you can. I'll probably be out cold so you won't hurt me. Tie my T-shirt round the wound as tight as you can. If it's got a major artery then there may not be much you can do. If it hasn't, I'll make it. Now go to it, girl."

Jenna's hands were shaking and the feel of the cord handle on her skin made her nauseous but, at High School she had been the top female athlete in her year. Several top Colleges had offered her an athletics scholarship but she had always known that as soon as school was over there was a wider world to see and she'd packed her bags for Vegas. But that innate strength, which had carried her through to the tape in the long distance events, remained within her body and now was the time to deploy it. Anchoring her knees in the wet earth she gripped that evil handle as tightly as she could so that it did not waver one centimetre as she pulled back hard and true, closing her ears to the animal scream that came from Pal's throat as he slumped sidewards, but hanging on to consciousness as the wicked weapon came free in her hands.

Getting blood-saturated clothing off an injured man with the upper torso of a fighting bull was heavy work but Jenna's determination was now taking control. In the darkness she could see the entry wound pouring, but not pumping blood, which might mean a major artery had not been hit. Vicious though the blade was, it was narrow and the appearance of the actual wound was less frightening than she had anticipated. Slashing the T-shirt into strips, she wrapped the wounds, binding them as tightly as she could, while Pal, who was already coming back to his full senses, urged her on.

"How bad is the pain?" she eventually asked

"It's changed now the knife's out," he replied. "It's throbbing but it's going numb. You're going to have to finish the job. There's a fertiliser bag in the car. It's very heavy. Weighted. It's got the guns and other stuff in it. Take it and that knife downstream."

"Yes, I know what to do," she replied. "A deep section of river and mid-stream."

"Yeah. When the Police find his vehicle and connect it to the body, they'll drag the river. So walk at least a couple of hundred yards downstream. They won't drag that far. Toss the bag and knife in different directions."

Jenna picked herself up from the ground, recovered the thick plastic bag from the Fiesta and heaved it over her shoulder, carrying the vicious throwing knife with Pal's blood running down its length in her free hand and hurriedly set off along the river path, relieved that the rain had at last relented.

Pal struggled gingerly to his feet, wrapped the combat jacket round his shoulders and threw his sweater into the Cadillac, noticing a small suitcase on the back seat when he did so. Then, walking the few yards to the hatchback, he extracted the full green petrol can with his right hand and carried it back to the Escalade. Jenna was gone a long time but by the time that she returned he was ready for the final act.

"Did you check inside that bag on the back seat of the Escalade?" he asked.

"Yes. It's an overnight bag. Change of clothes. Washing gear. That's all. He must have been away from home for a night," came the answer.

"OK. Get in the Fiesta, Jenna. You'll have to drive. Reverse it a safe distance from the Cadillac. It's got five gallons of four star all over it's leather upholstery"

Within a minute, sixty thousand pounds of Cadillac was a massive ball of flame, visible to no-one in the middle of the damp English countryside and consuming any clue it might have provided to solving the murder of its owner. The anonymous hatchback trundled its way peacefully back towards Birmingham while Pal fell into a deep sleep in the passenger seat as his body battled to recover from Millard's last throw.

Chapter 6

In the last hour of the full blackness of night the Motorway was carrying very little traffic and the ribbon of glistening road stretched out ahead of Jenna as, with frequent glances of concern at the dishevelled figure to her left, she steered them away from their mission of revenge. Millard's demanding voice echoed through her mind and the aura of menace he had generated sent a shiver down her spine. All she needed to know was that he had met his deserved punishment, so that they could now leave England and get on with the rest of their lives. If Pal wanted to tell her the details of the confrontation then she would listen but, as far as she was concerned, she would be content never to speak of Millard again.

Lost in her own thoughts she had no idea where the blue flashing light had come from. They were on a stretch of the Motorway that was several miles from the nearest town, she was driving in the inside lane and never wandering over sixty-five miles an hour. Either the Police had realised this was a stolen vehicle or something to do with Millard's body or the burning Cadillac had been already communicated to the white Range Rover that was now closing up on her rear.

"Pal", she shouted in alarm. "Wake up. The cops are pulling me over."

Awakening brought back the reality of the pain he was in and Pal groaned involuntarily as he opened his eyes, looked in the wing mirror and saw the white vehicle with its flashing light now immediately behind them.

"It may only be routine," he said unconvincingly. "We're tourists. American. We've been to Oxford. Met some friends and went back to their house. I'm asleep in the car. Keep them away from me if you can, they'll see the state I'm in."

Jenna pulled on to the hard shoulder and braked gently. The Range Rover immediately followed suit, coming to rest about forty yards behind them. Jenna swiftly reached on to the back seat, grabbed the navy blue cardigan she had brought with her, slipped it on and was walking briskly back along the hard shoulder towards the Police vehicle before either of the two Officers had even opened their doors. She was anxious for any discussion to take place as far away from the Fiesta as possible.

Only the passenger door of the Range Rover opened. Perhaps they could now clearly see it was a woman driving they would be less concerned. Looking at the whiteness of her blouse she could only hope that by some miracle she had not got any of Pal's blood on the front of it so as to raise their suspicions and pulled the cardigan more closely around her, thankful that the point at which she had thrown the bag into the river had allowed her to bend down and swill her hands in a more tranquil eddy at the water's edge.

Full uniform. Flat cap. Slim. Torch. Not very tall for a Police Officer. As he walked towards her she could see he wore glasses and had a moustache. Middle aged. No stripes. Never going to make the higher ranks and landed with the dog watch on the Motorway run. Perhaps Pal was right and it was only routine.

"I wasn't speeding, Officer," she called out.

"No, Madam. I'm not saying you were," he declared politely enough in a rural kind of accent she did not recognise as he came up to her and stopped. "Keep well over towards the verge. It's safer, love."

"Love". Millard had used the same term. It had not sat easily on his lips but in the Officer's more attractive burr it softened his approach and gave her hope.

"It's very late, Madam. Are you out alone?" he asked.

"No. My husband's asleep in the car. I'm trying not to wake him. He has a bad headache. Have I done something wrong?"

"American are we?" he responded.

"Touring. From New York," she answered calmly.

"Have you had a drink tonight?" he asked rather more assertively.

"Not a drop. Is that why you stopped me?"

"No. We stopped you because your offisde rear light isn't working," he finally announced, pointing back up towards the Fiesta to demonstrate his point. "That gives us the right to do a roadside alcohol test if we suspect you've consumed alcohol."

"And do you suspect me of having had a drink?" she enquired, relief now fuelling her confidence.

"No. I can see you haven't. But your shoes are covered in mud. Have you had some kind of problem? he asked with an edge to his voice.

Jenna's relief and confidence evaporated in an instant. Dog watch or not, his powers of observation were sharp enough and she hesitated before any kind of explanation could enter her head.

"Oh, dirty shoes," she laughed falsely. "We visited some College in Oxford and walked through the grounds. I stepped in the mud."

"Do you have any driving documents on you. Is it a hire car?"

Pal had explained to her that for some reason the British were not obliged to carry any driving documentation with them. No licence, no proof of insurance or ownership of the vehicle. Nothing. It was safe to say no.

"My husband arranged the car with some business associate. My licence and passport are back in our room."

"Right, Madam. I'll let you off the faulty light, but I'm going to give you a notice to produce your licence and insurance to a Police Station. It's only a formality. Do you want me to explain it to your husband?" he courteously enquired, now seemingly satisfied that all was well.

"No." Jenna responded.

Assuring her it would only take a few minutes, he ushered her back to the Range Rover, opened the rear door and helped her in before taking his seat and picking up a clipboard with a sheaf of papers on it.

"I just need a name, address, nearest Police Station and a signature" he announced. "Then you can be on your way."

"Susan Vance," she replied, instinctively using the name she'd trained herself to use over recent days. "We've got a room right in the centre of Birmingham. Not a Hotel. The name of the street is Gas Street," she lied nervously, using the name of a street she had seen near to where their service flat was. "But I don't know the number."

"I'll put down Gas Street, then. No number. And I'll put down your American address as well," he said, obviously trying to be helpful, as he began to write.

While her mind was racing to come up with an address in the States, the vehicle was suddenly filled with the piercing opening bars of "Battle Hymn of the Republic" set within the shrill ringing tones of a mobile telephone. With a growing sense of horror she realised that it was coming from her trousers pocket where she must have thrust Millard's phone in the frenzied seconds after Pal had launched the attack. Fumbling desperately to extract it from her pocket she knew that she had no idea how to cut it off.

"Sorry, Officer. Damned nuisance. I'll switch it off," she mumbled ineffectually, struggling to swing back the lid and cut off the ringing. Pressing buttons indiscriminately, the ringing continued for several seconds until eventually it stopped. "Sorry, Officer" she repeated. Then, flipping the lid closed she thrust it firmly back into her pocket.

"And the US address, Mrs Vance?"

"25 North 25th Street New York City", she lied nervously.

"The central Birmingham Police Station is Steelhouse Lane. I've put that down. Anyone will give you directions. Take the paperwork in during the next five days and you'll hear no more about it. If you'd sign the form at the bottom," he explained, holding the clipboard so she could easily see the document under his interior light. "Sign next to where I've written my name, the date and time. P.C. Gellick 4.54 a.m on Thursday the 10th."

As soon as she had scrawled "Susan Vance" on the form he handed her a copy while his colleague drove them slowly up to the rear of the Fiesta. P.C. Gellick insisted on seeing her into her car and in the Range Rover lights she could now see that the offside light plastic casing was actually broken and the bulb was smashed. It must have happened on the rough ground by the river, she thought to herself. Quickly slipping into the driver's seat she denied P.C. Gellick any opportunity to address the recumbent shape of her husband, the coat drawn tightly around his body and his head angled away from the road.

Wasting no time she started the engine and very correctly eased her way back onto the deserted Motorway while the Range Rover stayed courteously behind her to ensure her safe return to the road and then followed at a respectable distance.

"Broken back light," she half-whispered to Pal, as if the Police might hear her.

"Did they ask any questions" he asked urgently, keeping his head below the top of the seat as long as the Range Rover stayed behind them.

"Gave me a form to produce my licence and so on. But we've got five days, so it's not a problem. We'll be long gone by then. I gave a couple of false addresses in Birmingham and New York." Jenna assured him.

"Good girl," came the relieved response.

"Oh. There was a problem," she suddenly remembered. "His damn phone. It was in my pocket. I'd forgotten all about it. It rang when I was in their car. I couldn't get it to stop."

"Christ, Jen. That could be serious. Give it me now," he demanded.

Struggling to pull it from her pocket while she drove, it eventually came free and he grabbed it from her hand. There was a screwdriver in the glove compartment and flipping the phone lid back, he drove the screwdriver between the body and lid of the phone, wrenching them asunder before opening the back and pulling out the Sim Card.

"When we get back to Birmingham you cut this card up and dump it and the phone in the canal at the end of the road" he insisted. "Check the car seats for blood and clean it off. I'd intended to torch it as well but I can't ask you to do that. So dump the car on the outskirts of the City."

"OK. And I'll get rid of all the clothes we're wearing. I've probably got blood on the back of my blouse which is why I put the cardigan on. But, most important of all, we've got to clean that wound. Hydrogen Peroxide. It'll hurt like hell but we've got to avoid infection."

"I just need sleep, get the healing started and recover my strength. Then we get out. I doubt they'll find Millard that quickly. The Escalade will eventually lead them to him, but it's in the middle of nowhere so they may not find that for a day or two. And a burned out stolen car is no big deal. They won't hurry. It'll only start to matter when they find the body. Saturday we move on. Train to Fishguard and then the ferry to Larne."

At that moment Jenna looked in her rear view mirror to see the Range Rover indicating that it was turning off at the "Coventry South" exit, which was a location she recognised as being the town through which Lady Godiva rode naked in the full light of day in exchange for her husband, Leofric, reducing taxation on the populace. Jenna reflected wryly to herself that human beings hadn't changed much in the thousand years since Lady Godiva had strutted her stuff. Men could still influence women to perform foolish and extreme acts.

Chapter 7

Later, while Pal lay in a state of exhaustion in the Birmingham service flat and Jenna dressed and re-dressed the wound, Jake Kempner was driving his faded green Volvo up the same Motorway that Pal and Jenna had travelled but a few hours earlier. Len Barras was fifty-eight years of age and would probably never finish the thirty year sentence for murder that he was serving. His son, Martin, had pulled a bank job ten years ago, but a passer-by had seen him pulling off his mask as he jumped into the get away car, subsequently picking him out on an Identification Parade. Len had tracked the witness down and shot him in the chest. The shot was fatal and so was the Judge's sentence. Eighteen years for Martin for robbery and life, with a minimum recommendation of thirty years to be served, for Len.

Serving a prison sentence from which you never expect to be released presents two options. Either you knuckle down and direct your energies into softening the regime, or you resist and fight the authorities at every turn. From day one Len Barras had chosen the second option. If any opportunity arose to attack a warder, a weak inmate or a social worker, then he took it. Solitary confinement, sudden transfers, loss of privileges had all been tried and now he had stamped on a warder's head, fracturing his skull. Prosecuting him was a waste of time and money as he was never going to be released. So the authorities decided to give him a taste of the glass cell.

Originally reserved for the most dangerous criminals in the country, the glass cell was a free-standing construction in the middle of a an open area in the inner cell block of one of the toughest prisons in the United Kingdom. Other than for one hour's exercise a day so as to comply with the Human Rights legislation, the prisoner never emerged from the goldfish bowl. He was under observation twenty-four hours a day. Food was posted through a hole in the door. No-one spoke to him.

One telephone call had been sufficient to enable Jake Kempner to identify the face Salerno had been referring to and, whilst he didn't hold out much hope of getting any information out of Barras, he was prepared to try. Forewarned was forearmed and he didn't take kindly to the notion of Albright sending in the heavies. A second phone call had provided him with at least the pretence of a carrot to offer.

It took fifty minutes to pass through security. The stony faced prison officer checked Kempner's hair, under his arms, in his crutch and even inside his socks. A succession of electric doors eventually led into a yard where he and the escort were joined by two unchained alsatian dogs, each with their own handler. In a silent procession they headed for the inner nucleus and the glass cell.

It was a gruesome spectacle, as Barras could be seen pacing backwards and forwards across the few feet of the transparent cage, like some wild animal, stripped of all dignity, every last ounce of its freedom removed, yet its spirit unbroken. Cameras were trained on the Plexiglass cell while another officer sat at a desk, empty-eyed, staring at the prisoner, waiting for the change of personnel which happened every half-hour as the observation duty was so tedious.

Kempner had interviewed prisoners under draconian Death Sentence conditions at the Clinton Correctional facility in Dannemora, New York State where the restrictions were so severe that the inmates referred to the regime as "dying twice". In New York he had come to accept it, but found himself shocked to discover similar conditions in England.

The old Electric Chair from Dannemora had subsequently been moved to a training facility in Albany and his team of Detectives had been taken up there on a guided tour. Kempner realised he was currently experiencing the same feeling of deep disgust at State brutality in the name of justice as he had felt during that tour. With an undisguised sense of pride, a retired guard had shown them the obscenity, with its leather belts designed to run across the chest and limbs. Two copper electrodes sat on a shelf, one for the shaved leg and the other, set in a hideous helmet, for the shaved head, nestling alongside a leather face mask and a diaper.

One touch on the executioner's button and 2400 volts would be delivered, causing smoke to come out of the leg and head but, subtly, the amps were always kept at less than six, so that the body did not cook, yet transmitting enough voltage to destroy the brain and central nervous system. Every muscle in the body would have contracted, rendering breathing and heartbeat impossible yet, commonly, a second surge was required to finish the job.

"Cooks the brain," the self-professed expert had smugly declared. "Eyeballs pop out on to their cheeks while they sweat blood. Just like bacon sizzling on the hob."

Perhaps the glass cell wasn't quite as extreme as the Dannemore relic, but the mentality of the prison staff was too similar for comfort and, whatever Barras may have done, Kempner was shocked by the spectacle.

"You don't go in the Cube," the seated officer announced. "Speak through the hole in the door on the far side. I doubt he'll talk to you. He hates coppers worse than screws."

"I want to interview him about an old case. We think he may be able to clear it up. Something's turned up to suggest it may actually have been a natural death," Kempner explained, repeating the lie he'd given to the Governor to obtain permission for the visit."

"Please yourself," the guard grunted. "He ain't been told who you are, but he can smell coppers at a thousand feet, so watch out for his spitting. He's got a good aim."

Kempner walked round the structure to the far side where he could see the hole in the door. Bending his head down to the level of the aperture, he was about to speak when Barras, who had been staring intently at him as he approached, suddenly emitted a large globule of spit straight at his face. Kempner rapidly jerked his head back out of the line of fire and the disgusting mass flew through the hole before splattering on the floor.

"OK, Barras," he began. "That should make you feel better. And you're right. I'm a cop. But what I want from you will cost you nothing."

Barras was stocky and in good shape for his age and debilitating state of confinement; his head was completely shaved, but he had a tightly groomed beard and moustache and a large tattoo of an eagle on the left side of his neck. Other grotesque tattoos were fully exposed by the white vest and navy shorts that he was wearing.

"Fucking crazy are you?" he shouted. "Len Barras talking to a copper? If they let you in here I'd tear your head off your shoulders. Now, piss off."

"Spit, curse, do your worst, Barras. But in eighteen months Martin comes up for parole. The Police Report carries a lot of weight in that decision," Kempner said calmly.

The heavy forehead wrinkled in concentration and the beady eyes fixed on Kempner, exuding a contradictory mixture of contempt and interest. After a moment's consideration, he slowly eased himself towards the door.

"Are you so thick that you think the screws won't put it about that a cop came to the Cube? he sneered, although he now lowered his voice so that only Kempner could hear.

"The Prison's been told you can help us clear up an old enquiry. A death which may actually have been an accident, not a crime. No grassing," Kempner explained quietly. "It's a lie. The truth is I do want a name off you. But the low-life'll never know my source. This is a personal thing between me and him."

"What you say your name was?" asked Barras, his mind quickly reviewing all the prison talk he'd heard over the last few weeks.

"Jake Kempner. You've heard a heavy sounding off about a contract to do me over. I want his name. I'll deal with him man to man. Nothing official and no permanent damage. In exchange, I put a piece in the parole report on Martin. It'll help get him out. Your wife's struggling badly. With Martin out her life will improve. Yes or no? Now. Or the screw will start to think you're grassing."

"Fuck off, out of here and don't come back," Barras screamed, punching the glass wall and throwing himself on to his bed, causing the Prison Officer to get out of his chair and walk round to where Kempner was standing.

"Don't say you weren't warned," he said dismissively to Kempner. "I'll send for the escort so you can leave."

"Right," replied Kempner, catching Barras's discreet nod in his direction as the Prison Officer turned back towards his desk to phone for the escort. "But, I'll just have one last go."

Still lying on his bed and speaking so softly that Kempner strained to hear, Barras mouthed the words that Kempner had never expected to hear. "No big deal. Geezer just picked up a five stretch. Sounding off in Belmarsh that getting locked up had cost him a ten grand job but he'd found a replacement."

"What was the job?" breathed Kempner as Barras picked himself off the bed and came back to the door.

"Some big noise in the City wanted a copper called Kempner doing over," he whispered. "What's the guarantee on Martin's parole?"

"No guarantee. But a promise I'll try. Name of the replacement?" Kempner demanded.

"Tisdale. Bruce Tisdale," came the soft reply, immediately followed by a stream of abuse as Barras began banging his head forcefully against the glass door. "Get the bastard copper out of here" he screamed repeatedly as the escort arrived and Kempner turned away from the glass cell.

* * *

By late afternoon Kempner was back at his desk in the drab Victorian building just south of Eltham. The top brass in the Met had decided that giving the Regional Organized Crime Department their own local Headquarters might lift the sagging morale of the troops. Beeston House had become surplus to Local Council requirements, enabling the Met to acquire the balance of the lease at a knockdown price. Cold in the winter, stifling in the summer, mainly open-plan so it was hard to find any privacy, set out on three floors with a lift that seldom functioned and with a canteen that served weak coffee and under-filled sandwiches, it had soon acquired the sobriquet of "Bleak House."

Heading South on the Motorway Kempner had called Danny Rose. Detective Sergeant Danielle Rose belonged to the new generation of Police Officers. Leaving Liverpool University with a first class degree in Business Administration, she had immediately joined the Met on the Graduate Programme and rocketed her way up to Sergeant. Bright as a button and tough as teak, she belied her dainty appearance. Standing only five feet four and weighing less than a hundred and ten pounds she had emerged top of the class in self-defence and had already dealt with thugs twice her weight and a quarter of her brain power. Her female intuition had proved faultless. She had as much in common with the old Bobby image of Dixon of Dock Green as Mozart had in common with Madonna.

When she had first been assigned to Kempner there had been an immediate problem, for her soft face and red curls bore an uncanny resemblance to the girl he still thought of each morning as he awoke. In other circumstances, the obvious mutual appeal might well have had a future, but the folly of trying to revive a ghost, plus the Lauren factor, combined to stop him crossing the line, but Danny Rose had found it hard to disguise the feelings she was developing for him. Lately, they had taken to calling each other by last names as a kind of reminder that, whilst the job may demand total reliance on each other, emotional distance was to be encouraged if possible. In this respect, their efforts totally lacked success and the complexity of the relationship intensified by the day.

"Rose," he began when she picked up the phone on the second ring. "How was the Coliseum?"

"Fantastic," the bright voice came back enthusiastically. "Four days of gladiators, pasta and poets. But first day back's always a bit grim. What you up to, Kempner? Your phone's been off all day."

"I'm only an hour away. I'll explain when I get there. In the meantime I want you to run a check for me. Bruce Tisdale. Put him through the computer and get me the collator files on him," Kempner demanded.

"Wilco," she snapped in return, adopting the old bomber pilot lingo her father had always used at home throughout her upbringing, having picked it up off his own father who had flown the heavy Lancasters over the North Sea a lifetime ago.

"One other thing, Rose," Kempner added sharply. "Only you know about this. Don't run the checks in my name. No-one else is to see what you're doing."

"Very NYPD," she laughed, as he clicked off his phone.

By the time Kempner had parked the old warhorse Volvo in the yard at the back of Bleak House, the information on Tisdale was sitting in a brown sealed envelope on Kempner's desk. All the other officers were out in the field and Rose was alone when Kempner walked in. Her soft skin had the touch of sun upon it from the Italian trip and, as usual, he felt that sudden skip in his heart when he saw her, heralding an abrasive edge to his tone which they both knew was a cover-up.

"Done what I asked of you?" he barked in her direction, prompting a nod from her in the direction of his desk top and the envelope.

"Look before you speak," she observed reprovingly, smiling broadly at him at the same time.

"Summarise," he demanded.

"Easy," came the immediate reply. "Thug. Used to run with the big boys but got caught too often. String of previous for GBH. Does a bit of freelance now and again, but he's yesterday's man."

"Any current intelligence?" Kempner enquired.

"Hangs round his old haunts since his last release. Peckham mainly. Still has some notable criminal associates. Been seen with Gerry Walton several times in the last six months. Been seen a couple of times lately with Ray Millard."

As Danny Rose had anticipated, Kempner's ears had pricked up at the mention of Millard's name. Last year Kempner's team had targeted him for three months but had failed to gather sufficient evidence to move in. Kempner had grown to despise Millard during that time, not only for the massive scale of his Class A drug-dealing, but also because one night, when they had him under observation in an Edinburgh hotel room, they had had to endure the sounds of him giving his girlfriend a beating, unable to intervene for fear of compromising the covert operation. For all his New York veneer of toughness, Danny knew that Kempner was sickened by male violence towards women.

"What's his connection with Millard?" he asked.

"They go back a long way. You know that Millard was suspected of shooting a copper years ago. Some old intelligence suggests that Tisdale was there. No proof. But they're old mates."

Kempner picked up the envelope, sat himself down at his desk opposite Rose's and scanned the contents which she had so accurately and concisely summarized, unstapling Tisdale's latest arrest sheet which contained a copy photograph and slipping it into his pocket.

"OK. Shred the rest of it. I've got what I need," he ordered, tossing the empty envelope and papers on to her desk.

"Am I to share in the secret then?" she asked softly.

"It's unofficial. Albright has hired a heavy to give me a pasting. I've been to see some psychopath in one of the glass cells. According to him, Tisdale's the muscle."

"You'd better make it official, then. You can't watch your own back indefinitely," she replied, unable to keep the alarm from her voice.

Danny had met Lauren several times and, if the truth be told, she was jealous of her. Not of her beauty or success as an actress, but of her relationship with Jake. During long night duties Jake had spoken to her about his loss, how his mind wanted to visit places that no longer existed and how Lauren had become his refuge. But, from all he said, she recognized that Lauren was never going to leave her husband and Danny resented that. Lauren denied her a fair chance with Jake. So the lines had been drawn but there could be no denying how much she cared for him and a serious threat of violence from one of the old gangland heavies made her fear for him.

"I've thought long and hard about it. No official report. I'll deal with it my own way," he declared.

"How?"

"He'll have been told where I live and that it's on the fourth floor. He'll reason he can't safely break in. He'll know I operate out of Eltham. Albright knows all of that," Jake explained, re-analysing it as much for his own benefit as Danny's.

"You don't have to say anymore," Danny interrupted. "He's going to strike when you walk from your garage at the back of the flats. It's dark. It's secluded. You often don't get home until eleven of twelve at night."

"Exactly," Jake agreed. "He'll already have been tracking me. The job's been out quite a while already but this week I've been using the Tube."

"Until today," Danny remarked ominously.

"I've got a lot of paperwork to catch up on. . . ," Jake continued, deliberately ignoring her observation.

"So you'll be working late," Danny interjected, "giving the bastard the opportunity tonight. And I'm going to be out there in the shadows. You don't fly solo on this, Kempner."

"No way, Rose. This is my problem. You know enough to go after Tisdale if I'm found comatose in some dark corner. But that isn't going to happen. I'll deal with Tisdale. New York style," he declared emphatically.

"You won't learn, will you Kempner. This isn't New York. It's Blighty. Some of your methods can't cross the Pond."

Kempner looked up at the earnest young face, framed by those red curls and smiled across at her. "That old fighter pilot jargon you endlessly spout. What happened to your granddad then?"

"It's bombers he flew, not fighters. Lancasters not Spitfires," she announced defiantly. "And he got shot down in 1943 over Holland. Escaped capture and made it back to Manston. Flew dozens more missions. Made it through."

"And how do you think he'd have handled thugs like Tisdale?" Jake grinned.

"New York style," she replied unhesitatingly as they both started to laugh, before Kempner wandered out into the corridor to the coffee machine. It was time to draw the lines again.

Chapter 8

Fourth from the left in a row of eight garages. Nearly a hundred yards from the block of flats and down a poorly lit side alley that ran directly off the residential road. Kempner's eyes had scoured the approach to the garage but there had been no sign of any lurking figure in the shadows, nor any parked vehicle in the garage area that he didn't recognize. Pulling the Volvo into the empty garage, he turned off the lights and killed the engine. Silence. Activating the remote to close the garage door, he walked slowly away from the garage block, constantly straining his ears for any suspicious sound but all was quiet.

Towards the end of the alley, behind a low brick wall, there was a dustbin area housing a dozen bins alongside two large rectangular dumpsters in which the tenants were supposed to toss their rubbish that was suitable for re-cycling, although not many of them took the trouble to do so. He had looked with care in the direction of those dumpsters when he drove in and did so again as he walked by. Still nothing.

As he neared the alley's junction with the road he began to think that nothing was going to happen tonight when a bulky, broad-shouldered figure suddenly loomed into view from the street and headed slowly and deliberately towards him. Obviously, Tisdale didn't believe in the hiding behind a bush technique. This was going to be head-on. Kempner had no doubt it was Tisdale from the un-coordinated gait and the disproportionate size of the square-shaped head. Moreover, most honest London citizens didn't walk down side alleys at half past eleven at night with an iron bar in their hand.

Ten feet away from each other both men stopped and Tisdale raised the iron bar to shoulder level.

"It's showtime, Kempner," the gruff voice snarled, picking up his hackneyed lines from watching too many boxing matches. "No more screwing another bloke's wife, you bastard," he spat out as he lunged towards Kempner swinging the bar downwards in a vicious arc. "You gets your legs done now, next time it'll be your fucking head."

Whilst the years may have slowed Tisdale down and the movements may have become ungainly and clumsy, he still remained a formidable force. Dark alleys, iron bars, breaking bones and kicking heads had been his way of life since his father first took that leather strap to him and exposed him to the type of brutality that had dominated his life ever since. If Kempner had not been as keyed up as he was the bar would have shattered his leg. As it was, the very end of the heavy bar still caught him across the front of his thigh, thudding into the flesh but missing bone. It was Tisdale's only shot of the night. Drawing his arm back for a second blow, an athletic figure darted at him silently from behind, moving like quicksilver. A small hand grabbed the side of the thug's jacket, skillfully harnessing his own momentum as part of its attack, whipping his legs from under him and brought him crashing to the ground, the iron bar clattering uselessly at his side.

Danny Rose was astride the brute before he even realized he was down. The iron bar was now in her hands, held across his throat, restricting his breathing, while Kempner had drawn the Raven and was leaning over Tisdale, forcing the muzzle against his lips so that they were crushed against his teeth.

"One move, Tisdale, and you taste the bar or the bullet," he growled. "Nice move, partner," he added in his Sergeant's direction. "What do you call that?"

"Aikido. Victory at the speed of sunlight," she replied, enjoying the acknowledgement, pressing a little harder on Tisdale's windpipe with the bar, causing him to retch as he tried to gasp for air with the steel of a gun barrel burrowing into his lips.

"OK, Tisdale, we know who you are and who's bankrolling you,"

Kempner spat out. "Right at this moment you've got a problem with a Raven. Only four inches long. Fits into the palm of the hand snug as a bug. Teenage hoodlums love'em. Light and cheap. That's how I got this little charmer. Untraceable. Kept it for a rainy day. I'm going to pull it back now just a couple of inches. So you can speak."

"You've made your point," Tisdale said quietly, dragging oxygen into his lungs as the barrel retreated.

"I don't think I have," Kempner retorted immediately. "We can arrest you for attempted GBH and slot you back inside for a stretch. Or I can put a slug into each elbow. The cops won't believe you if you claim it was me. Or there's the third way."

"What the fuck's the third way?" Tisdale grunted.

"From here you go straight to 105 Bellhouse Gardens, Chelsea. I imagine he's dealt with you via a middle man. But that's his address and his name is Albright. You tell him that you were caught and confessed on our little tape recorder that he was paying ten grand to break my legs."

"What you on about? What fucking tape recorder?" came the bemused response.

"This one," Kempner laughed, holding up the micro-cassette recorder he held in his free hand. "And when you've told my little machine all about Albright, you'll go round and warn him that one more pop at me and the tape goes to my Superintendent and to the Press. That's the third way."

Tisdale's excuse for a brain carefully reviewed the choices and within five seconds made the selection. Still keeping the gun trained on him they led him to the brick wall where he duly mumbled his confession into the machine.

"On your way now, Bruce," Kempner ordered as he returned the recorder to his pocket, but still aiming the Raven at his belly. "With one other errand to perform as a bonus for my generosity."

"What?"

"Within twenty four hours from now, I want to know if your mate is still hitched up with that black girl he's been going with for a couple of years," Kempner said.

"Which mate?" Tisdale enquired nervously.

"Your old mate. The one who shot the copper. You know all about that as well. I'm not asking you to tell me what jobs he's done or he's planning. I just want to know if the girl is still on the scene. Else our whole deal's off and we'll run you in for attempted GBH now."

When Kempner had mentioned shooting the copper, Tisdale had been unable to prevent the shock from showing all over his face. This whole job was proving to be a disaster and he was now aware that he was well out of his depth. Telling Kempner whether or not Ray still had Alicia in tow wasn't grassing him up and he reckoned he could live with that if it got Kempner off his back.

"How do I get in touch with you?" he breathed.

"Here's my mobile number, Bruce." Kempner responded. "I'd already written it out for you. I knew you'd see it my way. By midnight tomorrow night I want to know you've dealt with Albright and if the black girl is still on the scene. If you fail to deliver on either, or don't call, then I'll be round with the cuffs. Now, beat it."

As the cumbersome figure sloped off into the darkness Danny and Jake sat on the wall, close together, letting the adrenalin subside.

"Why on earth do you want to know if Millard is still seeing that girl?" she asked in a puzzled tone.

"Because my instinct tells me that she may have an important part to play in getting at him. You know he knocks her around. Everything else we've tried has failed," he replied.

"You don't understand that type of woman too well, do you?" Danny asked gently.

"What do you mean?"

"Millard's a major player. One of the top few in the country. Vicious. Ruthless. And, as far as the girl is concerned, dominant," she explained.

"Are you telling me that she gets some kick out of his dominance?" Jake enquired.

"Precisely. And she not only accepts his violence but expects it. She sees it as his virility. She won't let him down," Danny concluded with a shake of her head. "Anyway, the mission's over. Time to head for home."

"It's midnight, I'll put you in a cab," observed Jake, looking at his watch. "On the other hand, you can stay at my place if you want," he added dangerously.

"And Lauren?" Danny snapped back.

"She's in Manchester until Sunday. The play's running up there before its London opening next week. And there's a spare room, you know," he answered.

Danny looked at the handsome American face, far from his natural home, set in the blackness of the London night, still recovering from the drama of the battle they had just fought with Tisdale. Those brown eyes looked sad with creases appearing at their corners and worry lines visible across the forehead. Being attacked by a brute wielding an iron bar wasn't something easily dismissed from the mind and she longed to take him in her arms and make him forget. But she knew it wasn't concerns about iron bars, thugs and gangsters that caused the sadness and the worry lines. It was a ghost. And she wasn't capable of exorcising that ghost. He had to do that for himself.

"The heart says yes," she eventually replied. "But the head says no."

"And which wins?" he asked apprehensively.

"The head, Kempner. So call me a cab," she declared, getting to her feet and walking towards the road, brushing away a tear in the darkness.

"Yea, I've ordered. What's happening?" Jake enquired, coming briskly to the point. Experience had taught him that Champagne enjoyed socializing and needed hurrying along.

"How's that actress lady of yours. Still playin' to full houses?" he asked with interest, ignoring Jake's question.

"Yeah. New play opens down here next week. 'When The Moon Stopped Smiling'. They're previewing in Manchester at the moment," Jake replied, attacking the tuna salad sandwich and cappuccino which had just been delivered to the table. "What's troubling you, maestro?"

"OK. Here's the picture," Champagne answered, pushing his long, lugubrious face across the table close to Jake and lowering the piping voice to a whisper. "At the weekends we employ twenty-five Security staff. Occasional changes, but faces mainly stay the same. We have a main man. Been a Scorpion ever since I laid my money down in Vibes and Margarita. Last week he tells me he's hiring outside the Scorpion at Margarita. I says Millard'll have the place torn apart and him with it."

"Did he give any reasons?" Jake probed.

"He says Millard's under heavy pressure. Money. He's probably going to sell the Scorpion Sting business off. So our main guy says he's got to look to his own future."

"Did he say who Millard was selling to?" Jake asked.

"As yet, unknown. As soon as I get a name I'll let you know and you can give me the feedback. But I reckoned you'd be interested. Particularly about him being under pressure."

"Thanks, Champagne. I am interested. People make mistakes under pressure. Keep me informed," Jake responded, getting off his stool. "Got to get back to the office. Good seeing you."

"Short and sweet, Detective. What about the social niceties?" came Champagne's retort.

"Got a lot on, maestro. And I can't help you until you get me a name. But anything about Millard's always appreciated. Ciao," Jake replied.

Champagne nodded. "OK. So long," he smiled, now turning his attention to the next iced mocha.

Crossing the river on foot over Blackfriars Bridge, Kempner picked up the Volvo from Waterloo car park and, as soon as he got on the road towards Eltham, pressed the button on his hands-free for Rose. She answered on the first ring.

"You made it home alright last night then?" he remarked.

"But I couldn't sleep," came her terse reply. "I was in the office by six and on the road to some village in Berkshire by seven. I tried to call you but your phone was off."

"What's taken you to Berkshire?"

"Some anglers were holding a fishing competition on a stretch of the river by this village. Amberley, it's called. When the first team arrived at dawn this morning they found a burnt-out Cadillac Escalade. Some American four-wheel drive monster." Rose explained.

"Why's that of any interest to us?" came the puzzled response.

"It had been deliberately torched. Gone cold long before the firemen arrived but they found the melted remainder of a plastic petrol can inside. They think it'd probably been done in the early hours of Thursday. They got the ID Number off the engine which led them to the owner's name. You're going to like this," she teased.

"Shoot."

"Raymond Leon Millard of Keeling House, Radford, Berkshire", Rose announced. "The local cops fed the name into the computer and it showed our boy was something of a celebrity. Our Department's interest in him is flagged up via the Collator's files. So they phoned Eltham and I thought I should fly up and take a look."

"And your verdict?" Kempner asked.

"The locks were never forced. The keys are still in the ignition. So it was pinched with the keys in it, or with Millard in it, or both. There's a small case on the back seat which had clothes and personal washing gear in it. All pretty much consumed by fire, but a part of one label is legible. Armani," Rose recited.

"Armani equals Millard. His preferred gear," Kempner observed wryly.

"Nothing else survived which throws any light on what happened. No-one was in the car. No sign of foul play. No-one lives within a couple of miles, so nothing was heard or seen. It's a pretty isolated spot. And it's poured the last couple of nights round here. There are some car tracks which obviously don't come from the Escalade but there are numerous others. Kids drive up here for a bit of passion in the car and at least a dozen anglers' cars had churned the area up by the time I arrived. That's about it," she concluded.

"What about Millard. Who's contacted him?" Kempner asked.

"I thought it better to get the local lads to do that. Didn't want Millard to know we came running that quickly just 'cos his wheels got nicked and torched. So they phoned his house. Millard wasn't there," Rose replied.

"Was anyone there?"

"Just a woman's voice on an answer phone giving a mobile number. They've been trying that all morning. Nothing. No answer. No message. As soon as I hear anything I'll let you know."

"Right. I'll be in the office in half an hour. I'll follow it up. Tisdale hasn't contacted me yet. Might learn something off him. If you were in at six, it's hardly worth you coming back to Eltham, is it. Your shift's over as it is," Kempner observed.

"OK. I'll head home. I'll keep my phone on in case you need me. Over and out."

"Over and out, Rose" Jake replied with a grin on his face. But Danny had already gone.

Back at Eltham there was a crisis over the paperwork for the covert surveillance job on the Japanese Bankers. It had taken

Kempner three hours of faxes, phone calls and form-filling to get things in shape and, by the time the final version was winging its way along the telegraph lines, Kempner was ready for his dinner. Sitting at his desk in the spartan office he looked up to see that all the other detectives had gone. He was alone. Lauren would be about to take the stage in Manchester. Danny would be in her flat cooking a Marks and Spencers microwave meal for one. Millard was bound to have learned about his Cadillac by now and would be fuming. Tisdale still hadn't phoned. Pushing his chair away from his desk, he decided it was time to head for home.

The contents of the fridge were singularly unpromising. Rustling up an inadequate omelette with a toasted bagel and a banana for dessert, he uncorked the bottle of Californian Zinfandel and slumped into the armchair by the window which, in the daytime, afforded him a narrow angle glimpse of Clapham Common. The lower end of the rental market didn't run to full frontal views and it was a real bonus to have even a peek of green, yet alone the luxury of a garage. Sipping from a thick kitchen tumbler, his mind wandered inevitably to thoughts of the girl with the tight, red curls. Carefully selecting a CD, he clicked the remote for Track 5 "The Only Living Boy in New York". The purity of Art's voice and Paul's haunting guitar carried him back to the City where everything had seemed possible and now existed only inside his head. She was gone. New York could never again be the place that he wanted. Lauren might still play an important part in his life but would never leave Albright. Jake felt the blackness descending. He couldn't afford to stop to think because, if he did, he always reached the same conclusion. His life was going nowhere. Catching big-time London villains was an exercise to stop him examining the realities of his own circumstances. Simon and Garfunkel had moved on to "Old Friends", yet another manifestation of their genius. Jake's problem was that, outside work and Lauren, he had no friends with whom he could grow old. His emotional downward spiral was gathering momentum when the phone rang. It was Tisdale.

"Kempner?" the gruff voice asked.

"That's me."

"The husband got the message. Not happy about it, but you won't be getting no more grief from that direction," Tisdale mumbled.

"And your other errand?" Kempner enquired.

"Ray and his lady friend shack up together at his place in the sticks. That's all I'm doing for ya, Kempner. We're quits," Tisdale declared aggressively.

"Did you get that from Millard himself?" Kempner persisted.

"Nah. I couldn't get hold of him nowhere. In the end I phoned his drum. She answered. She's worried. She'd been out looking for 'im. He drove to Newcastle on Tuesday. Some business deal. Due back late Wednesday but never showed. She ain't heard from him since."

"Very touching, Bruce. But you've cleared your debt," Kempner replied and rang off. Something was obviously happening in Millard's world but he wasn't likely to learn anymore from Tisdale. Before he'd had the chance to pour himself a second glass of wine, the phone rang again. It was Lauren. She was as high as a kite. Three curtain calls. Standing ovations. They had a success on their hands and she would speak properly in the morning. Off to the celebrations. She was in such a state of elation she hadn't even bothered to refer to her earlier message about Tisdale's visit to her husband the night before.

Then came the third consecutive call in the space of a few minutes.

"Kempner?"

"You got him."

"D.I. Braithwaite from Newbury Police Station," the voice announced in a clipped, precise tone. "We've got a body up here which we think may be of interest to your lot," he continued.

"That's off my patch, Braithwaite, what's the connection?" Kempner asked.

"I'm not keen to say much on the phone. A farmer came into his barn tonight to load his trailer for an early start in the morning. He found the body. Tough old guy, but it's shaken him up badly. We suspect it's a London villain who lives a couple of miles from here. Your Department targeted him some time ago and there was an incident in Amberley earlier today which one of your Sergeants attended. It's a bad one, I can tell you," Braithwaite declared.

"I'm leaving now. What's the exact location?" Kempner replied.

"Nolan's barn. On your left as you come up the hill towards a village called Radford in Berkshire. Pathologist's on his way." said Braithwaite.

"I'll be there by eleven. Thanks for the call," Kempner snapped back, cutting the line and instantly activating Danny Rose's number from his memory. Again she answered on the first ring.

"Rose. Get your farmer's boots on. We're going to visit a barn," he ordered.

"Speak in English, Kempner, not in crossword clues," she barked back.

"Newbury Police just phoned. They think they've found Millard. The computer's tied it in with our interest and the torched Escalade," came the reply.

"When you say 'found' him, do you mean dead or alive?" she demanded.

"The former, Rose. Very much the former. That's why I'm picking you up in fifteen minutes flat and we're heading for Nolan's Barn."

"You're commanding me to scramble, are you?" she laughed.

"Exactly. Scramble. The bandit's not at one'clock. He's bought it. On my way. Over and out," he snapped back at her, as her attractive laughter grew louder, before he cut the call.

Chapter 10

About a dozen vehicles were parked on the side of the road near to Nolan's Barn. Marked and unmarked police vehicles, an ambulance and a white Scenes of Crime Van, loaded with the latest equipment. Twenty yards each side of the gate was already cordoned off by police Crime Scene tape and the technicians had rigged up some lights which enabled the essential personnel to walk to the barn without using the path. Two uniformed officers were positioned at the gate, vetting and logging anyone entering or leaving the barn or the surrounding area.

Kempner and Rose were ushered through and told to make their way across the longer grass round to the far side of the barn. Coming round to the wagon doors in a wide arc, they could see that one door was half-open and was being guarded by another young, uniformed Constable, white-faced and still appearing queasy from whatever he had seen within.

A short, stocky man in a flat tweed cap, dark green anorak, blue corduroy trousers and wellington boots quickly emerged through the door and introduced himself as Inspector Braithwaite. Kempner suspected that precious little hair lay underneath Braithwaite's cap and was compensated for by a full, bushy, moustache which dominated the well-worn, ruddy-complexioned and rather kindly face.

"Pathologist's here now. And three Scenes of Crimes bods. I'm going to let you see the body in situ, Kempner, but your Sergeant may care to give it a miss," Braithwaite informed them.

"I've seen dead bodies before," Rose interjected, bridling at the exclusion.

"No slight intended, Sergeant. It's just that I doubt either of you have seen one like this. You needed to be warned. If you insist, then I'm not stopping you. Your call," he replied.

"Let's get it over with," Kempner said. "Rose's tough enough and I value her judgement."

"Like I said, your call. The body's been badly mutilated. The fewer people that have to be exposed to it the better. Stay on the footplates and then I won't have to ask you to put any protective suits on. I'll see you back at the gate," remarked Braithwaite, pulling the door open for them and then walking away back towards the road.

Powerful floodlights illuminated the interior of the barn like daylight. The SOCO Officers and the pathologist were in white protective overalls, head coverings like shower caps, surgical gloves and over-shoes, lending the whole scene a science fiction dimension. The masked pathologist was crouched over the body in the central area of the barn, while the technicians were on their hands and knees, meticulously picking their way over the whole interior, collecting anything of potential interest and capturing it in their endless supply of plastic containers.

Kempner and Rose stepped carefully across the footplates which led them to a position opposite the pathologist and a couple of yards away from the feet of the body. It was stretched out on its back, legs towards the main wagon doors. The shoes were medium brown with rounded toecaps. Matching brown socks were visible beneath the bottoms of the high quality tailored beige trousers and the upper body bore only a blue shirt. The clothing looked soaking wet. Despite herself, Rose was forced to draw a deep breath and, for just one second, her hand reached out to grab Kempner's arm as her balance was threatened by the impact of what she saw. Before Kempner had any chance to re-act she had steadied herself and got her breathing back under control. For his part Kempner stood motionless. He'd only seen it done once before. A gangland slaying in the New Jersey Docks. They'd known the name of at least one of the assassins but had never picked up a single useable piece of evidence. No-one was ever prosecuted for it. The savagery of the mutilation had served to terrify all and sundry into submissive silence.

Dr Mimura looked up at them over his face mask and raised his eyebrows, as if expressing disbelief that a human being could do this to a fellow creature. Kempner had worked with Mimura on one previous case. Based at one of the top London Hospitals he was only called out beyond London Central if the case threatened to be forensically complex. This one certainly satisfied that criterion. Half Japanese on his father's side and half-Welsh on his mother's, he was a strange mix. Short, squat, dark, bespectacled and supremely polite. Shrewd, with a sharp instinct, his feel for a case was sound and Kempner nodded back at him, approving Braithwaite's obvious decision to send for one of the better pathologists. Slipping his mask down, Dr Mimura got to his feet and stepped back from the body, avoiding the two large boxes of vials, test-tubes, probes, swabs and other paraphernalia of his trade in death.

"This is Sergeant Rose, Doctor," Kempner said. "Glad to see they sent for you".

"Good evening, Inspector. Good evening, Sergeant," Dr Mimura responded, not quite bowing to Rose, although there was an unmistakable oriental lowering of the head. "As you see, the killer has beheaded the victim. One blow. A very clean, forceful blow. With an instrument of extreme sharpness," he reported in the tone of an accountant totting up the company's profit and loss for the month.

"Any sign of the head?" asked Kempner.

"No. Nor the hands. Both hands have been severed with the same clean-cut force," Dr Mimura replied. "But I doubt that the beheading was the cause of death."

"Why do you say that?" Rose enquired curiously.

"Because there is no sign of any blood anywhere. You see over there," he said, pointing to the coiled up hosepipe in the left hand bay. "SOCO are confident that this whole area has been hosed down in an attempt to dispose of any blood."

"I'd noticed that the victim's clothing appears wet," Rose remarked.

"Correct," Dr Mimura confirmed. "Well, if beheading was the cause of death there would have been massive bleeding, not just on the floor but within spraying range, because the arterial thrust when the neck arteries and veins were severed, would have been very substantial. Like a fountain erupting. I find it hard to believe that every last vestige of blood could have been satisfactorily hosed away."

"So, are you telling us that your first thought is that he was killed by some other means. And he was beheaded and his hands were severed after death? Rose asked.

"Just so. Just so. No blood pressure. No pumping. Therefore localized blood loss. Leaving only a controlled and diminished blood flow which could easily be washed away," Mimura continued.

"And the blood and water would run away into the main system," observed Kempner. I can see the drains right there for sluicing the place out.

"There is no sign of any life-threatening injury to the torso so my money is on a head injury causing death. A blow to the head or a bullet. Without the head it will be very difficult to say which. Then, in death, the mutilation," Dr Mimura concluded.

Just at that moment one of the SOCO team called out to his colleagues that he had found evidence of blood on a support pillar some twenty feet or so from where the corpse lay, prompting Dr Mimura to step across the plates to inspect it with the scientist.

"Vertical smears," the boffin explained earnestly. "Too far from the body for even arterial, sprayed blood to have reached this pillar, wouldn't you agree, Doc?"

"I do agree," the Doctor acknowledged.

"That almost certainly means that either the attack began by this pillar and the scene moved to where he fell, or the attacker was by this pillar and was himself bleeding and grabbed the pillar," the boffin concluded.

"Will you be able to decide which scenario is correct?" Kempner queried.

"Probably," the scientist answered. "The lab can analyse the victim's blood and this blood on the pillar. If they're the same, the deceased was nearer to this pillar at some point while under attack. If the blood on the pillar doesn't match the deceased, then the attacker was himself injured."

"Which would lend itself more readily to your idea that the victim was shot," Rose injected.

"Exactly" said Dr Mimura approvingly. "Shot, at a distance of about twenty feet, while the attacker was bleeding from a wound by that pillar. After that, the attacker mutilated the body."

"And carried off the head and hands. Probably in one of those tough plastic fertilizer bags," observed the scientist, pointing to a small pile of fertilizer, seemingly emptied out at the edge of the nearest bay. You can see that one was probably opened and the fertilizer tipped out there."

"I'll get the body taken back to the morgue tonight and perform the post mortem tomorrow morning. After that we may be a lot wiser," Dr Mimura concluded, turning back to the piece of meat on the ground that was once a human life.

"Doc, if you give me a sample of the victim's blood now, I'll take it with me when we've finished," suggested the scientist. "That way I can tell you very early in the morning if it matches the blood swabs we'll take from this pillar. If they're different, then we may have the killer's DNA staring at us."

"I'll do it right now," the pathologist replied, kneeling down and selecting a needle and vial from one of his bags.

"There are some vehicle tracks running from the gate to both sides of the barn," the same SOCO scientist added. "Seems like several vehicles at different times. We'll photograph them but I don't expect much help. Courting couples can open the gate and the farmer's tractor has churned most of them up."

"OK, I get the picture," Kempner replied.

"There are some tools the farmer uses for tree cutting by the fertilizer bags. Axes and saws, but the whole area and the straw around it is soaking wet. I doubt we'll pick anything up," the scientist explained.

"All the pockets are empty," Dr Mimura volunteered, while he started to take a sample of blood from the right arm.

"No surprise there. How long before you move the body, Doc?" Kempner asked.

"I'd say another forty five minutes and I'll be ready to go. Why?"

"Because we've got a shrewd idea who the deceased may be and the sooner we get an identification the better."

"You've no head. So no face. So no dental records. You've no hands. So no fingerprints. What means of identification did you have in mind?" retorted the Doctor as he insinuated the needle into the deceased's forearm.

"If it's who we think it is, then he lives five minutes away. Lives with a woman."

"How's she going to identify a headless body? With nothing in its pockets. And no rings on its fingers because its hands have been chopped off?" Dr Mimura posed, with an unusually sharp edge to his voice.

"Height, body shape, colouring, distinguishing marks, genitalia. If this is the man she's shared a bed with over the last few years, she'll know," came the equally abrasive response from Kempner.

"And you're prepared to let the woman see the body in this condition to speed up your enquiry. I would respectfully suggest not,

Inspector. This spectacle has already made one of the young constables vomit. And your Sergeant's understandable reaction did not escape my notice. You risk traumatizing some woman for life."

"It's a crucial part of the enquiry and the sooner we get an ID the sooner I can point the investigation in the right direction. These first few hours are vital," Kempner urged.

"You're not talking first few hours," responded Dr Mimura, standing up with the sealed vial of blood now in his hands and beckoning for the scientist to take it from him. This body has been dead for a while. We'll never be too clear on how long. The body's soaking wet. But rigor mortis, libidity, rectal temperature all say well in excess of twenty four hours."

"I'd still like to see if we can get an ID here and now," Kempner persisted.

"Then medicine and detective work are in conflict. I would accept that a controlled identification in the morgue, with the body cleaned up and the head and lower arms covered, could probably be justified. But to let a loved one see the body here in this state disturbs me, I'm afraid. I may be doctor to the dead but I have a concern for the living as well," the pathologist earnestly explained.

"I get your message, Doc. Loud and clear. And I respect your concern. But you'd better let me check with Braithwaite on this. You see, it's likely that this stiff is one of the most feared men in London. The sensitivity factor is at the bottom of the scale. He controls his empire by violence and he takes that philosophy home with him. The girl's no shrinking violet. Let's get Braithwaite's take on this while you carry on with your preliminary examination."

While Dr Mimura returned to his grisly task, Kempner and Rose picked their way back across the footplates, exited the barn and stepped out into the sharp night air, relieved to escape the atmosphere of violent and sadistic death.

"Why cut off the head and hands?" Rose asked as they headed back towards the gate.

"I would guess for two reasons. One, it makes our job of identification much tougher. Two, it's a message. If it is Millard, then it's a very heavy hit indeed. The word will go out across London gangland that there's a new King. Someone who was not only able to eliminate Millard, but was also arrogant enough to stick two fingers up at his image and his crew," Kempner replied, spotting Braithwaite, leaning on the gatepost while pouring himself a hot drink from a large vacuum flask.

"Learned it from my first boss," Braithwaite called out as he saw them approaching. "Never attend a night job without a flask of hot coffee. Lifts the spirits."

"And they certainly need a lift after seeing that little lot," Kempner agreed. "Can we talk in detail later, Braithwaite? I'd like to press on immediately and get an ID."

"How?"

"The woman at the house. Bring her down. She'll be able to tell. I've explained it to Mimura. He reckons I'm a hard-hearted bastard. He's against it. I need your authority as Officer-in-Charge. I'll handle the dirty work with the woman," was the harsh reply.

"And will you handle the Complaints Department when she kicks up a fuss?" Braithwaite sniped back.

"We'll drown in PR. The Doc's got all kinds of gear with him. He can cover the body from the shoulders up and the lower arms. She won't see the mutilation or any wound. If I've got a territory war about to break out, I want to know immediately. Have you got a phone number for the house?" Kempner demanded.

"It's in my file in my car," Braithwaite said, nodding in the direction of the standard issue Rover saloon just down the road. "Come on, you can use my car phone."

Braithwaite's car was a cross between a travelling office and a mobile canteen. Pre-packed sandwiches, packets of biscuits, bags of crisps, cakes, and another vacuum flask were littered across the front passenger seat, whilst the rear seat was covered in files, papers and two briefcases. As soon as Braithwaite had located the number and punched it into the phone he handed it to Kempner.

"Who is it?" snapped a hard female voice.

"Detective Inspector Kempner. Sorry to trouble you so late, Madam but I need to contact Mr Ray Millard. . . ."

"He ain't here," the voice interrupted. "What you want with him?"

"We're concerned about his whereabouts. Do you know where he is?"

There was a long silence, eventually prompting Kempton to repeat himself. Still the woman remained silent.

"Listen, Madam. I need to see you. Can you give me your name?"

"Alicia. Alicia Daley. Where are ya?" came the response after another few seconds hesitation.

"Only a few minutes away. There's been an incident. It's better if I explain face to face. Can I come up to the house?" Kempner asked.

"What kind of incident? Are you saying something's happened to Ray?" she replied, the tone of voice moving higher and becoming more alarmed.

"Best I come and see you. Is that OK?' Kempner pressed.

"When you get to the gates, touch the word 'Visitor' on the keypad. I'll open the gates. Drive straight to the front door of the house. Don't nose around and don't get out of the car. I'll come out to you," the voice commanded.

"Why shouldn't I get out of the car?" he enquired.

"You'll see," she snapped and rang off.

Leaving Braithwaite sitting in his Rover munching on a sugared doughnut, Kempner and Rose set off in the Volvo up the hill, turned left at the church and came to a halt at the wrought iron gates, where Kempner touched the pad and the gates swung open.

"Like Fort Knox," he observed. "High walls, razor wire."

"And we've got company," added Rose. "Of the four-legged variety," pointing to the two Rottweillers now running alongside the nearside of the vehicle.

"So that's why we have to stay put," Kempner nodded as he accelerated up the drive, trying to put some distance between themselves and the dogs. A moment later the drive opened up as they came to the koi pond with the imposing statue as a centerpiece, now impressively illuminated by floodlights, trained upwards from beneath the water of the pool.

"You know what that statue is?" Rose laughed.

"Not a clue."

"It's Jupiter. Roman God. Protector of all Laws. Don't tell me our boy hasn't got a sense of humour."

"Reminds me of Solly Kettleman," Kempner smiled, pulling up at the foot of the stone steps which led up to the tall, arched doorway of the Tudor-style mansion, noticing that the dogs had stationed themselves on the top step.

"Who's Solly Kettleman?"

"East Coast racketeer. Legend says he ripped off fifty million dollars in one scam. Never prosecuted. I had to deliver some papers to him once. Penthouse on the sixty-sixth floor. Views out to Connecticut. Sat me on his sofa and gave me a coffee. Showed me a painting he'd had commissioned by a rock star who was also a dab hand with the brush," chuckled Kempner.

"And what was the painting of?"

"A portrait of Solly. Sitting on the same sofa I was on. In his twenty million dollar penthouse. With a caption reading "Crime Doesn't Pay.""

"Just like this set-up," smiled Rose. "And here comes the moll."

Alicia Daley was descending the stone steps, flanked by the Rottweillers, passing Bacchus and Hebe and heading to the driver's window, which Kempner lowered a couple of inches, quickly absorbing the spectacle of this tall, black girl, dressed in a white tie-up blouse, displaying bare midriff, tight jeans which sparkled with gold glitter and high heels. The hair was held back by a white bandanna round the forehead. The complexion was clear, the expression and the body language were manifestly hostile.

"I'm Kempner, Miss Daley. Can you give us some space from the dogs?' he asked as politely as he could through the narrow aperture, aware of the low growling he could hear from deep within the throats of both creatures.

"It's Mrs Daley," she shot back at him. "And the dogs stay."

"I'd rather explain inside the house," he persisted.

"You'd better get this straight. You ain't setting foot in this house. No copper ever sets foot in this house. Ray'd kill me if I let any of your lot in. Just state your business," she said angrily.

"OK, lady. I tried," Kempner snapped. "Let's take the hard route. There's a body down the hill in a barn. Murdered. We think it may be Ray. You got my drift now?" Kempner sensed Rose's body stiffening in shock at the brutality of his words and manner.

The girl stared back at him, her mouth open, instinctively bringing her hands up to her face, pressing hard on her cheeks with those long fingers whose nails were painted in screaming purple. Kempner noticed that the wedding and little fingers on the left hand were bound together in surgical tape.

"I ain't heard from him for a couple of days" she eventually whispered, the tone softer and the voice on the edge of tears. "Why do you think it's Ray?"

"I can't discuss this through a slit in the window with two brutes straining to have us for a late dinner. It's serious business, Mrs Daley. Let's deal with it," Kempner reasoned.

"Drive to the coach house entrance. I'll open the remote doors. Drive straight in. The doors will close immediately behind you. I'll walk through the house and see you in there," she conceded, heading back up the stairs and issuing an order to the dogs which sent them off in the opposite direction.

Almost immediately the central door of the coach house swung upwards allowing Kempner to drive straight into the garage, the movement activating the overhead strip lighting and bringing his eyes to rest on the Bentley, Mercedes, Ferrari and E-Type sitting in their bays like objets d'art at a collector's museum. Stepping out of the tired Volvo, Kempner realized that the floor was actually carpeted.

"The old Volvo fits in nicely, doesn't it? Rose remarked as her eyes drank in the surroundings. Oil paintings of Ferraris, Masseratis, Corvettes and racing Jaguars adorned the back wall. Large photographs of Millard sitting in private planes, helicopters and Formula One racing cars were displayed on each side wall. In the left bay was a twenty-five foot speed boat with two Mercury five-hundred horsepower outboard engines strapped to the stern. Alongside the Ferrari was a John Deere ride-on lawn mower and an all- terrain vehicle with chrome anti-roll bars.

"Solly Kettleman would have been suitably impressed," Rose finally declared, as the sound of Alicia's stiletto heels on the floor of the passageway leading off to the right announced her approach.

In the full glare of the garage lights, Rose could see that she was not quite as young as she had first appeared, but sexy as hell. Nearer thirty than twenty. The eyes were heavy, showing signs of having seen too many late nights. Long legs. Knockout figure. Abdomen as flat as a board.

"Why do you think it's Ray?" she repeated, pointing to some white plastic chairs stacked on top of each other in the corner

"Let me start with a few questions of my own, Alicia, and then I may be better qualified to answer yours," Kempner replied, pulling three chairs off the stack. "Is it OK for me to call you, Alicia?" he continued when they were all seated.

"For Christ's sake," she shouted. "Call me what you bloody want, but tell me why you think my man's dead."

"The murder is of a type which suggests ruthless criminals were involved. It's no good pretending that Ray didn't mix in that world 'cos all three of us here know damn well that he did. That's the starting point," Kempner began.

"Secondly," said Rose taking up the story in a gentler tone, "early this morning, actually we're past midnight, so it's yesterday morning now, I went to an isolated spot near Amberley off the M40. A black Cadillac Escalade had been torched. That vehicle has been traced to Ray".

Alicia had gasped at the mention of the Cadillac and her head was now down so that neither Officer could see her face.

"When did you last have any contact with Ray?" Kempner asked.

"He went to Newcastle on Tuesday and was staying over. I spoke to him on the phone on Tuesday and Wednesday. The last time was about eight in the evening on the Wednesday when he was on the road back about to stop to eat. Said he wouldn't be back until the early hours and if he felt too tired he'd check in somewhere," Alicia recounted, gradually lifting her head.

"Did you hear from him at all on Thursday or today?" Rose probed.

"I wasn't worried when I woke up on Thursday and he hadn't shown. Ray often has sudden changes of plan. But by the middle of Thursday afternoon I was a bit worried. I took the BMW into town and asked round the places Ray might have been. Nothing."

"I don't see a BMW here," observed Kempner, looking around.

"No. The garage is Ray's special place. My car's kept round the back. It's there now."

"Today I've been phoning all over the place. No sign of him. But Ray can look after himself. I was sure he'd be OK and he'd have gone crazy if I bought the cops in."

"We've got enough to make us believe that this body may be Ray. We've got to move forward, I want you to come with us down the road to this barn and see if you can make an identification," Kempner eventually suggested.

"You mean now?"

"Yes."

"In the barn where the murder happened?"

"Yes."

"With all the blood and that?"

"There is no blood. But that isn't to say that this won't prove very distressing for you. But the sooner I know if it's Ray, the sooner I can try to find out what happened. Unless there's somebody else who could do it?" Kempner enquired.

"He ain't got nobody else. No family. Just me. I'll do it. But I need to know how he was killed. I got to know what to fucking expect," she announced, the obscenity plainly creeping in to bolster her own resolve.

"We don't know how he was killed. The pathologists's first thought is that he was either struck fatally on the head or shot in the head. We don't know which."

"Some bloody pathologist if he can't tell the difference," she snapped.

"It's not that simple. After death the murderer has . . ." Kempner, even with his loathing of Millard, was finding it tough to tell a young woman that she was about to see her man spread-eagled on a barn floor with his head cut off.

"What?"

". . . has removed the head," he continued in as flat a tone as he could muster.

"Oh, my God!" Alicia wailed. "I can't fucking look at that. . ."

"We're not asking you to, Alicia," Rose intervened. From the shoulders up, the body will be covered. You'll see no sign of any injury. No blood. Just a body and legs. Do you have any means of identifying Ray from seeing only his body and legs?"

"Yes," the girl replied almost inaudibly.

"Right," said Kempner. "Sorry to rush you, but the pathologist will be nearly finished. I'm going to call Braithwaite and set it up. You'll need a coat and some more suitable footwear. We'll wait in our car."

Chapter 11

Within five minutes the Volvo was passing back through the gates with Alicia in the back seat, now wrapped in a full-length sable coat and rubber boots.

"What've you done to your hand?" Kempner asked.

"It's nothing," she mumbled. "Tripped over the dogs' bowl in the yard and fell awkwardly. As if you care."

"You said you were Mrs Daley. Are you still married?" Rose enquired as the Volvo descended the hill towards the barn.

"I'm a widow," came the unexpected response. I was married to a rapper." Your lot done for him."

"How do you mean? Rose asked.

"He got ten years for a robbery. He was only twenty-three. Couldn't handle it and topped himself in the nick. Ray got me through it. That's how we hitched up," she answered bitterly.

"It was hardly the Police's fault, was it?" Kempner interjected.

"Ray said the cops had hyped it all up. It was worth five, tops. Leroy would have handled five," Alicia retorted.

"We're just coming to the scene now, Alicia," Kempner said, keen to move away from her robber husband's suicide. "I've just spoken to Braithwaite. You won't have to go into the barn. The body's been moved into that black van at the back of the line of vehicles. That's where we're taking you. But there's one other thing I've got to tell you."

"What?"

"The murderer also removed the hands. I'm sorry it's so grim."

"For God's sake," exclaimed Alicia, her anger and alarm filling the car. "What else did you fucking forget to tell me? How am I going to cope with that?"

"The pathologist will have covered the lower arms. You won't see the injuries," Danny tried to assure her.

"You ain't got no idea, have ya?" Alicia snarled at Danny. "Forget what the pathologist has done. If it's Ray, I've got to live the rest of my days with the knowledge some fucking maniac chopped his head and hands off. You bastards ain't even thought about that."

Stopping just past the black van which Mimura had summoned from the mortuary, Kempner spotted Braithwaite talking to the pathologist on the opposite verge and rolled the electric window down.

"I've got Mrs Daley in the car with us," Kempner called across the narrow roadway. "Do we have authority to proceed?"

Braithwaite walked urgently across to the Volvo and the tweed cap and moustache thrust themselves through the window. His face was so close to Kempner that Kempner could see the crumbs which had adhered to the moustache from the most recently consumed sandwich.

"Good evening, Mrs Daley. I'm sorry you have to face this ordeal," he said gently.

"Cut the sympathy crap. You all hated Ray. Let's just get on with it and see if it's him," she spat back, getting out of the car and walking towards the van.

"Have you told her everything, Kempner?" enquired Braithwaite anxiously. Mimura's very unhappy about this. I don't want hysterics 'cos you haven't given her the full Monty."

"She knows," Kempner answered, as he and Rose got out and joined Alicia at the rear of the large mortuary van, where the technicians had rigged up one of the arc lights so that the whole area was almost like daylight.

"As Officer in charge of the case I have to do this formally, Mrs Daley," Braithwaite announced in solemn tones, pulling a battered notebook out of one of his numerous anorak pockets. "You've been informed that the body has had certain. . . ," he hesitated, struggling for an appropriate euphemism. ". . .certain extremities removed."

"You mean have they told me that his fucking head and hands have been chopped off," Alicia retorted angrily. "Why can't you lot ever say what you fucking mean?"

"We need to know how you will be able to say whether or not this is the body of Raymond Leon Millard," Braithwaite continued in his clipped tones and ignoring her protest. "You must tell us the possible means of identification before you see the body. Indeed, I shall note them down and we'll all sign the note before I open these doors."

"Ray's got a real bad scar where a knife went through his right calf. He's also got a tattoo on the inside of the thigh of the same leg, high up. You got to know exactly where to look, if you get my meaning. And, if you want any more than that, I know Ray's body, every last part of it, including his privates. I'll know if it's him. So put that in your little book," she declared.

"The scar and the tattoo," Braithwaite responded as he noted down her words. "You said the same leg. Which leg?"

"Right. And the tattoo's a frog."

"OK. I've got that," Braithwaite replied, beckoning at the same time in the direction of the pathologist, who was watching this scene being played out from the roadside. "Sign my book, please, Mrs Daley and these two Officers will also sign as witnesses. While you do that, I shall have to call Dr Mimura over as we may have a slight problem here."

Dr Mimura responded immediately to the Inspector's beckoning. His protective clothing now removed, his appearance had become less surreal although, in an ordinary civilian jacket and trousers, his oriental features made him look more like a Tokyo bank manager than an expert in death. After introducing him to the surly and agitated Alicia Daley Braithwaite informed him of the potential means of identification.

"Ah, I see why you needed me," he nodded. "When I spoke to

you in the barn, Inspector Kempton, I had not yet examined the legs. On the back of the right leg, the whole calf has been sliced off. As if by a surgeon's scalpel."

"Christ Almighty," Alicia exploded. "Can't you bastards get all the fucking facts together instead of drip-feeding me. What else are you going to tell me has been cut off? Just open these doors now. I've signed your bloody book. I want this over and done with."

Kempner sensed Mimura looking at him, no doubt recognizing the accuracy of Kempner's earlier assurance that Alicia was no shrinking violet, as Braithwaite pulled open the double doors of the mortuary van. White arc light flooded into the van's interior and a small set of steps descended automatically from the floor of the vehicle, enabling Mimura to step easily up and assist Alicia who followed. Braithwaite stood in the doorway and then climbed in alongside, while Kempner and Rose remained where they were but in earshot.

"I should point out that, contrary to my normal practice, I've had to cut off all the clothes for the purposes of this identification. Perhaps Mrs Daley can be shown the clothes after the body," Dr Mimura suggested.

"I agree," Braithwaite murmured.

"Why's he slice off the calf?" Rose whispered to Kempner.

"Same as the head and hands. Identifiable scar. To stop us finding out it was Millard. Or at least to make it harder," was the soft reply.

Inside the vehicle the collapsible wheeled stretcher had been fixed to the steel platform on the left of the van while a similar, empty stretcher was positioned on the right. Dr Mimura had now discreetly slipped on a fresh pair of surgical gloves and pulled back the sheet that covered the body. He had meticulously wrapped copious strips of polythene around the neck, wrists and lower right leg, then placed opaque bags on top of his handiwork, so as to hide completely the savagery that had been deployed. Accordingly, beneath the sheet, all Alicia could see, beyond the wrappings, was the form of a naked male body, lying on its back. Even spared the full horror, Dr Mimura heard her wince and then start to sob.

"How tall was Mr Millard", the pathologist asked?

"Six three," she muttered, trying to pull herself together.

"Yes. I shall be able to be more accurate when I'm back at the hospital and have access to my equipment and computer but my estimate was that this body is of a man between six feet two and six feet four."

"I know it's Ray," she cried. "I know it's him. The colour of the skin. The hair on his chest. The lean body. Ray was in good shape. Everything."

"Let's move to the thigh, Mrs Daley," Braithwaite suggested. Where exactly do you say this tattoo is?"

"Do I have to spell it out?" she protested.

"I'm afraid so, Mrs Daley. We must be sure," Braithwaite insisted.

"Right up the top. Inside. Next to his balls. Size of a gambling chip," she snapped back.

Dr Mimura's deft fingers slipped in between the long, powerful thighs, forcing the right leg to bend outwards and expose the inner thigh. Pulling the flesh round, the whole intimate area became visible. At the same instant Alicia Daley gasped and took a step backwards, prompting Braithwaite to grab her arm to support her.

"I knew it'd be Ray as soon as those two coppers came to the house," she sobbed. "I just bloody knew it. It's him, alright. You can see for yourself."

Dr Mimura quietly pulled the sheet back over the body with a sad shake of his head. The blue tattoo of an ugly frog was staring at three strained faces from the white, inner thigh of a headless corpse.

Chapter 12

Back inside Keeling House, Braithwaite, Kempner, Rose and a subdued Alicia Daley were seated on high stainless steel stools around the gourmet island in the kitchen. Faced with the stark choice of being taken immediately to Newbury Police Station to make a formal statement and answer questions, or to allow the Police into the main house, she had opted for the latter, cursing that Ray would never have forgiven her for allowing the filth into his house. Her final act of defiance had been to limit them to the kitchen, albeit a kitchen into which Kempner could have sunk his whole flat and still had room to park the Volvo.

The ceiling was carved out of cedar whilst the floor was constructed from Brazilian cherry wood. The gourmet island boasted two sinks, a built-in fondue, griddle and a butcher's block. A range of various ovens nestled against the one wall, while a sub-zero fridge big enough to house a buffalo sat against the opposite wall. A picture window ran the full length of the outside wall, looking out over the rear paved terrace which was dominated by a fountain consisting of a full-size nude woman with a water jug on her left shoulder, out of which the torrent ran into an artificial stream which wended its way around the entire perimeter of the terrace while the whole panorama was lit by floodlights strategically located amongst the surrounding trees.

Deliberately refraining from offering the Officers even a glass of water, Alicia had signed the formal statement of identification that Braithwaite had studiously written out, detailing the distinctive features of the body, the tattoo and the clothing, and she was now making it clear that she wanted to be left alone to handle her grief without their presence at the earliest opportunity.

"Back at the scene you also identified the clothing as Ray's. Can you be specific as to where he purchased any particular item?" Kempner asked.

"I recognized the shoes. He liked them rounded toecaps. But I don't know where he bought 'em from. The trousers were new. He only got 'em on Monday. Four hundred quid they were. Armani. From Harrods," she explained. "Listen, I've had enough of this for tonight. It can all wait until tomorrow. Besides, you ain't bothered who's done this to Ray. You've been after him for years and got nowhere. Now he's dead, you'll be cracking open a bottle back at the station."

"Unfair," Kempner retorted. "We don't want gang warfare breaking out. Whoever killed Ray is a monster. We want him off the street as badly as you."

"Bullshit," Alicia spat back at him.

"Listen, Alicia," Rose interposed in an attempt to soften the instinctive antipathy to the Police that dominated Daley's every move, "experience tells us that our best chance of solving most murders lies in getting hard information in the first few hours. We need to know who Ray's really dangerous enemies were. We need a more detailed account of your last contact with Ray. The pathologist is sure he's been dead well over twenty four hours. We need to know what attempts you made to contact him late on Wednesday night into the early hours of Thursday morning. Give us that to work with and we can leave the rest until tomorrow."

Alicia sat on her stool, still in her sable coat, her elbows on the granite top and her head in her hands. Looking at her carefully, Kempner realized that she was exhausted and, of course she was right, the sudden death of Millard was not going to provoke any tears in his Department. But this was a hideous crime and he did want the killer caught.

"I've heard that Ray was under pressure and that he was thinking of selling off the Scorpion Sting. What can you tell us about any of that?" he probed.

"Nothing. He did deals. He owed money and he was owed money. Pressure was the name of his game. I don't know anyone in business who hated him enough to do this to him," she replied.

"Then what about outside business? He hasn't got high walls, razor wire and dogs for fun, has he?" Kempner said.

"That's to stop you bastards from prying. He weren't seeing some other geezer's woman if that's what you mean?"

"What about someone with a score to settle from the past, something like that?" Braithwaite asked.

Alicia lifted her head and stared into space for a long time before answering. "Yea. He did have old enemies. There was one fella in particular. Ray said that he often found himself looking over his shoulder for this guy."

"Why haven't you mentioned this before?" Kempner asked.

"Because the geezer's dead, that's why. I answered the phone to Tommy Langham. Phoned from LA a few days ago to tell Ray that Pal was dead, 'cos he knew Ray would sleep a little easier," Alicia responded aggressively.

"Pal? What's his real name?"

"Paul Locke. 'A' was his middle initial. They all called him Pal. Long before my time. I'd never met him. He's lived in Mexico for years. The row went back half a lifetime. Anyway, he's dead. Died in Mexico."

"OK. He's dead. What about an enemy still alive and kicking?" Braithwaite enquired.

"I've told you all I know. Ray lived in a tough world. But I ain't got no names for ya of anyone who'd kill him. And I've had enough now. I'm kicking you out. If you need more you'll have to come back tomorrow, I ain't going anywhere," she declared in a tone which made it clear that the questioning was over for tonight.

125

"Fair enough," Braithwaite agreed, slipping off his stool and nodding his head at Kempner to indicate that he should follow suit.

"One last question before we go," Kempner said, gesturing towards the estate stretched out beyond the terracing. "Who will inherit all this?"

"I wondered how long it'd take you suspicious bastards to ask that one," Alicia replied, opening the kitchen door leading into the galleried hallway and ushering them out. "The answer is me. I do. The house is in my name already. But I didn't kill Ray, in case you hadn't noticed."

"Right. I'm going to ask you to give us Ray's toothbrush, hairbrush, comb, the sheets from the bed he slept in on Tuesday night and your mobile phone. Then, we'll leave and come back tomorrow when you've had some rest," Braithwaite declared.

"What do you want with all that stuff?" she asked.

"We can get his DNA. Just a belt and braces job to confirm your identification."

"Well, you'll have to make do with just the belt. All his personal toilet gear was with him on his trip. In a case. And one thing Ray was very particular about. His sheets. They've got to be silk. And got to be black. And changed every day. It's the first thing the help does when she arrives in the morning," Alicia informed them. "As for my mobile. . . ." her voice tailed away and her hand went to her mouth. "Wait a minute. Wait a minute. On Wednesday night I fell asleep watching a film on TV in bed. When I woke up and saw Ray wasn't there I phoned him. Let me try to think. . . "

"Take it slowly," Rose said calmly. "Bit by bit."

"I was half asleep. But the phone was answered and I heard a couple of words and then it went all muffled. I couldn't make nothing out. Just noise. I'd forgotten about this. Thought I'd misdialed or summat. I went back to sleep then and whenever I tried again the next morning I got nothing. You asking for my mobile has brought it back."

"What time on the Wednesday night was this?" Kempner demanded urgently.

"I dunno. Very late. The film didn't start until two in the morning and I remember watching most of it. My mobile memory'll tell you. It was answered, so it'll register as a connected call to Ray's number. It'll be the last one to that number that connected. And anyway I didn't try again until late Thursday morning. Is this important?"

"It could be. Can you get your mobile, please?" Braithwaite asked.

"Sure. It's in my bag in there," she said pointing back towards the kitchen and leading the small group back inside to where the distinctive light brown Louis Vuitton sat on the black granite countertop of the central island.

Plucking the phone out of the bag, she flipped the lid back, punched the memory buttons before declaring, "there it is. That's Ray's number. The one ending 6258. His ring tone is "Battle Hymn of The Republic. Right racket. There's the time of the call. 4.54 a.m. Bloody hell, I didn't realize it was that late."

"Show us," Kempner demanded as they all craned to see the entry on the small blue screen. "Right. This could be important. When the phone was answered, before it went muffled, what exactly did you hear?"

"Like I said, I'd fallen asleep. Then I thought I must have just dialed a wrong number and went straight back to sleep. I can't be sure of any of this. And I only heard a couple of words," she replied, furrowing her brow as she tried to recollect the detail.

"Come on, Alicia," Rose said encouragingly. "Close your eyes. Picture yourself back in bed. Was the voice male or female?"

"Female. And it said 'Sorry' in a way that didn't sound English. Aussie or Yank perhaps. . . "

"Sorry" Kempner and Rose repeated in unison. "Just sorry?"

"No. There was another word. It wasn't saying sorry to me. It said a name. An odd name. Like 'Ofsa' or 'Affsa'," she replied trying to recreate the word in her mind.

Kempner looked at her hard and banged his fist on the counter-top. "You're talking to a Yank. A Yank who served his time in the NYPD. Is what you heard 'Officer'? 'Sorry Officer'," he shouted in triumph.

"That's it. It sounded just like the way you just said it. Exactly like that. Why's it so important?"

"Because in the barn Ray's pockets were empty. When Danny went to Amberley the firemen had identified the case with clothing and toilet gear, but no remnants of a mobile phone. Even when the fire is bad, enough will survive of a phone to indicate what it was," Kempner explained.

"So that means that the woman who answered that call at 4.54 on Thursday morning was in possession of Ray's phone. We can safely assume he hadn't given it her, can't we?" Rose continued.

"You bloody well can. That woman must know who killed Ray or did it herself," Alicia cried out. "How do you find her?"

Taking his own phone out of his pocket Kempner barked out the answer. "Number one. When you phoned Ray at 4.54 your signal went from the nearest mast to this house to the mast nearest the location of Ray's phone. We have both numbers and the time of the connection. The mobile network company can identify precisely which mast it was. They can usually tell to within half a mile where that phone was when the call was received."

"But it takes those companies forever to come up with that detail," Braithwaite observed. "Weeks rather than days. And what good is it to us? The woman is hardly likely to be still standing in the same spot."

"Kempner said that was point number one," Rose interjected. "His number two will be that we know Ray was killed in Radford. A couple of miles away from his home. He must have been intercepted somehow as he came up the hill in the Escalade and killed. Someone, the murderer or an accomplice, must have then driven the vehicle to Amberley and torched it. Am I right?" Rose asked, looking at Kempton as she spoke.

"You've got it, alright. And to get to Amberley from Radford in a hurry you go north up the M40. A detour off the motorway to dispose of the Cadillac somewhere remote and then back on to the motorway and my money would be on the journey continuing north. Somewhere, driving north from Amberley, the murderer's car was stopped by the Police. We don't know why. Speeding probably. But we know the exact time it was stopped. 4.54 am. It's after two in the morning now. The Officers who stopped that car will be on duty again now. It's the same shift, but nearly forty-eight hours later. We want a message putting out to all the patrol crews on duty now in Oxfordshire, Warwickshire, Leicestershire, Worcestershire and maybe Nottinghamshire" Kempner explained.

"And Bingo," Braithwaite declared in admiration.

"But what's the message?" Alicia asked in puzzlement.

"The message is, which crew stopped a car on this shift Thursday morning at 4.54 and spoke to a woman with a New York accent and, while they spoke, her mobile phone went off and she said sorry to the Officer? There won't be many of those to the pound," Rose smiled. "That's what my Inspector's doing now. He's phoning Traffic Control. That message will be on every Police radio in those areas before we reach your front door."

"And I want a news embargo on everything concerning the state of the body. No references to decapitation, hands or calf or anything," Kempner barked as he waited for his call to be answered. "A body was found in a barn. Foul play suspected. Full stop. Nothing else. See to that, Rose. Now. And we want that stretch of river dragged. The weapon, the head etcetera. They've dumped them. In water is my guess."

Rose pulled out her own phone, nodding her agreement. Braithwaite was standing silently with his back to the window, observing the two London Officers with interest and approval. "Odd pair," he reflected to himself, "and there's some powerful chemistry at work there if I'm not very much mistaken. All that calling each other by their last names. Who do they think they're fooling? Themselves I suppose," he shrugged, setting off towards his car and that chocolate cup cake he'd been thinking about for the last ten minutes.

Chapter 13

Tradition dictated that all of the cast and production team should attend a post-theatre dinner, always held at the restaurant most currently in vogue in the city where they were performing. "Sister Saffron's Ethiopian Cuisine" was the sensation of Manchester and, even on a Friday night, a party of twenty-five could only be accommodated at half past eleven, which meant that Lauren was still eating and drinking at nearly two o'clock in the morning.

One of the many idiosyncrasies of a life treading the boards was that you had to learn to re-adjust the body clock and the normal rhythm of the day. With the adrenalin flowing and the spirits buoyed at eleven o'clock at night, sleep was out of the question. And most actors can never eat before the performance.

Milo, the Director, basking in his own sense of success, had turned his attention to Janet who only had a minor part in the production but had also won the position of understudying Lauren. During rehearsals Lauren had spent some time with Janet because the young girl had shadowed her every move, seeking to pick up any little morsel about the business. Over several cups of coffee, Lauren had learned that the girl's driving ambition to make it on the stage had taken her from being a cleaner at the Old Bailey in London, into repertory and on to a West End production. Still very naïve and inexperienced, it was clear that she was currently having trouble fending off Milo's semi-drunken attentions and that it was probably time for some maternal intervention.

"I'm calling it a day," Lauren announced. "Anyone want to share a cab with me back to the hotel?"

Right on cue Janet quickly accepted the offer, making her polite apologies to Milo, whose eyes immediately wandered around the table to locate the next contender. Back in the deserted hotel foyer after some welcome fresh air and the short taxi ride, Lauren invited the young girl to her suite room for a nightcap.

While Lauren went into the bathroom Janet's eyes drank in the luxury of the surroundings which was in stark contrast to her broom cupboard at the back of the hotel, overlooking the dustbins. Looking across the sitting room she could see the oriental vanity table on which Lauren's cosmetics, perfumes and jewellery were neatly arranged. It was impossible to miss the photograph in the silver frame that had pride of place in the middle of her bottles of Hermes Caleche and Clarins. Janet had seen Lauren's balding and bespectacled husband at one of the early rehearsals and he bore no resemblance to the man in the photograph who was younger with a full head of dark, shining hair and an open, but rather 'old-fashioned face. He reminded Janet of a Hollywood actor she'd seen playing the lead in one of the old Western series which were re-run endlessly on TV but she couldn't bring his name to mind.

When Lauren returned to the sitting room, she kicked off her Jimmy Choo's vermillion shoes and, tucking her long legs underneath her, relaxed in the plump armchair opposite Janet and looked affectionately across at the ambitious girl curled up on the sofa. Mid-brown hair, quite pretty with wide sparkling eyes and a clear voice, still with a little bit of Cockney to be polished out of it, Lauren knew that making it in the theatre was going to be a tough challenge for this rather gentle girl, but her commitment and determination were plain to see.

"So, tell me, Janet, how did you make the switch from being a cleaner to an actress? It must have been really difficult," she enquired kindly.

"I met someone who inspired me. That's how lives are changed," Janet replied.

"A man?"

"No. A woman. She taught me that all things are possible, whatever your origins. Coming from the bottom of the pile, I'd never believed that I had the right to shoot for the stars. Naomi inspired me to think differently," came the earnest response.

"How?"

"She was a barrister. I met her a few days before she was due to start her first case as a QC. While I wielded my duster we got to talking and I told her of my dream to go on the stage but would always stay a cleaner. She told me I was wrong. That she came from the same place as me. Same place in life, if you follow."

"I do follow. Carry on."

"Her father had been a miner. Never forgave her for breaking away from her working class roots. My father's much the same. But then she told me how her old headmistress had inspired her and she recited the words that her teacher had used."

"And what were they?" Lauren enquired, now intrigued by the story.

"*In most people's lives, there would probably come a time when they might have to take a big chance and, if they missed it, they might regret it for ever.* That's what Naomi quoted. And she told me that her chance had come and she'd taken it. And if I looked hard enough my chance would also come. She told me later that Miss Wickham, that was the name of her headmistress, had really taken Shakespeare's words in Julius Caesar '*there is a tide in the affairs of man*' and put them into language that Naomi would understand"

"Now I understand your choice of stage name, 'Janet Wickham'," Lauren declared. "You took the old teacher's name."

"I borrowed it. I'm really plain old Janet Kelly. But that's my way of recognising the lady I never met who inspired Naomi, who then passed on the inspiration to me."

"What became of Naomi?' Lauren asked.

"She's still a QC. Naomi Nicholas. I see her occasionally when she's doing a case in London. As a matter of fact, you look a little like each other. Blond, elegant. Beautiful speaking voices. She lives with an old footballer, Jack Farnham. He does a lot of TV work now. You've probably seen him on Sky."

"Yes, I have. It's quite a story. It makes me realise how lucky I've been. My family's never been short of money and my husband carries some clout in our business."

"That's not your husband in that photograph, is it? Janet enquired in a tentative tone. "Or are you going to tell me to mind my own business?"

"No. That's Jake. There's no great secret about it. My marriage has been unhappy for a long time. I met Jake when we were doing "The Chance of Life" in New York. It was the summer that the Towers went down. He's a cop. Was NYPD. Now he's attached to the Met."

"Does your husband know?"

"Yes."

"Doesn't he mind?"

"Yes?"

"So how does it work?"

"There's been some trouble while we've been up in Manchester. But that's unusual and I think it'll blow over. We play pretend marriage. I live at the Chelsea house but stay at Jake's when it suits us. A double life. Jake wants me to leave him but he knows I won't."

"Why not?"

"It's complicated. If Jake thought I really would leave James, I'm not sure what would happen. For all the tough guy image you see in that photograph, Jake's very fragile. He's in love with the unattainable. He lost someone but still loves her. Now he believes that he loves me. To a degree he does, but part of it is because I, too, am unattainable. If that changed . . . ," her voice tailed away and she drained the last wine from her glass. "You don't want to hear any more of my problems. Besides, it's time for some sleep," she added, slowly easing herself out of the chair and bringing the shutters down.

As Janet walked along the corridor, heading for her broom cupboard, it suddenly struck her who it was that the photograph had reminded her of. Dale Robertson. Tales of Wells Fargo.

Chapter 14

While Braithwaite headed south to Newbury, Kempner and Rose coasted up the M40 in the opposite direction towards Oxford, where it had been arranged that they would have the use of Oxford Central Police Station. The three minds in two different cars were all focused on the same subject matter. Alicia Daley.

"The trick cyclists could have a field day with her. More layers of defence than the Crown Jewels," Rose said.

"The hide of a rhinoceros and the cunning of a lynx," remarked Kempner. "Out of the gutter and into the world of fur coats and Ferraris, courtesy of the Devil. There's always a price to pay. She sold her soul, if ever she had one."

"Funny though. Devil or not, she loved him. Even you must have seen that."

"Depends what you mean by 'love'. Loved his money. Loved his power. Loved the fact that people feared him."

"Always the romantic," she laughed.

"Trouble is, Rose, I was a romantic once," Kempner sighed, casting a look at her over his left shoulder and seeing the red curls and the finely chiselled bone structure picked out by the headlights of an oncoming car. "And look where it's got me. A crummy rented pad, a Volvo that's coming up to a hundred thousand miles and a love life that's more complicated than 'Little George's.'"

"And who the hell is 'Little George'?"

"You mean you've reached adulthood and never heard of 'Little George Guinle', the Brazilian lover of Marilyn Monroe and Jayne Mansfield?" he asked in surprise.

"No, I haven't. But not quite the same complications that you face. What became of him then?" she asked.

"His fortune was frittered away. All due to the pursuit of women. But he must have thought it was worth it"

"How do you know that"?

"Because shortly before his death he told reporters, 'I might not have any money left, but when I sleep, I dream of Marilyn.'"

"And when you sleep, do you dream of Lauren?" she asked pointedly.

"No leading questions, Rose. You know the rules," he replied quietly.

"Sometimes the rules have to be challenged, you know. Otherwise you may find all you're left to dream about is what might have been and . . ."

Her sentence was suddenly interrupted by the sharp ringing of Kempner's phone on the hands-free console and in a second the voice of one of the operators at Traffic Control was filling the car.

"We've had a response to the message we put out," the female voice recited in a matter of fact tone. "4.54 a.m. on Thursday the 10th. Officers Waller and Gellick. Stopped a woman from New York in a Fiesta LX on the M40 Northbound. Gave a temporary address in Birmingham. The Officers have a note of the details provided and the notice to produce her driving documents at a Birmingham Police Station. Their copy of that notice is filed in Coventry."

"Where exactly did they stop her?" Kempner demanded.

"Three miles south of Coventry exit."

"Where are Waller and Gellick now?"

"At the time of their response they were approaching Daventry."

"OK. Contact them. Tell them we want to speak to them urgently. I want to see their notes. Ask them to phone in to Coventry and get someone to access the copy notice and read out any information that isn't in the notebook so that I get everything. They can put the blue light on and make it to the Banbury Exit in twenty minutes. We'll meet them on the overhead bridge. We're in a green Volvo. Got all that?"

"All of that's going through to them as we speak. Any problem I'll re-contact," the voice announced as it disconnected.

"Why didn't you ask her to patch you through directly to the patrol car? It would have saved time?" Rose asked.

"Because we're driving North and they're driving South. Meeting up will cost us half an hour tops. If I speak to them face to face there's a good chance that I'll pick something up that I might miss on the phone. These guys have seen and spoken to the woman who will crack this case wide open. I need to get the feel of it. Get the sense of her. Do you know what I mean?"

"I think I do, yes," she replied. "And, by the way, you're doing over ninety miles an hour," she added.

"I'm allowed to," he smiled. "I'm a cop."

"And a damn good one at that," she responded as they hurtled through the night towards the Banbury bridge. But she wasn't smiling.

The white Police Range Rover was visible under the yellow street lights on the overhead bridge for a mile before the exit and by the time the Volvo had pulled up directly behind it, Gellick had spoken directly to Coventry and got all the information that he anticipated the Murder Investigation Officers would require.

Climbing into the back of the Range Rover, Kempner made the introductions and then, under the bright interior light, pored over the notebook that Gellick had handed him before passing it to Rose for her to scrutinise.

"Describe her to me, Gellick. Everything you remember," he began urgently, as the uniformed Officer turned awkwardly over his shoulder to look into the back, giving Kempner the opportunity to weigh him up. Moustache, glasses, no spring chicken. How good were his powers of observation going to prove?

"Susan Vance. Mid to late twenties. Yank. Said she was touring. Spoke just like you. Black hair. Pale skin. Attractive in a sporty kind of way. Moved well, if you know what I mean. Some kind of cardigan on and dark trousers. That's about it, really," Gellick offered in his slightly rural accent.

"You've missed something," Waller unexpectedly interjected. "She had a beauty spot just above her upper lip. Right side, I think. Caught my eye."

"Did you ever see into the Fiesta? Did you see if there was anybody else in it barked Kempner?"

"She said her husband was asleep in the passenger seat. Had a headache. I saw a figure lying back in the passenger seat when I walked her back to her vehicle at the end. Never got a proper view though."

"OK. The mobile phone going off. What happened?"

"She got a bit flustered. Struggled to turn it off. I never saw the phone properly but it had a loud musical ring. She apologised for taking so long to turn it off," Gellick replied.

"What words did she use?"

"Just said she was sorry. That's all I remember her saying about it?"came Gellick's response.

"What tune did it play?"

"Can't call it to mind at the moment," Gellick said thoughtfully.

"Your notebook says she gave two addresses. One in Birmingham and one in New York, but they aren't in the book. Have you got Coventry to relay the details off the notice to produce?"

"Yea. I've jotted them down here," Gellick responded immediately, turning back towards the front to read from his observer's clipboard which was attached to the dashboard. "Birmingham first. She said they had a room bang in the city centre. Gas Street."

"Not a Hotel room, is what she said," Waller piped up. "I remember that. She was nervous. Couldn't give us a street number."

"And the New York address Kempner demanded."

"25 North 25th Street, New York City," Gellick read off his pad.

"Cute," Kempner laughed.

"What's so funny?" Rose asked.

"All Manhattan streets run East to West. Only Avenues run North to South. There's no such street as North 25th, he explained."

"Now to the Fiesta," said Gellick. "I've had the number run through the National Police Computer while we were on the road to meet you. It's not reported as stolen. Registered to a Steven Wieldstone of 22 Crossley Avenue, Sutton Coldfield. We didn't think it right to phone him up in the middle of the night to ask him. But we've checked him out. He's a Manager at Barclays Bank."

"The old trick," groaned Rose from the rear. "They've cloned the number. We'll have to run a check on all dark green Fiestas of this model reported stolen in the Midlands. It'll be the identical model to the Bank Manager's with copy plates on. Probably torched as well. Can you put that enquiry out now?"

"I'll see to it," nodded Waller

"And while you're about it call Birmingham Steelhouse Lane cop shop. There's no way she'll have taken any documents in there but they can get us a list of all non-hotel short stay accommodation in Gas Street and the surrounding streets. They may still be holed up there. The body was only found a few hours ago and there's been no publicity at all as yet. They'll think they're safe for a while."

"Are we heading on to Birmingham now?" asked Rose.

"Sure are. We'll go directly to Steelhouse Lane. Ask them to have the information on accommodation and stolen Fiestas waiting for us, would you Waller? And say we're requesting some manpower. Enough to handle the number of buildings we're going to have to visit."

"We'll set that up," Gellick replied, as Waller nodded in agreement, already connecting to Steelhouse Lane Police Station.

"OK guys, thanks. We're on our way," Kempner announced pushing open the heavy rear door and beginning to ease his way out.

"Just one other thing before you go," Gellick volunteered. "It's not in the notebook but it's been nagging away in the back of my mind ever since we got your call via Traffic Control."

"Let's have it then," Kempner said with interest.

"Her shoes. They were filthy. Fresh mud. I asked her about it. She laughed. Said she stepped in some mud in the grounds of an Oxford College they were visiting."

There was the little nugget that made the face to face to meeting worthwhile, just like Kempner had predicted, Rose thought to herself. Kempner looked at her as they headed back to the Volvo and suspected that he could see the beginnings of a smile appearing at the corners of her mouth. Just as they reached the Volvo Gellick's head appeared out of the passenger window of the Range Rover and he called back to them.

"The tune," he shouted triumphantly. "John Brown's Body. Battle Hymn of The Republic."

Driving off the bridge and back on to the Motorway Kempner sneaked a quick sideways glance at his partner. There was no doubt about it now. She was smiling.

Chapter 15

Jenna had spent the day scrupulously complying with Pal's detailed instructions concerning cleaning and disposal of the car and dumping the Sim Card and all the clothes they'd worn during the night. Every item of paraphernalia connected with the operation was abandoned, from her cardigan to his expensive Nighthawks, although she did keep her shoes, having wiped the mud off them. The large chemists in the centre of the town had stocked field dressings, laced with effective antiseptic, and a combination of these, together with regular applications of hydrogen peroxide, seem to have prevented any outbreak of infection. Physically debilitated by the wound and in a state of nervous exhaustion, Pal had actually slept through some of the dressing changes and had not shown any signs of properly waking up over the next twenty-four hours. Their small service apartment had a TV in the sitting room and Jenna had watched the main news bulletins and bought a variety of newspapers but there had not, as yet, been any reference to either the body or the burnt out Escalade.

The next morning Pal had started to show signs of recovery and had despatched Jenna up Broad Street to Haldane's, the rental office, to pay their bill in cash and to buy rail tickets for the following morning to Fishguard in Wales from where they would catch the evening ferry across the Irish Sea to Larne.

Their small bedroom overlooked the canal and, at just after nine on the Saturday morning, having packed their few remaining belongings, Pal, still a little unsteady on his feet, looked out of the window at the old, arched bridge which crossed the water and led to a cluster of wine bars and bistros which only brought the area to life at night. His eye happened upon the figure of a young woman, leaning casually on the wall of the bridge, seemingly passing a few idle minutes watching the water and the few early-morning passers-by. But there was an alertness in her posture, a rhythmic pattern in the movement of her head, that made Pal's eye linger upon her. Petite. Light. Jenna had an athletic build but this girl was more toned. He couldn't make out any detail of her features, but her appearance was dominated by her hair. Red natural curls, like a ragamuffin. After watching her for another couple of minutes he called out to Jenna.

"Come and take a look. The girl on the bridge. Just watch her."

"It's like watching a radar scanner at an airport," Jenna observed after a moment. "She's looking for something very specific."

"Us," Pal declared.

"Impossible," replied Jenna. "We've no reason to believe that they've even found the body yet, let alone made any connections to us."

"We're not hanging around to find out. If it links to the cops on the M40, they've never seen me. So they're just looking for a man and a woman together. We split up. You cover your hair. It's very distinctive. Only carry your handbag. I'll take the holdall."

"I can't believe she's anything to do with us. Will you be OK to walk on your own?"

"I'll have to be. We take no chances. Look, she's still there. It's not a good angle but I think she's speaking."

"To herself?"

"If I'm right, she'll have an earpiece under those urchin curls. We meet on the first floor of the bookshop opposite the station. If anything goes wrong, we make our way independently to Fishguard, get the ferry and wait for each other in Larne. Rendezvous at 'The Slug and Lettuce.'"

"And if we get stopped and questioned we've both got the same story that we've been over a hundred times, I know. But it isn't going to happen. I'll see you at the bookshop in fifteen minutes."

"Don't leave by the front door. Go down into the basement garage and use that exit. Cut down the alley which brings you into the square and on to Broad Street. I'll give you five minutes and follow suit".

"We've come a long way from Tamazula. We're not going to lose it now. Hasta luego," she whispered kissing him gently on the cheek and then, with her raven black hair tucked tightly under a pale blue baseball cap, she slipped out of the door.

Danny Rose was tired. Steelhouse Lane had given the night duty detective the job of following up the enquiries Waller had reliably communicated. When they had announced themselves at Steelhouse Lane, they had been left hanging around for nearly half an hour, sipping yesterday's coffee out of styrofoam cups, before anyone could even locate the detective who had slipped out for a bacon sandwich. Detective Constable Harry Colston, plump, dishevelled and bored, seemed to have as much interest in the case as a vegan would show for a rare filet mignon.

"Eleven LX Ford Fiestas stolen in the Midlands over the last eight days," he recited from a computer print-out. "Of those, three were dark green. Two of the three have been recovered and were returned to their owners before your woman was stopped on the M40. That leaves one outstanding. Belonging to a Mrs Elizabeth Lang. Lives in Stechford. Car stolen from a Service Station several days ago. Presumably, it's still sporting the Bank Manager's registration number. I've flagged it up on the Stolen Vehicles List. If you want to prioritise it, you'll have to speak to the Inspector. He comes on at eight."

"And the non-hotel lodging in the area of Gas Street?" Kempner fired at him.

"Gas Street runs off Broad Street which is the centre of the City's nightlife. There's blocks of yuppie flats along the canal basin at the back. Six of these buildings are registered as service flats where punters can rent, normally by the week. Three have front desks.

You'll have to phone them when someone comes on duty. Eightish I should imagine.

"And the other three?"

"They're operated via a rental office on Broad Street. Haldane's. Doubt they'll turn up before nine. If they turn up at all on a Saturday, that is."

"You know the area. How close together are these six buildings?"

"There's three in one street, two in another and the sixth is in the square."

"OK. Until the desk staff arrive and this Haldane's opens I want to borrow three officers. With you and us two, we can watch each of the six buildings. We're looking for a man and a woman. Almost certainly together. Rose will write out the description of the woman and give it to you for circulation."

"Hang on a minute. My shift's over. I've been on since ten last night. And we haven't got three bobbies I can just rustle up to hang around for a couple of hours. It doesn't work like that up here. I'll show you on the map where the places are and get you the phone numbers. Then, it's up to you. I've done bloody well to get you the information I have.

"You mean you've pressed two buttons on the Stolen Vehicle computer and spent five minutes looking in the registered accommodation manual. No wonder you're exhausted," Kempner snarled at him. "I haven't got the time to get your ass kicked or I would. Show me the map."

Armed with a marked copy of the map that Colston had grudgingly provided, Kempner and Rose had driven immediately to the area and positioned themselves in locations where anyone exiting from the buildings of interest was most likely to pass. It left two of the buildings completely uncovered but, as Rose had observed, it gave them sixty six per cent coverage and they could re-position when any of the staff had been spoken to. By eight-thirty, Kempner had spoken to the three front desks. No guest by the name of Vance was registered and no woman matching the description of Susan Vance was a guest. That had left the three buildings managed by Haldane's. Kempner had parked himself in the square which gave him a very restricted view of the largest, while Rose had taken up a position on the main canal bridge which gave her a good view of the block on the square, but only a restricted view of the third block. It was the best they could do in the circumstances.

As she leaned on the parapet of the bridge feigning disinterest in the few people around, her mobile phone vibrated and Kempner's tired voice came through the earpiece beneath her red curls.

"Yes", she breathed, trying not to move her lips.

"Haldane's don't open on Saturdays. I've phoned Steelhouse Lane and given them a blast. They'll try to get hold of one of Haldane's staff at home and get them to come in. In the meanwhile I've moved across to the fountain next to the French restaurant in the square."

"It's very quiet. Nothing of interest. Keep . . . ,"

"Action," Kempner's voice interrupted, suddenly stripped of its weariness. "There's a woman walking across the square. Blue baseball cap so I can't see her hair, but her face is pale. She's trying not to look around, but there's something furtive about her. Got to pass right by me. . . ." The voice tailed away, presumably as the woman came within earshot and Rose waited impatiently for it to resume.

"I think we're on to something. The back of one heel as she passed by me. You know what I think I saw?" Kempner continued after the figure had passed.

"Mud," Rose declared.

"Just a small splash. I could be wrong and I couldn't see if she had a beauty spot, her face was turned away from me. I'm going to follow. You stay put. I'll call again as soon as I get a better view. No sign of a man, though."

"Wilco," Rose acknowledged, pressing the disconnect button while keeping the phone in her pocket and wandering slowly off the bridge and down the side street that led across to the square where Kempner had been. There was a wooden bench, set back in a recess, with a metal plate bearing an inscription on it and she gratefully sat down for a rest, her eyes lingering on the carefully chosen words. *"What's the rush. Take a moment to sit and think while you still have moments. Ours have gone. Dennis Alsopp (1918–2004) and Lemmie, labrador and friend."* Rose tried to picture the old man, alone with his thoughts and his dog, who had sat watching the world go by from this bench, waiting for nothing. Suddenly, forty or so yards ahead of her, a noisy roller shutter began to judder upwards. Seemingly, it gave access to a basement garage in one of the buildings they'd been watching and she waited for a car to exit but, instead of a car, a male figure emerged tentatively from the garage, looked left and right and hurried away. It was impossible to judge whether he'd seen her on the bench tucked away in the recess, but Rose considered it odd that a pedestrian should make use of a basement garage exit.

The man had turned left at the top end of the street and disappeared from view and she moved off in pursuit. As she reached the corner, she could see him crossing the square. Carrying a holdall in his right hand. Odd gait. As if trying to walk quickly, but keeping his left upper body immobile with the left arm held unnaturally across his front. Still. Not swinging. He looked over his shoulder and she ducked back for a second into the side street. Decision time. Stay put as per Kempner's orders or follow the man. There could be any number of innocent reasons for him coming out of the garage, but her intuition made the decision for her. Keeping close to the building line, she walked briskly into the square and across it in the same direction that the man had taken on to the main thoroughfare. There was no sign of him anywhere. Rose quickened her pace, scanning the pavements and shop doorways trying to spot him but he had completely disappeared. On her left a walkway led to another bridge where several canal tributaries met, forming a large central basin containing a number of moored barges. Rose ran to the bridge and looked across the basin and beyond. Just past the last moored barge she spotted him, scurrying down the tow path, the unnatural gait even more noticeable as he endeavoured to run. Satisfied that he must have seen her and had chosen to flee, she was now confident that he must be Vance.

There was no way down to the towpath from this bridge and she had to run across the road, down an old flight of steps and then jump off a wall on to the path below. The jump was further than she had anticipated and, landing badly, she picked herself up and scoured the pathway for her quarry. He was probably eighty yards ahead of her, still on the tow path, at a point where the canal narrowed, with decaying, Victorian buildings crowding the waterway and obscuring her view. Making no further effort to remain inconspicuous, Rose broke into a sprint, the sound of her feet on the ground ensuring that he was alerted to the fact that the chase was now really on. It was obvious within a dozen strides that she was faster than him and the gap lessened by the second but, as she closed to a point where she had him clearly in view, the canal widened abruptly and she saw he was alongside a barge which was chugging its way northwards at the statutory four miles an hour. Taking the bargee at the wheel completely by surprise, the man leapt on to the deck, continued running up the length of the vessel, before leaping off on to the far bank and disappearing from view.

Rose was breathing heavily by the time she came up alongside the startled skipper and wasted neither breath nor time in providing any explanation, but simply replicated the actions of her quarry and leaped aboard. However, when she prepared to jump off on the other side, the distance was more than she had anticipated, forcing her to stop dead in her tracks, realising that the canal was at least ten feet wider here than at the point where the man had jumped. Shouting to the bargee that she was a Police Officer, she asked him to steer his vessel closer to the far bank and, with a nod of his bearded head, he immediately obliged, but valuable time had been lost and, crouched on the path, Rose could neither see nor hear anything of the man.

Walking back to where he must have landed, she saw that a dilapidated door into a warehouse type building hung almost off its hinges and she kicked it inwards, revealing an interior of damp-smelling, twilight darkness. Picking her way over discarded lumps of iron and broken bricks, she heard his breathing before she saw him and the breathing came from behind. As she turned, he threw a straight right aimed directly at the point of her jaw, with all his body weight behind the blow. Danny Rose was quick, but not that quick and, although she managed to sway back on her heels and pull her head away, the blow connected with the side of her head, knocking her off her feet and she felt the outside of her right thigh ripped open by some sharp object on the ground. Immediately aware that the man was closing in on her, she rolled further to her right and, as he swung his leg at her body, her hand snaked out and grabbed his ankle. The boot still landed in her ribs, but, rolling back in the reverse direction, she hung on to the ankle and, twisting and jerking simultaneously, she took the leg away from under him and he crashed to the ground. In an instant she was on top of him, her forearm across his throat, her knee coming down hard on his left shoulder, causing him to let out a scream of complete agony and she felt all the fight ebb out of him. The light was poor but she could see enough to realise that his eyes appeared closed and his face was contorted in pain, the breathing coming in short, shallow gasps.

"I'm a Police Officer," she shouted. "I'm arresting you for assault.

I'm getting off you, but if you make any attempt to resist I'll put you straight back on the ground. Do you understand?"

There was no response from the man and, even when she got to her feet, he remained on his back, his hand now clutching his left shoulder.

"Get up," she demanded, her ribs aching and aware of blood coming from her thigh, but now completely in control. The man remained silent and motionless. Rose's eyes had grown more accustomed to the light and, just beyond the prone figure, she could see a window in the wall which was covered by some kind of sacking. Keeping one eye on him and the other on the debris-littered ground, she stepped across to the window, grabbed the sacking and wrenched it away from the tacks that held it in place. A shower of dust filed the air, causing her to splutter and cough, but the light from outside flooded in, picking out the myriad of dust particles, but enabling her, for the first time, to see clearly the man she believed to be Vance.

He was wearing a check jacket that had fallen open and a pale yellow shirt, except that most of the front of it wasn't yellow any more, but was red and spreading fast. For a brief second, she was worried that somehow or other she had killed him, but as her eyes wandered up to the rugged face, she could see that his eyes were open and were following her.

"Did I do that?" she asked

Still, he said nothing, but, as she reached inside her pocket for her phone to call for assistance, she thought she saw him shake his head, as if to exonerate her from blame.

"Kempner," she breathed into the phone. "Can you talk?

"Just about, he whispered. "The woman's in a bookshop, showing no interest in buying a book. She's waiting for someone."

"The guy she's waiting for is flat out on his back in a derelict building by the canal. He's hurt. I need back-up and an ambulance. Can you do the necessary?"

"Are you OK?"

"Cuts and bruises. No worse. Arrest your woman, then see to me. This guy's not going anywhere in a hurry. I'll stand out on the tow path so they know where to come. Maybe a hundred yards north of the canal basin. See you soon."

"Roger, he whispered, moving swiftly in the direction of the woman with the light blue baseball cap and the beauty spot on her upper lip."

Chapter 16

Berkshire Police
Record of Interview
Place of Interview: Newbury
Person Interviewed: Susan Vance
Interviewing Oficers: Detective Inspector Jake
                                                Kempner
                                                Detective Sergeant Danny
                                                Rose
Others Present: Solicitor – Declined.
Tape Reference: JK/345/68/
Suspected Offences: Theft Of Ford Fiesta LX
                                                Murder Of Raymond Leon
                                                Millard

Kempner: I'm Detective Inspector Jake Kempner and this is Detective Sergeant Danny Rose. The interview is being tape recorded. What's your name?

S. Vance: Susan Vance.

Kempner: It's Sunday morning. Your husband will remain in hospital until the doctors are satisfied that the wound to his shoulder no longer requires in-patient treatment. Then he'll be brought to this Police Station for interview. In the meanwhile it's our intention to interview you. You've already been cautioned. You're entitled to a solicitor. Do you want one?

S. Vance: No lawyers.

Kempner: I arrested you in a bookshop on suspicion of the theft of a Fiesta LX and the murder of Raymond Leon Millard. On searching you I found two one-way rail tickets from Birmingham to Fishguard for use yesterday. Who were those tickets for?

S. Vance: Philip and me.

Kempner: Who is Philip?

S. Vance: The man you referred to as my husband. We aren't actually married.

Kempner: It's obvious to me that you're American. As an American myself I believe that your accent is New York. Am I right?

S. Vance: Maybe.

Kempner: Where do you live?

S. Vance: Here and there.

Kempner: In the United Kingdom?

S. Vance: I don't propose answering personal questions. If you've got evidence that I've committed a crime, then put it to me and I'll answer you. Otherwise I shall exercise my right of silence.

Kempner: Why were you going to Fishguard?

S. Vance: We move about a lot.

Kempner: Fishguard is best known as the ferry port to Larne in Ireland. Is that where you were headed?

S. Vance: No.

Kempner: Were you driving a green Ford Fiesta LX on the M40 in the early hours of last Thursday when it was stopped by a Motorway Patrol Range Rover?

S. Vance: Yes. No big deal. We were staying in Birmingham. We wanted to visit Oxford and hired a car off someone Phil met in a pub. We returned it to him. It was obviously a shady deal. Plus, I didn't have proper driving documents and we paid in cash. So I lied to the officers about my addresses.

Kempner: When you were talking to the officers a phone in your possession rang. We'll get the billing off the company in a week or two, but we can already prove that at 4.54 a woman called Alicia Daley telephoned Ray Millard on a mobile phone. Did you receive a call at that time?

S. Vance: My phone did ring while I was in the Police Range Rover, yes.

Kempner: Did you answer it?

S. Vance: I fumbled around with it and turned it off. It seemed wrong to accept the call while the Police were talking to me.

Kempner: Who would phone you at nearly five in the morning?

S. Vance: Friends. They know I'm not a good sleeper.

Kempner: What did you say to the Officers while fumbling with the phone?

S. Vance: No idea.

Kempner: Did you say "Sorry Officer"?

S. Vance: No idea.

Kempner: What sound did your phone make when it rang?

S. Vance: A musical sound.

Kempner: Any particular tune?

S. Vance: Can't remember. It's only a cheap Pay as You Go. I played around with the different rings and often changed them.

Kempner: Did it play "The Battle Hymn of The Republic." As an American, you'll be very familiar with that.

S. Vance: Can't remember

Kempner: Where is this phone?

S. Vance: It broke on Friday. I've thrown it into a dustbin somewhere. Like I say, it was a cheap Pay As You Go. No contract.

Kempner: And no records.

S. Vance: No.

Kempner: What was your phone number?

S. Vance: Can't remember. They're so long. I forget.

Kempner: Before the Police stopped you had you been to a small village called Amberley?

S. Vance: Never heard of it. We'd been in Oxford and were on our way back to where we were staying in Birmingham.

Kempner: Had you helped burn out a Cadillac Escalade near Amberley?

S. Vance: No

Kempner: Earlier, had you been to a village called Radford in Berkshire and helped in the brutal killing of Ray Millard?

S. Vance: Never heard of him or Radford

Kempner: When you were stopped on the M40 the Officer noticed you had a lot of mud on your shoes. When I saw you in Birmingham you still had a thin streak of mud on your shoe. Where had you been to get that?

S. Vance: Round the Oxford Colleges grounds. I thought that's what I told him on the Motorway.

Kempner: As an American in the UK where are your papers, your passport, any proof of who you are or the circumstances of your presence in this country or where you live in the UK?

S. Vance: Listen. I've already told you. I lied to the Motorway cops. You can have me for that. What I'm doing here and all that stuff is my business and not yours. If you want to get me kicked out of the country then go ahead and try. But as to murder and car theft, I've answered all your questions. If you've any evidence to put to me then do it now.

Kempner: When and how did Philip sustain the serious wound to his shoulder?

S. Vance: You'd better ask him. It's not my shoulder.

Kempner: I'm asking you.

S. Vance: Silence.

Kempner: What is your family name?

S. Vance: Silence

Kempner: Is Philip Vance a genuine name?

S. Vance: It is

Kempner: Does the name Pal or Paul Locke mean anything to you?

S. Vance: No

Rose: Listen, Susan. That phone call in the Police car will kill you. We're awaiting forensic on the blood from the murder scene. If that links Philip to the scene then both of you are in deep water on the murder charge. It may be that he killed Millard in circumstances which don't incriminate you in what happened. Don't be a fool and risk getting convicted of a murder he may have done and for which you're not responsible.

S. Vance: Do I look like I was born yesterday, lady? Save the "dump the other guy and save yourself routine" for someone else.

Kempner: We have enough evidence to charge you with murder. Unless you provide a satisfactory explanation to the questions we're asking, then you will be charged. Frankly, I'm tired of your bullshit.

S. Vance: I've answered. It's not bullshit. Turn your tape recorder off. We're through.

Kempner: Not yet. What did you do to the body after the murder?

S. Vance: I don't know anything about a murder.

Kempner: Which one of you mutilated the body? Or was it both of you?

S. Vance: Mutilated? How was it mutilated?

Kempner: You know. Tell me.

S. Vance: I've no idea what you're talking about

Kempner: There's been a news embargo on the details of what was actually done to Millard. Only the killer knows. You'd better tell us what Philip did to the body or you'll share responsibility for that as well.

S. Vance: No. You tell me.

Kempner: Millard was decapitated. His hands were cut off and the calf muscle was hacked off.

S. Vance: Christ Almighty.

Kempner: You've gone pale. Makes you feel ill now, does it?

S. Vance: Silence

Kempner: Rose. Get her a glass of water, would you?

S. Vance: No water.

Kempner: What was done with the head and hands?

S. Vance: I've no idea what you're talking about.

Kempner: We'd have found some residual forensic evidence of the head if it had been burned in the Escalade fire. There wasn't any. What did you do with it? Did you weigh the parts down and dump them in the river at Amberley or in another river or lake driving North?

Susan Vance: I've had enough. Your questions mean nothing to me. I don't want to hear any more. Like I said, we're through.

Chapter 17

Berkshire Police
Record Of Interview

Place Of Interview:	Newbury
Person Interviewed:	Philip Vance
Interviewing Oficers:	Detective Inspector Jake Kempner
	Detective Sergeant Danny Rose
Others Present:	Solicitor – Declined.
Tape Reference:	JK/345/68/
Suspected Offences:	Theft Of Ford Fiesta LX
	Murder Of Raymond Leon Millard

Kempner: It's Monday morning. I'm Detective Inspector Jake Kempner and this is Detective Sergeant Danny Rose. You've been brought here from Hospital where you were treated for a serious wound to your shoulder and your left arm is now in a sling. You were arrested by Sergeant Rose in Birmingham on suspicion of assault. I'm now formally arresting you and interviewing you under caution on suspicion of car theft and the murder of Raymond Leon Millard. Do you understand?

P. Vance: Silence

Kempner: What's your name?

P. Vance: Philip Vance.

Kempner: Where do you live?

P. Vance: Put me down as no fixed abode. And let's save a lot of time here. I'm telling you nothing about myself. You've got my name.

That's it. If you want to question me about specific allegations, I'll answer.

Kempner: Do you have something to hide?

P. Vance: It's a free country still, isn't it? If I shack up with some American girl and we do our own thing, whether we're actually married or not, then that's my business, not yours. So keep your noses out of my personal life.

Kempner: OK. Let's start with your arrest. Why did you run away from Sergeant Rose and then attack her?

P. Vance: I haven't been in Birmingham for a while. It's become a hostile place. I'd already been attacked in the street a couple of days earlier and injured. Our passports and money were stolen. On Saturday I knew a woman was following me. I thought it might be connected with the earlier attack so I tried to shake her off. She was very determined and when she actually tracked me down into that building I hit her. Self-defence. Fear of a robbery. That's all I've got to say about that.

Kempner: Your shoulder had a nasty wound. I've spoken to the Medics. It was an existing injury which had opened up in the struggle you had with my colleague. The Doctor says that a very sharp instrument had pierced you straight through that shoulder at least thirty six hours earlier and probably longer. How did you come by that injury?

P. Vance: I told you. I'd been attacked in the street. Robbed. Knifed in my shoulder.

Kempner: Did you report this robbery to the Police?

P. Vance: No

Kempner: Did you go to Hospital for treatment to the injury?

P. Vance: No

Kempner: Why not?

P. Vance: I rely on no-one but myself. I wasn't going to die. The Police would never have caught the robbers. Don't like hospitals.

Kempner: We've now located the service apartment you rented under the name of Vance. There's nothing there, nor in the rental form, nor in your pockets that establishes who you are. What is your true name?

P. Vance: Philip Vance.

Kempner: Your skin is deeply tanned. Not like two weeks on the Costa Brava, but the tan of a man who has spent years in a hot climate, yet your accent is very British. Where have you been living for the last few years?

P. Vance: Don't you listen? Ask me what you like about some crime you suspect me of but, as to my personal circumstances, they stay private.

Kempner: Do you know a man called Raymond Leon Millard?

P. Vance: Never heard of him.

Kempner: Were you in the green Fiesta LX stopped by the Police on the M40 in the early hours of last Thursday, driven by Susan Vance?

P. Vance: Yes

Kempner: Why was Susan driving?

P. Vance: I had a headache

Kempner: Was it because you'd already sustained a knife wound at the hands of Millard when you killed him.

P. Vance: Crap.

Kempner: Have you been to Radford in Berkshire?

P. Vance: Not to my knowledge.

Kempner: And into a barn at the side of a country lane?

P. Vance: No.

Kempner: In that barn Millard's body was found. So was blood from someone other than Millard. Scientists are analysing that blood. Will you provide us with a sample of your blood to compare against it?

P. Vance: No.

Kempner: Why not?

P. Vance: I have to prove nothing. I'm giving you nothing. You get no blood.

Kempner: We can't take blood against your will. We need your consent because blood is what the law classifies as an intimate sample. But, if you refuse to consent to blood being taken, the law allows us to take hairs from your head by force, DNA them, and compare them to the DNA profile raised from the blood at the scene.

P. Vance: Then you'll have to use force. I consent to nothing. And any bastard trying to pluck hairs from my head won't find it easy.

Kempner: As it happens, we don't have to go to those lengths. But your determination to try to stop us is very significant. If that blood at the scene matches your blood, then you were in the barn where Millard was killed and you were bleeding.

P. Vance: You try to prove it.

Kempner: We will. Your yellow shirt which you were wearing when my colleague arrested you is soaked in blood from the re-opening of your shoulder wound. We need no consent to analyse that. It's already at the lab.

P. Vance: Silence.

Kempner: Have you ever been to a village called Amberley?

P. Vance: Not to my knowledge.

Kempner: I believe that's where you were coming from when you were stopped. You'd just burned out Millard's Escalade.

P. Vance: Rubbish.

Kempner: Where did you get that Fiesta from?

P. Vance: Cash deal. In the pub. Rented it for fifty quid for a couple of days. We didn't have current licences or insurance so we did an iffy deal. Sounds like the fella had pinched the car but we gave it back to him on Thursday.

Kempner: Which pub? What was the man's name? Describe him.

P. Vance: Do me a favour.

Kempner: Millard was a well known and successful criminal. That kind of life-style attracts enemies. Were you one of his enemies?

P. Vance: Never heard of the bloke.

Kempner: We know that one of his most bitter enemies was a man we know by the nickname of Pal. Do you know anyone by that name?

P. Vance: No.

Kempner: We've been informed that Pal is dead. We'll check that out. But my instinct prompts me to believe you are Pal. Are you?

P. Vance: My name is Philip Vance. I'm often called Phil. But not Pal.

Kempner: Does the name Paul Locke mean anything to you?

P. Vance: No.

Kempner: Have you ever been to Mexico?

P. Vance: Is this a travel quiz?

Kempner: What's the answer?

P. Vance: Silence

Kempner: The evidence we have will lead to you being charged with murder later today. As soon as you are charged we have the right to take your fingerprints.

P. Vance: Is that a fact?

Kempner: Will you consent to that?

P. Vance: No. I'll refuse.

Kempner: Are you frightened that we may have the prints of Paul Locke on file and that yours will prove to be a match?

P. Vance: No prints.

Kempner: I am empowered to have your fingerprints taken by force. That will be done on my direction later today. By force if necessary. So I'm asking you once more. Are you Locke?

P. Vance: No.

Kempner: Do you know a man by the name of Bruce Tisdale?

P. Vance: No.

Kempner: What kind of mobile phone does Susan have?

P. Vance: Cheapo. Pay As You Go.

Kempner: What's it's ringing tone?

P. Vance: She changes it every five minutes. No idea.

Kempner: Your connection to the Fiesta on the M40, the incoming call, your injury, your attempted escape from Sergeant Rose and all of the lies we've listened to this morning mean that you will be charged with murder. When the blood analysis comes back I suspect your goose will be well and truly cooked.

P. Vance: Your opinion isn't what counts though, is it? I've no more to say and you're reduced to the "my goose is cooked routine". So let's call it a day."

Kempner: No. I've got a lot more to ask you about. I have to go into the details of what you did with the body.

P. Vance: What are you talking about?

Kempner: You know exactly what I'm talking about it. The mutilation. You hated that man so much that you mutilated his corpse. Now tell us, was he dead when you did all that?

P. Vance: You're crazy. I know nothing about any of this shit. Finish it here. I've had enough.

Kempner: No. I want to hear from you the reason why you mutilated the body.

P. Vance: Finish. No more questions. No more fucking questions. Get me out of this interview room right now.

Kempner: There's been a news embargo on the details of the murder. In fact, no report at all was broadcast or published until Saturday, by which time you'd both been arrested. I want the details of what you did to the body and why.

P. Vance: Pull the plug on this. Now. Pull the fucking plug. I don't want to hear anymore of this shit.

Kempner: The head, hands and piece of calf? Where did you dump them? In the river?

P. Vance: I told you. I've had enough of this shit. Finish.

Kempner leant across the formica-topped table, which was apparently the best that Newbury Police Station could run to, and pressed the red button on the tape-recorder which stopped it recording. Vance, his arm held in a sling across the white overalls that had been supplied by the hospital, was leaning back in the uncomfortable red plastic chair and watching every move. The reference to the mutilation of the body had produced quite a dramatic effect on him and had prompted Kempner to look at the tough face opposite him and stare into the deep-set eyes with interest. It wasn't an evil face. Knocked about by life for sure. Capable of profound anger, but lacking the look of someone with the capacity to chop a dead man's head off. Moreover, Kempner believed that he had recognised what he'd seen behind the mask that Vance presented. He'd seen the look of a man who'd got satisfaction. Whatever price he might have to pay for Millard's death, Vance must have suffered a terrible wrong at his hands, because the fact that he had succeeded in exterminating him obviously outweighed any other consideration and Vance rejoiced in the fact of his death. But he didn't seem to rejoice in the mutilation.

"We're off the record, now," Kempner said softly. "No tape. No notes. Just the three of us."

"Is that on your Scout's Honour that you won't use anything said?" Vance scoffed.

"I'm serious. I'm trying to help," Kempner insisted.

"And why should you want to help me?"

"Because I know Millard was a bastard. And although I couldn't have hated him quite as much as you obviously did, I still despised him," came Kempner's open response.

"So what are you saying exactly?" Vance asked

"I'm saying this. You'll be charged with murder. Susan'll be right there in the dock as well on a murder charge. The way you're playing it at the moment, you're a racing certainty for the drop and she's not far behind you."

"So if I confess, you'll go easy on her. Is that your line?" Vance spat back at him.

"Not entirely, no. It may be that Millard lured you into that barn. Attacked you with a knife and you killed him in self defence. You could have a defence, or at least enough to get it down to manslaughter. The mutilation could have been just to make it difficult for us to identify

Millard. In English Law, it's the intention at the precise time of the killing that decides if it's self defence or murder or manslaughter. Cutting the head off afterwards may have nothing to do with your intention at the second you actually killed him."

"What the fuck do you mean? Cutting his head off? What is all this mutilation shit?"

"The murderer cut his head and hands off. You know that. It may still leave you with manslaughter, that's what I'm really saying."

"Listen to me, Kempner and listen good. I never cut anybody's fucking head off. You get that into your brain once and for all. I've hired a pinched car. That's what you've got me for. Nothing else. No murder. No manslaughter. Nothing."

"You're in deep trouble and you'll likely take the woman down with you. You'll both get life and Millard isn't worth that. Give us something to hang manslaughter on and we'll persuade the wigs at Court to take it," Kempner spelled out to him, while Rose shifted uncomfortably in her chair at the risk he was running in putting a deal like that to a suspect off the record.

"I don't trust you and I don't trust her and I don't trust the wigs, as you call them," Vance spat back at him. "Right at the end of the interview you hit me with some shit about decapitation. Then you try to offer me a manslaughter deal off the record. Take your manslaughter and shove it where the sun don't shine."

"OK. Your choice," Kempner grunted. "And your funerals. Don't say I didn't give you a chance. Let's go. Back to the cells."

Chapter 18

"If he's Philip Vance then I'm Wolfgang Amadeus Mozart," Kempner observed with a grin, as they sat in Braithwaite's shabby office on the top floor of the Police Station. There wasn't even a proper desk in the room, just a cheap counter-top screwed into the wall under the window, with thick, unpainted wooden legs to support it. Amidst the papers strewn across it, Kempner noted three Kit-Kat bars and a packet of Cadbury's chocolate fingers. Braithwaite had laid on some tasteless coffee in thick white cups and, as he tipped a third spoonful of sugar into his, he stretched across Kempner and seized the biscuits.

"How do we prove he isn't Vance?" Braithwaite enquired, opening the packet in a trice and extracting a handful of the long biscuits in one deft move. "Help yourselves," he added, pointing at the packet which he had neatly replaced only within his own reach.

"Number one, we wait for the results on the fingerprints. Number two, we play my hunch. I find out some more about this guy, Pal," Kempner replied.

"Your hunch may well be wrong. Alicia was sure Pal was dead," Rose said.

"Possibly. Alicia Daley told us the report was that he'd died recently in Mexico. We've got a name. Paul A. Locke. You can contact the British Embassy in Mexico City and get them to run a check on all British deaths over there in the last couple of months. There won't be many. Find out if anyone by that name is on the list. Did you see the colour of that guy's skin? Tanned deeper than a Californian beach bum. I'll bet he's a dab hand at The Mexican Hat Dance. And send a photo of both Vances, just in case they can be checked," Kempner responded.

"And how do you get any proper information about this Pal? Alicia didn't know anything," Rose reminded him.

"Of all the people we've dealt with so far in this case, who has known Millard the longest?"

It only took Rose an instant to come back with the answer. "Tisdale", she fired back at him.

"Exactly. Bruce Tisdale. He's been a sidekick for Millard for over two decades. He'll know all about Pal. I'm going to track him down as soon as we get back to London. If it's alright with you, Braithwaite, I'll get Rose to follow up on this from our end and let you know the results."

"I'm happy with that," Braithwaite nodded, discreetly helping himself to another chocolate finger. "Do you want me to check on the woman from here? See if a Susan Vance was admitted to this country and through which port. The likelihood is that there's no such record because if he's a phoney then so is she, but it's routine stuff, I'll get one of my DC's to handle it."

"Yes. You do that. I'll also call a guy I used to work with at the Precinct in New York. She provided her fingerprints, didn't she?"

"She did. Unlike him, no fuss. The Custody Sergeant has them. If you want them sent out on the computer link to New York then give me the Precinct address before you leave," Braithwaite answered.

"OK. We'll be in touch later. Come on then, Rose. Back to London. Tisdale's our first port of call. As soon as we've dealt with him and I've called New York, I'm leaving you to chase up the other enquiries. Tonight, I'm going to the theatre. Lauren's play opens at Her Majesty's."

"Sounds interesting," Braithwaite remarked.

"Yes. Good friend of mine. She's got the lead role in "When The Moon Stopped Smiling." First night tonight. Mustn't miss it. She'd kill me," Kempner laughed.

"And then cut off your head and hands. Sorry, bad taste," Rose added.

"Is it dinner before the play or after?" Braithwaite enquired, seemingly unashamed at disclosing where his true priorities would lie.

"Neither. I'm on a diet," Kempner said, watching Braithwaite visibly wince at the sound of the dreaded word.

* * *

Phoning ahead to the Intelligence Section at Eltham, Rose got Tisdale's last known address from the Parole files and Kempner pointed the Volvo in the direction of Hackney. The curtain went up at seven thirty and he had to get home and change into an evening suit, so he needed to find Tisdale without too much trouble. The address given was a high rise tower block called Benton House. Twenty floors of slums piled on top of each other with lifts stinking of urine, walls defaced by obscenities and unemployed tenants pushing bawling brats in baby chariots or playing their music at full volume. Holding their noses up to the eleventh floor Rose banged on the red painted door of Flat 11K, while Kempner pressed his finger over the peephole. A moment later they heard the sounds of several locks being undone before the door cautiously opened a few inches. Tisdale's instinctive attempt to slam it shut on seeing the faces of his unwelcome visitors was met by the immoveable obstruction of Kempner's boot.

"Don't make this difficult, Bruce. We're not after you. Millard's dead," Kempner announced through the gap in the door. "We're on the same side for a change."

The door slowly opened to reveal Tisdale in a grimy vest and torn jeans, his large head leaning forward to check if any of his neighbours were on the landing. The arms were heavily tattooed and the muscles still bulged, but the hard face showed signs of genuine shock.

"Ray's fucking dead?" he grunted in disbelief. "When was this?"

"Can we just step into your hallway? It might be better if the whole landing didn't hear," Kempner asked.

The bulky figure retreated into the narrow hallway, allowing Kempner and Rose to enter the flat. It smelled of chips from the chip shop. The patterned carpet was thin and worn. There was a naked bulb hanging from the dingy ceiling. Rose closed the front door behind them.

"I can't tell you much. But he's dead alright. And he didn't die in his bed. He was murdered. Alicia, his girl, has told us that of all his enemies the one he really feared was a man called Pal. That's who we're here to ask you about," Kempner explained slowly.

"I can't fucking believe that anybody'd get the jump on Ray," Tisdale exclaimed. "He was as hard as fucking nails and twice as smart. How was he done?"

"Like I said. Detail's a bit sparse at the moment. But what about this guy, Pal? What can you tell us?"

"You're wasting your fucking time with him, Kempner," Tisdale grunted. "He's dead. Ray told me himself. And Tommy Langham told Ray. Tommy never gets it wrong."

"Who is Tommy Langham?"

"East End boy. Best connected thief you'll ever meet. Lives in the States now. His sources don't come up with crap. If Tommy says he's dead, then he's dead. Somewhere down in Mexico."

"Even so, I want to know about Pal and Millard. What's the story?"

"Pal picked up a fourteen stretch on a drugs charge. The same business when the copper got topped. Pal and Ray blamed each other for the drugs. Jury believed Ray. Pal vowed he'd have Ray and Ray took it serious. Pal was a handy geezer."

"Where did he come from?"

"Birmingham. But he'd been down in London for a while when I met him."

"Describe him."

"Like I said. Handy. Tough boy. Not too tall, but plenty of beef."

"Face?"

"Solid."

"Did you see much of him?"

"In the months before he went down I saw him quite a bit when I was out with Ray."

"I know this was a long time ago but do you think you'd recognise him if you saw him again now?"

"He's fucking dead. I told you. Tommy Langham don't make mistakes."

Been living in Mexico. That's where he snuffed it."

"Pretend for a moment that he wasn't dead. Could you pick him out on a Parade?"

"I reckon I probably could," Tisdale responded after a long hesitation.

"I want you to attend a Parade later this week. As you'll probably know, they're done on video nowadays. The suspect's video'd and put in with a video of nine other men. You just look at the video. Are you game?"

"If Pal's the geezer what's done for Ray I'm up for it. But you're barking up the wrong tree, Kempner. Pal's brown bread."

"If it isn't Pal who else might be prepared to kill Ray?"

"There's some who might think about it. But I wouldn't have reckoned they'd ever go ahead with it. Ray was still 'The Man' round here."

"Who might think about it?"

"I ain't saying. They're still alive and Ray's dead. They go where I go. I'll look at the video. That's different. Pal ain't had no clout round here in years. The others carry the muscle and one of 'em must have done for him. That's it. No more. You can hop it now, Kempner."

"OK. I'll be in touch for the Parade."

* * *

"I'm running late and we've still got a lot to do," Kempner said when they were back in the Volvo. "I want to call Joe Kritzeck in New York and get him working on Susan Vance. "Here, see if you can see his cell number in my book. KRITZECK," he spelled out while thrusting a well-thumbed diary from his inside pocket into Rose's hand.

"I got it," she murmured.

The connection was almost instantaneous and a deep, loud Brooklyn accent came hurtling three thousand miles into the Volvo's airspace, prompting Kempner to pull over, grab the phone from Rose's hand and shout into it before the car had even come to a halt.

"Joe. Its' Jake, how ya doing?

"Jake! The Limey Cop. Doing fine. You calling to ask if you can come back? 'Cos we'll take you, buddy, any time," the good-natured voice rumbled.

"No. Staying put. At least for the time being. I'm calling for a favour."

"Shoot."

"We've arrested an American woman for murder. Undoubtedly a New Yorker. She's given us a name. Susan Vance. Almost certainly phoney. I can get her prints and mug shot sent out on the computer. Can you run a few checks. See what comes up."

"Sure thing. I'll do the necessary. Get back to you if I turn anything up. How's your actress friend, buddy? Still on the map?" Kritzeck chuckled.

Kempner cast a sideways glance at Rose's face as it was inevitable that she could hear every word that Joe was bawling down the phone. Joe didn't do discreet. "Opening night tonight in a new play. On my way to see it. Got to fly. Love to Carol," he replied.

"We miss you, Jake. Both of us. Come and see us," the deep voice boomed out as he cut the line. Kempner knew that the reliable New York cop meant what he said.

"Did you hear all of that?" he asked Rose as he started to turn the car round and head back on to the main road.

"How could I not hear it? Anyway, I suggest you drop me at the Tube Station near your place," Rose replied. "I'll go home and phone Braithwaite and get him to send the Susan Vance photo and prints to your mate. The rest of the stuff I've got to do is all phone work and it's not worth going back to the office to do it. It's not like I've got a night out at the theatre to look forward to."

"Unfair," Kempner said softly.

"But true. First night and all that. Is her husband going to be there?" Rose asked dangerously.

"Probably. We'll just ignore each other. Particularly after Tisdale's efforts. I've been in that situation before. Lauren just has to be equally polite to both of us."

"And who gets to go home with her?" Rose fired mercilessly at him.

"That's a dirty question," he replied.

"But it's a hell of a good question, isn't it?"

"Yes," he replied sadly. "I'm afraid it is. Let's just talk business."

"Whatever you say, Jake," she said gently, watching his face intently as he turned to smile uneasily at her.

"Business, Rose. Just business."

Danny sat in silence, watching London move gradually towards the end of another working day. People scurrying along the pavements, bound up in the complexities of their own lives and seeking some kind of fulfilment. Tonight, she would sit at home alone, while Lauren would take the plaudits and then choose which of two men she would favour, in the knowledge that she would never really commit herself to either. She remembered what her grandmother used to say to her as a child when things went wrong. "Fair, Danny? Fair? Who said life was fair?"

"Right. Business," she said curtly, after the silence had endured far too long for comfort. "If Pal served fourteen years, for a crime committed by Millard, we've got our motive. I'll have the Locke file delivered to the office overnight and we can go through it together in the morning," she announced.

"Something worries me about that, though. Vance is no fool. If he's really Pal, he'll know we're bound to have Pal's prints on record from the fourteen year stretch. If ever he got stopped on this, he must have known the prints would fix him," Kempner pondered out loud.

"He didn't bargain on a broken back light and a pull from the Motorway boys. You can't cater for everything, can you? Else we'd never catch anyone."

"I've still got an uneasy feeling about that side of it. I guess we'll be a lot wiser tomorrow. Here we are," he said, pulling in at the side entrance to the Tube Station. "Your station. See you in the morning."

"Tell Lauren, break a leg," she replied cryptically, as she got out of the car and joined the other pedestrians. All of them hurrying nowhere.

Chapter 19

Jack Farnham had never enjoyed wearing a dinner jacket and, as he bent down to tie his shoelaces, he felt the familiar stab of arthritic pain shoot up his leg, the bitter legacy of ruptured anterior cruciate ligaments, which had prematurely ended his professional football career. Now a highly successful football broadcaster, with his own weekly chat show on cable TV and a football column in the most respected broadsheet of them all, he had passed through the indescribable agony of losing his wife in an accident caused by a drunk driver and moved on to another chapter in life.

Still handsome, although the hair was now flecked with grey, a day never passed without Jack reminding himself of the extent to which his recovery was a direct result of stumbling across Naomi, who had gently and slowly shown him that the world could smile again.

The daughter of an embittered class-ridden miner, Naomi Nicholas had had her own titanic battles to fight before arriving at the destination her old headmistress, Miss Wickham, had convinced her was within her reach. A career at The Bar. Five feet ten inches tall, naturally elegant, swept-back blonde hair and high cheekbones. Sometimes bursting with self-assurance and strength, yet at other times vulnerable and soft. Their life together had been idyllic until that dreadful time when she had thrown him out. Of course he had let her down, but the dilemma with which he had been confronted with was so awful that whatever he had done would have been wrong. Eventually, a chance meeting in a London hotel and the intervention of a sad old Hungarian musician had brought them back together and now, with Naomi a flourishing QC, they had sold their homes in Leeds and bought a two-bedroomed flat in Greenwich overlooking the Thames.

"Have you called for a cab?" Naomi asked, causing him to

abandon for a moment his struggle with the shoelace and look round at her framed in the bedroom doorway. She looked absolutely stunning. Her blond hair, held back by a deep purple braid, was shining and the white lace blouse and black mid-length Dior skirt showed off her figure and long legs to perfection. With matching Manolo Blahnik high-heeled shoes and her ramrod-straight back, she stood only about an inch short of Jack.

"You look spectacular, Naomi," he said enthusiastically. "Janet'll be proud of you."

"I hope so. We're the only people she'll have there so we won't let her down. And you didn't answer my question."

"I did call a cab. I got slowed down by the knee that's all. I'm ready. Let's go."

Predictably, the traffic was chaotic and there was only about ten minutes to curtain time when the cab containing Jack and Naomi eventually pulled up outside Her Majesty's. The canopy on top of the entrance had Lauren Callaway's name in capital letters above the title of the play but Naomi was delighted to spot Janet Wickham's name, albeit in much smaller lettering, on the posters immediately inside the foyer, which was heaving with people.

Even amidst the London glitterati, the arrival of the striking couple turned many heads and few failed to recognise Jack Farnham from the TV, with his broad shoulders and easy smile.

Lauren had ensured that Janet's guests had been provided with tickets in Row A and Naomi found herself seated next to a man who immediately reminded her of the old cowboy actor, Dale Robertson. Although his head had been buried in the programme when she approached her seat, he had instinctively looked up as she arrived and acknowledged her and Jack Farnham in an accent which sounded like it originated from Dale Robertson's side of the Atlantic.

"American?" she asked pleasantly.

"Guilty," he replied, smiling.

"Theatre buff?" Jack Farnham enquired.

"Yes and no. I live in London nowadays and just happen to know one of the cast," he answered.

"So do we," said Naomi. "That's why we're here. Janet Wickham. She isn't the same member of the cast that you know, is she?"

"No, ma'am. I don't know Janet Wickham. Anyway, let's wish them all luck," he replied.

"Not good luck. They don't like that," Naomi laughed. "Break a leg, that's what you have to say."

"Not to me, you don't," muttered Jack with a rueful grin, as the house lights went down, a hush fell over the theatre and that incomparable moment in an actor's life arrived. The curtain went up on the opening night of a West End production.

* * *

The upstairs bar had been closed off for a private reception after the play. Pretty young waitresses in mini-skirts dodged in and out of the crowd of producers, critics and investors, holding aloft their silver trays bearing glasses filled to the brim with Perrier Laurent pink champagne. Curtain calls and standing ovations had lasted for nearly a quarter of an hour and members of the cast, their faces flushed with success, circulated amongst the invited guests. James Albright, sweating profusely and with eyes darting everywhere across the room to identify who he should move in on next, had trapped Lauren's hand in the crook of his arm and was steering her around the room, lapping up the plaudits like he was the owner of the racehorse that had just won The Grand National.

Naomi Nicholas and Jack Farnham were surrounded by a knot of people clamouring to have a word with Jack and, even in these elevated circles, ask him to sign their theatre programme. Naomi had witnessed Jack dealing with the public in numerous circumstances and never failed to marvel at his patience and easy charm. But on this occasion, Naomi was concerned to discover what had become of Janet and, leaving Jack to talk about football, she wandered away, glass in hand, towards the recess at the far side of the bar to look for Janet. In fact the recess was deserted, except for a solitary male, sitting at a table and sipping from his flute of champagne.

"Hi," he said, jumping immediately to his feet on spotting her. "I'm taking five. To escape the frenzy."

"I know the feeling," she replied. "I can't find Janet and Jack is surrounded by people talking about Manchester United."

"Take a seat, ma'am," he responded, pointing towards the red leather banquette seat. "We sat next to each other all evening and I never introduced myself. I'm Jake Kempner," he added, offering his hand.

"Naomi Nicholas," she replied, gratefully lowering herself on to the seat opposite him.

"And presumably Jack is the gentleman sitting with you down-stairs?" he enquired politely.

"That's him. People never tire of talking football to him and he never tires of answering."

"I'm afraid I'm not into soccer. I was brought up on American football. Your friend, Janet, by the way, she did a grand job. You can be proud of her."

"She needs exposure. Good reviews and a long run. Which one was your friend?"

"They deserve good reviews," he responded, carefully ignoring Naomi's question and taking a sip from his glass.

"I was very impressed by. . ." Naomi began, before a female voice interrupted her as Janet came bustling around the corner of the bar.

"Naomi. I couldn't find you. I saw Jack and he said you'd gone looking for me," she said excitedly, throwing her arms around Naomi and kissing her on the cheek as she slid on to the seat beside her.

"Go on, Naomi," Janet added hurriedly, staring at her apprehensively. "Go on. Give me your verdict. I can't wait to hear what you say."

"You were brilliant, Janet. Just brilliant. Your voice filled the theatre and I'm so proud of you," Naomi enthused.

"Hear, hear," the male voice opposite declared. "You were a star."

Janet looked away from Naomi at the stranger on the opposite side of the table, now leaning back in the booth and observing the two ladies with great interest. It was as if she had been so intent upon finding Naomi and receiving her verdict that she failed altogether to notice the man at the table, but, as soon as she looked at him, she recognised immediately the cowboy from Wells Fargo.

"Oh, I'm sorry," she said. "I hadn't realised you were talking to Naomi."

"Not at all," he replied. "We just happened to sit next to each other in the theatre. Then we bumped into each other here, five minutes ago."

"You're Jake, aren't you?" Janet said.

"Guilty."

"I recognised you from a photograph Lauren has," Janet added, feeling as if an explanation was appropriate.

"So your friend in the cast is Lauren Callaway, is it?" Naomi observed. "You behaved just like one of my clients when I asked you before," she added with a laugh.

"How do you mean?" he asked with a twinkle in his eye.

"You know what I mean. You avoided the question," she grinned.

"Maybe," he smiled back. "And when you say 'one of your clients' what kind of clients are you referring to?"

"Criminals," she answered gleefully. "I'm a barrister. Murderers, rapists and burglars. I only mix with the social elite."

"Well, we do have something in common. They're my customers as well. I'm a cop," he chuckled, just at the moment Lauren's head appeared around the corner.

"Jake," she called. "Great to see you. Can I drag you away for a minute? Do you mind, Janet? she added.

"Not at all. But before you go, let me introduce you to my friend. This is Naomi Nicholas QC who I told you about."

"You were masterful, Lauren," Naomi declared. "It was a wonderful production."

"Thank you. And thank you for making it possible for Janet to be at my side," Lauren replied.

"OK, Lauren. Where are we off to?" Jake asked as he came round the table to join them.

"Just to meet a few of the others," said Lauren.

"You didn't mention the QC bit, did you, Naomi?" Jake called over his shoulder as he was being led away.

"See you in Court," she called back, laughing, as Janet took her arm and they settled down for a long chat.

Lauren took Jake by the arm and walked briskly along the edge of the crowd until they came to a door with a combination lock into which Lauren swiftly punched a code and they passed through into a dark and carpetless corridor.

"Cast only," she breathed. "It's like going into the staff quarters at a smart hotel. Shabby and downtrodden. All the money is spent front of house. OK. In here, this is my dressing room."

"More like dressing cupboard," Jake remarked, taking her into his arms as soon as the door closed behind them. "You were sensational, Lauren. Sensational," he added as he kissed her hungrily and she pressed herself responsively against him.

"Stolen moments are always sweeter," she whispered.

"Does that mean you're headed for Chelsea rather than Clapham when the lights go out?" he asked bitterly.

"The bastard's deliberately come by limo and asked the Ralstons back to the house. Ralston put up a quarter of million for this production. If I'm not in the limo with them it'll do a lot of damage. I'm sorry. After tomorrow's performance it'll be Clapham, I promise," she explained.

"And what if I'm tied up tomorrow tonight? It's a two-way street, you know."

"Come on, Jake. We both know it's difficult sometimes. Let's not spoil a wonderful night," she insisted, kissing him on the cheek and taking his hand. "Let's go and get another glass. James has done his stint of wheeling me round on his arm. He'll have moved on to chatting up the money men."

"Your call, Lauren," Jake replied. "It's your town and your call."

Chapter 20

He'd just finally managed to drop off into a fitful sleep when he heard the sound of his mobile phone ringing from somewhere in the flat. Jumping out of bed, he rapidly tracked it down to the countertop in the kitchen and grabbed it, looking at the clock on the microwave as he answered.

"Kempner," he barked.

"Jake, I got something for you," the booming voice announced.

"Christ, Joe, it's half past two in the morning here," Kempner groaned.

"Sorry, buddy. I wasn't sure how many hours you were ahead."

"What you got, then?" Kempner asked, now fully awake.

"I ran the prints on the State and Federal databases. No match. No rap sheet. She's never been in trouble with the Law," the voice began. "But I got a buddy. He's got access to private employment databases. Folks looking for security jobs, bank jobs, know what I mean?"

"Yeah."

"When they get taken on the payroll for those types of jobs prints are compulsory. He ran your lady's dabs."

"And?"

"Casinos, Jake. Casinos. 'The Imperial Palace'. Vegas. Three years working the craps tables. Jenna Zayer. That's her," he announced triumphantly.

"Zayer." "Not the Zayer family? The architects?" exclaimed Kempner in surprise.

"Just how I reacted, Jake. Just like you. I called the Zayer Foundation on Madison Avenue. Asked to speak to the big man himself. The secretary told me to take a hike, but when I said it was to do with a murder enquiry in England and I could make it hot for

182

the old guy she told me to hang on. Did I let anything out of the bag? he asked anxiously.

"No. There's no secret. She's already been charged."

"OK. Well the old guy came on. Jerome Zayer himself. I told him what I knew. Asked if he had a daughter called Jenna. Gave him the date of birth.

Told him she was for the high jump on a murder charge across the pond. Wanted confirmation it was her."

"And?"

"He told me he had a daughter called Jenna. If she was calling herself by another name, then he was delighted. He never wanted her associated with the Zayer name again and she hadn't been for several years. He hadn't seen or heard from her since she left New York after High School and he'd be very grateful if this didn't get into the Press unless it had to."

"That's our girl then, Joe. Worth waking me up for. I owe you one," Kempner acknowledged.

"I faxed Zayer the photo. He called back and confirmed it's her. Asked if I could help to keep the Zayer name out of it. Sounded a decent guy, Jake. I said I'd let him know. What's the score on that?"

"She's been charged as Susan Vance and will stand trial in that name but the fact she's using a false name will come out at trial. The victim was a gangster and not too many people are shedding any tears over him. It may not make a big enough splash to cross the pond. Except it's got a particularly gruesome angle to it. That's the best I can offer him," Kempner explained.

"OK. I'll relay that on to the guy. What you mean 'gruesome'?"

"Head and hands. Sliced off clean as a whistle."

"Holy cow! That'll hit the tabloids alright. I don't think I'll mention that part of it to the old timer," Kritzeck sighed. "Anyway, all you need do for identification purposes is call the Employment

Office at The Imperial Palace and they'll nail her to the name of Jenna Zayer. Nice work, eh, buddy?" he laughed.

"You're still The Man, Joe. Time for some shuteye. So long," Kempner replied.

Back in bed, he tried to get some sleep but his head was filled with female faces. Lauren, Danny, Jenna Zayer, Naomi Nicholas, Janet Wickham. All spinning in space. Detached from their bodies. Ethereal. After a while they all seemed to merge into one amalgamated kaleidoscope of faces and he couldn't tell them apart.

Chapter 21

"Do you want the good news or the bad news first?" Rose asked sharply.

Waking up with a headache, Kempner had decided to take the train to Eltham and, rather than face the dishwater in the office, he'd stopped at Luigi's on the corner and ordered a double espresso. Having savoured the hot, strong coffee he'd headed into Bleak House where Rose, transparently refusing to ask about the play, had hit him with her prepared opener.

"I'll take the good first," he snapped back. "And a very good morning to you, as well."

"The blood from Vance's shirt recovered from the hospital," she responded, ignoring the sarcasm. "It's a match for the blood on the wooden pillar in the barn. It absolutely destroys him."

"And the bad?"

The file on the Locke trial. It's on your desk there," she pointed. "You can see, it's barely a centimetre thick. There's hardly any paperwork at all. It's all evaporated in the system. All the statements, Police Reports, everything. Gone. They didn't keep the details for very long in those days. We're left with the charges, the verdicts and the sentence. Millard was only on the drugs charge and was acquitted. Locke was acquitted of murder but convicted on the drugs charge and got his fourteen years. That's it."

"We can live with that. It's not particularly bad."

"I haven't finished," Rose said sharply. "In those days the finger-prints were re-taken after conviction and filed manually. They didn't put them on a data base. When Locke was released on parole after ten years, they realised that his prints had been lost. There's a copy letter in the file demanding that he report at a Police Station and provide a fresh set. The letter says if he failed to attend he'd be arrested in breach of parole, returned to prison and his prints taken by force."

"And?"

"He never turned up. He'd kept all parole appointments up to that time. He was never heard of again. He scarpered," said Rose.

"Did he ever receive that letter?"

"Oh yes. It was sent Recorded Delivery. He signed."

"So he always knew that we didn't have the prints of Paul Locke. We've got nothing to compare the prints taken off him at Newbury with. The crafty bastard. At least we've got Tisdale. He'll do the business on an ID Parade."

"Probably. But who would you put your money on in Court? Some smart-alec QC or Tisdale?"

"I met a QC last night, as a matter of fact," Kempner volunteered. "At the event you're at such pains not to ask me about."

"Who was he?

"Not a 'he'. A 'she'."

"Name?"

"Naomi Nicholas. Have you come across her?"

"You bet I have. She prosecuted a Government hatchet man at the Old Bailey awhile back. She's a class act. I went to part of the trial. She was questioning the hatchet man."

"And?"

"She took him to the cleaners. So you met her at the play, did you?"

"Yes."

"And is it a hit?"

"I thought so. The audience thought so. But I read the reviews in the papers on the train. Not that good. Unkind. No complaints about the acting, more an attack on the author."

"Too bad."

"What about the Embassy in Mexico?"

"They're not easy people to deal with. It took forever to get to speak to someone who was prepared to help. Pedro Guiterrez. We swapped names and Email addresses. He's got the mug shots and all the details. He'll Email the results about Pal as soon as he gets them."

"When will that be? Manana?

"Exactly."

"You've been busy, Rose. Does Braithwaite know about all of this?"

"Yes. I phoned. He'll set up the video of Pal today so we can get Tisdale in for a Parade tomorrow. Pal will be remanded to Bellmarsh. The woman will go to Risley in Lancashire. Have you ever been there?"

"No."

"Don't."

"One piece of information for you now," said Kempner. "Susan Vance is the daughter of one of New York's most influential architects. Jerome Zayer. Not quite Frank Lloyd Wright but still a major player."

"Who is Frank Lloyd Wright?"

"You don't know your Simon and Garfunkle do you? He was a genius. Like them. Except he designed buildings, not dreams. Like the Guggenheim Museum."

"OK. So she's Susan Zayer?"

"No. She's Jenna Zayer. She obviously flew the coop long ago and upset daddy in the process. Went to Vegas and worked at one of the big Casinos. Then she must have met Pal. Let Braithwaite know about that as well. Tell him, once the pathologists's report, the forensic and the Mexico information is in, we can prepare the file for Crown Court. I think we've got a wrap."

Chapter 22

Standing 6 feet 5" in his stocking feet and weighing in at 18 stone, Ronan Cadogan QC took up a lot of courtroom space. A massive presence with a booming voice tinged with a Southern Irish lilt, he dominated any forum in which he appeared and he used his bulk and noise to maximum effect.

At school he had been a formidable second row forward and at Trinity College, Dublin he had represented the University in the heavyweight wrestling division. Twenty five years on, his frame had lost much of its shape but had retained and added to its bulk. Those who had known him as a boy, and later in adult life, would have all agreed that he had also retained one overriding characteristic. He was a monumental bully.

Dominating and subjugating his wife, so that her own once-sparkling personality was suffocated beneath his mass, he had proceeded to belittle and humiliate their son until all confidence was shattered.

There were times when the bully in him temporarily abated and he would charm and flatter and the house had a calmer atmosphere, but his mood could turn with the wind and the hectoring and tormenting would then begin anew.

In court, the witnesses, other barristers and even Judges would often wilt beneath the verbal assault, intimidated by the sheer size and volume of the man. Of course, not all would give way and his appearances were littered with savage and bitter exchanges.

Some years ago he had tangled with Mr Justice Bessant. Roland Bessant was a slight man, bespectacled, short, in his seventies and soon to retire. A High Court Judge who had been trying Criminal cases for as long as anyone could remember. In 1945, still only a teenager, he had won the Military Cross when, alone, he had killed four German soldiers with his bayonet in total blackness in a French sewer. After that experience, any encounter with a belligerent barrister held little fear.

Cadogan had pulled a stunt in Court in front of Bessant who had reported him to the Bar Council. Six weeks later Bessant suddenly dropped dead of a heart attack in the library and the whole complaint had died with him.

A few years ago he had defended a man for murder at Leeds Crown Court and confronted an adversary who had once cheated him in a case and Cadogan had sought his revenge. None had watched the unfolding drama with more horror and distaste than Cadogan's Junior, Naomi Nicholas, who Cadogan had relished treating with complete contempt.

Unless the case was very high profile Cadogan always refused Legal Aid cases, accepting only those that were privately paid. Now he had been offered the brief to represent an American woman charged jointly with her boyfriend with the murder of a London gangster, paid for under the Legal Aid scheme. In a fury he had sent for his Clerk, Alistair Quail, and threatened him with the sack for even contemplating accepting such a Legal Aid case.

To his surprise, the following week, Quail had knocked sheepishly on his door in chambers and nervously crept in clutching a sheet of paper. This new breed of Clerk was all computers and technology, Cadogan reflected angrily to himself. This latest specimen that Chambers had somehow acquired was too young, earnest and useless.

"Good morning, sir," the thin voice began, staring at the giant who was leaning back in the high-backed ornate chair behind the antique desk and gazing out of the sash window over Temple Gardens and beyond to the river.

"What do you want, Quail?" the voice boomed.

"That case you were offered last week, Mr Cadogan. Susan Vance. Two-handed murder. I did what you told me. I phoned the solicitors and said that there was no question of you accepting a Legal Aid brief."

"Well?"

"They've sent a fax. I think you should read it," he said, meekly thrusting the paper towards the massive paw that now reached out across the desk.

Attention of A. Quail Esq
Clerk to Mr Ronan Cadogan QC

Chesney, Mellor & Statham
Solicitors
The High
Oxford.

R v Susan Vance : To be tried at Oxford Crown Court

Dear Mr.Quail,

Further to our telephone calls concerning the above case we confirm that you have informed us that Mr Cadogan QC has declined to accept the brief if his fees are to be paid by the Legal Aid Fund. We informed our client that we would instruct another Leading Counsel who was prepared to accept the brief under the existing Legal Aid Certificate.

However, to our surprise, we received a communication yesterday from New York to the effect that she must only be represented by Counsel of the very highest quality. Our enquiries disclose that Mr Cadogan's success rate in criminal defence trials is second to none. His fee will be met on a private basis from New York.

We therefore communicate herewith our wish to instruct Mr Cadogan in this trial which will take place at Oxford Crown Court next month lasting three to four days.

Accordingly, we would wish to meet with you to discuss the appropriate fee. We would be grateful if, having discussed the matter with Mr Cadogan, you would telephone our Senior Partner, Selwyn Statham, before the close of business today, so that we may arrange a meeting in your chambers tomorrow morning.

Yours sincerely,

Selwyn Statham

"Phone Statham," Cadogan barked. I want the name of the person providing the money and proof it exists. Tell Statham to bring that proof to chambers at nine-thirty sharp tomorrow morning, together with the brief. I shall then assess the amount of work in the brief and decide my fee. He will then have until the close of business tomorrow to get approval from New York. Is there the slightest possibility that you can actually remember any of that or should I write it all down in your crayoning book?"

"I'll see to it immediately, Sir," Quail replied, before fleeing from the room, leaving the bully looking out towards the river, his size fourteen feet now resting comfortably on the desk. Three days in Oxford. That lovely pub right on the river and within walking distance of the Court. Naming his own price, courtesy of some well-heeled New Yorker. There was only one possible cloud on the horizon. Bellinger. Mr Justice Rodney Bellinger. He was sitting at Oxford this term. Bad-tempered, prosecution-minded, wise to the old tricks and arrogant. Cadogan removed his two tree trunk legs from the desk, opened the central drawer and poked around until he found one of the diaries containing the Court Centre phone numbers and reached for the phone.

"Criminal Listing Department," the young female voice answered.

"Crown Prosecution Service here," Cadogan barked. Case of Vance and Vance. Murder. To be tried at your Court next month. I require the name of the Trial Judge," he demanded.

"Just a moment, Sir. I'll look it up," the girl replied. "Yes, I have it here. It's been allocated to the High Court Judge. Mr Justice Bellinger will be trying it."

Cadogan's finger came down hard on the phone's disconnect pad.

"Damn," he cursed silently. "Rodney Bellinger, a barrister himself long ago, belonged to the breed of Judge who developed 'Judgeitis' the moment he got his appointment. Pompous, preening and intolerant, he turned against the Bar as soon as his fleshless rear end lowered itself on to the red-crested leather of the judicial chair. Promptly christened "Bellicose Bellinger", he bullied the youngsters, despised successful barristers and, most intensely of all, he hated Cadogan.

In his last year before being appointed to the High Court Bench Bellinger had been Head of Caxton Chambers, which was run by a cabal of selfish, self-seeking back-stabbers who excelled in poaching tenants from other chambers as soon as they had started to develop a practice of their own. A prime suite of office space had become available in The Temple attracting a bid from Caxton Chambers which, by chance, had co-incided to the penny with a bid made by Cadogan on behalf of his chambers. On learning of this, Cadogan, skilled in mimicry, had phoned the vendor's agents and, pretending to be Bellinger, withdrew their bid. That same afternoon he had exchanged contracts with the owner of the property. When Bellinger emerged from the Royal Courts of Justice at the end of the day, he was met on the steps by his flustered clerk who had informed him of the startling development.

Bellinger had marched round to Cadogan's chambers in a fury, barged into his room and threatened to sue unless Cadogan withdrew from the deal. Grabbing Bellinger by his scrawny throat, still bedecked in its starched wing collar, Cadogan had pinned him to the wall and told him that any attempt to sue would lead to public exposure of all the poaching scams that Bellinger had orchestrated. No proceedings were issued and the two men had never spoken again.

The following morning, when Selwyn Statham, seated in Cadogan's room, had reluctantly coughed up the name and certified Bank Statements of Jerome Zayer, Cadogan did the mental mathematics, building in an extra twenty five thousand pounds on the brief for the Bellinger aggravation factor.

"Very well, Mr Statham. I've looked at the brief," Cadogan announced. "I shall require three hundred and twenty five thousand pounds on the brief and refreshers of twenty thousand a day. I shall also require a Junior. Quail can provide you with someone suitable. Only a nominal fee for him, as his purpose is simply to carry my messages and my bags. Please let my clerk know of Zayer's decision by the end of the day. I've been offered an alternative case for that week which, to be frank, has rather more going for it. Good morning."

Selwyn Statham blinked and swallowed hard, but remained seated as he pulled a calculator from his briefcase and punched some figures into it. "There's no need for further communication with Mr Zayer," he declared after completing his calculations. "I have written authority to meet your demands up to a certain figure and you've not gone above that. You are now formally retained to represent our client."

"You mean I could have gone higher?" Cadogan said acidly.

"Jerome Zayer is a very astute man, Mr Cadogan. I'm sure you realise he will have done his homework on you. At the present rate of exchange, your fees are lower than the ceiling Mr Zayer imposed."

"How much lower?" Cadogan demanded.

"Forty three dollars exactly. I'll leave the brief with you. Good morning."

"Forty-three dollars," Cadogan's voice boomed out, as the fleshy jowls started to vibrate. "Forty-three dollars," he repeated as his humourless laugh began to erupt from within the barrel chest. "Mr Zayer sounds like my sort of guy." "And," he added silently to himself as the mean laugh filled the room, "the cute bastard worked it out without even knowing about Bellicose Bellinger."

Chapter 23

It had turned into such a late night that she hadn't completely removed all of her mascara when they went to bed and now, as she sipped from the big breakfast coffee mug, he could see streaks of the black cosmetic running down from the corners of her eyes where she had wiped away the tears.

Sitting at his breakfast table in jeans and a T-shirt, she looked younger and more vulnerable than when she was dressed in all of her finery and Jake got up, slowly walked round the table and stood behind her, putting his hands gently on her shoulders, seeking to protect her from another of life's raw deals, but powerless to do so.

"Not even a month. We won't even have lasted a month," she sighed. "And you saw for yourself the reception we received on opening night."

"It's no reflection on the production. The critics went after the writer, not the cast. It's like our job, Lauren, you close the file, shrug your shoulders and walk on to the next case. You won't be short of offers," he said reassuringly. "What does 'you-know-who' have to say about it?"

"He's very disenchanted with Milo. Says it's his fault that we brought it to the West End so early. Should have done a full provincial tour and built up the momentum. He's very stressed about the whole thing. At least he isn't blaming me."

"Or me," Kempner added, bringing his mug of coffee back to the table and sitting down.

"He never mentions you at all now," she replied. "No sarcastic remarks, no rows. He just behaves like you no longer exist. As a matter of fact, he's been rather supportive during all the upset about the play which makes life a bit less complicated."

"Do you think it's being getting so complicated that you'd be better off if you saw less of me? he asked pointedly.

Her eyes stayed down and she studied the almost empty mug held cupped between her two hands, waiting a long time before eventually answering. While he awaited her response, Kempner pictured their situation from the outside, looking in. A cramped kitchen in a cheap flat. An attractive woman consumed by permanent indecision. And a man, no longer young, who was directionless. It was a cameo of sadness.

"I don't want to see less of you, no. But your roots aren't here. You've no-one to fall back on. You're only here because of me and you only get me part-time. You deserve better than that," she declared slowly, never lifting her eyes from the bottom of her mug.

"I knew the score when I made the move. We're all masters of our own destiny. I could go back if I wanted. When I spoke to Joe Kritzeck recently, he made it clear they'd like me back. It's my choice to stay," he replied.

"For the time being, anyway," she smiled. "No decision lasts forever. Other people's lives always seem so much simpler than one's own, don't they?" Look at that barrister you sat next to on the opening night. Beautiful. Mega-successful. And has no problem at all with simply living with that old footballer while each of them forges ahead with their careers. No soul-searching."

"You don't know if all of that is true. She may have had serious difficulties about which you know nothing," he answered.

"I don't think so. She's in control."

"Well," he grinned, suddenly changing the mood. "I can tell you this. She's got one hell of a problem coming her way the week after next."

"How do you know?" she asked in surprise.

"Because she's been briefed to defend Philip Vance at Oxford. He hasn't got a feather to fly with. So I can't see her talking her way out of that one," he laughed.

"I should love to see that," said Lauren.

"Then you shall. I'm staying up there. You must come up, watch some of the trial and we'll enjoy Oxford together. How does that sound?"

"Interesting. Who's on your side in this contest?"

"That's a bit of a worry. Prosecuting Counsel has been selected by a new female CPS solicitor in Oxford. And she's chosen Luther Farlow QC."

"Why's that a worry?"

"Because he's got a full head of black curly hair"

"So what?"

"Which is permed and has extensions"

"Oh!"

"He wears suits that cost more than my car."

"Not difficult."

"His eyes are never still. They range up and down a woman's body like a yo-yo on a string."

"Oh, dear."

"He's got a permanent tan, from a bottle or a salon. And do you know what they call him?"

"Go on."

"Lothario Farlow. But, god damn it, he is incredibly handsome and he knows it. So the girls fall at his feet and he always obliges, I'm told, even for the ugly ones."

"But is he any good as a barrister?"

"Actually, he is. Very good. So long as you manage to keep his eye on the ball. But if there's a chance of a conquest, he becomes distracted."

"Perhaps he'll be distracted by Naomi Nicholas," Lauren observed.

"Maybe. But I suspect she'd give him short shrift. We'll just have to hope that he manages to last three or four days without mishap," Kempner concluded.

"Or that someone in the case doesn't know of his weakness and uses it," she said. "Who's the barrister defending the woman in the case?"

"No idea," he replied. "We'll just have to hope it's a man. Then we'll be safe."

Chapter 24

Danny Rose had already been at her desk in Bleak House for an hour when Kempner walked through the door, clutching a cup of Luigi's filter coffee in each hand.

"Brought you a decent brew," he smiled, as she lifted her head up to look at him. She was in an olive-green two piece suit which contrasted well with her natural colouring and accentuated the curves of her body. Normally, for work, she wore clothing which tended to disguise her femininity, but this morning she looked stunning. Nevertheless, Kempner recognised that the suit was more Marks and Spencers than Chanel, and he found himself subconsciously comparing its quality with the type of clothes that Lauren was able to afford. Rebuking himself for such an unkind thought, he put the coffee on her desk and, when he was close to her, he realised she was wearing both make-up and perfume.

"Opium?" he asked.

"Correct," she answered. "Not the Hermes Caleche that you're probably more accustomed to, but I don't go for bags of swank."

He winced at the accuracy of her barb and pulled his chair over to sit directly opposite her. "What've you got for me, Rose?" he asked gently. "And, by the way, you look a million dollars."

"I've heard from Pedro Guiterrez at the Embassy in Mexico City. He phoned late last night. I was still here," she replied, ignoring the compliment, but unable to stop herself from blushing. "The records show that Paul Arthur Locke is definitely dead. He bought it a few weeks back in a place called Tamazula. I've got all the details. The death certificate was signed by a registered medical practitioner, Dr Luis Hidalgo. Cardiac arrest. Natural death."

"Where's the body?" he asked.

"Cremated."

"Goddam it," he muttered.

"What about Hidalgo? Can he describe the body? Age, size, distinctive features? Anything to show it couldn't have been Locke?"

"Actually, Pedro Guiterrez was surprisingly efficient. He'd got Hidalgo's phone number and called him. Asked him if he remembered any details."

"And?"

"Guiterrez said he was next to useless. The word he used was 'borracho'. Do you know what that means?"

"Oh, yes. I know alright," he replied.

"Apparently, he did remember going to the house. The man was dead in the bedroom. And he remembered a distressed Senora but he couldn't describe her properly except for one thing."

"Go on."

"He remembered that she had a beauty spot over her upper lip. He remembered nothing about the corpse except it was a natural death and the body showed all the hallmarks of a heavy boozer. So the question is, do we drag him over from Mexico to say that the woman had a distinctive beauty spot?" she concluded.

"That's a decision for Prosecuting Counsel," he replied. "Tisdale picked Vance out as Pal on the Parade. So we've got that. Given that Hidalgo's described as a 'borracho', it may not be worth the candle to bring him over."

"Why not?" she asked. "What is a borracho?"

"A hopeless drunkard," he replied. "Just like the corpse."

Rose removed the top off Luigi's coffee and took a sip, before grimacing and continuing. "A couple of other developments. The blood on the pillar in the barn. The DNA result is back. The chances of that blood coming from someone other than Philip Vance are negligible."

"Then he's dead in the water. Naomi Nicholas isn't going anywhere with this one. "What else?"

"We already knew from the last forensic report that they eventually dug a 9mm bullet out from a pillar behind the body. No other forensic on it, but a downward trajectory lining up with the pillar where Vance's blood is," she said. "So Mimura was obviously right about it being a shooting."

"So the recovered bullet may be a miss or it may have been the fatal shot and passed through Millard, any blood being lost on its impact with the pillar," Kempner postulated.

"Correct," Rose nodded. "But the fatal shot to the head and the injury to Vance's shoulder could have been almost simultaneous. As Vance shot, Millard could have thrown a knife at Vance. The exact chronology is impossible to ascertain forensically. Only Vance can tell you. Still, on any analysis, he's heading for the drink."

"OK. Let's move on. I've got a much more important question for you," Kempner declared, pulling his chair even closer to her. "Why are you dressed to kill?"

Danny Rose pushed her chair back and stood up, coffee cup in hand, and walked over to the window. There was only one other Officer in the area and he was right at the far end of the room, his head buried in a computer screen. Leaning against the window she looked back at Kempner. "I've been meaning to tell you for a while," she finally announced. "I put in for my Inspector's exams and I lied to you."

"How do you mean?" he asked, the worry showing on his face.

"When I told you I went to Rome, I didn't. I took the exams," she confessed.

"But you had a tan?"

"Tanning salon. Kensington High St."

"I see. So all that stuff about gladiators and pasta was just junk?"

"Fraid so."

"And the exams?"

"I got the results two days ago."

"You don't have to tell me. You passed with flying colours."

"Yes. I won the gong. And this afternoon I'm being interviewed by Superintendent Yelland for a new job. Uniform. But a base wallah."

"What's that mean?"

"Inside. No field work."

"That's not for you. Who is this Yelland? I've never heard of him."

"I'm not surprised. He's Yorkshire Constabulary. He's down here to interview several Officers with a view to them being transferred to Leeds."

"Leeds? That's two hundred miles away, Danny. You can't do it. I'd never see you."

"That's the whole point, Jake. You look at me and you never see me. I sat at home in the evenings when I knew you were with a woman who never truly wanted you but didn't want anyone else to have you. I decided I could only wait so long."

"We can't have this conversation here," Kempner insisted, nodding in the direction of the Officer at the end of the room whose attention they now seemed to be attracting. "Let's talk about it this evening, after work, after your interview."

"It's too late. Too late," she whispered, her voice trembling."

Kempner had felt his heart sinking in his chest while she had been speaking to him. Suddenly, the full extent of her pain was exposed and the more he looked at her, the more he saw another similar face under red curls, looking helplessly back at him. Getting out of his chair, he walked over to the window and took her hand in his, feeling the tremor it caused in her. "Danny, please. Tonight. Just the chance to talk. I need a while to think and then the chance to talk. Privately and properly."

Slowly withdrawing her hand, she returned to her chair, sitting with her back to him so that he couldn't see the tears on her cheeks. "OK," she said softly after composing herself, still not facing him. "OK. Tonight. But you need to know that my mind is made up. We'll just be making it even more painful."

"Thank you, he breathed. Thank you. I'll pick you up from home at half-seven.

Rose tossed her empty coffee cup into the waste paper basket. She hated Luigi's coffee.

Chapter 25

While Danny Rose was being interviewed by the Yorkshire Constabulary, Ronan Cadogan was turning his nose up at the smell of body odour, industrial disinfectant and stale cigarette smoke that always permeated the Visitors Area at Risley Gaol. By the time that Cadogan arrived, Selwyn Statham was already positioned in the interview room with Junior Counsel and the client. Wearing a black Crombie overcoat that came down to his ankles and an old-fashioned bowler hat, the towering figure completely filled the room as soon as he opened the door and stepped inside. Cadogan was a firm believer in the power of the dramatic entrance and his choice of clothing was considered and deliberate. Without uttering a word, his presence dominated the room and the people in it. The unfortunate Junior, some wet-behind-the ears youngster that Quail had put forward, busied himself helping to remove the giant's coat and, because it weighed almost as much as him, struggled to lift it up high enough to hang it on the peg on the side partition of the rabbit hutch they had been allocated.

Meanwhile, in silence, Cadogan had taken his seat opposite the woman, removed his papers from his briefcase and taken stock. Green eyes, watching him like a hawk, naturally pale skin made even paler by several weeks inside, black hair, tied back and an expression that spelt defiance.

"I'm Ronan Cadogan," he eventually announced, extending his hand for the briefest of handshakes. "Do I call you Zayer or Vance."

"Vance. I haven't used Zayer in a long time. I'm the black sheep," she answered in a strong voice. "Do I call you Ronan or Mr Cadogan, I don't know the rules here?"

"The latter. At all times," he barked back at her. "Black sheep or not, your father's putting up the money to have you properly defended."

"Conscience money. I was a teenager when I left home. He never tried to mend the fences."

"If I may point something out, Mr Cadogan," Statham respectfully interposed, thrusting a piece of paper in the QC's direction. "I received this fax from the Police this morning. I think you should see it."

Cadogan devoured the contents in a few seconds, before looking up and staring directly at his client's mouth. "Dr Hidalgo seems to have remembered your beauty spot," he exclaimed with a sneer. "How did a young woman of your privileged background learn how to buy a corpse?"

"I don't know any Dr Hidalgo or anything about corpses," she replied, seeming to turn even paler at the realisation that the Police had tracked down the old Mexican medico."

"Sombreros, tortillas, donkeys and crooked Police! That's my image of Mexico," he retorted. "Is that a fair description of Tamazula?"

"Could I say something?" the nervous voice of the Junior piped up.

"What's your name?" Cadogan enquired in an irritated tone. "I've never met you before."

"Spiller. Mark Spiller. I'm in your chambers as a matter of fact."

"Then you should have made it your business to find out that I don't welcome interruptions in conference. What is it?"

"Sorry. Just to say that the fax states that the Prosecution haven't decided they will definitely call this Dr Hidalgo."

"Thank you so much, Spiller. We're indebted to you. We all feel much better now, I've no doubt. So, Ms Vance, do we run this case pretending that the Tamazulan corpse was the exiled Brummie, or shall we start calling Vance by his real name of Locke and begin to construct a proper defence?" he asked acidly.

"What's a Brummie?" she enquired.

"A native of Birmingham, that centre of culture, sophistication and learning," Cadogan replied, his sarcasm likely lost on his increasingly bewildered client.

"Until this case I'd never heard of the man Locke. Philip and I have been together pretty much since I left Vegas. That's his name and, given that we've knocked around together for quite a while now, I took his name."

"Then why did Jenna become Susan?" Cadogan snapped.

"I never liked the name Jenna, that's all."

'Where did you live with this man?"

"All over."

"Where?"

"I don't intend to say."

"Why not?"

"Because it's got nothing to do with whether I was involved in a murder or not."

"Why were you staying in Birmingham?"

"Like you said, an interesting town."

"I was being sarcastic."

"I wasn't."

"Where had you been when the Police stopped you on the M40?"

"Oxford. Looking at the Colleges. Having dinner."

"Why did you avoid giving them the proper address of where you were staying in Birmingham and a false New York address?"

"Because of the business over the car."

"How are you going to explain the call made by Alicia Daley to Millard's phone when the Officers will tell the jury that the timing, the ring and the words used by you, all coincide with what Daley says?"

"Coincide was a good choice of word. Coincidence"

"Why were you carrying two tickets to Fishguard?"

"Going to visit."

Whilst she had done her best to withstand the barrage of questions that he had unleashed, Cadogan's puffing and blowing and failure to make a single note of any of her replies, made it clear that, sooner or later, his very limited supply of patience would come to an end and, seemingly, it was the empty Fishguard answer that marked the end of the line.

"Right, madam, I've listened to sufficient gibberish for one afternoon," he exclaimed, putting his pen back in his pocket and leaning forward across the table, so that she could see the patchwork of narrow bad-temper lines on his brow and around the corners of his mouth. "It's time for the serious business. I don't lose cases. I don't do failure. I couldn't give a fig about the state of your relationship with this loser Locke and I don't give a damn about what happens to him. I do winning. Am I making myself clear?"

"Very."

"Splendid," he replied, a hollow, false smile flashing across his lower face, but never remotely nearing the small, pig-like eyes, which were so disproportionate to the overall size of his face. "So let's put this defence in some kind of order, shall we? First, I need to explain that, unlike lawyers in your country, I'm not allowed to suggest a defence to you. Do you understand?"

"I think so."

"Spiller," he said, turning his attention momentarily to the eager young man at his side. "Just pop out to the canteen, will you? Get us all a coffee from the inmate in charge there. I'm sure Mr Statham will re-imburse you from the client's account."

"Of course," Spiller mumbled, scurrying out of the door, both anxious to comply with the Master's command and relieved to have a short reprieve from the oppression that Cadogan's manner created, particularly in such confined circumstances. When Quail had put his name forward for this brief he had been elated, despite the miniscule level of his fee, but words of caution had soon been directed his way when people learned that he was to be led by Cadogan. The warnings had ranged from the light-hearted to the dire, but nothing had prepared him for the withering contempt that the man displayed towards everyone, including the client. As soon as Spiller had closed the door behind him the QC picked up where he had left off.

"Now, Ms Vance, you need to understand that I am bound by certain rules. I can only act on your instructions. I am merely enquiring whether perhaps the following is a possible interpretation of events. Number one, Vance is Locke. Number two, he told you he had a score to settle with Millard. Number three, you lent yourself to a silly deceit, at his insistence, that Locke was dead. Number four, you believed that Locke would simply give Millard a beating, nothing too serious but enough to settle the score. How am I doing so far in my interpretation of the evidence?"

"Go on," she breathed uneasily, beginning to see for the first time where he was coming from. The clue had been the rapid insertion of the words "at his insistence" in his seller's pitch.

"Perhaps you drove with him to the barn to which, somehow he had lured Millard. Millard's Escalade was parked outside. You stayed outside. Locke went in alone and emerged badly injured, carrying a bag, saying Millard had attacked him and he'd struck back. Then you drove the Escalade to Amberley."

Pausing momentarily for breath, he took a quick glance in the direction of Statham to observe if any reaction to this particular approach was visible from that quarter, but Statham's head was down, concentrating on his file. Susan Vance remained silent, waiting for the QC to get up steam again.

"Are these the instructions I am receiving?" he asked.

"I need to hear the full analysis before I say anything further," she replied quietly.

"Very well. He followed in the Fiesta. He burned the Escalade, got into the Fiesta with you, handing you a mobile phone saying it must have fallen to the floor in the struggle and he'd picked it up. Somewhere, perhaps in the river at Amberley the bag containing the gun and head and hands were dumped. You then drove and were stopped by the Police and panicked. You had no idea at all of what he'd actually done to Millard in the barn until you were arrested. The only intention, as you understood it, was to give him a beating. I think that represents the general theme as I would see it," he concluded.

"And where would all of that leave me?" she asked.

"Instructions along those general lines would leave you safe in my hands," was his cryptic reply.

"What does that actually mean?"

"It means that, at the end of this little trial you'd have a sporting chance to take tea at Benton's on the High in Oxford, accompanied by those delightful little cream scones that Americans believe we English have brought to us by our maids every afternoon. In short, it means you'd be in with a genuine chance of freedom, madam. Freedom, that most precious of gifts," he declared emphatically.

By this point Selwyn Statham was visibly squirming in his seat, as he, like his client, began to fathom the way that Cadogan operated. At that moment the door opened and Spiller re-appeared, balancing four plastic cups of coffee on his Counsel's notebook.

"Ah, young Spiller with our best Risley coffee," Cadogan boomed out, pushing his papers and notebook aside to make room for the brown-grey liquid that Spiller had paid for out of his own shallow pocket.

"Right, now we have Spiller back, what are our instructions?"

"Can I summarise my understanding of the position Mr Cadogan in my kind of language?" she enquired very politely.

"But of course," he said, in what was meant to sound like a sympathetic tone, but which resonated with condescension.

"Does it come to this? You're telling me that my best way out of this is to shit on Philip? she asked angrily.

"Crudely put, my dear, but accurate," he replied.

"That's what I thought. So let me spell it out. No deal. No way. Take that particular defence, Mr Cadogan, and, if you'll forgive the Americanism, 'shove it'. You've got my instructions. As already given to Mr Statham. Phil is Philip Vance. Not Paul Locke. We'd been to Oxford. Travelling about. He got knifed in Birmingham by a street robber. We were off to Fishguard. Sightseeing. I suggest you go earn my father's money with those instructions," she fired back defiantly at the QC.

"Very spirited. Very loyal. So good to see in these days of greed and selfishness. But remember this. You didn't kill anybody. You didn't decapitate anybody. Nevertheless, you're at serious risk of being convicted of murder and paying the same price as the man who did it. My advice to you is to reflect very carefully on what we've discussed this afternoon. I hope we'll all see the same way forward by the time of the trial."

"One other thing before you go," she suddenly declared angrily. "This business about decapitation. And dumping the head and hands. It's crap. Is that clear enough English for you?"

"Absolutely, my dear. Like I said, the time for serious reflection now arises."

Susan Vance remained in her seat while the lawyers gathered up their papers and belongings, feeling as if she now inhabited an alien world. Grey walls, grim faces, foul food, strange accents, empty days and now this giant of a lawyer that her estranged father had hired for some exorbitant fee. He talked in language from another time and his manner was insufferable, but, according to Mr Statham, who had sat stony-faced throughout the conference, he was the best QC in London and had the skill to extricate her from this catastrophe. Now, she began to realise that he saw Pal's downfall as her best route of escape and the starkness of the choice she may have to make appalled her, unless Cadogan could produce some other rabbit from the hat.

"You know, Mr Cadogan, I had to have a lawyer in Vegas when I had a car accident on Paradise Road. He took pride in describing himself as a Nevada shark. But, compared to you, he was a babe in arms," she said.

"I'll take that as a compliment," he replied. "But I do trust he was a lot cheaper than I am. Good afternoon," Cadogan smiled, opening the door and walking out into the main area as Spiller hurriedly emerged, carrying one of the plastic cups and bringing Cadogan to a halt.

"You haven't drunk your coffee, Mr Cadogan," he said apprehensively.

"No, Spiller. One of the Cadogan Golden Rules to be assimilated and stored away by those fortunate enough ever to be his Junior. Never, but never, drink anything whilst inside one of Her Majesty's Penal Institutions," he proclaimed.

"Why not?"

"Because inmates always make a point of piddling into drinks supplied to official visitors. Particularly lawyers."

"Then why did you send me to get them?" came the puzzled response.

"To give the client space, Spiller. Room to think."

"And did it help?"

"Not yet. But it will. Pop back in to the room, would you. I appear to have left my hat and coat. You can carry them to my car," he directed.

As Spiller scurried back to do Cadogan's bidding, Selwyn Statham seized the opportunity to raise his concern at the QC's so-called 'analysis' of the evidence. His researches had disclosed that, whilst Cadogan's track record was formidable, he was a universally disliked figure, but he had not appreciated that he would be quite so overbearing with the client, trespassing perilously close, if not beyond, the bounds of propriety.

"If I may just say, Mr Cadogan, I think we must let our client choose her own line of defence," he ventured.

The giant turned to face Statham square on, scowling at him, causing the jowls to descend even further down his face as the corners of the sour mouth turned down in scorn.

"Is your firm receiving generous remuneration for this case, Mr Statham?

"Yes."

"Did your charges increase as a result of my fee?"

"Really, I don't think it's at all appropriate. . ."

"Fair enough," Cadogan interrupted, "but we want to justify those fees, don't we? We have to win. That is why you came to me and why Zayer approved your choice. You don't want to seek an alternative QC, do you?"

"Certainly not," Statham insisted, not wanting to have to explain to Zayer that he'd lost the best QC in the business.

"Excellent, Mr Statham. Sometimes Counsel has to deliver robust advice. Time to head back to London, I think. Robust advice to the lay client. Focuses the mind. Good day to you."

Chapter 26

Danny Rose rented a tiny basement flat on the edge of Camden Town and when Kempner walked apprehensively down the stone steps to the heavy front door, he was wearing his best New York suit that he'd bought at Bloomingdale's just before he crossed the pond. Single-breasted, light grey, with a plain white shirt and pastel blue tie. Danny responded to the doorbell almost immediately and Kempner was both surprised and disappointed to observe that she was in a pair of blue jeans, a pink Everlast boxer's T-shirt and bare feet.

Stepping through the door brought him straight into the twelve by twelve sitting room with its two-seater floral-patterned sofa and one matching armchair, coffee table and TV. He'd been inside several times before, but only now did it strike him that this was a lonely person's room.

"Come on, Danny," he began. "Get your glad rags on. I've booked a table at 'Les Tres Canards' for eight o'clock."

"Then you'd better pull the plug on it," she replied, sitting herself down on the small sofa. "I've no intention of playing along with the romantic candlelit dinner scenario. You said you wanted to talk privately. We can do that here. There's an opened bottle on the side there with a couple of glasses. Bring them over. I'll get you some cheese and biscuits if you're really hungry."

"You're a tough guy, aren't you?" he smiled, pouring two glasses of wine and putting them on the coffee table as he sat opposite her in the hard, uncomfortable armchair. "How did the interview go?"

"Uniformed Inspector. Leeds Central. To start immediately after the Vance trial is over. I have until the end of this week to let Yelland know my decision."

"OK. Best not to beat about the bush. I can sense you just want the facts," he began, picking up his glass of red wine and tasting it.

"It was a big move coming over to England. It was only because of Lauren that I made it. And it took me a long time and a lot of anguish before I accepted she really wouldn't ever leave Albright. All the time that was happening, I was working alongside you. Attracted to you. But every time I got close, you put the barriers up because of Lauren. I was torn between New York and London and I was torn between Lauren and you. I was in a relationship with Lauren that had no direction, but I was in there up to my neck."

Danny had tucked her legs under her on the sofa and was watching him closely, her glass of wine untouched on the table. She could sense that he was waiting to judge how his opening remarks had been received before he was prepared to venture further, so she gave it to him straight.

"I thought you said no bull," she said harshly. So far you haven't told me anything I didn't know."

"I don't want you to go to Leeds. Stay in London. OK, you're going to be an Inspector now. You won't be working directly along-side me, but there are lots of Inspectors jobs going down here. Then we could continue to see each other. Is that a straight answer?"

"No. Because you haven't answered the real question, have you?" she said harshly.

"You mean Lauren?"

"Of course I bloody well mean Lauren. You can't handle this Jake, and I'm not spending what's left of my youth sitting in the hangar watching you decide which plane you're going to fly. I know you lost your wife and it knocked you sideways. And I know that you were right in there at Ground Zero. But, as a result, you only go after what you know you can never really have, because if ever you got what you thought you wanted, you'd be terrified of having it wrenched away from you again. . . "

"Hold on there, Jake interrupted, staring at her, horrified.

"No. I'll finish. You can never really be part of London like you were part of New York. That's part of the reason you're here. You can never have Lauren in a normal relationship. That's why you stay with her. I knew what I felt about you within a week of starting to work with you. And I didn't put up the barriers. You knew what I felt and all you had to do was face up to reality over Lauren. It's because you knew you could have me that you always held off. I had no other man, no strings. You knew I'd commit. That's why you never dared make the decision. And now, when I'm about to become unattainable, suddenly you want me more than ever."

The words had just tumbled out, pent-up within her for months, but now she had uttered them, she felt an enormous sense of regret. When she had finished, the sad little room was filled with complete silence. Danny leant over and picked up her wine glass and took a large uncomfortable swallow of the cheap supermarket Rioja. She knew that her face would have gone bright red, because she had cursed her colouring a thousand times before for displaying the intensity of her emotions. Everything she had said to Jake was true and she well realised how deeply it would have hurt him, but she remained unsure whether he had any real concept of how her heart had ached for him, night after lonely night. Perhaps if she had lost him to a woman who truly loved him and wanted to spend her life with him, then, hard though it may have been, she would have come to accept it. The heartbreak here was that she had never felt like this about a man before and she knew that he wanted her, but Lauren would not let him go. He would spend his life forever in love with the ghost of his wife, seeking fulfilment from a woman who would be equally unattainable and never knowing whether he belonged in New York or London.

"You know where to hit, don't you?" he eventually said, in a low, flat voice.

"It's not an ultimatum. I'm not trying to punish you for seeing me as second best. In fact third best. I've just been honest and honesty can sometimes be the worst policy. It just leaves everybody hurt," she answered.

"It's time I need. . ." he began but she didn't allow him to finish.

"No, Jake. You've had time. The risk you're running is that you'll spend the rest of your life just filling time, without ever really taking hold of it."

"I can't just finish with Laura like returning a library book. They're pulling the plug on her play, she's down. I can't just stick the knife in."

"But you can let me go?" she retorted.

"I don't want to. . ."

"Come here," she interrupted, swinging her legs round on to the floor and patting the empty seat next to her"

Kempner moved the few feet across the carpet and sat next to her. Without any warning she took his hand in both of hers, turned her face up towards him and kissed him long and hard, conveying an intensity that he knew Lauren could never match. Although he responded, he recognised that she was completely in charge of the situation. Her mouth became soft and urgent and in one kiss, she communicated to him the extent of what she felt for him and what she had to offer him. As she drew away, he saw that she was crying and he moved to put his arm around her, but, in an instant, she was on her feet, looking down at him, the tears now running freely down her cheeks.

"Goodbye, Jake," she said kindly.

"You're confusing me. I don't understand," he responded.

"I just wanted you to know how I really felt. I think you know now. It's best you go."

Kempner got to his feet and looked down at her. In bare feet she seemed so small. Her room was sad and, outside work, her life was empty and now he knew he could and should have filled it. "Is there anything I can do about this?" he asked plaintively. "If I came to a decision about Lauren before the end of the week. . ."

"Goodbye Jake. I fly solo", she responded, walking the dozen steps to the front door and opening it, standing aside as he slowly moved past her and out into the night air, going nowhere, acutely aware of the emptiness behind him to which Danny was now returning. Alone.

Chapter 27

Although it invariably proved to be a pig of a journey, Naomi Nicholas always drove to Belmarsh High Security Prison so that, when she later got out of the wretched place, she could immediately have some space of her own in the car and lift the inevitable mood of depression that the soulless institution generated. Amongst the criminal classes it was known as Hellmarsh, reflecting the extreme harshness of the regime that prevailed behind the high walls and watch towers. The last time that Naomi had visited a client there Ronnie Biggs, the Great Train Robber who escaped had just been sent there after returning to England as an old and broken man. The cons had been particularly bitter about the authorities sending Ronnie to one of the toughest nicks in the country when he was plainly in such poor health and no threat to anyone.

"He offended against the Establishment," her client at the time had remarked. "And if you offend against them, then they never forgive. That's what it's all about". It was just about the only topic upon which she had agreed with her client during the entire conference.

Eventually passing through the tedious security procedures, she walked along the miles of echoing corridors to the interview area with its row of glass-walled interview rooms containing the prisoners in orange dungarees, sitting waiting for their lawyers, penned in like cattle in their stalls. Bob Tomlin, her instructing solicitor, was waiting for her outside one of the cubicles. Naomi knew that the real reason Bob briefed her was because he was an avid Arsenal supporter and, on the last two occasions Naomi had done a case for him, Jack Farnham had taken Bob up into the commentary box and allowed him to watch the match from there.

Tall, thin, round-shouldered and almost bald although not yet thirty, his long face broke into a smile as soon as he saw the elegant, black-suited figure approaching.

"Good to see you, Naomi," he began. "And how's Jack?"

"If you mean is he commentating at Highbury on Friday night, then the answer is yes," she laughed. "And when I told him you'd sent me this brief he said to tell you to call his mobile half an hour before kick-off and he'd try to oblige. Is that what you wanted to hear?"

"Music to my ears. Thank him very much," Tomlin enthused.

"How about work? Is that our punter in No 14?" she enquired, peering round Tomlin's narrow frame to identify the appropriate orange blob.

"No 14. Correct. He's an oddball I have to tell you. As you can see from the brief I've been here four times to try to get some decent instructions from him but he's extremely defensive, virtually monosyllabic and he doesn't trust lawyers as far as he can spit.

"Sensible fellow," she smiled. "Is Junior Counsel coming to this conference or shall we just press on?"

"Junior Counsel is tied up in a case in the Family Division and sends her apologies.

"Her?"

Yes. It's a youngster called Fiona Breslaw. We send her some of our less well-paid family cases and thought it was time to thank her by sending her something decent where she didn't have to actually make any decisions. She's a nice girl, but a bit impulsive and I thought if she watched you in action she'd learn a lot.

"You're making me feel old," she laughed, nodding towards the Prison Officer who had stood patiently waiting to open the appropriate door. Other lawyers were now arriving and being slotted into their pens.

The rugged, solid face looked up at her as she took her seat opposite him, shifting along to enable Tomlin to lever his long legs under the desk. There was an air of mystery about the face, the skin still sun-weathered, despite several weeks on remand in this hell-hole. Naomi found herself reflecting that the ladies on the jury might find Philip Vance quite an attractive proposition.

"This is Naomi Nicholas," Tomlin said to him. "Like I told you before, our firm think she's one of the best QC's around, so you're lucky to get her.

"How do you do, Mr Vance" Naomi responded, offering her hand, which he took and nodded at her.

"OK. To business. You say you're Vance. The Prosecution say you're Locke. We've recently been served with a statement from a Dr Hidalgo in Tamazula who certified Locke as dead, not long before Millard was killed. He can't give sufficient descriptive detail of the body to prove it wasn't Locke and so they haven't finally decided whether or not to call him."

Vance simply nodded his understanding.

"But Hidalgo did have one clear recollection," Naomi continued. "He dealt with a woman while he was examining the corpse. He remembers that this woman had a very distinctive beauty spot above her upper lip. Does Susan have such a beauty spot?"

"Yes."

"Then, if I was prosecuting I'd call Hidalgo. They say you're Locke and a woman giving Locke as the name of a Mexican corpse is sitting in the dock alongside you. Dangerous stuff, isn't it?"

"But you said they haven't made up their minds whether to bring him over."

It was the first full sentence she had heard him utter. The voice was rather mellow, but the accent was completely unidentifiable. He'd spent too much time in too many places.

"My opinion is that they'll call him. And they'll certainly call Tisdale who identified you as Locke on a video parade. Once they prove you're Locke then they have their motive. Millard put Locke inside for a crime committed by Millard. Powerful incentive, wouldn't you say?" she asked.

"I'm not Locke. My name is Vance. If I was Locke, a convicted criminal, they'd have my fingerprints on file. They took my prints at Newbury. Compare the two and there's your answer."

Naomi started to laugh. "If you're Locke, then you know they cocked it up and lost the prints long ago. They've got the letter from the Parole Officer ordering Locke to attend for them to be re-taken. He never showed up."

Naomi spotted the beginnings of a sheepish smile around the corners of his mouth. He was a cut above the normal type of murderer she represented, she thought to herself, even though he was prepared to hack someone's head off.

"So what do I put to Tisdale when he says its you?"

"You put his record. It's as long as your arm. He's a gangster's hard man."

"How do you know that?" she fired back at him.

"Intuition," he grinned. "But the cops in this case must have had something else going on with Tisdale – he hasn't just crept out of the woodwork. You've got to dig around."

"That's possible. Can you set up an enquiry agent on that, Bob? Naomi asked. Find out if there's any word on the street about Tisdale's activities around the time he identified Mr Vance."

"Yes. I'll call Harry Edgington as soon as we leave the prison. His network of contacts in the East End cess-pit is legendary," Tomlin replied.

"Right, let's move on to the real cruncher," Naomi continued, carefully placing her pen down on the open page of her notebook and watching intently for Vance's reaction. "The blood on the pillar in the barn. The scientist will say that DNA analysis puts the chances of it not being your blood at less than one in a quarter of a million."

"Coincidence," he muttered.

"No, Mr Vance. That just won't wash."

"OK. How about this? You'll tell the jury what a ruthless bastard Millard was. The Prosecution's own case is that he put Locke down for a fourteen stretch to save his own skin. And the jury'll believe he killed that young cop. Your job is to make them hate him. Hate him so much that even if they think it is my blood in that barn, at least some of them'll say the bastard got what he deserved."

"And let you off?"

"Yeah."

"Even though the evidence says you did it?"

"I didn't do it."

"You think they'll sympathise with someone who chopped the head and hands off a corpse?"

For the first time in the conference Vance actually became animated and moved to get out of his seat, causing the Prison Officer on the other side of the glass to walk quickly up to the door, but Naomi waved him away and gestured to Vance to stay put. "That decapitation business," he shouted, "it's garbage."

"Alright. Calm down. I understand you deny it. But you've got to face up to it. The head, hands and calf muscle have been hacked off the corpse and taken away. They'll suggest you did it to make identification of the corpse hard but, more importantly, as a sign in the world of organised crime, that someone had taken their revenge."

"They can suggest what they like. I told you. It's shit," he replied angrily.

"Those body parts have been dumped after the murder. Probably with the murder weapon. You need to know what will be put to you."

"They dragged the river at Amberley, didn't they?"

"Yes. And found nothing. But there are other stretches of river you could have stopped and got rid of the evidence," she answered.

"But I didn't. I know nothing about this. Nothing," he declared vehemently.

"OK. So let's move on. Where had you been when the Police stopped you on the M40?"

"Oxford. Nice town. Day trip to see the sights."

"Why didn't you hire a car in the proper way?"

"This way was cheaper. And neither of us had a driving licence."

"Where do you live normally?"

"Around. Some of the time in England. Some of the time abroad."

"Do you have a passport then?"

"Did have. Both Susan's and mine were stolen when I was robbed in Birmingham."

"Why didn't you report it?"

"Pointless. Anyway, I'd taken a blade in the shoulder. That was more of a problem."

"Why is Jenna Zayer calling herself Susan Vance?"

"Ask her. I call her Susan. People are entitled to their secrets. I'll bet you've got one or two."

"But I'm not in the dock."

"Listen, I've told you the line. The extermination of vermin. Even the copper hated Millard's guts."

"Kempner?"

"Yes?" Do you want to know what he said to me off-tape at the end of the interview?"

"Yes."

"He said you'll both get life and Millard isn't worth that. Give us something to hang manslaughter on and we'll persuade the wigs at Court to take it."

"Slow down. Let me get all of this down," she responded with interest, picking up her pen to make a verbatim note of everything Kempner had said off tape at the end of the interview.

"In view of what you say Kempner offered are you interested in me trying to get you a deal on manslaughter?"

"How long would I get?"

"On the basis that there was an armed confrontation between two criminals and one ended up dead and the other wounded, then there really isn't a basis for manslaughter, it's still murder. But if the Police encouraged Prosecuting Counsel to lend himself to a fudge because Millard was so despised, then you'd normally get something like twelve. Add in the mutilation of the body and I'd say you'd end up with a sentence like the one you had before."

"Fourteen years?"

"Or thereabouts. Maybe sixteen or seventeen. Paroled around half."

"So, if the Prosecution are right, and I'm Locke, I'd have spent fifteen to twenty years of my three score and ten inside. All because of Millard."

"Yes. But if you're convicted of murder you'll get life. You may never get out again. You'll probably take Susan down with you as well. If they took manslaughter off you, they might reduce her charge down to a nominal accessory. A couple of years or so."

"At least you give straight answers, Miss Nicholas. I respect that. Now here's mine. I'm not Locke, I'm Vance. Someone else has blood just like mine. I'm not guilty of murder and I'm not guilty of manslaughter. And I didn't cut the bastard's head off. Is that clear enough for you?"

Naomi started to collect her papers together from the desk and tie them up with the customary red tape, nodding that she had well understood the emphatic position that Vance was taking, when he asked a final question.

"Whose Susan's brief then, Miss Nicholas?

"I'm sorry. I don't know, nor do I know who's prosecuting. We'll learn in the next couple of days," she replied, standing up and offering Vance her hand.

Before he could take it, Tomlin interjected. "I've got that information. The Court faxed it to me this morning. Hang on, it's in here somewhere," he continued, rifling through his file. "Right, here it is. Mr Justice Bellinger is the Judge."

"Bellicose Bellinger," Naomi groaned. "Irascible and unfair."

"Luther Farlow QC prosecutes," Tomlin continued. "Do you know him, Naomi?"

"Never heard of him."

"And Ronan Cadogan QC appears for Susan," he announced finally, reading from his piece of paper.

Naomi Nicholas felt the colour drain from her cheeks and suddenly felt obliged to sit down again so as to recover her composure. Bellicose Bellinger was bad enough news. Having Cadogan in the case was just catastrophic.

"Are you alright, Naomi?" asked Tomlin with genuine concern in his voice. "You've gone very pale."

"It's nothing, I'm fine. It'll pass in a moment. Just a headache coming on," she lied.

Vance had been watching her keenly throughout these exchanges and, when he saw her colour begin to improve, he spoke.

"So this brief, Cadogan, do you know him? I want her to be properly looked after."

"I know him," she replied.

"And is he any good?" Vance pressed anxiously.

"As good as they come," she answered. "With one proviso."

"What's that?" asked Vance.

"He's treacherous. Victory at any price."

"And what's wrong with that?"

"He'll use anything, anyone, any method in pursuit of victory. I wouldn't normally speak to a client about another barrister so frankly. But you need to know. He won't care who suffers so long as he wins his case. Be warned," she said, now getting back to her feet. "See you in Oxford."

When the two lawyers finally emerged into the fresh air and were making the long hike to the Visitors' Car Park, Tomlin took her gently by the arm and brought her to a halt. The whole area was exposed and a thin east wind was picking up force, making Naomi draw her jacket tighter round her shoulders.

"I've never heard you be so disparaging about another barrister to the lay client. What's that all about?" he asked.

"I told Vance because, if necessary, Cadogan will throw him to the dogs. He needs to know that. Ronan Cadogan is the most formidable QC I've ever encountered. A few years back, before I took silk, he led me in the defence of a murderer up in Leeds. I saw at first hand how he operated. He's prepared to cross the line. And he did. He's completely fearless, ruthless and, like I said to Vance, treacherous."

"Bad news for us then."

"Probably. It depends how he sees the case."

"How do you see it?" he asked, as they started walking towards the cars again.

"Do you want the truth or the diplomacy, Bob?"

"The truth."

"Somewhere between hopeless and impossible," she answered as they approached her Mercedes CLK 320. "And something else you should know. I prosecuted Cadogan at the Bailey not that long ago. A Government hatchet man was in the dock. And Cadogan had become even more deadly."

"Some food for thought then on my drive back to the office," Tomlin observed as he helped Naomi into her car. "I'll phone Harry Edgington immediately and set him on to Tisdale. Try to give you something to fight with."

"See if you can come up with something that stops me from being stabbed in the back while you're at it," she smiled, as she started the big engine.

"You're referring to Cadogan I take it?"

"Yes. He's particularly averse to me because I've seen his tricks from the inside and he and Jack had a bit of a set-to. Nearly came to blows."

"Well, Jack would have seen to him, there can be no doubt about that," Tomlin said confidently.

"Actually, I wouldn't like to pick a winner. Cadogan was a champion wrestler. He's six foot five if he's an inch. And he's a bully."

"And I suspect he's wary of you, Naomi, because you're tough enough and good enough to stand up to him. Let's hope he deploys his weaponry against the Prosecution and not us. Be in touch," he called, closing her door for her and watching her drive away.

With the grey edifice of Belmarsh looming in her rear view mirror, she pressed the button on her CD to listen to Johnny Cash singing 'Fulsom Prison Blues' to the inmates at San Quentin. Now there was a man who would really have known how to deal with Cadogan.

Skipping lunch, she spent the afternoon in the Temple library researching all the recent cases concerned with DNA analysis based on blood, but by six o' clock she was back to square one and her stomach was rumbling so loudly that she believed the other library users must be able to hear it.

Half an hour later saw her kicking off her shoes back at the Greenwich flat and gazing through the twilight across the river towards the warehouses on the opposite bank, while Jack prepared one of his special dry martinis for her. Apparently, there were more rumblings at the Football Association Headquarters and heads were about to fall, which meant that both the landline and Jack's mobile never stopped ringing. As he left her alone to answer the phone in the hall for about the tenth time since she'd walked through the door he shouted to her that the call was for her.

"Bob Tomlin," he mouthed as she loomed into view.

"Hello, Bob. Bit late to be still at the office, isn't it?

"Yes, but I've got Harry Edgington with me now and I thought you should hear what he's found out. I'll put him on"

"Good evening, Miss," the sharp little voice declared. Shall I just fire away?"

"Please do."

"Struck lucky on this one. It's common knowledge that Tisdale drinks down 'The Plume' in Hackney. I know a little grass hangs out there so I arranged to meet the geezer. It cost two hundred quid to wheedle it out of him but, the story is, Tisdale was going to pick up a few grand for giving someone a pasting," he related.

"How does that help?" asked Naomi.

"The fella on the receiving end was a copper. Been messing about with some toff's wife. And the copper was the copper in your case. Name of Jake, is that right?

"Yes."

"My guy didn't know the copper's last name, nor the whys and wherefores, but seems the whole deal went pear-shaped. Somehow the copper nailed Tisdale and it all died a death."

"So Jake may have some kind of hold on Tisdale. Not to do anything about the deal to beat him up, in exchange for a favour owed. Is that the flavour of it?"

"That's more your territory than mine, Miss. I've told you all I got. How you and Bob use it. . . ."

"Quite right," she interrupted. "Well done. Just one other thing. Did your source know the name of the toff who hired Tisdale?"

"No. All he knew was that the woman in the middle of the mess was an actress. Quite well-known actress, by all accounts. But no names," Edgington replied.

"Thanks, Harry. Put Bob back on, would you?"

"Is it of any use?" asked Tomlin as soon as he came back on to the line.

"Maybe. I'd like to think about it. It's a dirty line of attack on Kempner. In effect we'd be accusing him of not prosecuting Tisdale for conspiracy to assault, in exchange for identifying Vance as Locke. Pretty fanciful. And dirty," she concluded.

"We're in a dirty business, Naomi, aren't we? But I don't have to tell you that. Tell Jack, I hope to see him at Highbury on Friday. Ciao."

Naomi wandered thoughtfully back into the sitting room. Jack had opened the French windows and was resting against the arm of one of the all-weather patio chairs that they kept out there, still talking into his mobile phone. Naomi retrieved her drink, freshened it up and went outside to join him. Darkness had now fully descended on the city and the myriad of lights on the opposite bank reflected off the blackness of the Thames. It had taken her a long time to come to terms with life in London after an upbringing in the North and her early professional years in the more comfortable atmosphere of a provincial city. Jack, on the other hand, had taken more easily to London, enjoying the bigger stage, but she had noticed the changes it had produced in him. Surviving in the jungle of the world of television had stripped him of some of the softer edges of his character that had always appealed to her. The people he mixed with now spent the entirety of their energies in forging networks of connections, always greedy to log the next phone number or Email address into their palm tops for future use. Using people, and other people's connections, was the oil that greased the engines of their ships, but it made for an ugly spectacle. Jack disliked it as much as she did, but in the worlds of both broadcasting and football administration the sycophants, the self-seekers and the nakedly ambitious now made up the power base.

Eventually his call came to an end. "That was Steadman, one of the FA moles," he groaned. "Another bloody scandal."

"Sex or drugs?" she enquired.

"Both," he replied.

"Are you too busy to spare me five minutes then?" she asked, slipping into the chair.

"Of course not," he replied, turning his phone off and closing the French windows, so that he couldn't hear the house phone.

"You remember when we went to Janet's play I sat next to an American. You exchanged a word or two with him?"

"Vaguely."

"Well, upstairs in the bar afterwards, when you'd been cornered by some football people, I met him again while I was looking for Janet. Turned out he was an Inspector in the Met. Name of Jake Kempner. Rather a decent guy, I thought."

"Yes."

"As it happens, he's the Officer in charge of this case I'm starting soon at Oxford. I hadn't been briefed when I met him."

"The case you described as a no-hoper?" Jack asked.

"That's the one. And that call I just had was to tell me that a thug of a witness called Tisdale, who claims to identify my client as a man with a motive strong enough to kill the victim, has had dealings with Kempner outside school hours. Apparently, Tisdale was paid by an angry husband to beat Kempner up because he's having an affair with the guy's wife."

"Sounds like the world of football," he observed with a smile.

"The beating never took place. Somehow Kempner outmanoeuvred Tisdale but never did anything about prosecuting Tisdale for conspiring to attack him."

"Then Kempner's a sensible fellow. As if he'd want to broadcast all the sordid details," Jack remarked dryly.

"Except that one possible analysis is that Kempner held off. In exchange for Tisdale identifying my client," she replied.

"Deliberately fed him information enabling him to pick out your client? Is that what you mean?" Jack asked.

"Possibly. It doesn't have to be that sinister. It may be that the favour was just to attend the Identification Parade. Normally Tisdale wouldn't be seen dead doing anything to help the Police."

"So what are you asking me?

"If I use it, is it below the belt?"

"Of course."

"But it may make the jury doubt Tisdale's identification. My job involves casting doubt on that identification."

"It's a tough decision."

"There's more. I'm sure that Kempner's lady friend is Lauren Callaway who Janet introduced me to in the bar. It'd be pretty excruciating to drag all of that out in the trial," she sighed.

"Surely you can do it without going into that kind of detail?" Jack suggested.

"Yes, I can. But it may prompt Counsel defending the co-accused to start poking around."

"But how could it possibly help the co-accused to delve further. It's your client that Tisdale's evidence affects, no-one else," Jack said.

"Agreed. But it's a really grubby line of enquiry and the barrister who follows me is a master at exploiting the grubby. Ronan Cadogan."

"Well, there's your answer. With him in the case it's no-holds barred. Go for anything and everything. He will. Do you want me to come up to Oxford one day and show my face? That's bound to upset him."

"Let's see how we go. I feel a bit sorry for Jake Kempner though."

"I'm sure he can look after himself, he's a big boy."

"Not as big as Cadogan", she replied ruefully. "No-one is, not even you. Come on, let's go inside. I'm getting cold. And with all this talk about that bastard I need another drink."

Chapter 28

Whenever he returned to Oxford by road, Luther Farlow QC always made a point of approaching the city from the East, so that his very first glimpse of the skyline would be Magdalen's Great Tower. Standing one hundred and forty four feet high and nearly five hundred years old, it brought the scintillating memories of his three wild undergraduate years flooding back. A virtually limitless supply of nubile female students, breaking free from the domestic reins for the first time in their short lives, curious, enthusiastic, willing and, most importantly of all in his estimation, grateful. Sitting at the wheel of his brand new Mercedes, with its hood down despite the chilly weather, the V12 engine purring under the bonnet while the 6 disc CD changer switched from Pavarotti to Meatloaf, he sailed impressively along and, as the magnificent Tower grew ever nearer, he was young again. Oxford always did that to him.

"*Fritillaria meleagris*" he repeatedly recited to himself out loud, like a long-forgotten mantra that carried in its sound the elixir of youth. He'd never forgotten the name. The snakeshead fritillary lily which appeared every spring in Magdalen Meadow. He would often stop to gaze at their beauty as he walked back to his room, with the half-light of first dawn already outlining the far horizon, reflecting on the countless pleasures he had just received from last night's conquest. It was as if the sweet scent of the Meadow's floral wonders was filling his nostrils this very minute, mixed with a hint of that mysterious natural perfume that could only be generated by those delectable cherubs in their black gowns, bursting with promise like newly ripening fruit.

Dropping his bags off at the Lodge, he parked the car in the garage in Abingdon Rd before wandering slowly back towards the

High, crossing the river at Folly Bridge, just before the original Morris Garage, now the Crown Court where he was to be performing tomorrow, and onwards to Magdalen, where his room awaited him on the north side of the Cloister Quadrangle. Standing quietly alone at the edge of the Quadrangle, he surveyed the Old Library, the Chapel and Founder's Towers. The stunning panorama was timeless and made him feel like one of John Keats' lovers, frozen in time in the exquisite artwork of the Grecian Urn, never able to seize the prize, but forever able to retain his youth.

He could remember clearly from his College days the poignant words of that magnificent but tortured poet, dead at twenty-five and buried in Rome with no name upon the gravestone. Unembarrassed by the odd passer-by, he spoke them out loud.

"Bold Lover, never, never canst thou kiss,
Though winning near the goal – yet, do not grieve,
She cannot fade, though thou hast not thy bliss,
For ever wilt thou love, and she be fair!"

He'd read English, not Law, at Magdalen and, in the summer vacation at the end of his first year, he had travelled around Italy, visiting the tiny room overlooking the Spanish Steps, where the young poet had died a desperate death from consumption, alone but for his faithful friend, Joseph Severn. Later, he located the cemetery near to the Pyramid of Caius Cestius where Keats was buried. *"Here lies One Whose Name was writ in Water"* was the poet's chosen epitaph and, Luther Farlow had, unashamedly, shed a tear.

How blessed he felt, compared to Keats himself, or the Grecian lovers etched upon the Urn, to pursue the fairer sex and achieve the goal. Every trip to Oxford brought the promise of yet another romantic adventure and the luxury, courtesy of one his old professors, of borrowing a room on the Quadrangle for the duration of the case, significantly increased the chances of encounters with the female members of the College. As he grew older, his genuine interest in English Literature became an increasingly useful device allowing him to classify himself as a Romantic, rather than a lecher.

Both of his opponents in this case were strangers to him. When he'd made appropriate enquiries around The Temple, the reports he'd received on Cadogan were all of a kind. Showman. Extremely dangerous. Bordering on the invincible. But Farlow hadn't been too depressed at this information because Kempner had made clear that the Police viewed the female Defendant as a bit player in the drama and were not overly excited whether she was convicted or not. And, to counter-balance the daunting reports he'd obtained on Cadogan, the feedback on the other QC in the case, Naomi Nicholas, had excited the Farlow taste buds. Not only was she widely respected, straightforward and well liked, but she was also, by all accounts, a stunner.

Extremely keen to make her acquaintance on a social basis, and also duty bound to raise the question of manslaughter, as Kempner had specifically asked him to do, Farlow decided to kill two birds with one stone and had invited her to meet him in his rooms at Magdalen, at seven thirty on the Sunday evening to share a bottle of 2001 Bourgogne Rouge and to discuss various evidential aspects of the case, assuring her that he would be extending the same invitation to Cadogan. The richness of her voice had further stimulated his interest and, although making no attempt to disguise her profound dislike of Cadogan and reluctance to have any social contact with him, when he had emphasised the help it may be to the conduct of the case, she had graciously accepted. When he had immediately phoned Cadogan to offer a similar courtesy, the reaction had been a distant and disinterested refusal.

After his shower and body lotion applications, Farlow had selected the salmon pink Kenneth Cole shirt with the French cuffs, the light grey slacks and hand stitched leather brown casuals he'd bought in Paris at Easter. Just a touch of Eau De Sauvage, and he was almost ready to receive his evening guest. Then, realising he had left all of his CD's in the Merc, and not keen to trek all the way back to Abingdon Rd, he perused the eclectic collection of the room's usual tenant, eventually finding himself reduced to a choice between Chopin's Sonata for Piano Number 1 in C Minor or Neil Diamond. He opted for the latter and was just in the process of working out how to operate the CD player when there was a knock on the door.

Those colleagues who had described her as a stunner in response to his enquiries were guilty of a serious understatement, he thought to himself when he opened the door and set eyes on her for the first time. Simply dressed in a lilac sweater and a pair of designer blue jeans, with a Gucci handbag slung casually across her shoulder, her shining blonde hair was worn loose, framing a face of chiselled high cheekbones, intelligent blue eyes and an immediate smile.

"Naomi Nicholas, please enter my modest quarters," he began, with an extravagant, welcoming gesture. "Luther Farlow, delighted you could make it."

Reciting the social niceties, Naomi walked into the room, absorbing the quaint surroundings and décor and rapidly weighing up her opponent. There could be no doubt that he was a handsome specimen, dark, curly hair, sparkling white teeth against an olive skin and quite immaculately attired, but Naomi had learned the hard way which men could be trusted with women and which could not. Instinct and experience told her that Luther belonged to the latter category, although she suspected he would back off easily enough if resisted, so as to protect his own ego.

Perching on the edge of the loveseat in the window, she accepted the glass of Bourgogne Rouge that Luther had swiftly produced and proceeded to get down to business.

"Where's Cadogan?" she asked.

"Rebuffed my invitation. Too late for me to let you know, I'm afraid," he lied.

"I wish I had known," she remarked. "I've spent most of the day expending nervous energy at the prospect of seeing him again. You could have spared me the anguish."

"Sorry. Is he really that bad?"

"Yes. But, make no mistake, he's exceptionally able. Anyway, I can relax a little knowing he's not coming. What's the evidence you want to discuss."

Naomi had felt a little uncomfortable at giving her opponent any inside information on the Counsel of a co-accused but her intense dislike of Cadogan ran so deep that she was incapable of hiding her feelings and, she reflected, the more unnerved it might make Farlow feel. The prospect of spending time alone with him in this delightful little corner of Magdalen had not particularly troubled her at first but, as she spoke, she had observed his eyes travelling around the contours of her body with increasing interest and, sooner or later, she suspected a sharp word was likely to be required. The simplest answer, she determined, lay in getting down to work, but the more she tried, the more he talked of other things.

"Were you at Oxford?" he enquired.

"Manchester. Now, is it the pathology you wanted to talk about?"

"I was here," he replied. "Magdalen. Riverside walks. The deer herd. Wandering across the Meadow. And '*Fritillaria meleagris*'. Have you heard of them?"

Observing her shaking her head, he continued. "The snakeshead fritillary lily. Magdalen's always been famous for them. Unfortunately, it's the wrong time of year or I could have shown you some."

"Too bad," she said. "Time to talk business, I think."

"Right," he finally agreed, reaching across from the armchair to his notebook which was on the nearby table. "Firstly, did you receive the cell site analysis evidence? It's quite complicated"

"I've got it. I've left my papers at the Hotel, but I don't need them. I've been through it all."

"It shows that when Alicia Daley phoned Millard's mobile number at 4.54, the mast through which the call was directed to Millard's phone was the one on a church steeple between Daventry and Coventry. That church stands within one mile of the location on the M40 where the Police stopped and spoke to Susan Vance," he recited with relish.

"Yes. I'm familiar with all of that. I'll have to deal with it," she responded, not wishing to sit and listen to her opponent extol the strengths of his own case.

"It's all logged on computers. You can't challenge it. Will you admit it so I don't have to call all the experts to Court?" he asked.

"I could but I won't, because I can assure you that Cadogan will admit nothing. So whatever I say, he'll want the witnesses at Court."

"I see. And it is pretty deadly against his client. And, of course, we have the DNA. . . ."

Hang on a minute," she interrupted. "I didn't accept your invitation just to hear you tell me how strong you believe your case is. I'm not wet behind the ears, you know."

No, no. You're misunderstanding me," he protested. "There's a purpose in what I'm saying. It's the main reason I wanted us all to have this little chat before we got to Court so that there's time for you to think about what I'm going to say."

"You'd best make your pitch then, I think."

"Point taken," he replied with a smile. Naomi had watched his face closely during these exchanges. She hadn't bothered to look him up in the Bar Directory before coming to Oxford and therefore didn't know how old he was. But, on careful scrutiny, beneath the tan, the tell-tale wrinkles suggested he was not only older than she'd first thought, but also he'd had the odd little surgical snip to maintain the image.

"As I see it," he continued, "both Defendants, particularly your client, are at serious risk of being convicted of murder. Chopping the head and hands of a corpse won't exactly endear your fellow to the jury. . . "

"You're doing it again. . . " she retorted.

"Just hear me out. What I'm trying to say is that despite all the evidence Kempner would settle for a plea of guilty to manslaughter from Philip and assisting an offender from Susan. That's what I wanted to discuss."

"Why's Kempner interested in manslaughter?" Naomi enquired. It now sounded very much like Vance was telling the truth about the off the record offer. This put Kempner in serious breach of the rules.

"Two reasons. Millard was the absolute pits. Vicious. Kempner's not pretending he isn't relieved to see the back of him. He knows manslaughter will be a shabby compromise on the evidence. On what we've got it's murder. But he's a pragmatist. He reckons a long stretch for manslaughter, rather than life for murder, meets the rough justice of the case. Decent fellow and damned generous offer. So there you have it."

"You said there were two reasons," she reminded him.

"Oh, yes. The other reason is that Alicia Daley is playing up. She doesn't want to come to Court and give evidence and, as you can imagine, she's quite a handful. Any woman who shacked up with Millard must have the hide of a rhinoceros."

"So the reality is that Daley may not show. That weakens your case considerably. Is that what all this is really about?" Naomi fired back at him.

"No. It isn't. Daley will show. Even if the Police have to drag her here. But it's just another factor which makes a plea to manslaughter attractive because she wouldn't have to come to Court to give evidence, that's all," he declared.

"OK. I've got the picture. Thanks for making the offer. But I can tell you, without a doubt, that my client won't plead to manslaughter. We touched upon it in conference. Just as a hypothetical exercise, you understand," she explained untruthfully. The last thing she now wanted to do was to alert Farlow to the fact that Kempner had been reckless enough to raise manslaughter with the Defendant himself off-tape. Kempner would have to pay a forensic price for that misjudgement and she wanted to keep her powder dry. There was no way that Kempner would have volunteered his indiscretion to Farlow.

"Very well," he replied quietly.

"Anyway", she continued, "I can also tell you that Cadogan won't let his client plead guilty to anything. Not even riding a bike without lights. He fights everything to the death. Not on, but thanks anyway," she concluded, swigging back the last of her wine and glancing at her Cartier watch.

"C'est la vie," sighed Farlow, "every cloud has a silver lining. If you'd accepted, I'd have done myself out of a few days in Oxford and all the delights on offer here, including your company."

"Did the Police turn anything up when they dragged the river?" she asked.

"The odd boot or bike, but no head or gun," he laughed. "Your lot probably dumped the evidence well downstream at Amberley. There's a limit to resources, the Police divers only dragged a relatively short distance."

"Are you calling Hidalgo?" she enquired, fearing the worst.

"He's been jetted Business Class from Mexico City to Heathrow. It'd be a shame to bring him all that way and keep him on the substitute's bench, wouldn't it?" Farlow quipped. "But enough talk about the case, let's have another glass, shall we?" he suggested, jumping to his feet and reaching for the bottle.

"No. Thanks all the same. It's time to go back to my hotel. . . "

"But I absolutely insist," he exclaimed, already refilling her glass and simultaneously pressing the 'play' button on the CD, heralding the introduction of "Neil Diamond".

"Alright, just this glass and then I'm off," Naomi conceded, well alive to the sudden change in atmosphere, as Farlow switched into seduction mode.

"*Venus in Blue Jeans*," he oozed. "What an appropriate selection of song", he laughed, now squeezing himself alongside her on the loveseat, rather than returning to his armchair.

"You're showing your age, Luther," she replied cuttingly. "Venus in Blue Jeans was sung by Bobby Vee, not Neil Diamond, and it's early Sixties. This is *Forever in Blue Jeans*."

"But the sentiment remains the same," he responded, undaunted.

"Bugger the sentiment, get your facts right. You should know that," she answered, now being forced into the hard corner of the love seat and observing his arm stretch out along its back, ready for the next inevitable move."

"What do you think of the wine. I actually visited this particular chateau last summer. The Girardin family in Santenay," he said, the arm now being gently lowered on to her shoulders."

"Come on, Luther, she laughed easily. "Switch off the charm. Back to your own chair. Your wine is delightful, much better than your chat-up lines. I'm here to defend a man for murder not to play games."

"Oh dear", he responded in a deflated tone, quickly slipping away and returning to his armchair. "I've been misinterpreted, I'm afraid. I hope I haven't offended."

"Not at all. Like you say, just a misinterpretation on my part. So now we can both enjoy a second glass of your excellent wine and then I can go back to my room to prepare to do battle with you tomorrow. And, do you recognise the song that Neil Diamond is singing now?" she asked with a smile.

"Not sure that I do," he replied after a few seconds listening.

"It's called '*Solitary Man*'," she informed him, keeping her face straight as his ego deflated a notch further.

Chapter 29

The astronomical prices that the British seemed prepared to pay for hotel accommodation never ceased to amaze him. Lauren had insisted that she wanted to stay at "The Speckled Newt", an up-market pub in the Oxfordshire countryside where the rates were outrageous, but it was only for the one night as she had to return to London on Monday afternoon for the evening performance. For the rest of the trial he'd found a cheap place on the Banbury Road, called The Wayfarer's Hotel. The spartan accommodation of the weekdays should soften the extravagance of the Sunday. His tentative suggestion to Danny that she might also like to consider staying at The Wayfarer's had been met with a severe look, signifying absolute refusal and was swiftly followed by her purchase of a rail pass for daily commuting between London and Oxford.

The arrangement made was that he would meet Lauren at "The Speckled Newt" at around five with the much-prized window table overlooking the Thames booked for seven forty five.

Kempner had deliberately arrived very early, as he relished the prospect of a couple of hours tranquillity exploring the English countryside on a Sunday afternoon. Tranquillity and serenity seemed to have disappeared from his life altogether and, for that matter, from modern society generally.

'The Speckled Newt' was at the end of a narrow, country lane which was badly signposted but was idyllically located on the river's edge. On the far side of the expanse of gently moving water, green fields and woodland stretched as far as the eye could see, the occasional group of cows surveyed their lush pasture and he quickly appreciated the wisdom of Lauren's insistence that this was the only place to stay. It was not really a pub at all, but a historic country house, lovingly and tastefully restored and maintained, in a setting that epitomised England at its finest.

Impatient to be out in the fresh air and wandering the by-ways, he hurriedly unpacked the few clothes he would require for the one night that they would be there and set off to explore. Finding the path that ran right along the water's edge, he marvelled at the myriad of wild flowers and small waterfowl and birds whose names he would never know. After Clapham, Bleak House, Albright, Tisdale and the other depressing features of the daily grind, Lauren had pointed him to a temporary paradise.

Eventually, circling back towards the pub, he came across a garden bench alongside a splendid boathouse where a small, elderly figure was seated, gazing at the far bank. As he grew nearer, he realised it was a neat, bespectacled lady in a green felt hat with a gold band around its brim, a plaid overcoat and, incongruously with her rather smart attire, a pair of muddy, walking boots.

"Mind if I join you for a moment?" he enquired politely.

"Of course not, young man, you're most welcome," came the immediate reply, as she slid herself along the bench to make room to accommodate him.

"Scottish accent," he declared with a smile, turning to look at her after he had sat himself down.

"Edinburgh," she replied. "Born and bred and still living there at eighty-four. But even a Scot has to recognise the beauty of this part of England. I've been coming to 'The Newt' since the end of the War."

"Has it changed at all?"

"The prices have changed. I used to come for a week but it's so expensive now, I have to settle for three days. But I wouldn't miss it. Ratty and Mole, you know, it's around here that their magic began," she continued.

"Ratty and Mole," he repeated thoughtfully. "Do you mean 'The Wind in The Willows'?"

"But, of course. 'Hang spring cleaning' she exclaimed excitedly. "No child I ever taught failed to be captivated by their wonderful story. Kenneth Graham was a Scot, you see, like me. Born in Edinburgh but, after a dreadful childhood, he came to live with his grandmother down here in Oxford. This is the stretch of the river where he created them all. Badger, Mole, Ratty, Toad. Hang spring cleaning," she laughed. "Am I bringing it all back to you?"

"You certainly are," he said.

"And you're an American," she responded. "Kenneth Graham brought joy to children all over the world with that wonderful story. Strange, isn't it, that a man whose own life was blighted by tragedy, had the gift to give such joy?"

"Why? What happened to him?"

"When he came to Oxford, he fell in love with the idea of going to the University. But there was no money left in the family. The 1870's. You needed money. It was his dream and he never fulfilled it," she answered.

"But, that's hardly a tragedy, is it? I'd have loved to have gone to Yale but my folks didn't have the funds. It's a common enough situation, even today."

"True," she countered, "but you didn't let me finish the story. He got a dry old job with the Bank and began a relationship with a woman. Elspeth. It was a miserable affair. They were seldom happy. Stayed together. The relationship was a sham. But they never separated to the end."

"I see," Kempner observed, as images of Lauren and Albright immediately flashed through his mind.

"The only good thing that emerged from their relationship," the old lady continued, now delighted to have such a responsive audience to this story which plainly meant so much to her, "was the fact that they had a son, Alistair, and he won a place at Oxford."

"So the son fulfilled the father's dream. There's much consolation in that, isn't there?" he asked the earnest little lady.

"None," she replied emphatically. "None at all. When he was only nineteen years of age, Alistair threw himself under a train."

"Hell, I wasn't expecting that," Kempner responded, shocked at the ferocity of the feeling with which she had delivered such a devastating conclusion to her narrative. "That's just awful."

"I never used to tell the children that side of it," she said. "The magic of Ratty might have been spoiled. But there's a lesson there, isn't there, for all of us?"

"What lesson is that?"

"Don't waste life. He lost his son, then spent the rest of his life trapped in an unhappy relationship, with no proper direction. And yet he created magic."

"I'll bet you were a wonderful schoolteacher," Kempner said to her, recognising how uncomfortably close she unwittingly was to his own dilemma.

"What's your name?" she suddenly asked.

"Jake. Jake Kempner," he answered, offering her his hand which she gently took.

"Well, I'm Mary. Mary MacLeish. Do you have any children?"

"No," he said, shaking his head sadly.

"Well, I'm giving you a word of advice," she continued, still holding his hand. "If ever you want to open a child's eyes to the wonders of the written word, pick up Mr Graham's offering and read it out loud to them. You'll fire their imagination. Now I'm off for a nap in my room. It's been nice talking to you, Mr Kempner."

"I'm wiser for having met you," he smiled, standing to help her get to her feet. "Let me walk you back, I'm staying there tonight as well."

Taking his arm, the odd couple, a disillusioned NYPD cop and a retired Scottish schoolma'am from another time, walked slowly across the beautifully manicured lawns to the old country house, each lost in their own thoughts.

By seven o'clock there was still no sign of Lauren and no message. His messages on her answering service had provoked no response and he was starting to grow anxious. Sitting in the back bar with a glass of bourbon his phone rang, the illuminated face spelling out Lauren's number.

"Where are you?" he asked urgently.

"Still in London. There's a problem. I can't make it. I'm so sorry," she responded in a tone that made him even more concerned.

"Are you ill?" he enquired anxiously.

"No. I'm OK. It's James. He's had a heart attack. That's why I couldn't phone. Luckily, he was in a cab near St George's Hospital when it happened and the cabbie drove him straight there. Otherwise, he may not have pulled through. It was a bad one," she explained.

"Couldn't you have let me know earlier? I've been worried something had happened to you," he responded angrily.

"I'm sorry. The Hospital phoned me, giving me precious little information, so I raced over here and it's been chaotic ever since. I'm just too exhausted to drive up to Oxford and, besides, I wouldn't be very good company."

"You can't expect me to be overly concerned about him. It's you I worry about."

"I've spoken to him now the immediate crisis has passed. He wants me to help him through it. There'll be about six weeks of home nursing after he's discharged. He wants me to do it, not some hired help. And after next week the play will have run its course."

"What exactly are you telling me Lauren? The dutiful wife role comes as a bit of a surprise, if you don't mind me saying. He's using the heart attack to stop you seeing me. He could afford the best home nursing in London," Kempner responded harshly.

"It's hard to explain. I just felt so uncomfortable, scheming to get away to see another man, while he was lying in a hospital bed with wires and tubes everywhere. I just felt I had some responsibility."

"He's playing the guilt card and you're falling for it," Jake retorted.

"Maybe, but I just feel that I should make some effort to help him through this, whatever the poor state of the marriage. My feelings for you are unchanged. You'll have to give me some space on this," she tried to explain, her voice now developing an edge of irritation.

"Well, tonight's ruined. I recognise that's not your fault. But the idea of you nursing him for six weeks doesn't sit too easy with me. We'll talk about it when we've both slept on it."

"OK. Good night," she replied curtly.

Returning his phone to his pocket, he slumped down dejectedly into an armchair in the corner of the room, more confused and uncertain than ever, and knocked back the remnants of his drink in one hit. The bastard would milk the heart attack for all it was worth. The sympathy card. He'd already played his opener, about Lauren nursing him through it, within hours of the attack. Once he'd realised it was working, he'd really turn the screw. Where aggression had failed, weakness may prevail. Sooner rather than later, Lauren was going to have to face up to all of this and so was he.

"A penny for your thoughts," a friendly Scottish voice declared from the middle of nowhere.

Almost hidden behind a tall house plant, sat Mary MacLeish, eyes twinkling behind her gold framed glasses, sipping daintily from a glass of sherry.

"Oh! Good evening, Mrs MacLeish," he replied. "I never saw you tucked away behind the foliage."

"It's called '*Ficus Benjamina*', The Weeping Fig. And please call me Mary," she replied.

"Or Ratty, perhaps," he said smiling. "And you call me Jake. Now tell me this. Have you had your dinner yet?"

"No. I usually take dinner in the small restaurant at eight. Table for one. It's Miss not Mrs, you see."

"Well, tonight, Mary, I'd be delighted if you took dinner as my guest, in the big restaurant, at the best window table. It's all booked. My friend's had to cancel. So, what do you say?"

"What a treat," she answered enthusiastically, rising out of her chair with surprising agility for an eighty-four year old and taking his arm. "Dinner with a handsome young American. You know what Mole would say, don't you?"

"Hang spring cleaning," they recited in unison, both laughing as they headed for the best table in the big restaurant, although behind the laughter Kempner was saddened that someone with so much to offer had seemingly gone through life dining at a table for one. Might the continuing pursuit of Lauren deal him a similar hand? Chance meetings with strangers sometimes provided a sharp insight into one's own destiny.

Chapter 30

"I particularly asked for Lady Bellinger's breakfast to be taken up to her room, Mrs Haskins," Mr Justice Rodney Bellinger declared angrily, over-enunciating each syllable, as he spat out the words at the unfortunate housekeeper at the Judges' Lodgings. The usual Lodgings, closer to the city, were being re-wired and the Lord Chancellor's Department had been obliged to rent an estate about ten miles away, where security arrangements could more easily be implemented. As a result, temporary staff had been hired from the small village nearby.

Jennifer Haskins had not wanted the job of housekeeper in the first place, but with an idler of a husband and a daughter who was getting more expensive by the day, she had accepted the three month post. The Department had shipped in a butler from the Lodgings in Birmingham, but he was only required to oversee the dinner arrangements. Her responsibility covered the overall housekeeping and breakfast.

Within twenty-four hours of taking the job she had realised that this Judge would never be satisfied with anything she did. In his whining, sanctimonious voice he complained about the cleanliness of the rooms, the strength of the coffee, the delay in being served and the failure to satisfy his wife's latest demands. Every time he mentioned his wife, to anyone, in any context, he always referred to her as 'Lady Bellinger', as if there was a risk that her exalted status might somehow be temporarily forgotten. Each morning, when the limousine arrived to transport His Lordship to the Court, she would sidle in beside him, enormous feathered hat perched on top of her lacquer-stiffened hair, and accompany him to the Courtroom where, apparently, she sat alongside him, as he chastised the daily flow of barristers and consigned the ragged classes in the dock to the various penal establishments of the realm. Mrs Haskins had tried talking to the butler about their Master, but he treated her as if he, too, was a member of the Ruling Classes. "Temporaries," she would hear him mutter, as he walked away, after she had tried to ask for help.

"I'm s-s-sorry, My Lord," she stuttered. "I must have misunderstood the note about where her Ladyship would take breakfast."

"It's too bad, Mrs Haskins. I'd be grateful if you'd see to it immediately. I'll breakfast in the dining room as usual, but a tray for Lady Bellinger, as a matter of urgency," he whined. "Did you bring my copy of *The Times* from the village or did that slip your memory as well?"

"It's on the breakfast table, My Lord. There's some papers from the Court in a big, brown envelope as well. They'd been left at the Estate Lodge on Saturday. I've brought them up the drive this morning."

"Very well. See to Lady Bellinger. I'll have to pour my own tea," he declared, walking off towards the galleried dining room, where an antique oak dining table that seated fourteen was laid out for breakfast for two.

"Incompetent female staff," he thought to himself as he settled down with *The Times* and his peach yoghurt. Monday morning was always peach yoghurt. At least the stupid woman had got that right this week. Tuesday was lemon, followed by strawberry, raspberry and vanilla on Fridays. It was a routine he'd followed religiously since his appointment and Lodgings all over the country were familiar with the barrage of complaints if ever there was an error in the sequence. Brown toast and Earl Grey tea had to follow.

Almost as ritualistic as the yoghurt sequence was the order in which he devoured the contents of *The Times*. Firstly, he would turn to the Legal Appointments to check on any names that might have received the holy call. Most days the section was confined to the lower ranks of Deputy Judges and Circuit Judges, in which he had little interest. His concern was on the very occasional day when a new High Court Judge was appointed or, even rarer, when a High Court Judge, was appointed to the Court of Appeal. That was his next target and Lady Bellinger had been directing great energies in her dinner invitations to increase the chances of achieving even higher rank.

When a new High Court appointment was announced, his reaction was invariably the same, regardless of the quality and reputation of the appointee. "How the hell did that dullard ever make it to the High Court Bench?' he would exclaim in disgust to Lady Bellinger and she would dutifully nod her agreement at the wisdom of his judgement. Scouring the column on Monday mornings was usually stress-free, as Mondays only rarely produced an announcement.

The next journalistic port of call was the Obituaries. Who had died? Were there any Judges in the Court of Appeal who had expired, thereby producing an opening? How old? From what? Did they have a spouse and heirs? If no spouse, then could he identify anything in the nuances of the obituary to suggest that they might have been gay?

Mrs Haskins walked timorously into the grand dining room just as he finished the last obituary to inform him that Lady Bellinger's breakfast had been safely delivered to her room and to enquire whether there was anything else she could do for him.

"Butter's too hard," he muttered. 'And where's that envelope you mentioned? I can't see it."

"It's on the sideboard, My Lord. I'm sorry, I should have put it with your newspaper," she said, hurriedly fetching it and offering it to him.

"Could you open it?" he asked sharply.

Once the housekeeper had carefully and neatly slit open the envelope with an unused breakfast knife, she handed it to him and he pulled out two foolscap sheets of paper from within and briskly scanned them.

"The week's list of Oxford cases and Counsel," he mumbled, half to himself, before an outburst of temper erupted that shocked Mrs Haskins to the core. "Fuck," he exploded. "That bastard. In my Court. Defending. Excuse me, Mrs Haskins," he said, taking control of himself. Forgot you were there."

Picking up *The Times* again, he pretended to read it while the useless woman fluttered around, pouring him another cup of tea, removing his empty peach yoghurt carton and scuttling away towards the kitchen. But Mr Justice Bellinger wasn't absorbing the latest news about the forthcoming election. He was cursing silently but violently at the prospect of having to confront once again that despised enemy from yesteryear, Ronan Cadogan QC.

Before he had had adequate time fully to regain his composure, the wretched woman re-appeared, holding the cordless telephone from the hall table.

"It's Gerald, My Lord. Will you take it at the breakfast table?" she asked nervously.

"I suppose so," he responded, holding out his hand by way of command for her to deliver it to him.

"Yes, Gerald," he barked down the instrument to his latest Clerk.

"I'm at the Court, My Lord. I thought I'd better give you an update on the arrangements for the procession. Major Linton has directed that four trumpeters from the Regiment attend. Is that sufficient?"

"I would prefer six," he answered.

"Only four available, I'm afraid. They'll be positioned just inside the main entrance. The dignitaries will wait in their cars outside the main doors until Your Lordship's limousine arrives. When it does, I will line them up behind you. Firstly Lady Bellinger, followed by the High Sheriff, then the Lord Lieutenant, then the Chaplain and I shall bring up the rear. As soon as the procession moves forward into the building, the fanfare will be sounded."

"You've put the High Sheriff in front of the Lord Lieutenant. Wrong. Switch them around. Otherwise, all is in order. My limousine will arrive at ten twenty five precisely. Anything else, Gerald?"

"No, My Lord," came the reply, accompanied by an audible sigh of relief that the Judge seemed relatively satisfied with his efforts.

Handing the phone back to Mrs Haskins, the Judge pushed his chair back and made his way into the galleried hall, towards the grand staircase and upstairs to inform Lady Bellinger of the procession order and to get robed.

Today was the official first day of the Legal Term and, at Court Centres all over the country, the arrival of the High Court Judge and local representatives, appointed by the Queen within the particular county, would be heralded by fanfares as the formal processions made their way into the Court buildings, always led by the Judge himself in his full-bottomed wig. The barristers, solicitors and public would line up inside the building to witness the occasion and all barristers were required to bow as the procession passed.

Unusually, Mr Justice Bellinger had already been sitting at Oxford Crown Court for the two weeks preceding the first day of Term, but this did not in any way obviate the necessity for the official opening of the new Term being marked by the normal formalities. Bellinger's early presence at Oxford had been for the purpose of trying an urgent case which had been given high priority from the powers that be. A young street-level criminal from Blackburn Lees, the local trouble spot where young car thieves raced stolen vehicles, had been pursued by a Police car, lost control and caused a fatal accident. In normal circumstances, he would have been charged with death by dangerous driving, but, as the fatality was a Police Officer, the direction from above had been to pursue the youth for murder and every stop had been pulled out to convict him of murder.

Massive manpower and resources, way out of proportion to the enquiry if the victim had been anyone other than a Police Officer, had been poured into the enquiry. Every device, proper and improper, had been deployed to secure the required pound of flesh. The final piece in the jigsaw had been the selection of Bellinger to try the case. Unfair from beginning to end, ruling constantly in favour of the Prosecution, he had ensured that the inadequate black youth was duly convicted of murder and consigned to society's waste bin. Bellinger's extra two weeks at Oxford had achieved the Establishment's objective and the Police felt better.

Now, with that task successfully completed, Bellinger believed that, as the new Legal Term began, he and Lady Bellinger could begin to enjoy fully the pomp and the numerous social advantages of sitting in Oxford. The procession was an important symbol of the beginning of that time.

Chapter 31

As a consequence of the heavy volume of work at Oxford Crown Court, the Robing Room was packed to the rafters. Long and narrow, with a central table running its length, there was hardly any space to move. Bags lay scattered selfishly across the table top, leaving no room for others to place their belongings, suitcases were dumped carelessly round the walls and everybody, from the most junior pupil to the leading QC's was thrown in there together, pushing and shoving. Whilst Naomi Nicholas immediately noticed Cadogan's empty wig box positioned in the middle of the table, she was extremely relieved to observe that there was no sign of the man himself. Positioning herself by the window, which looked out over the front of the building and across to the Police Station on the far side of the road, she battled for a bit of room to put on her Court attire. The entrance to the Courts lay immediately beneath her, with a small semi-circular driveway to allow the official cars to drive up, disgorge their privileged cargo and move on. The canopy above the main entrance door was just below the window through which she was peering and, to her absolute disgust, she saw that a carpet of cigarette ends lay on top of it, thrown out of the window by barristers over what must have been a period of years, judging by the depth of the obscene mass. Little would Bellinger realise that, as he made his triumphant entrance, surrounded by the trappings of authority and class, above his bewigged head, lay a ton of butt end detritus.

At a quarter past ten, Gerald, manifestly uncomfortable in his new morning suit, marched into the Robing Room and tried to make himself heard above the hubbub of noise. The word in The Temple was that no clerk could last more than one term out on Circuit with Bellinger and, so far, he had been responsible for two resignations and three early retirements. Picking up a heavy hole-punch from the table, Gerald banged it down hard, so as to gain the room's attention.

"Mr Justice Bellinger requires all members of the Bar to line up inside the main hallway no later than ten twenty five for the Judicial procession," he announced in stentorian tones. "The trumpets will sound at exactly half-past. Please begin to make your way down there now."

Naomi smiled to herself as she saw Farlow hurriedly heading for the stairs so that he could place himself right by the main door where the Judge could not fail to notice him. Following along with the crowd, she descended into the hallway and stood alongside Fiona Breslaw, her Junior. The entire hallway was lined with Court staff, members of the public and the barristers, all wigged and gowned. At the actual entrance itself stood the trumpeters, two on each side of the doorway, resplendent in full livery and carrying shining ceremonial trumpets at their sides like rifles, with Farlow pressed in, right up against them and Gerald feverishly issuing directions to all and sundry.

From the street outside, Naomi heard a College bell strike the half-hour and, with precision timing, the four long trumpets swung up to the horizontal and the brass fanfare began, filling the building with an ear-piercing sound. Right on cue, in his red ermine-trimmed robe, full-bottomed wig and white gloves, Bellinger appeared, poised to lap up the scraping and bowing as he processed the length of the hall. But, to Naomi's amazement, from out of a side door, the massive figure of Cadogan suddenly emerged, in silk's wig and gown, followed by his Junior carrying his Leader's podium. Cadogan neatly slipped in a few feet ahead of Bellinger and proceeded, at funereal pace, to walk the length of the corridor, acknowledging the crowd, whilst Spiller, head down and in a state of excruciating embarrassment, tried to look as if he wasn't really there. Bellinger was blocked from Naomi's view by the enormous bulk of Cadogan who, as he came level with her, nodded superciliously in her direction. It was only after he had passed that she was actually able to see Bellinger's thin face, white with anger and screwing his gloves into a tight ball in his fists. Behind him, in a sickly yellow hat with a half veil, came Lady Bellinger, her fat legs finding it hard to adjust to the absurdly slow pace her husband had been reduced to, so as to avoid walking right into the back of Cadogan. The other dignitaries, in costumes that belonged in a museum and carrying swords so long and ridiculous that they actually touched the ground, followed behind, unaware of the outrage that was occurring ahead.

As he neared the end of the hallway, Cadogan, still followed faithfully by the lapdog Spiller, suddenly veered up the stairs towards the Robing Room, leaving the Judge a final few yards of encumbered progress.

From bitter experience Naomi knew that Cadogan was the master of the dramatic entrances, but this time, she thought, he had excelled himself and she anticipated with relish the fireworks that would inevitably follow when Bellicose sought to impose his punishment.

By the time that she had collected her papers and made her way into the Courtroom most people were in place. On the front row, furthest from the jury box, sat Luther Farlow, who waved his hand in greeting and winked at her, while simultaneously nodding in the direction of Cadogan, as if to signal that he expected some repercussions.

Cadogan was at the other end of the row, closest to the jury box, head buried in his papers. The Juniors and solicitors sat in the rows behind. The Judge's throne-like red leather chair bearing the Royal Crest and the prisoners' seats in the dock stood empty.

The Public gallery had filled and an air of expectation grew when the Judges' Clerk appeared on the dais. However, instead of calling the Court to order in anticipation of the grand entrance of the Judge and his entourage for the reading of the Letters Patent, the Clerk came down into the well of the Court and approached Cadogan.

"Mr Cadogan" he began, putting his hands on the desk and leaning down towards the QC so that his voice did not carry far. "The Judge requires a letter of explanation and apology for what happened. He requires it by the end of the Court day. Four-thirty. He'll then decide what action he proposes to take"

Slowly rising from his seat, the QC pulled himself up to his full six feet five and peered down at the hapless clerk.

"Gerald, isn't it?" he replied calmly. "I don't believe we've met before. Ronan Cadogan. Delighted to meet you," he continued, offering the clerk his hand. "Have you been with this Judge long?"

"No, sir. Now I've delivered the message may I tell him that there'll be a letter?"

"I'm afraid not, Gerald. I've no idea what the Judge is referring to. Perhaps he'll let me know. In person. Rather than putting you on the spot. Now, if you'll excuse me, I have to defend a woman for murder. Priorities are everything, aren't they? So nice to have had a chat."

While the clerk headed disconsolately back towards the Judge's Chambers to report his failure, the Court staff took their places for the reading of the Letters Patent. After a considerable delay, presumably while Bellinger tried to regain at least the outward appearance of calm, a loud rapping on the side door to the dais heralded the entrance of the entourage, led by Bellinger, followed by Her Ladyship and then the other Office bearers.

While the Letters were read aloud by the Court Clerk, Bellinger, still in a cold fury at Cadogan's stunt, conducted a mental assessment of the Counsel he was going to have to deal with over the next few days, quickly deciding that the female QC could only possibly have got silk because she was so strikingly attractive. Probably slept her way up to the top, he thought to himself. Farlow, on the other hand, was a complete unknown. He'd looked him up in the Law List. Magdalen man, so he should have a brain. The problem may be, looking at his deep tan, dazzling white shirt and ostentatious chunky, gold cufflinks, that he had too high an opinion of himself. The third QC required no analysis. Cadogan had to be confronted early on, publicly rebuked and, hopefully, suppressed.

At the end of the charade, the entourage withdrew and then returned, with the Judge having replaced his full bottomed wig with his every day Court version and, seemingly, ready for business. The only missing ingredient of the drama was the prisoners and, at a given signal from the Court Clerk, the clanking of keys could be heard and the heavy door behind the security glass of the dock swung open to disgorge Philip Vance, with a Prison Officer on each side, from the bowels of the building.

Looking uncomfortable in a white shirt, green tie and cheap brown trousers, he walked to the centre of the dock. The skin that had summered for so many years under South and Central American skies, had, in the few days since Naomi had visited him in Belmarsh, at last begun to surrender its dark hue and the eyes appeared tired and sad. Taking his seat between the Officers, the Court awaited production of the female prisoner.

Kempner had directed, from the moment of their arrest in Birmingham, that the two Defendants were to have no means of communication. They had not been allowed to speak to each other or receive letters from each other in prison, and they were kept apart in the custody areas at Oxford Crown Court. When, a couple of minutes later, Susan Vance was escorted into the dock by a female Prison Officer, she was visibly taken aback by the spectacle of lawyers and the Judge in wigs and gowns, which were alien to anything she had seen before. As she absorbed the starch formality of these bizarre surroundings, her eyes sought out those of her fellow prisoner and she was saddened to observe the fatigue in his general appearance. For her part, the worst features of Risley had been the emotional emptiness of each day, while the physical deprivations had been quite easy for her to cope with, so that she still looked lithe and relatively fit.

For all the time since their arrest, she had wanted to ask Pal every detail of what had happened in that barn. In the days immediately after the shooting, having spent so much time and emotional energy in plotting Millard's death, the aftermath had been dominated by seeing Pal through his injury and, ironically, neither of them had wanted to pick over the gruesome details of the actual confrontation. However, after Kempner's bombshell in interview about the decapitation, one grisly topic had pre-occupied her ever since. Why had he mutilated the body? What had he done with the head and hands? Why hadn't he said anything about that? Were they in that bag with the guns which he'd weighted down? There were a score of unanswered questions.

But any hope of contact had been dashed.

The two Defendants stared straight ahead of them as the theatre of their trial commenced and each saw, for the first time, the QC that fate had thrown up for the other. Pal had expected the Prosecution to open the proceedings but it was Cadogan who levered himself to his feet and came directly to the point.

"I object to the Prosecution calling Dr Hidalgo," he announced. "He will say the woman he dealt with in Tamazula had a beauty spot that co-incides with that of my client. In short, the Prosecution seek to use him to identify Susan Vance as the woman in Tamazula. If they want to do that, they should have held an Identification Parade as they did with Philip Vance and Tisdale. They didn't. Your Lordship should rule the evidence inadmissible."

"I needn't trouble you, Mr Farlow," the Judge responded. "The argument raised by Mr Cadogan is without merit or substance. The evidence will be called. Moreover, I make it clear that frivolous applications of the kind I regret I have just had to listen to, are not to be repeated. Swear in the jury."

After the jury had been sworn, Farlow proceeded to open the case for the Prosecution in the terms that the tabloids would relish.

"A story of revenge and brutality," he began. "Manufacturing the ultimate alibi of death, Paul Locke, with his female accomplice helping him every step of the way, lured his old enemy, Ray Millard into a barn near to Millard's home and shot him in the head before mutilating the body in the most barbaric way. . ."

As the jury listened in horror to the gruesome tale being related to them, Cadogan turned to run his eyes slowly along the two rows of six. By reputation, Oxford juries were normally more astute and prepared to convict than some of their big City counterparts. The QC's analysis was that there were four middle-aged, respectable women, three academic males, two what he termed "blokes", an elderly Asian in a turban, a pretty young girl and an anti-authority, heavily tattooed male youth. "Not without promise," he smiled to himself as Farlow continued to lay on the blood and gore with a trowel.

Turning back to the front, Cadogan realised that the Judge's narrowed eyes were fixed on him, watching his every move, still seething at the way in which his precious procession had been turned into a laughing stock. That dreadful woman who followed him everywhere, with her endless supply of completely tasteless hats and frocks, was also peering down at him, like a zoo visitor leaning over the enclosure parapet to watch the lion in his lair.

Eventually Farlow reached the end of his peroration, announcing the name of his first witness with the same flourish as a boxing ring impresario introducing the fighter in the red corner. "All the way from Tamazula, Mexico, Doctor Louis Hidalgo."

As the Court awaited the entry into the witness box of the Mexican Doctor, Susan Vance managed to catch Spiller's attention and called him over to the dock where he wrote her whispered instructions in his Counsel's notebook before scurrying back to his seat just as the Doctor entered the Court room, dressed in a crumpled, white linen suit, his face creased with deep lines of fatigue.

While Farlow began taking him through the introductory formalities of his evidence, Spiller tugged at Cadogan's gown, causing the QC to turn round in his seat, glaring at the Junior in irritation.

"What is it?" he growled.

"The client gave us some last minute instructions from the dock, I've written them down," he whispered, thrusting a piece of paper into the large hand of his Leader.

As he read the few words that Spiller had recorded, his face broadened into a smile of approval. The woman was obviously picking up the tricks of the trade, he thought to himself. The note had read 'Old soak'. That was all that someone of Cadogan's calibre required. By now, Prosecuting Counsel was approaching the critical part of Hidalgo's evidence.

Oxford Crown Court Transcript Ref 244 Hidalgo/Farlow

Farlow: Please take this copy of the Death Certificate we have obtained from Tamazula courtesy of the British Embassy in Mexico City.

Dr Hidalgo: I have it. I signed it.

Farlow: Do you remember the circumstances of signing it?

Dr Hidalgo: I went to the house in Tamazula. I remember the cadaver. White man. On a bed. I spoke with a woman. Natural death. Heavy drinking. Heart. I signed.

Farlow: Where did you get the dead man's name from?

Dr Hidalgo: The woman. She said he was Inglese.

Farlow: You are speaking in clear English here. Did you speak to the woman in English?

Dr Hidalgo: Yes. I spent four years in Nogales. On the border with America. I learn English. She spoke English, sounded American. I only remember she was quite young. Black hair but not dark in the skin, but her hair was very dark. And, she had a lunar. De la piel. Above her lip.

Farlow: Lunar?

Dr Hidalgo: Like a mole. On the skin.

Farlow: Thank you.

Oxford Crown Court Transcript Ref 245 Hidalgo/Nicholas

Nicholas: Do you remember much about the corpse?

Dr Hidalgo: Drinker. I could tell. And the woman. She said drink. I write forty one years on certificate. He looked older. And the woman told me his name was Paul Arthur Locke.

Nicholas: This may sound a silly question, but I assure you it is not. There is no doubt at all, is there? Paul Arthur Locke was dead?

Dr Hidalgo: What you saying? I sign Death Certificate for man who is alive? A live man with rigor mortis? He was dead, senora.

Oxford Crown Court Transcript Ref 246 Hidalgo/Cadogan

Cadogan: You say you saw the signs of a heavy drinker. What signs?

Dr Hidalgo: The veins in the face, the skin, colour, eyes. A Doctor can tell.

Cadogan: Are you an expert in the effects of drink? Do you drink?

Dr Hidalgo: A lot of people drink.

Cadogan: Did the Police pay to fly you here from Mexico?

Dr Hidalgo: Yes

Cadogan: Did you drink on the plane?

Dr Hidalgo: One or two. It's a long journey?

Cadogan: Presumably the Police are paying for your Hotel. If we send for the bill, which we can, will it show you have been drinking a lot in the Hotel?

Dr Hidalgo: A few.

Mr Justice Bellinger: What is the possible relevance of the Doctor's drinks bill at the Hotel or on the plane? I suspect this is just a gratuitous attack on a respectable Doctor's reputation.

Cadogan: I propose exploring the state of the Doctor's sobriety at the time of the signing of the certificate. His drinking habits are highly material to such questioning. Is Your Lordship intending to stop me ascertaining if the witness's recollection may be distorted by drink?

Mr Justice Bellinger: Are your instructions then that the woman Dr Hidalgo met was your client and she can say he had been drinking?

Cadogan: Absolutely not. My instructions are that Dr Hidalgo and my client have never met in their lives. I raise drink because the witness's hands are trembling, his eyes are bloodshot and there are thread veins in the face. The jury can see this for themselves. I am entitled to explore it.

Mr Justice Bellinger: Stop giving evidence.

Cadogan: Your Lordship accused me of a gratuitous attack. I am answering that charge. And Your Lordship, with respect, gave evidence that the Doctor had a respectable reputation.

Mr Justice Bellinger: Enough, Mr Cadogan. Get on with your questions. Confine them to what is relevant.

Cadogan: Are the trembling hands, bloodshot eyes and veins in the face in any way connected with drink?

Dr Hidalgo: Not really.

Cadogan: Had you been drinking when you went to view the body in that room in Tamazula?

Dr Hidalgo: How can I remember?

Cadogan: It was about four in the afternoon. The time is on the Certificate. By that time is it likely that you would have been drinking?

Dr Hidalgo: Maybe one or two tequilas with lunch.

Cadogan: Did you come into this case when British Embassy contacted you?

Dr Hidalgo: Yes.

Cadogan: Did they send you any photographs?

Dr Hidalgo: Maybe. I think yes. At some time. A man and a woman. I did not recognise the man. The woman was a possible but not sure.

Cadogan: Look at the man and woman in the dock. Are those the two people whose photographs the Embassy sent you?

Dr Hidalgo: Maybe. I think so.

Cadogan: So when you speak of a lunar, is it possible that you had already been sent a photo of a woman with a lunar?

Dr Hidalgo: Possible. I cannot remember when I first saw the photos.

Cadogan: But it may have been before you told anyone you remembered a lunar?

Dr Hidalgo: Maybe.

Cadogan: You would never be able to recognise again the woman you spoke to in that room in Tamazula, would you?

Dr Hidalgo: I would not recognise her again, no.

As Dr Hidalgo shuffled his way out of the witness box, sweating even though he was accustomed to a far hotter climate, Farlow angrily scribbled a note to his Junior, Oliver Carne, telling him to go out of Court and demand an explanation from Kempner for the Embassy sending on the photographs to Hidalgo before any consideration had been given to the question of an Identification Parade or the existence of a distinctive characteristic like the beauty spot. Carne had hurried away and managed to return before the next witness had been brought in from the Witness Waiting Room, which was on the side of the building furthest from the Courtroom.

Leaning over Farlow's shoulder from behind, Carne swiftly relayed the information that Kempner had provided.

"Cadogan was just guessing. It was a bluff. Hidalgo never saw any photos until well after he'd phoned Pedro Guiterrez at the Embassy and told him about the beauty spot. He'd always said he wouldn't be able to recognise the woman for certain, but he was adamant about the beauty spot. So it was clear that an ID parade was never a runner."

"Then why was Hidalgo prepared to say he may have seen the photos first?" Farlow retorted angrily.

"Kempner said he's very easy to confuse. Drink. That was always the worry about calling him. Somehow Cadogan knew which button to press," Carne replied.

"Somehow?" grunted Farlow. "Someone, you mean. Jenna Zayer. She'd obviously got the medicinal whiff of tequilas at four in the afternoon. How does Cadogan accept that kind of instruction while still advancing the case that it wasn't her? Talk about sailing close to the wind. And now we've got to run the gauntlet of Hackney thuggery at its best. Bring on The Brain," he sighed as the lumbering figure of Bruce Tisdale loomed into view and crossed the well of the Court, causing the end of Lady Bellinger's nose to twitch in disdain and, to Cadogan's delight, having a similar effect on a couple of the middle-aged ladies on the jury.

East End villains traditionally kept a special, conservatively cut, dark suit for their appearances in Court and the old muscle proved no exception. Normally, the attire was reserved for the dock but, on this unusual occasion, its destination was the witness box. Despite the fact that his most useful days on the hard streets were behind him, Tisdale still looked the part, as his shoulders and hefty forearms made the cheap fabric of the suit stretch at the seams and the large, square head instinctively ducked this way and that, forever replaying the experiences of the gnarled fists and iron bars that had thudded against it over the years.

Despite the old-fashioned menace of his appearance, his emphatic confirmation that the man he'd picked out on the recent Parade was Pal came over as completely genuine. "Ray and I used to see a lot of him. Most days. OK, he's heavier now. Less hair an'that. But I recognised him in a flash. He was always goin' to do for Ray if he got the chance. I seen the look when they was at the Bailey together."

Farlow gently nudged him through the story of the cut-throat defence twenty years ago and the consequent vicious enmity between the two men, while Tisdale liberally threw in repeated inadmissible references to the threats it was rumoured Pal was making about what he'd do to Millard when he eventually got out. The Judge made no attempt to control the damaging hearsay Tisdale was freely disseminating and protests from Defence Counsel received mere judicial lip service.

When Naomi Nicholas stood up to cross-examine him, she was aware of an audible whisper from her right. "The bludgeon, not the scalpel," the giant murmured, as if to himself.

Oxford Crown Court Transcript Ref 248 Tisdale/Nicholas

Nicholas: Ray Millard was a close friend of yours, wasn't he?

Tisdale: Over many years.

Nicholas: You have numerous convictions for serious crimes of violence. Did you commit any of those on the instructions of Millard?

Tisdale: Nah.

Nicholas: Weren't you one of his paid heavies? Broken heads and bones bought and sold?

Tisdale: My fights was my own fights. Where I grew up if you didn't fight you was nothing. Ray could handle himself. 'Cept if some nutter with a gun popped him one. Like Pal, there.

Nicholas: You claim to have picked my client out as Pal on the recent identification Parade. When had you last seen Pal?

Tisdale: In the dock at the Bailey when he drew his fourteen. I was there. Drove Ray home. Ray hadn't done nowt and the jury said so.

Nicholas: About twenty years ago?

Tisdale: Some boats you don't forget, lady. Some looks neither. I seen the look in the Bailey dock. That geezer is Pal, sure as I'm standing here.

Nicholas: I suggest you're wrong. Maybe just mistaken but, much more likely, lying.

Tisdale: You do your suggesting. That's what you get paid for, ain't it? I'll tell ya the plain fact. That's him.

Nicholas: Where were you when you were first asked if you would attend a Parade?

Tisdale: At home.

Nicholas: Who asked you?

Tisdale: Kempner. And his sidekick. The one with the red curls.

Nicholas: Had you had any dealings with either or both of those Officers before?

Tisdale: Do ya mean had either of 'em ever nicked me? Nah.

Nicholas: I don't mean that. I mean had you had contact with either of them, particularly Kempner, over another matter? A private matter.

Mr Justice Bellinger: You're wasting valuable time again. Beating about the bush. Cryptic half-questions. Please try to assist the jury by putting your client's case, whatever that might be, and not dancing around the point.

Nicholas: Did you accept money from someone to attack Kempner over a personal matter?

Tisdale: Rubbish.

Nicholas: But did it go wrong and, in exchange for Kempner not taking it further, did you owe him a favour?

Tisdale: Like I says, rubbish.

Nicholas: And was the favour to attend the Parade and pick out the only man who looked like he'd seen the Mexican sun.

Tisdale: Crap.

Nicholas: You tell us two Police Officers came to your home and invited you to attend the Parade. Were you immediately prepared to be so co-operative with the Police?

Tisdale: OK, I don't like the cops. But Pal had done for Ray. I didn't need no persuadin' to help see him go down for that.

Nicholas: I suggest you are a violent accomplice of the deceased, embroiled in some other agenda with Kempner, and those reasons lie behind your false identification of Vance as Locke.

Tisdale: Suggest what you like. Don't make it true.

During lunch Naomi, keen to avoid any chance contact with

Cadogan, steered clear of the Court dining facilities and took Fiona for a sandwich at the French Boulangerie opposite the entrance to Christ Church College. It was the only Oxford College about which Naomi knew very much because, long ago, she had gone out with a boy from Manchester who was reading Maths there, and he had told her about Tom Tower. She remembered that it had been designed by Christopher Wren and contained a bell, known as Great Tom, which weighed over seven tonnes and rang one hundred and one times every evening at five past nine.

Fiona seemed to have more interest in consuming the two baguettes that she had ordered for lunch, rather than listening to Naomi's half-remembered stories about Tom Tower. Her lusty appetite was obviously responsible for her carrying a few extra pounds around the hips and thighs and, although she wasn't without some physical attraction, she fell just short of being pretty. Closer scrutiny revealed that she was already beginning to develop a double chin and a plumpness around the cheeks. But she seemed a bubbly girl and her presence behind Naomi in Court had already attracted the Farlow eye now and again during the morning session.

"The jury didn't seem too impressed with Tisdale, did they?" Fiona remarked between mouthfuls.

"I didn't think so. And we'll show he's lied when we get Kempner in the box," Naomi answered, taking a sip from her glass of freshly squeezed orange juice.

"But how are you going to deal with the blood? That evidence will be called this afternoon and we still haven't got any plausible instructions to throw doubt on it, have we?" the Junior asked.

"We've got nothing. So we'll have to imply they've mixed up the exhibits," Naomi said with a smile. "Bellinger will doubtless interfere but fortunately, at the moment, he's so incensed with Cadogan that the judicial spotlight isn't focused too much on me."

"The Judge is completely unfair. And rude. I didn't expect to see High Court Judges quite so offensive and prejudiced," Fiona declared indignantly. "But, if you ask me, he's no match for Ronan Cadogan. The upstaging of Bellinger's procession was a master stroke. And the way he sliced the old Mexican quack apart, presumably with hardly any decent instructions, was brilliant."

"Oh! You're a Cadogan fan now, are you?" Naomi chuckled. "Well, take a word of warning. He's brilliant alright, but he's untrustworthy and extremely dangerous."

"Come on, Naomi, that seems a bit harsh. Anyway, we're on the same side in this case, aren't we?"

"Are we?" Naomi responded quizzically. "Depends which way the wind blows, I suspect."

"Actually, I'm staying at the same place as him. Ten minute walk from the Court, along the river. I managed to get a cheap single room there, but when I checked in last night and told them I was at the Crown Court, they said they had a very important QC staying there this week, he'd booked the only suite they have. Turned out it was Ronan."

"What a good job I didn't book in there then. Staring at that monster over the breakfast table would be a fate worse than death. I'm at the four star on the Abingdon Road. Anyway, lunch over," Naomi said, finishing off her drink and squeezing out from behind the little round table with its neat, blue check tablecloth. "Let's get back to headless and handless corpses. The oriental doctor of death is first on this afternoon. Should be fun."

Chapter 32

Farlow: So what were your final conclusions?

Dr Mimura: There were no signs of any life-threatening injury to the torso. All vital organs were healthy. A head injury caused death. The discovery of a bullet at the scene suggests the deceased was shot in the head. Then, in death, the mutilation. As to time of death, I can only approximate. In excess of twenty-four hours. The body being drenched in water makes it harder to judge.

Farlow: As you know, blood coming from a source other than the deceased, was found on a pillar on the opposite side of the body from the pillar in which the bullet had lodged. Does that fit with the scenario as you see it?

Dr Mimura: The discovery of the bullet in the other pillar, its trajectory lining up with the position of the body, and the position of the killer's blood on the opposite pillar, all support my opinion that the deceased was shot. The recovered bullet may represent a miss. Even it had hit the deceased and passed through him and into the pillar we would not expect forensic evidence to be on it.

Farlow: What can you tell the jury about the physical details of the deceased?

Dr Mimura: Lean. Six foot three. Give or take an inch either way. The absence of the head makes precision impossible. Fortyish. I was present when Mrs Daley identified the body by the tattoo the jury have been told about. The body hair and its pattern and volume confirmed her identification and also support the proposition that the man was of dark appearance.

Farlow: We know that the head has never been recovered. If the head and hands and flesh from the calf had been inside the burned out vehicle, would you expect some residual evidence to have been found?

Dr Mimura: The circumstances of the burning of the vehicle cannot be directly equated to the intensity of a cremation when the body is wholly consumed. The idea that a vehicle fire could have destroyed the entirety of a human head and hands, but particularly the head, does not find favour with me. I believe obvious skull residue would have remained.

Oxford Crown Court Transcript Ref 251 Mimura/Nicholas

Nicholas: As the jury know, blood from someone other than the deceased was found on one of the pillars. If that is the killer's blood, then you cannot say, can you, who was injured first? The killer or the deceased?

Dr Mimura: No. Without the head I cannot tell if the fatal injury would have rendered the deceased immediately dead, or might have allowed him a few seconds to strike back in some way.

Nicholas: So the sequence of events may be that the deceased did serious injury to the killer, causing blood loss in the area of that pillar, and thereafter the killer responded in a way which led to death?

Dr Mimura: Possible. As is the converse. Killer struck first, but the deceased had a few seconds of consciousness during which he may have thrown a knife at the killer. Without the head, the pathology cannot establish the sequence.

Nicholas: You have concluded that the deceased was shot. Is it not possible that he was killed by a blow to the head?

Dr Mimura: The presence and trajectory of the bullet in the pillar suggest a shooting.

Nicholas: Was a major consequence of the mutilation to make both identification of the deceased and the mode of death much more difficult to establish?

Dr Mimura: Of course

Nicholas: So, setting aside the gruesome nature of such conduct, the mutilation does not necessarily have any bearing on the killer's state of mind at the time of the fatal injury? Indeed, the mutilation may have occurred several minutes after the fatal injury.

Mr Justice Bellinger: This witness is a pathologist, not a mind reader. His expert opinion is on the cause of death. Not on any hypothetical state of mind of the killer. Kindly ask questions within his expertise.

Nicholas: The rest of my intended questions go to that issue. I would submit that it is important for the jury to hear from the Pathologist that the mutilation may be an irrelevance on the issue of intent.

Mr Justice Bellinger: Is it your client's case that he caused the death but did not have the intent for murder?

Nicholas: Your Lordship knows that my client's case is that he had nothing to do with the killing. But it is my duty to explore many avenues.

Mr Justice Bellinger: You're not exploring that one any further I can assure you.

Mr Cadogan, I don't suppose you wish to cross-examine Dr Mimura at all, do you?

Cadogan: Has Miss Nicholas finished then?

Mr Justice Bellinger: Oh, yes.

Cadogan: Despite Your Lordship's most welcome indication that such is the weakness of the evidence against my client that I might not even wish to trouble the pathologist, I do have just a few matters to raise.

Mr Justice Bellinger: I gave no such indication. Get on with your questions.

Oxford Crown Court Transcript Ref 252 Mimura/Cadogan

Cadogan: Is it your normal practice to allow the distressed female partner of a mutilated corpse to make an identification in the back of the morgue van at the scene?

Dr Mimura: No. I was not keen to do so.

Cadogan: Then why did you allow it?

Dr Mimura: The Police felt there was a chance of an immediate identification which would have given their investigation invaluable information at a very early stage.

Cadogan: When you say the Police, do you mean one Officer in particular?

Dr Mimura: I suppose I do. Inspector Kempner was pressing me.

Cadogan: Did you consider the risk of losing evidence, cutting off clothing from the deceased at the scene, instead of within the laboratory conditions of a post mortem?

Dr Mimura: I told you, I was not in favour of this.

Mr Justice Bellinger: What is the purpose of these questions?

Cadogan: I wish to expose the serious shortcomings of the Police in this investigation. Pressurising the pathologist into permitting a purported identification by a loved one in such gruesome circumstances may be extremely relevant.

Mr Justice Bellinger: I think not. The jury will not be helped by further repetition of the distress that Mrs Daley must have endured. Do you have any other topic of enquiry?

Cadogan: Do I take it that Your Lordship is stopping me from pursuing this line any further?

Mr Justice Bellinger: Correct

Cadogan: Then I must move to another topic. Libidity. The gathering of the blood in the body after death. After circulation ceases with death, does the blood lie static within the body?

Dr Mimura: Yes. Like a bottle of water on its side, the liquid will gather. This may demonstrate the position in which the body has been since death.

Cadogan: Did it do so in this case?

Dr Mimura: To an extent. The body was found effectively on its back. The libidity would confirm that is fundamentally the position it had lain in since death, although I cannot exclude it having fallen in one position and then been moved on to its back or moved generally.

Cadogan: Perhaps you can be more certain about my next point. Would you agree that, putting the forensic findings and your findings together, there is nothing to suggest that at the time of this killing anyone other than the killer and the deceased were present?

Dr Mimura: That is right, I can. . .

Mr Justice Bellinger: Just a minute. How can this be a question for a pathologist?

Cadogan: Some killings show clear indications that more than one person participated. Indications that a pathologist can identify. Different shoe treads where there has been a kicking death.

Different calibre bullets where there has been a shooting. I am seeking to establish that every indication here is that only killer and victim were present at the time of the crime.

Mr Justice Bellinger: No, Mr Cadogan, I shall not allow it. The examples you cite where the Pathologist can properly be asked your question do not arise on the facts here. In any event, the case against your client is that she helped her co-prisoner in the arrangements, in the planning, driving him away after the burning of the vehicle and so on. She is guilty of murder if she did these things, regardless of whether she was actually in the barn when the victim was killed. You will not pursue this line further.

Cadogan: Your Lordship is most helpful. Am I to take it that establishing whether there is any evidence of my client being present at the time of the killing is now, in the light of Your Lordship's intervention, deemed to be an irrelevance?

Mr Justice Bellinger: That is not what I am saying, as well you know. Either move to another topic or resume your seat.

Cadogan: Then I shall, as Your Lordship puts it, resume my seat.

As the acrimony between the Judge and Cadogan became increasingly obvious to the jury, Farlow began to grow anxious. Experience had shown that constant judicial intervention aimed at the Defence seldom helped the Prosecution. Juries did not like bias in a Judge and Bellinger not only made his profound personal dislike of Cadogan painfully apparent, but he was also sniping at Naomi Nicholas who Farlow recognised the jury would instinctively like. It was a remarkable state of affairs, Farlow reflected to himself, that very clever men with the acuity to make it to the High Court Bench, often had so little understanding of how ordinary members of the public, such as sat on juries, would bridle at the spectacle of the Judge using the imprimatur of his position to gun down a barrister trying to do his job.

The next witness was John Whitely, the scientist who examined the blood on the pillar and had calculated that the odds were very substantially in favour of it being Philip Vance's blood. As Farlow called him into the witness box, he found himself praying that Bellinger would keep his nose out of it when Naomi cross-examined the witness. Everyone knew what a tough point it was for her to deal with, but if Bellinger started publicly crowing at its potency and belittling her attempts to find a way round it, then the strength of the Prosecution's best point in the case might be significantly reduced.

Whitely efficiently listed a summary of the findings made by the Scenes of Crimes Officers in the barn and the conclusions that could be drawn. Addressing the jury like a lecturer with his students, he explained that the body and the whole floor area had been thoroughly hosed down after the killing, leaving the body and its clothing soaked. They had examined the farmer's saws and axes to see if any one of them may have been used for the mutilation but they also had been blasted with the hose and the straw beneath them was saturated.

Tyre marks running from the gate to the barn had come from several different vehicles, but the gate was not locked and it was not uncommon for cars to use the area. The only safe conclusions he could draw was that the farmer's tractor tyres were identifiable and some other large vehicle, like a four wheel drive, had at some time recently also driven down at least the first part of the track to the nearest double doors.

Oxford Crown Court Transcript Ref 253 Whitely/Farlow

Farlow: Did you carry out DNA tests on the blood found on the pillar in barn?

Whitely: Yes. I can say with absolute certainty that the pillar blood did not come from the deceased.

Farlow: Did you have access to blood from the Defendant, Philip Vance?

Whitely: He had refused to provide a blood sample but the Police recovered his blood-soaked shirt from the hospital which I used to raise a DNA profile.

Farlow: How did it compare to the blood from the pillar?

Whitely: It was a match. The odds of the pillar blood coming from someone other than Philip Vance are in the region of one in a quarter of a million.

Oxford Crown Court Transcript Ref 254 Whitely/Nicholas

Nicholas: Would you agree that the current population of the United Kingdom is about sixty million?

Whitely: Roughly

Nicholas: So how many matches for that DNA profile would you expect to find in the United Kingdom?

Whitely: One hundred and twenty

Nicholas: Why do you say that? There are four matches in every million and therefore two hundred and forty potential matches.

Whitely: I am assuming the population to be equally divided between males and females. That halves the number.

Nicholas: On what basis do you exclude a woman as being the source of that blood?

Whitely: On no evidential basis. On the other hand, within a population of sixty million, tens of millions will be either children or very elderly. In reality, they can be excluded as being the killer.

The presumptions made in favour of the Defence make no allowance for that. My figures are conservative. Also, the male Defendant in this case was known to have a wound which bled. Statistically, this increases the chance of the blood being his.

Nicholas: Doesn't that analysis depend exclusively on the blood on the pillar definitely coming from the killer?

Whitely: Yes

Nicholas: So if, for example, a child had been playing in the barn and had cut himself and left the blood, then your analysis is completely worthless?

Whitely: My analysis is a scientific comparison of highly detailed profiles. They match. The statistical conclusions depend upon a host of variables. But for that blood not to have come from your client would call for a most remarkable set of circumstantial coincidences.

Nicholas: Was the work of raising a profile from the bloodstained shirt done in the same laboratory as that in which the work on the blood from the pillar was done?

Whitely: Yes. By the same team of laboratory technicians.

Nicholas: Is it the fact that if there had been any contact between the swab taken from the barn and the swab taken from the shirt, then possible contamination of one by the other would invalidate your whole analysis?

Mr Justice Bellinger: Do you have any evidential foundation for such a suggestion? Are you accusing the scientists of negligence in a murder enquiry?

Nicholas: It is for the Prosecution to prove that there was no contamination. Not the other way round. I submit that I am entitled to explore whether or not there was any risk of contamination occurring?

Mr Justice Bellinger: The jury may not be impressed by such fanciful excursions off the path of the proven evidence.

Whitely: There was no contamination. All samples and tests were kept apart from each other at all times. You've seen our notes, I'm sure.

Mr Justice Bellinger: That would seem to dispose of your point, Miss Nicholas.

Nicholas: No. I asked, in the event of contamination, would the analysis and alleged match be invalidated. That was my question to which I am entitled to an answer.

Whitely: The answer is yes. You're right. The analysis would be worthless. The defect in your question is that I can assure you that there was no contamination.

Nicholas: Unless there was human error which is lost within your notes

Whitely: Yes. Human error. The problem for you is that there was no human error. Every step of every procedure is monitored and noted. Our system is absolutely meticulous.

Nicholas: According to you?

Mr Justice Bellinger: Enough. Enough. This kind of exchange does not help the jury.

Oxford Crown Court Transcript Ref 255 Whitely/Cadogan

Cadogan: Is it the fact that out of all the extensive scientific and forensic tests carried out by the Scenes of Crimes Officers and the Forensic Laboratory that not one single piece of scientific evidence, not one shred, has emerged which links Susan Vance with this crime?

Whitely: No scientific evidence, no. But I understood the case against her to depend on other evidence.

Mr Justice Bellinger: So did I, Mr Whitely. And so did Mr Cadogan. And, no doubt, so did the jury. We shall now adjourn until ten-thirty tomorrow morning.

Completely ignoring the Judge, smiling sweetly at the jury, then directing Spiller to collect his papers and to meet him outside the building in a few minutes, Cadogan walked out of Court and into the public area, only to find Gerald hovering by the coffee shop, with obvious instructions to waylay him.

"Mr Cadogan," he called.

"Sorry, a lot of work to do," Cadogan boomed back, taking giant strides down the corridor towards the Robing Room, with Gerald scuttling along in his wake trying to stop him.

"Mr Cadogan, you must stop," he finally shouted, actually running round the QC and positioning himself right in his path, prepared to be mown down by the unstoppable tank if necessary.

"The Judge," he panted. "The Judge demands that you go straight to his Chambers. Now. I'm instructed to order you to attend."

"Are you enjoying your new job, Gerald?" Cadogan asked. "Is this what you expected? A prefect chasing the naughty schoolboy across the playground. Come on, before you expire on the spot. March me to the inner sanctum."

Punching the combination into one of the doors that led to the Judges' Chambers, the clerk anxiously escorted his prisoner to the Judge's lair, knocked timorously on the door, and, directing the aloof QC to wait outside until summoned, he crept nervously inside, only to re-appear within seconds, gesturing Cadogan to enter.

Bellinger was sitting bolt upright in the large chair behind the modern, light wood desk. At a separate table, pushed up against the desk, was the stony-faced Court Logger with her portable tape recorder in front of her, a tape obviously already whirring inside, designed to be scrutinised later by the Judge for more ammunition against his bete noir. In the corner sat Lady Bellinger, like a tricoteur, teacup in hand, lips pursed and silent, whilst Gerald perched himself on the edge of a chair beneath the window. Cadogan alone was left standing, like the soldier escorted before the Court Martial. The Judge was still in his robes but had removed his wig, his cup of tea and old-fashioned teapot sitting on the blotter on his desk. His face remained white with anger, but Cadogan did not miss the tremor in his hands, nor in his voice, when he spoke.

"Do you have anything to say?" he began in that whining tone.

"Only that, if I'm also to be offered tea, I prefer lemon to milk," the QC replied sweetly.

"Don't be so impertinent, Cadogan," he spluttered furiously. "Your outrageous demeaning of the Judicial Procession this morning was an insult to Lady Bellinger and the dignatories. And, of course, to the Office that I hold. You're a disgrace to the profession."

"Would Your Lordship explain what it is that I am supposed to have done?" Cadogan asked politely.

"You walked in front of the Judicial Procession," the Judge exploded. "At the very moment the fanfare was sounded."

"Did I? I had no idea. Head full of other things. Like defending a woman for murder. I suppose the call of the trumpets is more important than a life sentence for murder. How very careless of me."

"I see no point in a prolonged discussion," spat the Judge. "You are determined to add deceit to discourtesy. For the record, I gave you an opportunity to explain and apologise both this morning and now. You may expect to be reported to the Senior Bencher at your Inn of Court, Lincoln's Inn, for appropriate disciplinary action to be taken against you. I shall write the letter to him immediately. Do you understand?"

"I do."

"Is there anything else you wish to say?"

"I think not."

"Very well. My clerk will escort you to the security door."

Gerald jumped obsequiously to his feet and scurried across to the door as Cadogan turned on his heel to leave. Just at the second that the door was opened for him, the QC stopped and, turning back to face the apoplectic figure at the desk, he smiled and then spoke.

"Oh! Just one thing, Judge."

"What?"

"I am the Senior Bencher at my Inn. If you like, I could wait and save you the cost of the stamp."

"Out. Out of my chambers, Cadogan. Get out," the thin voice shouted, now almost out of control.

As the QC walked ahead of Gerald back towards the security door, the clerk gazed at the impressive shoulders and straight back towering above him. Gradually he noticed that those broad shoulders were beginning to move up and down with increasing speed and intensity, until the whole frame was shaking as it walked along. As they reached the door, with the QC's back still towards him, it slowly dawned on Gerald that the giant was laughing.

Chapter 33

By the time that Cadogan reached the Robing Room all the other barristers had gone, except for Farlow who was grooming himself with the utmost care in the full-length mirror, checking that every hair was in place and that the knot in his tie was symmetrically perfect.

"Trouble from Bellicose?" Farlow enquired with great interest, giving the knot a final pinch, as he observed Cadogan's entry into the room.

"Not at all. Asked me in for a quick cup of tea. We go back a long way," he replied. "Now what about this Daley woman? Is she going to give evidence or not? You've no case against my client at all without her, and precious little with her."

"You can rest assured that Kempner will get her here. So you'll have to deal with John Brown's Body playing out on the old mobile. Anyway, got to dash. Staying up at Magdalen and they'll all be heading back to College now from lectures. Must check out the talent, one of the perks of doing a case in Oxford. See you in the morning," Farlow said cheerily, as he headed for the door, unencumbered by any paperwork to attend to overnight.

When he emerged into the corridor, Kempner and Rose were waiting patiently for him, carrying some of the case papers.

"We expected a conference with you, Mr Farlow, at the end of each day," Kempner began. "Can we just step into this conference room?"

"Five minutes then. Not really necessary tonight," Farlow replied, anxiously looking at his watch, as he hurried into the nearby room, deliberately remaining standing once he had got inside and Rose had closed the door behind them.

"Any work for us to do overnight?" Kempner asked.

"No. Just make sure you get Alicia Daley to Court, that's all. I suggest first witness tomorrow morning. Maximum impact. Shut Cadogan up. He's hoping she won't show."

"She's moved," Rose informed them. "She's sold everything up. The house. The cars. The lot. She's living in a flat in Kilburn with some old girlfriend. She's playing her face about coming to Court, alright, but we'll get her here one way or the other. I can go round this evening, if you, like. I'm going back to London."

"Good idea," Farlow nodded. "One thing I should mention. Naomi Nicholas put some junk to Tisdale about him being paid to beat you up, Inspector, over a personal matter and, when it went wrong, owing you one. Hence the fact he picked Pal out on the ID Parade. Some rubbish her client has dreamt up, no doubt?"

Kempner and Rose looked at each other with some alarm at this revelation and there was a short silence before Kempner spoke.

"I think we'd better talk about that, Sir . . ."

"Not tonight, if you don't mind. Load of tosh anyway, I'm sure. We'll have a proper talk before the Court sits tomorrow morning. Got to go," he said, putting his hand on the door handle. "Oh, one thing. The Mexican quack. Like that Embassy fellow warned you. Bit too fond of the sauce. Cadogan spotted the boozer's shakes. Did him a bit of damage, I'm afraid. Not to worry, Daley does for Jenna and the blood on the pillar just about finishes Pal off. See you in the morning."

After his departure Kempner and Rose were left alone together in the small confines of the conference room. During the day they had been waiting in the Police Room, but it had contained a constant flow of other Officers involved in different cases in the building. Now, an uneasy atmosphere immediately descended as soon as Farlow closed the door behind him. It was Rose who eventually broke the silence.

"What do we say if Nicholas asks us about Tisdale and Albright?" she asked anxiously.

"We'll have to discuss it with Farlow. But he's too bloody interested in other things at the moment. Raise it with him tomorrow. I suppose, if we're pushed on it, we'll just have to tell the truth. It's got nothing to do with this case and we'll say so," Kempner responded.

"OK. I'm going to get the five thirty back to town. I'll try to see Alicia tonight and travel up with her in the morning. If there's a problem I'll call you. Unless you intend to spend the night cruising the town with lover boy," she said in a tone of obvious disapproval at Farlow's order of priorities.

"Before you go, can I ask? Any change of heart? Is Leeds a certainty now?"

"Signed and sealed. But I'll just be flying a mahogany Spitfire."

"A desk job? You can't take it," he exclaimed.

"I told you. I've signed."

"Albright's had a heart attack," he found himself blurting out.

"Who cares?" she responded.

"Lauren cares. He's persuaded her that she should have a conscience and she's bought it. Going to look after him when the show comes off in a week or so," he relayed to her in a flat tone of voice.

"So you've got no-one to play with, is that it? Listen, Jake. The die's cast. I don't want to hear about Lauren or Albright. You've had your chances and you never knew which way to jump. Well, I've bailed out now. See you in the morning," she declared aggressively, before marching off towards the stairs and the Railway Station. Kempner couldn't see her biting hard on her lip, nor did she let him know that Leeds was the last place she wanted to go. As she stood on the platform, with an emptiness in her heart, waiting for the five-thirty commuter train, he was trudging across Oxford towards a tired, dingy, one star hotel where they rationed the soap and the toilet rolls and filled their cubicle-like rooms with the lonely people.

Chapter 34

On the other side of town, in very much more comfortable surroundings, Naomi ate dinner alone in the restaurant before retiring to her room and working on the case until just before midnight, when Jack called on the room phone to see how she was faring.

"Sorry it's late," he began, "but I knew you'd still be up working. I've been hard at it as well. How are things?"

"The Judge is getting up everybody's nose. Particularly the jury's. And, he and Cadogan detest each other. It's wonderful to watch. It's actually taken some of the sting out of Cadogan's attitude to me, but, as we know, sooner or later he'll pull the fast one. Just have to hope it's Farlow or the Judge he's after, not me," she answered, remembering run-ins that Jack himself had had with the giant."

"Well, it's not as if you've got much chance of being acquitted anyway, is it?

"Unlikely, but you never know in this game."

"I've got some news for you. Next Saturday night. On the show. I'm interviewing the England Manager. That's what we've been working on tonight."

"Now that is big news. Is it no-holds barred or best behaviour?" she asked mischievously.

"We've got a meeting with the FA's man tomorrow. The PR blazer. That'll set the ground rules. But the fee is so outrageous I take the view that we've paid for the no-holds barred. You can help me prepare the cross-examination," he chuckled.

"Can't wait. Talking of which I've got some cross-examination to finish off preparing now and it's getting late," she said.

"OK. Sleep tight. Ciao."

"Night, Jack," she replied.

Half an hour later, too tired to do any more work, she quickly got ready for bed, slipped gratefully between the sheets and, within minutes, was on the edge of sleep, when the shrill tone of the room telephone rang again. Switching on the light and looking at the bedside clock in annoyance, she saw that it was nearly quarter to one in the morning.

"Hello," she barked into the mouthpiece. "Who is it?"

"Is that Naomi Nicholas?" a deep male voice with a completely unidentifiable foreign accent breathed down the other end.

"Why?" she demanded, anger now being replaced by concern. The tone of the voice sounded too much like that of the kind of people she spent her time defending.

"Is that Naomi Nicholas, the QC?" the voice insisted aggressively.

"Yes," she said reluctantly.

"Are you defending Pal?"

"I'm not discussing a case with some unknown stranger at one o'clock in the morning. Who are you and what the hell do you want?" she shouted.

"No names. We meet. I got some information."

"If you've got information you take it into my solicitor's office. His name's Bob Tomlin. Tomlin and Bailey, Kentish Town. They're in the phone book. Don't phone me again. And how did you find out where I was staying?" she demanded.

"You need to fucking listen, lady," the voice announced, menace accompanying the words down the phone lines and into her room, making her tremble as she now sat bolt upright on the edge of the bed, feeling vulnerable and exposed in her thin nightdress, as if the voice had eyes.

"I'm listening," she said quietly.

"I can help Pal. But only through you. No fucking solicitor. Just you. We meet tomorrow night. I'll come to Oxford."

"No. Under no circumstances will I meet you. And certainly not alone. If you've got useful information you take it to Tomlin and . . . ." The sentence went unfinished as the line went dead.

Naomi replaced the phone in its cradle and stared at the image of herself in the mirror on the opposite wall. Her face was white. In her job you mixed with dangerous people but, when you walked out of Court, or out of the prison cell, you left them behind. They never crossed the line from their dark world into hers. Now this sinister voice had found her and had visited her bedroom. She was frightened.

Chapter 35

Back in the same conference room at nine o'clock the next morning, Farlow and the two Officers assessed the latest disturbing news about Alicia Daley. Both Officers had been encouraged to find a very different Prosecuting Counsel on the job this morning. Focused, sharp and decisive.

"I left half a dozen messages on her phone but she never called back. At ten o'clock I actually went to the flat. No lights on. No reply. I even knocked a couple of neighbours up, but you know what they're like. See no evil. Hear no evil." Rose explained dejectedly.

"Without her we're in all kinds of trouble. She identifies the deceased and we need her to prove she made the 4.54 call and that Millard's ringtone was The Battle Hymn," Farlow reasoned.

"I don't understand why she's playing up," said Kempner. "We're on her side on this one. I can only suppose it's the whole idea of the Courtroom that's made her wobble. Wigs, juries, barristers, it has that effect on some people."

"Do you think it may be that she's frightened of Pal seeing her?" Farlow enquired. Don't forget, they've never set eyes on each other. He doesn't know what she looks like and she may prefer it to stay that way."

"It's a possibility. She may have frozen on the stick," Rose agreed.

"OK. If that's the problem we can put her mind at rest. This Judge will allow her to give evidence from behind a screen without either Defendant being allowed to see her. He'll allow anything the Prosecution asks of him. You've got to get in touch with her and tell her that. I suggest you release Sergeant Rose from staying at Court today, Inspector. She can give evidence tomorrow morning," Farlow announced firmly.

"If you give me all day on that, I'll find her. That's a promise," Rose assured them.

"Right. I'll go along with that," said Kempner. "I can tell you if Danny promises something, then Danny delivers. But before she goes, we want to deal with that matter you mentioned about Tisdale. You've got to know the facts in case I'm cross-examined about it."

"Fire away, then," Farlow said.

"Tisdale was paid to give me a beating. Nothing to do with Police work at all. When he tried it on, Danny was with me and she put him on his back. We told him to warn his paymaster off and we'd call it quits. It had nothing to do with the eventual ID parade of Pal at all," Kempner explained as economically with the facts, as he dared.

"You mean Sergeant Rose overpowered that bruiser?" Farlow exclaimed in disbelief and undisguised admiration.

"Oh yes," Kempner smiled. "You saw how tough she is from her arrest of Vance. Never underestimate her because she's small. I don't. She's the best Police partner I've ever worked with. Met or the NYPD."

"Very impressive," Farlow remarked. "I should like to hear more. Perhaps after Court tomorrow when you're back with us, Sergeant Rose? he suggested."

"I don't think so, Mr Farlow," Kempner said before Danny could even contemplate accepting an evening in Lothario's company. "We've a lot of work to cover and I need her full time."

"I see," Farlow replied, looking carefully from one to the other and getting the lie of the land. "Then perhaps I should just ask this. When you say Tisdale was hired to work you over, do I take it that there's a woman in the middle of all that?"

"Yes," Rose jumped in. "There is."

"But not you?" Farlow asked her.

"No, it's not me," she answered quietly.

"Alright. Thanks for telling me. If Nicholas puts any of this to you at least I'll know what's going on," Farlow said, getting up to bring the discussion to an end.

"But how do I answer?" Kempner asked.

"With a bare minimum of fact. And within a few questions on that topic, she'll have Bellicose on her back, so between you and the Judge I reckon you'll see her off," Farlow assured him.

"Bellicose? That's what you call him is it? That was the operational name of the first bombing shuttle raid by Bomber Command, re-loading in Algiers," Rose commented.

"You never cease to amaze, do you Sergeant Rose? Well you go and find Millard's moll and we'll look forward to seeing you tomorrow," he said, picking up his wig off the table and setting off for the coffee bar. Last night had proved extremely disappointing. A very restricted choice. Two polite refusals and one short, sharp obscenity was all he'd had to show for his sartorial and social efforts. He'd been in bed by ten thirty. Unaccompanied. But today was another day and the young barristers in the other cases would all be calling by the coffee bar by now. Time to make the morning check.

After Farlow had left them, Rose went down to the Police Room to collect her briefcase and then set off yet again for the London train to continue her search for Daley. When she walked out of the main doors of the building, Kempner was standing on the pavement waiting for her.

"Sorry you're having to go backwards and forwards to London," he said.

"That's not why you're waiting here for me though, is it?" she replied.

"No," came the immediate and honest response."

"OK, I'll tell you what the answer would have been if you'd allowed me to speak," she smiled.

"Go on. What would you have said to him?"

"I'm not going to be another notch on your bedpost, you canteen cowboy. That's what I'd have said," she laughed.

"See you later then, Danny," said Kempner with obvious relief in his voice.

"I've had a thought. Where's your car?" she suddenly asked.

"In the street outside the flop house I'm staying at. Fifteen minute walk away. Why?"

"If I drive to London I can go via Radford. Check out Keeling House. See if anyone there has got any information about her. You never know."

"Sure. Take the Volvo. Come on. The Police Station's right here. One of the lads'll give us a ride up to where the car is and then he can bring me back."

As they crossed the main road towards the Police Station, a taxi drew up outside the Court and deposited Naomi at the main doors with her bag containing her papers and a suitcase. She'd had a poor night's sleep and had phoned Jack in the morning to discuss the mystery caller. His advice had been to raise it with Bob Tomlin and move hotel, booking in under his name, so she'd made a reservation at The Wesley in the town centre and checked out of the other hotel. Now it should prove impossible for any nutcase to track her down. Almost on cue, Bob turned the corner and loomed into view and helped Naomi take her luggage up to the Robing Room. At the top of the stairs, she led the way into one of the small conference rooms and relayed the content of the nocturnal call.

"I'll check with the office during the day to see if anyone's been in touch about the case, but they certainly hadn't been up to ten minutes ago because I was speaking to my secretary," he informed her. "It sounds like a nutter to me. You know how these cases attract them."

"That's what Jack said. And I'd booked into the hotel under the name Nicholas so I suppose if he phoned around all the better known hotels and asked for me by name then, sooner or later, he was going to get lucky. Let me know if anyone does contact the office though."

When the Court convened at ten thirty, Cadogan waited with interest to hear the name of the first witness to be called. By his reckoning, this was the optimum time to call Alicia Daley. Her evidence against Jenna Zayer was lethal and with the jury now well into the facts of the case and fresh and alert first thing in the morning on the second day, this was the time for her dramatic evidence. If Farlow had Daley under control then he would call her now. To his delight the name called was not hers, but Roger Lancing, the Assistant Sales Manager at the Mens' Department of Harrods. Armed with his computerised sales receipts, he was able to tell the jury that the trousers recovered from the body on the 11th had been sold by him personally on the previous Monday. Handed the garment in a sealed polythene bag he was invited to don disposable gloves to examine it closely. Blood-stained, screwed up and cut by the knife of Dr Mimura at the scene, he was nonetheless able quickly to locate a Harrods stock number on the labelling which matched his till receipt and computerised record of the sale on the Monday, also showing his employee number on the document.

"I sold this garment to a Raymond Millard who paid by Visa Card on that Monday," he declared reading from the piece of paper. "They are Armani trousers, mohair, beautifully cut and cost four hundred pounds. I have sold to this customer before and I remember him. Tall gentleman. Usually had a most attractive young black lady with him."

Farlow then spent a good chunk of the morning calling the cell site telephone expert to prove which mast had connected Alicia's 4.54 call to Millard's phone, then the firemen who had examined the Cadillac and the divers who had dragged the river for nearly a hundred yards in each direction without recovering anything of significance. Cadogan's well founded suspicions that Alicia had gone walkabout were confirmed when Farlow's final witnesses of the morning were the Motorway Patrol Officers Gellick and Waller, for there was no logical way that he would ever have chosen to call them before the jury had heard from Alicia giving the details of her 4.54 call to Millard's phone. Cadogan tweaked their tails about being able to remember so clearly the words 'Sorry, Officer', being said by Susan Vance but they stuck manfully to their guns. By then, the Judge was thinking more about his lunch than the case and Cadogan could only hope that the jury were of a like mind.

While events at Oxford Crown Court had moved forward at a fast pace, Danny Rose had not. Having collected Kempner's Volvo, she had headed out on to the Ring Road where she ran into a massive traffic jam. The result was, that by the time she was heading up the hill past Nolan's Barn towards Keeling House, it was already after half past eleven.

It was a very different scene from the last time she had passed that way and the barn, appearing serene and picturesque, gave no hint of the macabre events it had witnessed on that awful night. Today, the iron gates to Keeling House were standing invitingly open and a large 'Sold' notice stood at the end of the drive.

Driving up to the house in broad daylight, Danny was able to see it in its full splendour and wondered how many millions Alicia must have got for it. On the other hand, she thought, she had no idea how much Millard owed in a hundred different directions and so there may not have been much left for the girl in the end. Directly outside the main door stood an Electra Glide Harley Davidson motor bike and seated on the steps down which Alicia had come on the night of the murder, an untidy male in jeans and a white T-shirt emblazoned with the logo *My Loyalty Depends on the Options* was observing her approach. When she reached the bottom of the steps, alongside Bacchus and Hebe, he wandered slowly down them to meet her, enabling her to see that the jeans had holes in the knees and were tucked into long, black, Faded Glory leather boots. The grey hair, thin at the front, was tied at the back in what was meant to be a pony tail, but looked more like a rat's tail. The lines were deep and creased round the eyes, but the lived-in, seen-it-all face was generous and open.

"Morning darling," he said in an accent that owed more to Bow Bells than Nashville, but contained a hint of both, with a touch of Bondi Beach thrown in for good measure. "If you're a punter I'm afraid the pile's sold."

"No," replied Danny, getting out of the car and leaning on the door as she looked up at the tall figure. "Do you think I'd be seen in an old Volvo if I could afford to buy a place like this?"

"Never judge a book by its cover, look at me for instance, I ain't as low down the food chain as I look" he countered, holding out his hand at the same time. "Name's Marty Stetler, by the way"

"Danny Rose," she responded, shaking the hand, noticing the long, artistic fingers as she did so. "Actually, it's Detective Sergeant Danny Rose. I need to see if the former owner left a forwarding address."

"Well, they've certainly changed the mould for coppers since I was fined fifty quid for smoking pot at Glastonbury," he said, beaming appreciatively at her. "Come on in. There's something written down somewhere"

"What are those statues at the bottom of the stairs?" she asked as she walked in between them.

"Odd pair. Whoever chose'em," he replied. "The geezer on the left's Roman and the girl's Greek."

"She's beautiful," Danny observed, gently running her finger over the marble.

"She should be, darling. She's the goddess of youthful beauty, the daughter of Zeus and Hera. Nearly as beautiful as you," he laughed as he went up the stairs. "And the other one's Bacchus, the Roman god of wine and intoxication," he added.

Inside the magnificent house was now completely bare, except for dozens of tea chests and sturdy aluminium cases piled up in the centre of the grand hall.

"Are you the new owner?" Danny asked, standing in the middle of the vast reception area with its galleries and high ceilings, while Stetler poked around through various bundles of paper thrown carelessly on top of some of the cases.

"In a way, darling. The group's bought it. We're going to turn it into a production studio. No-one'll actually live here full time. Here, I found it," he exclaimed, holding up a bright yellow sheet of paper with a flourish. "I knew she gave us something. Alicia Daley. I couldn't find it when I looked for it earlier this morning. Is that what you wanted?" he asked reading off the paper.

"That's her," said Danny, looking at the details as he handed the paper to her. "Yeh, there's two addresses here. I've got the Kilburn one already, but not the Brixton one. I'll just copy that down if you don't mind."

"OK. Got your detective's notebook and pencil I trust", he laughed. You might be as pretty as a picture for a gumshoe, but you still got to have your notebook."

"I've got one. Gumshoe? Where did you dredge that up from? Micky Spillane or Raymond Chandler? And why were you looking for Alicia's address earlier?" she asked as she wrote down 83 Bevington St, Brixton in her book.

"I come up in the mornings to sort out the gear that's starting to arrive," he answered, gesturing towards all the crates and cases scattered around. "Earlier, a guy turns up. Asks the same question as you. But I couldn't find that piece of paper. He was an impatient bugger. Just cleared off without a thank you. Didn't take to him. He wasn't as pretty as you, neither. Anyway, let's go back outside, Danny. I'm going to take you for a little spin on the Harley. Within the grounds. If ever I saw a gal who belonged on the back of a Harley, it's you. Come on."

"I can't," she answered, as they both walked outside again and stood on the stone steps. "It's not that I'm scared, but I've got to drive to Brixton now and try to find Alicia. I promise you, but for that, it'd be chocks away."

"No problem," he replied with a mischievous grin, producing a card from his back pocket. "Here's my number. When you get a chance and we're up and running, you call me and we'll do it."

"Wrecking Ball And Chain" she said, reading from the card. "Is that your group?"

"That's us. You come out when we're set up and watch the wrecking."

"Thanks. I will. But I've got to get going now. One thing though. This guy looking for Alicia. Can you describe him?

"Ugly. Tough as hell. Odd accent. Couldn't place it. No name. Surly. Late twenties, that's the best I can do, darling,"

"Thank you, Marty," you've been really helpful. I'll be back for a spin on the Harley," she said as he opened the Volvo door for her.

"What's she done anyway, this Alicia?" he asked

"She's a witness in a Court case," Danny told him.

"Steer clear of Courts, I always say. Anyway, so long, darling," he said cheerfully. "See you soon."

Wondering who had been looking for Alicia and why, Danny started the engine and drove away, watching the old rocker in her mirror, as he polished away an imaginary mark on the gleaming chrome of his Harley. Perhaps she would be back for the guided tour and the ride, she thought, but, for the moment, she had other fish to fry.

Chapter 36

Farlow found himself starting to filibuster at about a quarter to three. Kempner was the only witness he had available to call that afternoon unless Rose got back with Alicia and, so far, there had been no word from her. The last thing he wanted was to have Bellinger turn on him because his two remaining witnesses had disappeared and half the afternoon's sitting time would be wasted. Kempner was alive to the necessity for a slow tempo and he went through the arrest of Susan Vance and the subsequent interviews as slowly as he dared, but by quarter past three Naomi Nicholas was nearing the end of her cross-examination.

Oxford Crown Court Transcript Ref 272 Kempner/Nicholas

Nicholas: After you had finished your tape-recorded interview of my client I suggest that, because you were worried about weaknesses in your evidence, you offered my client a deal.

Kempner: That would have been improper.

Nicholas: Perhaps you thought you were helping?

Mr Justice Bellinger: You certainly aren't helping the jury, Miss Nicholas. Stop fencing with the witness. Put your case and move on.

Nicholas: Very well, if that is how Your Lordship sees it. Inspector Kempner, I put it to you that, off tape, you said to my client: "You're in deep trouble and you'll likely take the woman down with you. You'll both get life and Millard isn't worth that. Give us something to hang manslaughter on and we'll persuade the wigs at Court to take it,"

Kempner: I must disagree with that, ma'am.

Nicholas: Is that a fair reflection of how you see this case?

Kempner: How I see it is irrelevant. It's how the jury sees it that matters.

Nicholas: Was Millard a serious, high-ranking criminal?

Kempner: Oh, yes.

Nicholas: I want to ask you about Bruce Tisdale. Was he also a serious criminal and a hireling of Millard's?

Kempner: Yes.

Nicholas: When you and Sergeant Rose went to his home to ask him to attend an Identification Parade involving my client was he immediately prepared to attend the Parade or did he need some persuading?

Kempner: He needed persuading.

Nicholas: So Tisdale's evidence to the jury that he didn't need persuading was untrue.

Kempner: Or Tisdale and I have different understandings of 'persuading'.

Nicholas: Did Mexico come up in your discussion with Tisdale?

Kempner: Yes. It did.

Nicholas: So did Tisdale know that the man you had under arrest, who you believed to be Pal, had lived under a hot sun for years?

Kempner: I suppose so. Indirectly. If Tisdale could actually work out that it's sunny in Mexico.

Nicholas: Have you had any dealings with Tisdale other than in your capacity as a Police Officer?

Kempner: I'm not quite sure how you mean.

Nicholas: Have you met him in circumstances which were part of your private rather than your professional life?

Kempner: I can't really answer. Your question's not clear to me.

Mr Justice Bellinger: Nor to me. I won't tolerate fishing. If you've something relevant to put, then do so.

Nicholas: Did you learn that Tisdale was being paid to give you a beating?

Kempner: Yes.

Nicholas: Was the reason to do with your private or public life?

Kempner: Private.

Nicholas: Did he attack you ?

Kempner: He confronted me and he was dissuaded from taking it further.

Nicholas: Did you report it?

Kempner: No. As it was private and no harm had actually been done, I used my discretion. And, if I may say so, I'm surprised that you're prepared to introduce that here. It has nothing to do with this case.

Mr Justice Bellinger: So am I surprised. I don't like it. Unless you maintain it has any relevance you will move to another topic.

Nicholas: I do so maintain. I suggest that Tisdale was left owing the Inspector a favour for not prosecuting him for conspiracy to assault. He's paid off the favour by falsely picking out Mr Vance as Mr Locke to suit the Prosecution case here on motive. And I respectfully remind Your Lordship that Tisdale denied there were references to Mexico and that he'd been paid to assault the Inspector. That is in conflict with the evidence of the Inspector.

Mr Justice Bellinger: Stop commenting on the evidence. Your question implies that the Inspector must have told Tisdale who to pick out. So are you suggesting Inspector Kempner has attempted to pervert the course of justice?

Nicholas: I can't say. It may have been deliberate or it may have been some inadvertent observation about my client that enabled Tisdale to pick him out.

Mr Justice Bellinger: I suspect someone put you up to this line of questioning against your better judgement. Deal with it Inspector.

Kempner: Tisdale picked Vance out as Locke without any help or pressure from me.

Mr Justice Bellinger: Very well. Your questioning on this topic is now over, Miss Nicholas, do you understand?

Oxford Crown Court Transcript Ref 273 Kempner/Cadogan

Cadogan: I want to pursue this further.

Mr Justice Bellinger: You may want to but you're not going to. It can have no bearing on your client's case.

Cadogan: The defence of my client and the defence of Philip Vance may not necessarily travel in the same direction. I wish to elicit what other private arrangements Inspector Kempner may have with other witnesses.

Mr Justice Bellinger: Unless you have some specific allegation to put, supported by evidence or by your client's instructions, you will sit down.

With still no sign of Alicia Daley, an embarrassed Farlow was obliged to ask the Court to adjourn early and after much huffing and puffing the Judge ungraciously agreed. Farlow wandered thoughtfully out of Court to check with Kempner if any news had been received from Rose. As he passed Cadogan's end of the bench he caught a snatch of Cadogan's observation to Naomi.

". . . they've lost Alicia. And I did enjoy your attack on Kempner."

Bellicose thought I'd put you up to it but I do believe a bit of the Cadogan magic has rubbed off on you. . ."

Farlow smiled to himself. Nicholas and Cadogan couldn't stand each other. Sooner or later, if Cadogan had his way, he would try to ride his client out on Pal's back. Tomorrow would be an interesting day. So long as Rose had found that wretched Alicia Daley.

When he got down to the Police Room Farlow could hear Kempner talking on the phone and so he wandered down the corridor and considered his options for the evening. Tomorrow and Thursday he would have to cross examine both Defendants and make his closing speech. He really should make a start on it tonight but there was a Magdalen Drama Club Wine and Cheese Party which he'd seen advertised on the Notice Board in the quad kicking off at eight. A magnet for the nubiles. Very hard to resist, he thought to himself. While considering his decision, Kempner emerged from the Police Room, spotted him waiting and beckoned him in, encouragingly putting his thumb up at the same time.

Police Rooms in Court Buildings were generally a shambles. They were used to provide phone facilities and as a Waiting Room for Officers due to give evidence. As a result, by the end of the day, numerous well-thumbed tabloids lay scattered across the seats, overflowing ashtrays were dotted hither and thither, dozens of used plastic coffee cups sat on tables, shelves and the floor whilst the air reeked of stale smoke. Wincing at the whole atmosphere of the place, Farlow removed a greasy edition of *The Sun* from a chair and sat himself down to receive the latest tidings.

"I told you. If Danny promises something, she delivers," Kempner announced with a grin. "In her words everything's tickety-boo. She's got her. There's a black guy called Honey Hogan. Was one of Millard's latest generation of enforcers. Lives with a girl in Brixton. Apparently, Alicia's been staying there quite a bit since she sold up. That's where Danny is right now."

"And why's she been keeping out of the way?" Farlow asked.

"She's nervous about Pal. He's never seen her. Alicia would rather it stayed that way. She didn't know we might be able to get her screened from the dock. Now that Danny's put her right on that, she's promised she'll come to Court in the morning, but Danny doesn't trust her. Gave her the choice of a night in the cells as a reluctant witness or the spare bed at Danny's flat where there's no chance of her slipping away. She chose the flat. They'll be here by nine," Kempner reported.

"I have to say I'm very impressed by Sergeant Rose. Very impressed indeed," Farlow observed, picturing the fresh, attractive face under those red curls and the lithe, agile body.

Kempner immediately recognised the look in Farlow's eye and, making little attempt to keep the irritation out of his voice, swiftly brought Farlow back to the realities.

"One other thing Danny picked up. Some heavy was trying to find Alicia yesterday. Went to Keeling House. Certainly nothing to do with Hogan. So maybe Pal's got someone out there trying to nobble her because her evidence is so damaging. Fortunately, for tonight at least, she's in good hands."

"Very good hands," Farlow agreed. "I can't wait to tell Cadogan we've found her but it'll have to wait until tomorrow. You hang on to that Danny Rose, Inspector, she's a gem," he finally declared, getting up from his seat. "See you in the morning."

Before he had even reached the stairs his decision about the evening's activities had been reached. Now that Alicia's attendance was guaranteed, the Prosecution case was unanswerable. He could easily put together his cross-examinations and a speech tomorrow evening. He could taste the Chablis and a sharp Cheddar already. What other delights may follow only time and a sense of adventure could answer.

Chapter 37

A brisk walk up to Folly Bridge and then left along the river for less than a quarter of a mile and there stood one of those glorious old pubs that are tucked away in discreet corners of Oxford. Right on the water, "The Stinging Nettle" was a Free House always offering a variety of Real Ales from independent breweries, an outstanding wine list, excellent food in the big, noisy bar, seven residential bedrooms and one suite. As soon as Cadogan had accepted the brief, he had directed Quail to reserve the suite for the week and, with the Court rising early today, he had done three hours intense work on the case before wandering into the bar and dining on 'The Nettle's' speciality, their exquisite roast duckling with fruit stuffing and wild cherry and wine sauce.

Returning to his very comfortable quarters, he had done some more work, leaving himself with half an hour before the bar closed to sample the 1967 Old Midleton Irish potstill malt whisky the landlord had been enthusing about at dinner. Seated alone at a prominent central table, enjoying a large tumbler of the malt, he noticed a figure walk through the door who seemed familiar. Dressed in a short skirt exposing legs that didn't quite make the grade and a green suede jacket, several seconds passed before it registered with Cadogan that it was Naomi Nicholas's Junior. At Court her hair had been tied back but was now worn down and it was that feature that made her look different. As she turned towards the door leading from the bar that was exclusively for residents he called over to her and she responded immediately.

Jumping to his feet he turned on the charm that, when it was necessary, he could engender.

"Fiona. What a delight to see you in mufti. Come and join me for a glass. Are you staying here as well?"

"I am. The little room at the back. They told me you were here, Mr Cadogan," she replied, rather overawed at the warmth of the attention he was bestowing upon here.

"Please sit down," he gestured. "And you forgot the Golden Rule. No 'Mister'. It's Ronan. Now, I don't know if you're familiar with Irish Whisky but this is as good an example as you'll ever find. Would you like to try it or would you prefer one of those weird coloured drinks with paper umbrellas in them? he laughed.

"I've never had an Irish Whisky, but I'm game for anything," she replied, slipping off her jacket and putting it on the back of her chair.

"The flavour is a mixture of fresh oak and butterscotch," he explained, catching the barman's eye and holding two fingers up to signify his order. "Matured over thirty five years. See what you think."

As soon as the two large malts arrived, Cadogan moved into full flow, regaling the young girl with his legal anecdotes, flattering her by showing interest in her progress at the Bar and sending for another round when the barman called for last orders.

"So how do you think the case is going Ronan?" she asked, now very comfortable in his company and wondering to herself how Naomi could have got her assessment of him so obviously wrong.

"As I see it," he answered, lowering his voice to an intimate whisper, "we both have different problems. Your fellow is struggling on the blood and my sweet lady is in her cell tonight praying that Alicia Daley doesn't show. But, one problem we share is Luther Farlow. He's a fine performer, don't you think?

"He's nothing like as effective as you," she replied honestly.

"How kind. But I still say he's very impressive. And the ladies on the jury are just fascinated by him," he said with a twinkle in his eye. "But, to be flippant for a moment, his eyes are trained in another direction, aren't they?"

"You mean Naomi, I suppose. She's just gorgeous," Fiona said.

"No, no, no, my dear. I meant you. Bowled over, I should say. Splendid fellow. But, as I say, he has the capacity to do us both some damage in Court."

While Cadogan chatted away to her Fiona kept hearing the phrase he had so casually thrown away resounding in her brain. ". . . I meant you. Bowled over, I should say." The dashing, dark and handsome QC was apparently looking in her direction. After two large Midleton malts this trip to Oxford was proving seriously exciting.

"Well, time for bed," Cadogan reluctantly announced. "It's been a pleasure to spend a little time in your company. I'll see you in the morning. Not at breakfast. I always take breakfast in my room. Time honoured habit," he said, getting to his feet and beaming down at her.

"Good night, Ronan. I'll just take a minute to finish my drink so carry on. Thanks very much for the whisky. It was a new experience," she said, feeling more than a touch light-headed and so preferring to make her way to her room without him seeing her unsteady on her feet.

"I've got an idea," Cadogan declared. "We're both in the same residence. The food here is quite magnificent. How about dinner tomorrow tonight? As my guest? In the best traditions of the Bar we eat together whichever side we're on, although in this case we're actually on the same side. Would seven o'clock suit you?"

"That's very kind of you. If you're sure."

"Absolutely. Seven o'clock sharp. Delightful. Good night."

Nodding his thanks towards the barman and landlord, Cadogan passed through the Residents Only door and wandered slowly along the corridor towards his suite. Although he had consumed three doubles of the Irish, his brain was working overtime and when he got to his room, he threw the French windows open and walked out on to the small terrace, which led down to the river bank, so as to get some fresh air. There was a small wrought iron table and two chairs immediately to the left of the windows and, picking up one of the chairs he carried it to the edge of the paving stones and sat down for a few moments to reflect, staring at the water.

The river, black and running fast, was only about twenty yards away and, for the first time during his stay, he noticed a difference in its sound. It seemed to have an urgency about it tonight and had lost all serenity. There was no longer a lapping and a rippling, but a coursing which harboured some dark purpose. As he listened closely to its rhythm he half-thought he detected another sound which seemed actually to emanate from the water itself. Except it did not. It came from behind. It was so controlled and so indistinct that he experienced a few seconds of doubt before he was sure it was the sound of breathing. Then, with quite exceptional speed and agility for a man of his enormous size, in one movement he leapt to his left, picking up the heavy chair in his right hand and swinging it hard at the source of the sound. As he swung, he turned and saw a massive white hand snake out and grab the leg of the chair, taking its full impact with ease and wrenching it from Cadogan's grasp as if it were plucking an apple off a tree. Releasing the chair and dancing backwards on the balls of his feet, Cadogan prepared himself to fight, now able to see more clearly the magnitude of his task.

Picked out by the light from the bedroom, the figure appeared almost square. So vast were the chest, shoulders and neck that the head seemed disproportionately small. Standing several inches shorter than Cadogan, the man nevertheless exuded such an aura of brute physical strength that Cadogan, for the first time ever in his life, was not sure that he could handle his opponent.

"I'm not here to fight" the man suddenly said, stepping backwards, putting the chair down and holding both hands up, palm forwards at shoulder level, to indicate that he did not intend violence. "I'm here to help. Are you Cadogan?"

"I don't want the kind of help that creeps out of the night,"

Cadogan barked, circling so as to put the table and remaining chair between him and the heavy.

"Give me ten minutes. I win your case for you. Nicholas was scared of me. I can't find Daley. You're the one," the hard voice spat out in an accent not even the astute Cadogan ear could fathom.

"You know all the names, don't you? How about yours then? Cadogan demanded.

"Not out here. Other bedroom windows are near. In your room. I give you what you need."

"And rob me," Cadogan sneered, although in fact beginning to think that the man was not some footpad robber. Knowing the names was making the QC very curious indeed.

"If I want to rob or fight I'd have slugged you from behind two minutes ago. Either we go inside or you fucking lose what I've got," he snarled.

"Right. You walk into the bedroom. You sit on the floor in the middle of the room with your hands on your head facing the French windows. Then, I'll walk behind you and, at all times, you stay on the floor. Have you got all that?" Cadogan drilled at him, now starting to feel that he could exert some control over events and recognising that what the man had said was right. He could have cracked him over the head from behind and stolen whatever he wanted at his leisure.

"I do it. Just to start. When you hear what I say, things change. Let's do it," he replied, turning his back on Cadogan, walking into the room, dropping on to the carpet with an athlete's ease and putting his hands on his head. Cadogan waited until the man was still and then, closing the French windows behind him, he also entered the room, circled the man and stood by the door with his hand on the handle ready to move quickly into the corridor at the first sign of any trouble. Staring at the back of the man's neck, which had thick ridges of muscle running horizontally across it, he could see, beneath the jacket, the rippling power in the shoulders and the bulging lateral muscle structure which was clearly visible because of the man's hands being held on his head. Then the mystery man began speaking in his guttural baritone and Cadogan listened. After two minutes, the QC told him that they could both sit in chairs now. After twenty minutes he sent the man on his way with precise instructions as to what he was to do. Plan B was beginning to take shape. And it was brimming with theatrical appeal, he thought to himself. And juries just loved theatrics.

Chapter 38

Naomi's enforced switch of Hotel had not proved a success. The room was too hot and the shower was out of control, directing water all over the floor and soaking the bath towel. Delighted to get out into the fresh air, she had left by half past eight and walked through the town, down past Christ Church and had the Court in sight by ten to nine. When she was about fifty yards away she observed an old green Volvo drawing up in the semi-circular drive-way right outside the doors and a slim, young black female getting out of the front passenger door, followed immediately by the familiar figure of Sergeant Danny Rose from the driver's side. Naomi had never met Danny, but she'd noticed her in the building over the last couple of days, occasionally going off with Farlow and Kempner so Naomi knew exactly who she was. Moreover, Naomi had read about her pursuing and arresting Pal and had recognised that this was the spirited kind of girl she liked.

Moving like a cat, Danny came round the front of the Volvo, slipped her arm through the crook of the other female's elbow and disappeared through the doors with her into the Court building. To the casual observer, they appeared like friendly young women, arms linked, walking together. To Naomi's eye, Danny Rose was keeping a hold on Alicia Daley as tight as an eagle's talons held its prey. By-passing the Robing Room, Naomi headed for the coffee bar. She hadn't even wanted to risk the Hotel's orange juice and so this was to be her first drink of the day. To her surprise Fiona was already in there assiduously poring over Philip Vance's proof of evidence which set out the detailed written account that he was expected to stick to when they called him into the witness box later that morning to give evidence.

"Two early birds," Fiona said, looking up as Naomi came over with two fresh cups of coffee.

"Four actually," Naomi replied. "Danny Rose and the elusive Alicia have just flown in. Very bad news for Cadogan. Here, I bought you another coffee"

"Thanks, Naomi, I can use that. My head's not too clear this morning. Your bete-noir saw me in the bar last night and bought me two double Irish whiskys. I've never drunk whisky before and when I got to my room I just fell asleep. I'd meant to re-read the proof of evidence as well, that's why I'm doing it now. Potent stuff," she said.

"I told you he's dangerous. What did he want? Did he try to pump you about what our client's going to say?" Naomi responded, irritated that her Junior did not seem to have heeded the warnings she had issued about Cadogan.

"I think you've got him wrong," Fiona retorted. "He was charming. The only time he mentioned the case was when I raised it and he just said we've both got our problems and started talking about something else."

"Mark my words. He's clever, ruthless and as cunning as a riverboat card shark. Watch him," Naomi declared emphatically. "I've been in two high profile cases with him. He always strikes. The only question is when."

"OK. If you say so," Fiona answered disbelievingly, but deciding that it was probably prudent not to mention that she had agreed to dine with the old fox tonight. He'd obviously upset Naomi badly in the past, but that didn't mean that, even as a QC in the same case, she could impose some veto on any social contact that occurred between the barristers. Cadogan had made her laugh and maybe he'd let slip a little more inside information on Luther Farlow's intentions in a certain direction.

"There's only Alicia and Danny Rose to call before the Prosecution closes its case. Our client will be in the box by eleven thirty. I've arranged to meet Bob Tomlin down by the entrance to the cells at twenty past nine so that we have over an hour to go over Vance's evidence with him for the last time. I'll go and get changed. See you down there," Naomi declared, finishing her coffee and heading towards the Robing Room, leaving Fiona a few minutes to re-read the details of what Vance was intending to say.

While Naomi had been in the coffee bar, Farlow had been seeking out Cadogan, anxious to see his face when he was informed that Alicia was now waiting in the wings. Last night at the Wine and Cheese party he had been within an inch of success when fate had cruelly intervened. Having invested the whole evening in open pursuit of a moderately desirable undergraduate from Aberdeen, who was responding with some show of interest, he was just about to invite her back to his room to sample the 2001 Bourgogne Rouge, when the girl's brother rang asking her to join him for a late supper in twenty minutes. Cursing his luck, Farlow had skulked back to his quarters.

Reflecting to himself on life's inequities, he suddenly spotted Cadogan sitting alone in one of the conference rooms, huddled over his phone. Courteously waiting until he had obviously finished the call, Farlow knocked on the glass window and walked in.

"Morning, Ronan. Just to let you know that the grieving Alicia has materialised. She's ready for action," he announced with a disarming grin.

"How fortunate for justice," Cadogan replied enigmatically, his expression giving away precisely nothing.

"She doesn't want either Defendant to see her. I'll be making an application to Bellicose for her to give evidence screened from the dock," Farlow informed him.

"I shall object. Bellicose will ignore me and you'll get your way," Cadogan answered, seemingly completely unconcerned. "But on a more important topic, we haven't had a chance to take a glass together during this case. I'm staying at "The Stinging Nettle" on the river. Food is outstanding, as is the wine and the Irish malt. Come and join me for dinner."

"Very decent of you but I'll have to decline. I simply must put some work in tonight. I'll still have a chunk of my cross-examination of Philip Vance left for tomorrow morning. Then I'll have to cross examine your client and make a final speech. Perhaps we could do it tomorrow night?" he answered.

"Tomorrow's no good. I've got to travel down to London immediately after Court for a long standing function," he lied. "And the case will all be over on Friday. Never mind. No doubt we'll do another case together. But the opportunity for opponents to dine together whilst out on Circuit seems to come up so rarely nowadays. Next time, then."

"For sure. Next time. I'll go and tell the Judge's Clerk that we'll want to argue about screens for Alicia before the jury are brought in," Farlow said, opening the door to leave and walking out into the corridor.

"Oh, Luther," Cadogan suddenly called out, "I've just had a first class idea. Why don't you get an hour's work in after the Court finishes today. Come over for a really early dinner, say quarter to seven. Last night the duckling with fruit stuffing and wild cherry sauce was three star Michelin. We'll limit ourselves to one glass of the red stuff each and you're back at the books by eight? Should leave you plenty of time to polish off the Vances."

"You're a very persuasive fellow, Ronan. Very persuasive. I admit I'm tempted," Farlow replied, working out the time table, while also picturing roast duckling with wild cherry sauce. "OK. You're on."

As he wandered off to find the Judge's Clerk, Farlow's mind went back to Sunday night and Naomi Nicholas's dire warnings about Cadogan. She seemed to have got that character assessment round the back of her neck, he thought. Seemed a very decent fellow. Still keen to keep alive the best traditions of the Bar. Dinner and a glass with the opposition amidst the heat of battle. A very civilised chap, Farlow decided. Naomi must have just come across him on a bad day.

Naomi, Fiona and Bob Tomlin were seated in the cells by half past nine, awaiting the arrival of Philip Vance, whose daily trip in the prison van from Belmarsh had meant he'd had to be up at five in the morning.

When he appeared a few minutes later, still in the same ill-fitting clothes that the prison had supplied, he was smiling.

"They transferred me," he remarked cheerfully, manoeuvring himself into the vacant chair facing the door. "Instead of going back to Hellmarsh last night, I was taken to the Top Security nick near here. Means I haven't been on the road for hours."

"Good. Today is a very important day indeed," Naomi announced solemnly. "The Prosecution case will end sometime this morning and then it will be your turn to give evidence. I want to give you some advice on how to conduct yourself in the witness box."

"How's it going then? Are we winning?" he asked.

"No. We're not winning. You've never dealt with the blood on the pillar. Whitely was good and I had no worthwhile instructions. That's why I've tried to leave myself some argument at the end that, even if they believe it was you in the barn with Millard, then at least they may think he attacked you first and there may be a basis for manslaughter rather than murder."

"But that's not my defence. My defence is I wasn't there. Why do you keep banging on about manslaughter?" he said, making no attempt to disguise the irritation in his voice.

"Because I'm a realist. You'll tell the jury you weren't there. I'll argue you weren't there as forcefully as I possibly can. But if they believe the blood is yours, then you need a fall-back position to still try to save you from a life sentence for murder. I'm entitled to argue for that, even if it isn't your primary defence" she explained patiently.

"I've told you before, just like I told Kempner, I'm not interested in manslaughter. I want not guilty full stop. I'm not serving any manslaughter sentence for Millard. You go for the first prize, not the second," he insisted, leaning across the table and tapping his finger on its top to emphasise his point.

"Let's concentrate on the evidence you're going to give. Leave the argument to the jury to me later," she responded calmly. "Now, you must understand Farlow will hit you with everything he's got on that blood. Have you anything else to add to your answer that it's just a coincidence?"

"No. But you needn't worry about my answer to those questions?" he informed her.

"Why not?" she asked in surprise.

"Because I'm not going anywhere near that witness box. As I see it, Cadogan showed that the Mexican quack was a drunk, you exposed Tisdale as one of Millard's bonecrushers and you did as good as anyone could on the blood. I'm not going to improve on that," he reasoned. "I've been thinking about it ever since you came to Belmarsh."

"You've got to give evidence," Naomi replied vehemently. "It's your only hope. The jury's got to hear you speak, see you look them in the eye, get some feel about you. At the moment they think you're a monster who shot Millard and cut his head off. You've got to show them you're a human being. With feelings. Sow some doubt. It's the only hope. If you just sit in the dock, silent, they'll be sure you're Pal and sure it's your blood. They'll think you just can't answer the questions."

"No. You're missing important bits out. The jury know Millard was a big-time crook. Ruthless and violent. Hired men like Tisdale to hurt people. Hurt them badly. They won't want to convict me if you show them a way of avoiding it."

"Only you can do that," she replied pithily.

"No. I can't. Everything I've got to say I said to Kempner in interview. I can't add to that. But you can."

"What do you mean?" she demanded.

"You can make them hate Millard so much that they won't convict me," he reasoned.

"Hating him isn't enough to explain away the evidence. And you refuse to face up to this. The body was savagely mutilated. The jury won't forgive you for that however serious a gangster Millard may have been. You've got to humanise yourself in their eyes. Let them hear you speak to them."

"But you've got more than Millard being a gangster," he insisted.

"What?"

"The Judge. He's a rude, prejudiced, pompous bastard. The jury can see that too. I'm watching them. If I don't give evidence he'll push even harder for them to convict me. They'll go the other way."

"I absolutely disagree with your decision" Naomi responded emphatically, looking at Fiona and Bob for support, which was communicated by animated head-nodding from them both. "My advice in the strongest possible terms is that you should go into the witness box and give evidence."

"No. My mind's made up. I'm leaving it to you. Make them hate Millard so much it hurts. Do that, Miss Nicholas and we'll win," he announced in a tone which left no room for further debate.

"I haven't finished," she continued determinedly. "There's another very important dimension to this decision. If you don't give evidence, Susan will. And she, and more importantly Cadogan, will have the chance to dump you. She can say she may have driven you about, but she didn't have the slightest idea you were going to kill. Your failure to testify will give her a free hand to save her skin at your expense."

"You mean like Millard did twenty years ago?" he blurted out without thinking.

"Are you admitting then that it was you in the dock with him twenty years ago?" she retaliated, capitalising on his slip.

"I'm admitting nothing," he mumbled.

"Then give evidence."

"No."

"You'll be pilloried by the Prosecution and by your co-Defendant. The Law is that the jury can infer guilt from your failure to testify. That's what the Judge will tell them and he'll lay it on with a trowel," she re-iterated.

"Not by my co-Defendant. You don't know Jenna. She'll never let me down. Never."

"You're still not understanding. I know what the Judge will tell the jury the Law is. And I may not know Jenna, as you now call her, but I do know Cadogan. Only too well. He'll call the shots in her defence, not her. He'll do everything in his power to persuade her to throw you away."

"Let me ask you, Miss Nicholas, are you married?"

"No."

"But have you got a fella, you know what I mean?" he asked in a softer tone.

"I know what you mean."

"Just imagine. If it was you and him in the dock. Forget the whys and wherefores of the particular case. But life sentences depending on it. Would he let you down?"

"No," she replied without hesitating.

"OK. Now you understand where Jenna'll be coming from. And let me tell you this. The only way you'd have got me to go into the witness box is if you'd said to me that my evidence may save her. And you've never said that, have you?"

"No. It wouldn't be true."

"In fact, I could only make it worse for her, not better. True?"

"Probably."

"That's it then. It's all down to you and Cadogan. Between you, both Jenna and I will be free"

"Cadogan will shaft you."

"Jenna won't let him. You make that jury hate Millard, Miss Nicholas. Hate. That's your mission and that's my defence."

"Bob, I'll want Mr Vance's refusal to give evidence in writing, signed by him," Naomi told the solicitor.

"I'll do it now, Naomi. And I'll record that he's taking this decision against your advice, knowing that the Law is that an inference of guilt can be drawn from his failure to testify" came the reply.

"The prisoner wouldn't listen to me, eh. All in writing and signed. Professional self-defence, eh, Miss Nicholas?" Vance chuckled.

"Perhaps it is self-defence. And that's the defence you should have run, Mr Vance," she replied curtly.

"When you came to see me in Belmarsh I was wary of you. Wary of all lawyers. But now I've seen you do the business in Court. You're OK by me. I'm happy with the defence I'm running. Millard. He's my defence."

As the trio of lawyers shuffled out of the cell and back through the security area back towards the Courtroom, Naomi could not stop shaking her head. She'd tried as hard as she could to impress upon Vance that he had to give evidence and she'd failed. It wasn't Farlow that she was now worried about. Nor the Judge who would savage Vance for not giving evidence. It was Cadogan. This move was like putting a bag of sweets in the hands of a child and telling him not to eat one. Whatever Jenna's depth of loyalty, Cadogan wouldn't be able to resist gorging himself on jelly babies and dolly mixtures.

Chapter 39

When the Court reconvened two large portable screens had been wheeled into place and Alicia Daley was already seated in the witness box. Rejecting all defence objections, Bellinger had directed that she should give evidence seated and hidden from the dock and the public gallery. Having spent a sleepless night in a strange bed in Danny Rose's cramped little flat with no opportunity to select her wardrobe for her Court appearance, Alicia was not looking her best.

Ironically, not being done up to the nines in the way she would have chosen, made her look much less the gangster's moll and rather more wholesome than was in fact the case. The youngest of four sisters, she was the only one who hadn't given birth to a child before she was eighteen. Observing the lives of her older sisters, each dragging up a child in a drab council flat without any sign of the father or any prospect of anything but a life of empty drudgery, she had realised that the only way out was with money.

In one year on the sleazy lap-dancing circuit she had managed to save fifteen thousand pounds, while learning how to fend off the greed and lust to which she was exposed on every shift. Allocating ten thousand of her savings to professional singing and dancing lessons, she had started to get one-nighters in some of the crazy South London hip-hop and rap clubs. Her melodic voice had an unusually wide range and some of the session musicians were soon putting her name about. That was how she'd got to perform at 'The Steel Ring Zone' which had become the hottest spot south of the Thames attracting some of the big-time artistes.

The auditorium was a fifty foot high cylinder with a small, circular stage set at the base. A staircase with a high guard rail spiralled its way round the walls leading down towards the stage and the crowds of revellers stood pressed up against the rail screaming their approval at the performers below. For those who actually made it down to ground level there was a dance floor around the stage and the numbers and the frenzy could get to the point where the musicians were in danger of being crushed. Accordingly, the stage was surrounded by a ring of steel bars which gave the performers protection and the Club its name.

It was at 'The Steel Ring Zone' that she had met Leroy who, under the stage name of 'The Leopard' was one of the up and coming stars of the sub-culture of rap. Leroy had swept Alicia off her feet and soon she was simply accompanying him around the circuit, rather than developing her own career. Leroy was into everything. Rapping, money, sex, clothes, cars and cocaine. Alicia learned things about sex that she hadn't even imagined could be done and when Leroy was flying high Alicia was taken along for the ride. The idea that he should ever do anything as conventional as get married had never occurred to her but, suggesting it on the Sunday and doing it the following Saturday was how Leroy operated. Leroy had introduced Alicia to Ray and Ray had introduced Leroy to robbery. Spending big money faster than he was earning made the idea of ripping off one of his coke suppliers at gunpoint irresistibly attractive. When it all went wrong and Leroy picked up his ten years, that length of time behind prison bars proved too much for him and, at twenty three, he turned his miserable steel bed up on its end, tied a strip of sheet round his neck and hanged himself.

Ray had looked after her. A flat. Money. Jobs in the Clubs. Then, once sex with Ray had started and she deployed some of the techniques that Leroy had taught her, she was quickly shipped into Keeling House and had never looked back. She was Ray's girl and had the lifestyle that went with it. Ferraris, speedboats, designer clothes, endless supplies of coke together with broken arms and black eyes. Now, in a room full of rubber-necking strangers and toffs in wigs, she had to describe how Ray was reduced to a hunk of raw meat in the back of a mortuary van on the side of the road.

Farlow was fascinated by her. With a minimum of make-up the natural clarity of her skin could be seen and her big eyes, such a pure white against her black skin, captivated him. The hair was worn in big loose curls and hung down to her shoulders. Wearing a light blue blouse with one button too many undone, Farlow could see the fullness of her figure and feel the rawness of her appeal. But what spoiled her was her manner. Even before she spoke, the surliness was apparent in the way she held her head and slouched in her seat. When she spoke, the voice not only revealed her tiredness, but also her resentment of the Police and the class and type of people that populated the Courtroom. Farlow led her through the early history, Millard's failure to return home and then brought her to the 4.54 am phone call.

Oxford Crown Court Transcript Ref 274 Daley/Farlow

Farlow: Did Ray's phone have a musical ringtone?

Daley: John Brown's Body. Battle Hymn of the Republic. Right row.

Farlow: The jury have a copy of your phone billing with calls to Ray's name highlighted. The last answered call was at 4.54 in the morning. What was said during that call.

Daley: At first I couldn't make out what was being said. Then I picked up a couple of words. 'Sorry, Officer.' Took some thinking about it to work it out but them's the words. Female voice. Yank. That bitch had got my Ray's phone.

Farlow: In the mortuary van were you called upon to identify the body?

Daley: I was. It was horrible.

Farlow: Before you were shown the body did the Police ask you how you believed you would still be able to identify the body?

Daley: They did. Ray was six foot three and in good shape. I knew every inch of his body. The skin colour, the body hair and everything. But he also had a very unusual tattoo. Got it done in Bangkok before I met him. A frog. Blue. Right up the inside of the right thigh.

Farlow: The jury have a picture of that, Mrs Daley. It's necessary for you to look at it.

Daley: Right. I've got it. Yeah, that's it. That's the clincher it was Ray.

Farlow: Were you shown clothing taken from the body?

Daley: Yeah. Wet and cut and bloodstained but I'd been with him on Monday when he'd bought those Armani trousers. Four hundred quid he'd paid for them. And he'd only had those shoes with the round toe caps about a month.

Farlow: So can you positively identify that body as Raymond Leon Millard?

Daley: That was Ray, as sure as I'm sat here.

Oxford Crown Court Transcript Ref 275 Daley/Nicholas

Nicholas: When Ray heard that Pal was dead, was he delighted?

Daley: More relieved, I should say.

Nicholas: Did you have razor wire and Rottweller dogs guarding the house?

Daley: Yes.

Nicholas: Was that because Ray had so many violent enemies?

Daley: No, it was because he feared Pal may try to do what he'd been threatening for years.

Nicholas: I suggest that the truth is that Ray was a man of extreme violence with a number of violent enemies, any one of whom may have killed him.

Daley: Rubbish.

Nicholas: Were the defences also to keep the Police out?

Daley: Nah.

Nicholas: Isn't the truth that Ray despised the Police?

Daley: He weren't a big fan. Suspected they might fit him up with something if they got the chance?

Oxford Crown Court Transcript Ref 276 Daley/Cadogan

Cadogan: Is it not possible to download various ringtones from the Internet?

Daley: I'spose so.

Cadogan: And 'The Battle Hymn of The Republic" is a very popular choice, isn't it? Anybody could choose it?

Daley: The only person I knew who had it was Ray.

Cadogan: Is the truth that you actually have no idea at all about what was said on the other end of that phone at 4.54?

Daley: I picked up two words. Spoken by a woman.

Cadogan: For all you know, Ray Millard could have been somewhere in the Daventry or South Coventry area with another woman?

Daley: That's crap.

Cadogan: In a hotel room or in the back of a car?

Daley: I said that's crap.

Cadogan: And fumbled around to turn his phone off, knowing it would be you who was calling?

Daley: You're just making this up.

Cadogan: Fumbling because he was otherwise engaged?

Daley: You mean screwing some other woman?

Cadogan: Yes.

Daley: Bullshit. Ray loved me.

Cadogan: Were the words you heard perhaps 'Sorry Ray'?

Daley: No way.

Cadogan: After the various post mortems had been carried out did the Coroner release Raymond Millard's body to a Funeral Director of your choice?

Daley: Yeah.

Cadogan: And was there a funeral?

Daley: Course there was. He was cremated. He had no family so I had to make the decision. Ray never spoke about death, but I reckoned he'd rather have been cremated than stuck in a hole in the ground. Thanks to them vicious bastards in the dock there weren't even a complete body to bury anyway.

Cadogan: Did Ray ever hit you?

Daley: Ray was a good man. Anyway, what kind of question's that?

Cadogan: One you should answer.

Mr Justice Bellinger: Why should she answer it? It would seem to have precisely nothing to do with this case?

Cadogan: It may have.

Mr Justice Bellinger: Do you have any evidence to suggest that the deceased did hit her?

Cadogan: No. Not direct evidence.

Mr Justice Bellinger: Then I shall not allow you to distress the witness further with that type of question. Move on.

Cadogan: If your Lordship is forbidding me to ask such questions then. . .

Mr Justice Bellinger: I am.

Cadogan: Very well. Madam, Do you assure us that the body is that of Raymond Millard?

Daley: Of course it bloody is.

Cadogan: Do you maintain there is no chance of error?

Daley: None. I know my man's body. All of it. And I'm one of the very few people who even knew Ray had that tattoo. Given where it was. I've seen it plenty of times I can tell you. It was unique that was.

Cadogan: I suggest you're wrong. While you were living with Ray Millard did you have any relationship with any other man?

Daley: You've got a bloody cheek. I didn't cheat on Ray. He gave me everything I could want. And vice-versa.

Cadogan: Like Miss Nicholas I suggest Ray Millard was a man with enemies. Violent men.

Daley: He had one bloody enemy I knew about. Pal. Ray knew Pal'd come after him one day.

Cadogan: What about other enemies? People he owed money to? Or who owed him money?

Daley: He was owed a lot. And he owed others a lot. Fact of life.

Cadogan: Did he owe a man called Don Ecklund an enormous sum of money?

Daley: I ain't got the slightest idea. Ray never went into business details with me.

Cadogan: Did you know Ecklund?

Daley: I'd met him.

Cadogan: Did you ever have a relationship with Ecklund?

Daley: I told you before I never cheated on Ray.

Cadogan: Were you ever intimate with Ecklund?

Daley: The answer's 'no'. But I've had enough of this.

Cadogan: Did you ever see Eklund in scanty attire or naked or. . . .

Daley: For Christ's sake. My man's been murdered and you're calling me a tart.

Mr Justice Bellinger: Calm down please Madam. Your anger and distress are justified, but I shall deal with Counsel. I'm warning you, Mr Cadogan, trying to deploy titillating and scandalous suggestions to offset the impact of a witness's evidence is a technique I both deplore and forbid. This woman lost her partner and is giving evidence in traumatic circumstances. I will not tolerate your tactics.

Cadogan: Do I take it that Your Lordship is stopping me from pursuing this line of questioning?

Mr Justice Bellinger: Yes.

Cadogan: So be it. I am compelled by Your Lordship's intervention to conclude my cross-examination.

Mr Justice Bellinger: Then the Court will rise while Mrs Daley leaves and the screens are removed. Five minutes.

As the ushers scurried around to clear the Court and discreetly escort the witness out of the side door and into a secure part of the building, Cadogan walked outside into the corridor directing Spiller, who was hot on his heels, to obtain a printed verbatim note of Daley's evidence. When the Court reconvened Danny Rose was called to give evidence about her pursuit and arrest of Philip Vance and at just before mid-day Farlow closed the Prosecution's case. The jury shuffled in their seats and looked at the dock in the expectation of Philip Vance making his way towards the witness box. Naomi knew from experience that the whole atmosphere of a case changed when the Defendant went into the witness box and that the jury expected it and felt an enormous sense of frustration and anger if it didn't happen. Trying her best to make her announcement in a very matter of fact tone of voice, she rose to her feet and dropped the bombshell. Her client was not going into the witness box. The Judge, in his most sneering tone, asked Naomi to confirm that she had explained to her client his failure to give evidence could be used against him whilst the frustrated jury shook their heads.

Oxford Crown Court Transcript Ref 279 S. Vance/Cadogan

Cadogan: My Lord, I was unaware of this development. It had been my intention to conduct a final conference with my client at lunchtime when, of course, I had anticipated the male Defendant would still be in the witness box. I would ask for some time to enable me to speak with my client at this stage.

Mr Justice Bellinger: You have had ample opportunity to hold conferences with your client. You should be ready now. Proceed.

Cadogan: Until two minutes ago I was wholly unaware that the male Defendant was not intending to give evidence. Even if I had seen my client a dozen times in conference during the trial I should consider it imperative that I discuss with her the possible ramifications of her co-accused's failure to give evidence. I request an adjournment until two forty-five.

Mr Justice Bellinger: I am unimpressed but you give me no alternative. The Court will just have to lose valuable time. Two-forty-five.

While the Judge flounced out of Court, making no attempt to disguise his anger at having to accede to a Cadogan application, which everyone else in the trial, including the jury, knew was a perfectly reasonable request, the QC picked up his note book, beckoned towards Spiller and Statham and headed for the cells with a beam upon his face. Everything was falling perfectly into place. Nicholas's inability to force her own client into the witness box was likely to prove disastrous for him and, potentially, extremely beneficial for Susan Vance. And the Judge's absurd resistance to allowing him some time to discuss this development with his client who, after all, was on trial for murder, had been viewed with obvious distaste by the jury. With most of the necessary pieces in place the time was drawing near for some Cadogan magic.

When the trio finally arrived in the small female section of the cell area where Susan Vance was being held, the Prison Officers had already given her what passed for her lunch. A yellow plastic mug of weak, tepid tea and one cheese sandwich made up of cheap sliced white bread which looked like cardboard and a sliver of some obscure processed cheese. When the lawyers squeezed in to her cell, which was the only place available for a conference, the sandwich was sitting on a paper plate on the wooden bench.

"Are you actually intending to eat that?" Cadogan asked, as she picked it up to make room for him to sit down while the other two hovered in the doorway.

"I've got to keep my strength up, somehow," she answered, taking a bite and forcing herself to chew and then swallow the fodder they had foisted upon her. "You can talk while I eat."

"Right. Come into the cell properly and close the door," he barked at Spiller and the hapless solicitor. "We don't want our tactics being debated by the Prison Officer's Association down here. Now, as you just heard, your co-defendant has chosen not to give evidence."

"Yes."

"This is very good news for us."

"Why?" she asked, already moving on to the second half of the excuse for a sandwich.

"His lies would only have made the case worse for both of you. The jury have no doubt that he's Pal and no doubt that it's his blood in the barn," the QC declared confidently.

"Let's hope not."

"Hope never won a case. It's time for the serious business. When you give evidence the Prosecution will concentrate on your alleged contact with Dr Hidalgo, the phone ringing in the Fiesta, your alias and why you're in the UK. I've taken your detailed instructions on those matters. Now is the time for you to change those instructions," Cadogan announced in a tone of voice which indicated that he would brook no dissent.

"What do you mean?"

"As I told you before, your story won't be believed. You'll take yourself down with Locke."

"His name's Vance," she snapped back aggressively.

"Whatever name you choose to call him, he's in deep trouble. Also getting yourself convicted of murder out of loyalty is the decision of a fool. Do you think he wants you to be convicted?"

"No."

"Do you think he doesn't know that he's at serious risk of a murder conviction, whatever defence you run?"

"He'll know. But are you telling me that if I say I was with him, knowing he was going to do some violence to Millard, that I won't make his position worse?" she asked.

"Of course you'll make it worse. But it's bad enough already. Don't go down with the sinking ship," he warned.

"Didn't I make myself clear when we met at Risley?"

"Things have changed. He hasn't given evidence. You've got a clear run. Admit all the Prosecution case except your state of knowledge. When you say you had no idea he'd kill, decapitate and the rest of it, they'll have a doubt. In my hands, with a gangster as the victim and a viciously biased Judge, I'll win. You'll be acquitted."

"But it'll guarantee Phil is convicted," she retorted angrily.

"Probably," Cadogan conceded. "But, like I say, don't go down with the Titanic. Jump into the lifeboat. It's waiting for you and it's got one space left."

"When you gave me similar advice at Risley do you remember what I said?"

"As if it were yesterday, my dear. You told me to 'shove it'. But you're wiser now, aren't you? You've seen what I can do in Court with a little bit of ammunition."

"What do you say, Mr Statham?" she asked, turning towards the solicitor who was standing leaning on the cell wall, looking like a startled rabbit caught in the headlights.

"I must defer to the advice of Leading Counsel," he mumbled, quite unable to withstand the dominance that Cadogan was exerting in that confined space.

"And you, Mr Spiller? Would you sell your lover's soul? Have you even got the guts to say what you really think or will you roll over like Statham?"

"I can only agree with Mr Cadogan," came the pitiful reply, his eyes fixed firmly on the floor.

"Spineless. A pair of spineless jerks. And you, Mr Cadogan, in your cushioned, comfortable world, you're the barrister equivalent of Millard. There's nothing to choose between you. I'm not interested. I stay exactly where I've always been. I give evidence as per the instructions you've got. Final answer," she fired at him, displaying both her anger and her disgust.

"Very well, my dear. You've made your position commendably clear. I do like that. You'll be in the witness box at two-forty-five sharp. I'm aiming to finish my questions at a time when it's too late for Farlow to cross-examine you this afternoon. No doubt the Judge will try to interfere with that but I'll handle him. So no cross-examination until the morning," he replied with absolute calm.

"Why are you so bothered about the timing?" she asked in puzzlement.

"Because sticking to your original instructions and refusing to take my advice means that I must now fully activate Plan B to get you acquitted. It's much the tougher route and timing will play its part," he answered with a smile, getting to his feet.

"What is Plan B?" she demanded. "I want to know exactly what you're up to."

"Plan B is what I've been looking for all along. It combines fatigue and surprise. Much of it is already in place. You see, I never expected you to give me the instructions I wanted. Loyalty. A splendid quality. But the barrister's nightmare. I do hope you enjoyed your lunch."

Almost knocking Spiller and Statham over, he strode out of the cell, looking at his watch. Not yet one o'clock. Squeezing even longer than he could possibly have needed out of Bellicose meant he now had time for a leisurely stroll across Christ Church Meadow and then he'd make his phone call before returning to Court. Nothing could beat the sense of complete power and control as he moved the human chess pieces on the board. And the beauty of this particular game was that most of the pieces didn't even realise they were being moved.

Chapter 40

When Cadogan called Susan Vance into the witness box, a tangible sense of satisfaction could be felt emanating from the jury. Brought up in New York and having survived in the jungle of the Las Vegas, she presented herself as a woman of substantial self-assurance and, for almost an hour, Cadogan prompted her through her colourful life story, never asking a single question about how or where she came to meet her co-Defendant. Then, at quarter to four he switched the scene abruptly to her presence in Birmingham and proceeded to take her briskly through the same sketchy account that she had given to Kempner in interview, never lingering on any of the difficult questions. Spending less than twenty minutes on the real evidence and skating over it with skill and speed he approached his final questions.

Oxford Crown Court Transcript Ref 280 S. Vance/Cadogan

Cadogan: What is the name of the man with whom you had taken up?

Susan Vance: Philip Vance. I took his name. He's been good to me. He's never been known as Paul Locke.

Cadogan: Why were you on the M40 in a car for which you had no documentation?

Susan Vance: We were touring. We'd made Birmingham our base for a week. We hadn't got driving licences so Phil did an iffy deal in a pub. We'd come here, to Oxford, to visit some of the Colleges. Then we were going to Fishguard.

Cadogan: Did your phone ring while you were with the Motorway Police?

Susan Vance: Yes. My friends call me at all times of the day and night. And I know a bunch of people with that ring tone. It's an American song after all. Then I lost the phone. No big deal. It was Pay as You Go. Cost peanuts.

Cadogan: Did you have anything to do with a man being killed in Radford on that night or a car being set on fire?

Susan Vance: Nothing to do with me. Or with Phil. Then he got attacked in Birmingham. This trip's been a disaster but, apart from driving that car when I shouldn't have done, I've done nothing wrong. I'm not involved with murdering anybody.

Cadogan: Thank you, Madam.

My Lord, that completes my questions of the witness. I have deliberately moved at pace so as to make up the time lost earlier for which Your Lordship held me responsible. It's now ten past four and I have managed to leave twenty minutes for Mr Farlow to make a start on his cross-examination. I am most anxious that he does so. I particularly want the jury to have my client's evidence-in-chief fresh in their minds when Mr Farlow begins.

Mr Justice Bellinger: I am tending to the view that it is better for the jury to listen to all of the cross-examination in one go tomorrow morning.

Cadogan: I am pressing as hard as I properly can for Your Lordship to let Mr Farlow begin now. . . .

Mr Justice Bellinger: No. Cross-examination will be in the morning. I have assumed, Miss Nicholas, that you did not have any questions of the witness.

Nicholas: None.

Naomi was astounded at Cadogan's performance. His client had made no attack at all on Philip Vance and nor had Cadogan made the slightest attempt to encourage her to do so. Moreover, he had directed most of his questions towards irrelevant material about her history, confining his questions on the real issues to a few questions which she'd met with inadequate half-answers. Then, quite transparently, he had provoked the Judge into putting Farlow off until the morning. She had to admit that she had no idea at all what he was up to. All she knew was that, being Ronan Cadogan, he was up to something.

Chapter 41

By ten to seven that evening Cadogan and Farlow were seated at the best table in the restaurant. Not only did it provide a view across to the lights on the other side of the river, but it was also just the right distance from the roaring fire in the enormous wrought iron grate. Cadogan had chosen the chair nearer the fireplace which gave him an unobstructed view of the 'Residents Only' door which led off the other side of the room. Farlow was in fine spirits. As he saw the situation, Philip Vance's failure to give evidence made it almost inevitable that the jury would convict him and, very conveniently, it saved Farlow the time and effort of having to prepare a cross examination of him. Now all that he had to do this evening was prepare his final speech and his cross-examination of Susan Vance. Surprisingly, Cadogan had done little to encourage his client to elaborate on any of her half-answers to the important questions and had left the field wide open. Dressed in an open-necked, light blue Ralph Lauren shirt and off-white canvas trousers by the same designer, he felt relaxed as he decided against the duckling and ordered baked wild pheasant with burgundy sauce and wild mushrooms. Cadogan was also in good form, seemingly resigned to Farlow being able to slice his client apart in the morning and, very fairly, insisting that they both start with only a glass of lime and lemon, so that they could stick to their promise of just one glass of wine with their early dinner.

At precisely the moment that the waitress brought their drinks to the table, a heavily made-up Fiona Breslaw emerged from the 'Residents Only' door and, observing Cadogan raise his hand in her direction, headed towards him. In an instant Cadogan surveyed her appearance and decided he couldn't have chosen better if he had been asked to act as her wardrobe consultant. Her skirt was tight and short, the tailored cream top was particularly low cut displaying her very satisfactory cleavage which was further accentuated by a small emerald which dangled from a gold chain and danced provocatively over the valley upon which Farlow's eyes were now riveted.

"Good evening, my dear," Cadogan called out, jumping to his feet as she neared the table. "Lovely to see you. Luther has joined me for an early dinner and I'd be delighted if you did likewise."

Already blushing deeply as she realised Luther Farlow was at the table and was making no attempt to disguise his pleasure at what he was seeing, she looked back at Cadogan.

"Had you forgotten you'd actually . . . " the girl began, before Cadogan's stentorian voice interrupted her, booming out across the bar for the waiter to bring their new guest a glass of the malt and to lay an extra place at the table.

"Luther and I are on rations. One glass of red each. But you can afford a little self-indulgence. The advantage of being a Junior," he laughed, busying himself to place her directly opposite Luther at the table.

"We've hardly had a chance to talk," Farlow began, gazing into her eyes. "I think it's so important for the Bar to socialise when out on circuit. Instructive and, when the company is so delightful, very rewarding," he oozed, as he opened a menu and passed it across to her, letting their hands touch as she received it.

"Ronan has plumped for the Beef Wellington," he continued, "but I've chosen the pheasant. See what you fancy," he continued.

"I'll have the same as you, Luther," she announced immediately, without even troubling to look at the menu.

Cadogan beamed at them both, as if savouring the general camaraderie of the occasion, but, recognising the fact that, in but an instant, he had become deliciously superfluous to proceedings.

Looking out across the river he pictured an angler on the far bank, casting his line with a deft flick of a skilled wrist so that the hook and bait landed mid-stream. Within a second, the line had jerked and tightened. The bait had been immediately taken. All that was left was to reel the line in and land the trout in his net. And once the hook was embedded, Ronan Cadogan never let the prey get away.

At precisely eight o'clock, when all three diners had eaten an excellent dinner and the two men had consumed only one glass of wine apiece, Cadogan sent for the waiter and, despite Farlow's gallant protests, insisted that the bill was put on the Cadogan account.

"Come on, Luther," he declared, pushing his chair back and getting to his feet. "Eight o'clock. You and I must head for the books. Delighted you could join us, Fiona. See you in the morning"

"Yes. Thank you Ronan. Actually, I think I'll just stay and have a quick coffee with Fiona before I go back to Magdalen. But you carry on. We shan't be long. Good night," Farlow replied before immediately turning back to gaze again at the young girl, whose flushed face demonstrated that she was already on her fourth drink and, as far as she was concerned, the night was still young.

Cadogan returned to his room and worked on the case until one in the morning. When he had finally completed his preparation, he headed out of his room, along the corridor and towards the back of the hotel where he had learned the cheap single room was located. Creeping up to the door marked '7' he pressed his ear against it. From within he could hear a female voice giggling and a cultured male voice reciting, "*Beauty is truth, truth beauty*"

'Music to my ears' he whispered to himself, not referring to the giggling and the poetry, but to the rhythmic creaking of the old bed, building up speed and ready to withstand a night of considerable activity.

Chapter 42

In a shabby hotel room on the other side of Oxford, Kempner was on the phone to Lauren. Next week the play would end its run and, she explained a touch nervously to Kempner, the deal she had finally struck with her husband was that if he arranged for someone to come in during the daytime, she would be prepared to be on hand at night time for four weeks and no longer.

"Whatever you think," he replied flatly with a resigned shrug of the shoulders. "This case is taking all my time at the moment and next week I'll be busy getting used to a new Sergeant because Rose is being transferred to Leeds. Let's just see how we go."

"You sound a bit down. Is Naomi Nicholas going to get her fellow off after all?"

"I very much doubt it. But we had problems getting our star witness to Court and Lothario's interest factor changes with the wind. Life's just a bit frustrating at the moment, I suppose. I'll get over it," he sighed.

"Is Naomi as good as Janet tells me she is?"

"As a matter of fact I'm not very happy with her. Somehow she knew about your husband's attempt to send Tisdale round to warn me off and started questioning me about it. I'd like to know who gave her the story," he said.

"What a filthy trick," Lauren exploded indignantly. "Who do you think told her? It certainly wasn't me."

"I'm not suggesting it was. And the Judge shut her up anyway. But she's certainly prepared to dish the dirt if she thinks it helps. Fortunately, her client hasn't got a prayer. He didn't even go into the box."

"Fatal," Lauren answered. "Anyway, I've had a piece of good news.

There's talk backstage that they may be auditioning next month for a new production. It's all a bit hush-hush at the moment but at least we're starting to look forward again. Hopefully you and I will be back to normal soon as well."

"Depends what you mean by normal," he grunted.

"You do need cheering up. I'm going to come round on Sunday to see you. How about a drink at 'The Grapes' at lunchtime and then we can talk. I'll be alright to leave him alone for a couple of hours."

"OK. I think we do need to talk. Say one o'clock."

After he had put the phone down Kempner sat in the window of the miserable room and tried to take stock. Gradually, over the last few days, he had begun to admit to himself that the harsh words that had fallen from Danny's lips in her flat that night were dangerously close to the truth.

He replayed them in his mind.

"You can never really be part of London like you were part of New York. That's part of the reason you're here."

New York was in his blood. He could never be intimate with London like he was with New York. There was something about London, its multi-layers, its culture, its heartbeat, that he would never really get hold of. It was out of reach. And Danny was right. That was why he was there.

"You can never have Lauren in a normal relationship. That's why you stay with her."

Cursing to himself he climbed into the single bed, its lumpy mattress shaped by a thousand different bodies and thought it through. "Goddam it," he said aloud, "What a mess. Big time."

Chapter 43

In Court the following morning the press benches and the public gallery were full. The cross-examination of the Defendant by Prosecuting Counsel was often the highlight of any trial and Susan Vance, or Jenna Zayer, as the tabloids had now taken to calling her, was not the usual kind of customer to be seen in the dock at Oxford Crown Court and the hacks were drooling in anticipation.

Cadogan had correctly identified the areas upon which the attack would be most heavily concentrated and, whilst her answers were delivered firmly and clearly, they never even began to deal with the evidence against her. But, eager to relish the spectacle of her being forensically shredded, the spectators were left deeply frustrated. Prosecuting Counsel never followed up when she was on the ropes. He never asked her how she had got into the country. He simply picked up his Junior's notebook and read out the Prosecution evidence to her, asserting that it was true. He didn't delve or probe. There was no scheme or pattern to his questioning, as if he had applied no time or mental effort at all in considering what he intended to ask. The jury began to show they were disturbed by the emptiness of the questions, the hacks put down their pencils and shook their heads, the Judge grew angrier by the minute but Ronan Cadogan leaned back in his seat, silently basking in satisfaction at a strategy brilliantly executed. Farlow was well and truly knackered.

Oxford Crown Court Transcript Ref 281 S. Vance/Farlow

Mr Justice Bellinger: I would be grateful, Mr Farlow if you refrained from merely reading out the evidence we all heard from Dr Hidalgo on Monday and concentrate on putting questions to the Defendant.

Farlow: I am putting questions. In my own way. Madam, are you seriously telling the jury that it is just coincidence that your phone had exactly the same ringtone as that of the deceased?

S. Vance: Apparently.

Farlow: That is nonsense. That was the deceased's phone. That is why you have made up a cock and bull story about losing it. Who phoned you at nearly five o'clock in the morning? Who do you know in this country who would phone you on that number?

S. Vance: Which question do you want me to answer? Who said the call I received came from someone in England? I've got friends in America. It wasn't yet midnight in New York at the time of that call. That's not late by my standards.

Farlow: So an unnamed friend called you at exactly the same time as Alicia Daley was calling the deceased. Just coincidence you say?

Mr Justice Bellinger: That is the third time you have referred to 'coincidence' in the last dozen questions. Kindly leave coincidence for the jury's consideration, Mr Farlow, and put questions on the hard evidence. There's enough of it.

Farlow: How did you travel to England?

S. Vance: By ship.

Farlow: Which ship?

S. Vance: I don't know the name. A cross-Channel ferry from France. I'd flown into Paris a few weeks earlier.

Farlow: Which airline

S. Vance: I don't remember

Farlow: How convenient

Mr Justice Bellinger: You know that isn't a question. Ask questions.

Cadogan smiled approvingly in the direction of Bellicose, irritating the Judge even further as Farlow's transparently ill-prepared and inept cross-examination blundered along, failing to press home most of the decent evidential points that he had against her. At one stage Cadogan stole a quick glance at Fiona Bresslaw, who was sitting behind Naomi gazing with carnal pleasure and admiration as she watched her lover in action, presumably reflecting on his nocturnal, rather than his forensic, performance.

Nevertheless, while Farlow had failed to slice Cadogan's client up for the jury's consumption, they were probably well capable of doing it for themselves in their own minds, given the strength of the evidence and, as Prosecuting Counsel asked his last question, Cadogan knew that he must now play his trump card. Turning round to Spiller he whispered his orders and the Junior hurried out of Court, returning a moment later carrying a small cardboard box and followed by a white man with a shaved head, dressed in a charcoal grey suit which struggled to contain the fifteen stone of honed muscle that had ridden bulls in the prairie towns of Canada and fought brutes like himself in the cages of Bangkok. Spiller slipped back into his seat, putting the cardboard box at his feet, while the bruiser headed for the witness box and took the oath in an accent hewn out of chunks of the Urals and the Rockies.

Oxford Crown Court Transcript Ref 282 Miskin/Cadogan

Cadogan: What is your name?

Miskin: Shrader Miskin

Cadogan: What is your job?

Miskin: Manager. Of investment company. I work for Mr Ecklund.

Cadogan: Who is Mr Ecklund?

Miskin: A business man in London. He tell us he was going to Sydney to look after the new office there.

Cadogan: When did he tell you that?

Miskin: A couple of days before I hear Ray Millard got killed

Cadogan: How did Mr Ecklund tell you he was going to Sydney?

Miskin: He'd been talking about it for months. Everything arranged in London office for him to go. But he went suddenly. Phoned me in afternoon and said he was going. Driving cross land to Singapore in the Land Cruiser. Then ship to Perth. Then land. Said not to expect news from him for couple of months. Maybe more.

Cadogan: Have you ever heard from him again?

Miskin: Never.

Cadogan: You mentioned Ray Millard. How did you know him?

Miskin: He owe Mr Ecklund big money. Millard came to see Mr Ecklund soon before he phone to say he was going to Sydney

Cadogan: Why are you here?

Miskin: Because I read in paper on Tuesday about trial. I not know much about the evidence before. I read the evidence of the Doctor who look at the dead body. I read about the body. And then I know it is Mr Ecklund.

Cadogan: How?

Miskin: Because only two people in world have tattoo of that kind of frog on inside of leg.

Cadogan: Who?

Miskin: Mr Ecklund and me?

Cadogan: How do you know there are only two?

Miskin: Because we have tattoo done at same time. Hong Kong. Mr Ecklund take photograph of frog. They are very rare. Mr Ecklund love them.

Cadogan: My Lord, I would ask that the jury turn to their large photograph taken by Dr Mimura of the tattoo on the body

Mr Justice Bellinger: Why? Where is this evidence leading?

Cadogan: I shall submit that it is leading to my client's acquittal. This evidence will demonstrate that the jury cannot be sure that the corpse is Raymond Leon Millard. A defect which is fatal to the Prosecution case.

Mr Justice Bellinger: Distractions help no-one. I shall allow you to proceed a little further. I shall consider later whether it has any relevance at all.

Cadogan: Mr Miskin, can you confirm that you have never been shown any photograph of the tattoo on the thigh of the body?

Miskin: I seen nothing. I don't even have photo in witness box

Cadogan: That is deliberate on my part. While the jury compare your words to the photograph they have, I want you to describe this rare frog.

Miskin: It is the poison dart frog. From Columbia. They make poison out of their skin as defence. They are blue. Two, maybe three inch long. They are only frog which cannot swim. You look at toes. They have no . . . I don't know the word . . . no kind of skin between toes. All frogs have this skin. Except blue poison dart frog.

Cadogan: The jury can doubtless see that the frog in the tattoo is exactly as you describe. Is the word you were looking for 'webbing'?

Miskin: That's the word. No webbing.

Cadogan: How tall was Mr Ecklund?

Miskin: Six foot three. Same size as Millard. Millard and Ecklund dislike each other. Millard get heavy when Mr Ecklund press for his money.

Cadogan: How can you assure the jury that only you and Ecklund have this tattoo of this particular frog?

Miskin: This is very rare frog. Tattoo man say he never done this one. Mr Ecklund have to pay him lot of money. It is in unusual place. I cannot say one hundred percent. Who can? But I not in doubt. This body is my boss. We never hear from him again. I phone Sydney when I read about tattoo. He never arrive. They thought he was on long trip.

Cadogan: If Mr Farlow, Prosecution Counsel suggests you are inventing this story about a frog would you be prepared to show the jury your tattoo?

Miskin: I show them now. Like I show you in hotel. I just need undo belt and . . .

Mr Justice Bellinger: Stop. Do your belt up. I will not have my Court debased by Mr Cadogan's theatrics.

By the time that Cadogan had sat down, Naomi realised that the identity of her late-night mystery caller was now revealed and, with his revelation, the pieces began to fall into place. That's why her client had become so animated at the suggestion he had decapitated Millard. The decapitation and removal of the hands were designed to make it look like the body was Millard, not that it wasn't Millard. She kicked herself for never questioning why the killer had gone to such enormous trouble to wash away the victim's blood when the answer had to be that the blood he washed away wasn't the victim's. Now she began to appreciate that even before Miskin had decided to drop his bombshell, Cadogan had already worked out that it wasn't Millard's body and had tried to cross-examine both Dr Mimura and Alicia Daley along those lines. She remembered how the Judge had interrupted and stopped him and how meekly Cadogan had succumbed. Of course, he had wanted to be stopped. He couldn't have known about Miskin then and so would be left only with innuendo, which he would doubtless have raised in his argument to the jury. Once he had Miskin, the whole scenario changed. There was now positive evidence to make the jury doubt the identity of the corpse. And, she anticipated, Bellicose was about to pay the price for his interventions. Just as significantly from the point of view of her client, she could now argue that Alicia Daley was in this plot up to her neck. The value of all Alicia's testimony could be undermined.

On her left Farlow was already floundering. His cross-examination of Susan Vance had been jaded and ill-prepared but now he was completely ambushed and didn't know which way to jump. She doubted that Bellicose could keep out of it for more than a handful of Farlow's inept questions.

Oxford Crown Court Transcript Ref 283 Miskin/Farlow

Farlow: How do you know Raymond Millard didn't have the same tattoo?

Miskin: Mr Ecklund's business was to do with betting. We give you odds of million to one that Millard have same rare frog, same place.

Farlow: Why didn't you take your information to the Police?

Miskin: I only read about it Tuesday. Frog never in paper until Tuesday. You think I should go to Police in middle of trial and say you got wrong body? They shut me up. I go to defence.

Mr Justice Bellinger: Mr Farlow, I wish to raise an important matter with Mr Cadogan.

Mr Cadogan, this story that you have seen fit to produce, like a rabbit out of a hat, at the very end of the evidence in the trial, if the jury are to be seriously invited to take any notice of it at all, then you should have suggested to Alicia Daley that she had wrongly identified the body as Raymond Millard. Your failure to do so renders this evidence fanciful. It was your duty to put it to her and to explore the question of identification with the Pathologist more closely.

Cadogan: I tried to raise it with Alicia Daley

Mr Justice Bellinger: What stopped you?

Cadogan: Your Lordship stopped me. My learned Junior has obtained an exact transcript of the relevant passages. I shall quote :

"Cadogan: Very well. Madam, Do you assure us that the body is that of Raymond Millard?

Daley: Of course it bloody is

Cadogan: Do you maintain there is no chance of error?

Daley: None. I know my man's body. All of it. And I'm one of the very few people who even knew Ray had that tattoo. Given where it was. I've seen it plenty of times I can tell you. It was unique that was.

Cadogan: I suggest you're wrong.

Cadogan: Were you ever intimate with Ecklund? . . . or see Eklund in scanty attire or naked or . . .

Daley: For Christ's sake. My man's been murdered and you're calling me a tart

Mr Justice Bellinger: Calm down please Madam. Your anger and distress are justified, but I shall deal with Counsel. I'm warning you, Mr

Cadogan, trying to deploy titillating and scandalous suggestions to offset the impact of a witness's evidence is a technique I both deplore and forbid. This woman lost her partner and is giving evidence in traumatic circumstances. I will not tolerate your tactics.

Cadogan: Do I take it that Your Lordship is stopping me from pursuing this line of questioning?

Mr Justice Bellinger: Yes"

Cadogan: I also have the transcript of my attempts to question Dr Mimura about the circumstances of Alicia Daley's purported identification of the body and, again, I quote:

"Cadogan: Do I take it that Your Lordship is stopping me from pursuing this line any further?

Bellinger: Correct"

Mr Justice Bellinger: You are blaming me for the deceitful way in which you intended to raise this particular hare. No doubt the jury will form their own opinion of such an approach. Continue, Mr Farlow.

Farlow: Do you say you knew Ray Millard?

Miskin: Yes

Farlow: So is the truth that you and Millard used the same tattoo artist. Probably in Hackney rather than Hong Kong?

Miskin: Rubbish.

Farlow: I suggest you knew that you and Millard had the same tattoo and you are making this up to confuse the jury?

Miskin: Rubbish.

Farlow: You probably picked the picture of the frog out of the tattoo artist's book.

Miskin: Rubbish. We picked the frog out of Mr Ecklund's tank and took picture of it.

Farlow: So now you're claiming Mr Ecklund actually kept these poisonous frogs as pets are you?

Miskin: Yes.

Farlow: To use your word, Mr Miskin, I suggest you're talking rubbish.

Miskin: No. Like Mr Cadogan tell me, I bring two frogs from Mr Ecklund's tank this morning. They are in cardboard box. Please give me box. I have gloves . . .

Mr Justice Bellinger: My Court is not going to be turned into some kind of circus act. Put the box down, Mr Spiller.

Cadogan: My Lord, the jury must be allowed to see inside the box. Mr Farlow's cross-examination is to the effect that it is rubbish that Ecklund had these rare frogs. The answer to that allegation lies in the box. The jury must be allowed to see inside.

Mr Justice Bellinger: Absolutely not. Miskin could have bought them from any pet shop. I refuse to allow it . . .

Usher: My Lord there is a written note from one of the jurors.

Mr Justice Bellinger: Very well. Pass it up, usher.

Cadogan: Would Your Lordship please read it out to us?

Mr Justice Bellinger: Silence.

Cadogan: We would be obliged to know the content of the note. As, by law, we are absolutely entitled to.

Mr Justice Bellinger: It reads "we want to see inside the box".

Cadogan: Thank you so much.

As the usher passed the box along the two rows of six they could see how carefully Shrader Miskin had perforated the cling film he had placed across the top so that the two blue poison dart frogs could breathe and yet be clearly visible to those who wished to look. The Judge, visibly in a fury, declined Defence Counsel's courteous offer that the box should be passed up to him on the Bench for his inspection. Retrieving the lid from Spiller, Cadogan closed the box and, at the same time, closed the case for the Defence. While the frogs hopped, the Judge seethed, Farlow cringed and Cadogan and Nicholas smiled as victory beckoned. Plan B seemed to have been well received by the jury.

Chapter 44

Kempner and Rose had been in Court as the dramatic developments had unfolded and, apart from being disgusted at Farlow's overall performance that morning, Kempner was now deeply troubled by Miskin's evidence. Some aspects of the case had just not fitted and it had been a mistake to put any faith in Daley. Her reluctance to come to Court was now explicable. Her indecently rapid sale of all the Millard assets would be so that the proceeds could be spirited away to wherever Millard was. And he remembered what Champagne Lamoise had told him about Millard being under heavy financial pressure and having to sell off the Scorpion Sting business. If Miskin was right, then this Prosecution for murder was a mistake. At that moment Farlow, looking worn out and shell-shocked, emerged from the Courtroom and beckoned the two Officers towards one of the empty conference rooms.

"Why hadn't you got any wind of the existence of this fellow Miskin?" Farlow barked at them, looking for someone to blame for his own lame performance.

"During the investigation, even after Inspector Braithwaite gave us complete control of the enquiry, the name Ecklund and the name Miskin never came up," Kempner answered.

"The quality of the investigation can now be seen to be pathetic. The jury aren't sure the body is Millard. We've spent half of our time proving Vance is Locke and Locke hated Millard, hence he killed him. There's no motive at all for Locke to kill Ecklund. We're in deep trouble and it's all down to poor Police work," Farlow declared angrily.

"If we're going to get personal about this, sir, then I'll be blunt with you about our view. We think that your cross-examinations of

Susan Vance and Miskin were far poorer than the Police work in the case. At least we tried. You'd never even thought about how to question that woman and, looking at you, it's obvious why not. You were too busy screwing some broad. It's written all over your face. If you want to get rough with me, then I get rough back," Kempner drilled at him, as the QC's tired face grew paler by the second.

"Don't you take . . ." Farlow began.

"Can it, Mr Farlow," Kempner interrupted. "Don't go standing on your goddamned dignity. You know I'm right, so let's get on with deciding how we're going to handle this."

"What do you suggest?" Farlow asked in subdued tone.

"I suggest we face reality. I'm far from sure that the body is Millard, so how can we ask the jury to be sure?" came the stark response.

"You mean chuck our hand in? Never. Not on. I'm not giving up and the Judge wouldn't let me if I wanted to. And I don't want to," Farlow asserted emphatically.

"May I say something?" Rose interjected softly. "We've charged these two with murdering Millard. We seem to be struggling to prove that Millard was in fact killed. But Pal was in that barn in a scene of extreme violence of one kind or another. Why don't we amend the charge to conspiracy to murder Millard? That way we don't have to prove that it is Millard's body, just that these two agreed to murder Millard and, on the evidence, either succeeded or had a damn good go at it."

"Neat," Kempner said nodding. "And probably near the truth. I like it."

"Well I don't," Farlow responded. "The jury will see that we've accepted Miskin's evidence. We'll look like fools. Not sure which horse to ride. We've spent three days proving motive, proving it's Millard and then, when some shaven-headed gangster has appeared from nowhere, we've jumped on to yet another horse and changed the substance of our whole allegation. Cadogan'll crucify us if we try to amend the charge. And there's no guarantee we'd be allowed to. Even this Judge will be reluctant to meddle with a murder count at the end of the evidence. He's made it clear that he views Miskin as an example of Cadogan theatrics. He'll dismiss Miskin in his summing up as a liar. A Cadogan stunt. That's the way to fight on. And, we can win it yet."

"But what about the truth?" Kempner queried. "What if you do win? And what if the body is Ecklund? Pal and Jenna will be serving life sentences for something they didn't do."

"They killed Millard or Ecklund. Spare your sympathy for a better cause, Inspector. My mind's made up. I make my speech this afternoon. I still go for murder," Farlow concluded, getting up and walking straight out of the room.

"He's suddenly got his energy back," Rose observed wryly.

"At the wrong time, for the wrong reasons," Kempner declared.

"Conscience at a job badly done?" asked Rose.

"Exactly. So we find ourselves in an absurd position," he said with a sigh.

"You mean we pray we lose?" she asked.

"Right on, Danny. We pray we lose."

Chapter 45

Over the rest of the luncheon adjournment Farlow locked himself away in a windowless room at the back of the building and, feeling deeply ashamed at his appalling performance in Court that morning, strived manfully to put together a final speech which might yet save the day. Kempner's justified criticism of him still made him go hot and cold and he cursed himself for his own weaknesses. All of his contemporaries, except for those who were gay, were married or in serious relationships while he spent all his energies on trying to retain his looks and behave as if he was still twenty-one. Time after time it had got him into trouble and still he made the same mistakes. Forever craving the thrill of the chase and, when the conquest came, allowing it to remove all sense of responsibility and priority. Yet, he knew that he was not a fool. A Magdalen scholar. A good lawyer. QC before he was forty. With the bit between his teeth he could sway a jury and, given this morning's performance, he was determined to give it everything he'd got. In one hour of intense application he constructed the final speech he should have been working on last night. This was now a personal battle. Kempner's words had shamed him. He must deploy every last vestige of his skill to earn Kempner's respect. Or, perhaps more significantly, regain his own self-respect.

When he opened the door, his notes in his hand, he was rejuvenated. The fatigue had passed. The brain was alive once more. The adrenalin was flowing. He was ready to let the jury have it. Lock, stock and barrel. As he swept down the corridor, passing the coffee bar on his left, a female barrister appeared from nowhere and grabbed his arm. Looking down at the face that really wasn't anything like as pretty as it had looked at four in the morning and catching a glimpse of the white legs that, truth be told, were more than a little on the heavy side, he quickly brushed the hand away.

"Sorry, Fiona," he breathed. "Another time."

When the Court reconvened Farlow moved into action, establishing that Philip Vance was Locke, with a burning hatred of Millard and, in Jenna, an accomplice who would follow him across the world to do his bidding. He savaged Philip Vance for his failure to give evidence, submitting that only a guilty man would not have laid his story before the jury. In short, he had no explanation for his blood being in Nolan's Barn. Miskin, he submitted was a fairground side show to be dismissed with contempt. Developing the arguments with flair and skill, he faced up to the fact that Millard was a crook but, he contended, Locke was even worse, prepared to engage in a grotesque act of mutilation to cover his crime. Jenna, he submitted was annihilated by the mobile phone evidence. The jury listened with care and, to Naomi's dismay, with numerous nods of approval at some of the powerful points Farlow was now making.

After an hour and a half of eloquence, reason and strength, his voice now reaching a crescendo, Luther Farlow QC made his final pitch.

"But for the chance of a broken rear light being spotted on the Motorway these Defendants would have got away with murder. They thought they could fool the Police and now they think they can fool you. Jenna Zayer had tried to talk them both out of it on the M40 and, now, holding you the jury in the same contempt that he held the Police, Pal Locke has shamefully let her try to talk them out of it in Oxford Crown Court. But you will not be fooled. Guilty," he concluded. "Both of them. Guilty of murder."

When he sat down the Judge, nodding enthusiastically in his direction, offered him the Court's appreciation for his submissions. Coupled with his own poisonous summing up which would be delivered immediately before the jury retired tomorrow, Bellicose

Bellinger reckoned the crisis of the morning had passed and Nicholas and Cadogan could be safely put to bed.

"Must be on something," Cadogan grunted to himself. There was still plenty of work left to be done here. Farlow had come alive and the verdict was far from assured.

Oxford Crown Court Transcript Ref 284 Speeches/Nicholas

Nicholas: My Lord, it's nearly four o'clock. The jury have been listening to Mr Farlow for over an hour and a half and must be tired. Would Your Lordship allow me to make my speech in the morning.

Mr Justice Bellinger: I think you underestimate the jury's powers of concentration, Miss Nicholas. Let us, in the interests of justice, maintain the momentum. Proceed.

Inwardly cursing Bellicose, Naomi was forced to deliver her speech. Every barrister in the business knows that to address a jury after four o'clock in the afternoon, when they have already listened to one long speech, and making them sit on until five o'clock when they have children to collect from school, dinners to cook and business to attend to, is the kiss of death.

Adopting her client's firm belief that one route to success lay in making the jury hate Millard, she painted the picture of the dangerous and ruthless world he inhabited, aided and abetted by other gangsters such as Tisdale. When she came to the blood in the barn matching that of her client and, even though she kept her voice strong and assertive, she knew that she was struggling badly in this area of the case. Some of the jury had begun to yawn and one of the women was looking anxiously at her watch, no doubt worrying about little Tommy waiting at the school gate. Several times Naomi tried to catch Bellinger's eye to communicate the blatant unfairness of making her proceed at, what was now a quarter to five, with a tired and distracted jury. The Judge smiled back at her, hypocritically nodding his head, as if actually concentrating on the substance of her speech, instead of relishing her problem in seeking to maintain the jury's concentration.

Towards the end of her speech, she submitted that, even if the jury were against her and were convinced that it was her client's blood in the barn, then they still had no idea what had actually happened. Millard may have been the aggressor and attracted an over-reaction in his opponent who may have struck back in circumstances amounting to manslaughter rather than murder. Then, she dealt with Miskin. Knowing that Cadogan would cover this part of the case in detail, she limited herself to the bald, but powerful, argument that Miskin's evidence undermined the whole basis of the Prosecution case.

When she sat down at five past five and the Court was adjourned she was seething with anger. She'd tried to show the jury that the Judge had been unfair but they had lost sight of whose fault it was that they had been kept late and had simply been straining at the leash for her to finish.

Subconsciously they would blame her. It was her voice that had been filling their heads, not the Judge's.

Directly outside the Courtroom Jack Farnham was waiting and, as Naomi burst through the doors, still in a cold fury, she walked straight into him, surprised that he had managed to get up to Oxford but still incensed at the treatment meted out to her by the Judge.

"I've just been completely stitched up," she reported angrily. "Bellicose gave me the graveyard shift for my speech. All the jury could think about was their meat and two veg."

"I was in there for some of it. You did a good job. They'll remember what you said," Jack tried to assure her, putting his arm around her. "But I didn't understand all that business about the frog and . . . "

"It's the footballer," a booming voice, exuding condescension, rang out, preventing Jack from finishing his sentence.

Jack turned and looked up at Ronan Cadogan. They had crossed swords twice before. Once at Elland Road in Leeds, when they had nearly come to blows, and a second time at the Old Bailey. Jack's face hardened and his fists instinctively clenched but Cadogan, ambling right past him, continued without even pausing for breath.

"No need for any heroics, Farnham," he sneered. "We're singing from the same hymn sheet this time, aren't we Naomi?"

"Lord knows how," she answered.

"Because of Plan B, my dear. So good to see you, Farnham," he called back, disappearing round the corner.

"I just don't know how you can spend days on end sitting next to that insufferable bastard," Jack sighed, visibly relaxing now that Cadogan had gone.

"I've got no choice. And I get paid to do it," she replied. "But this morning, he pulled one of his stunts. You know that mystery call I got in the night? Well, the fellow obviously tracked Cadogan down. That's where the frog you were asking about comes into it. Cadogan called this minder to say the frog tattoo on the body proved it wasn't Millard who's been killed, but some guy called Ecklund."

"He's always got a stunt though. Anyway, the Judge has done us one good turn. Your speech is finished, so there's no more work for you to do. We can have a night on the town. You know it's the big match tomorrow. That's why I came up here today. On the off chance we could go out for dinner. And it seems we can," Jack said enthusiastically, as they began to make their way down the corridor.

When Naomi reached the Robing Room there was no sign of any of the other barristers in the case. Quickly getting changed while Jack waited outside, she looked out of the window, gazing across the sea of cigarette ends, which had doubtless acquired an extra layer during the course of the week, and up the street towards the town. Two figures were strolling along the pavement arm in arm, presumably heading for Magdalen College. Both had their backs to her but she recognised them immediately. Now she realised why Farlow had made such a hash of cross-examining Jenna and Miskin. While Farlow was more than capable of arranging his own assignations it flashed through her mind as she slipped on her jacket, that perhaps someone else may have played a part in the apparent barristerial union and its timing. It's just the kind of thing he'd do, she thought to herself. No doubt that was part of what he referred to as his 'Plan B'.

* * *

After yet another excellent dinner at "The Stinging Nettle", Cadogan headed for his room to complete work on his final speech. Tonight, dining alone, he'd chosen the rich Tournedos Rossini, followed by crème brulee, but, with serious work to be done, no alcohol passed his lips. By a quarter to eleven he'd finished. The speech was a masterpiece. Short but lethal. Wandering back to the bar he could now allow himself the indulgence of another splash of the Irish malt. It was the landlord himself who was behind the bar as closing time approached and he was in a particularly chatty mood.

"Seems the Midleton '67 was well appreciated by you barristers," he chuckled. "You've knocked a hole in my supplies but at seven pounds fifty for a large glass I'm not complaining."

"Cheap at the price," Cadogan replied, reflecting on the outrageous fee he'd negotiated for this case.

"That Miss Breslaw put a few away, didn't she?" he continued. "Sorry we've lost her."

"What do you mean 'lost her'?" Cadogan asked.

"Some friend of hers turned up, she says. Offered to let her stay up at Magdalen for the rest of your trial. She checked out after Court this afternoon."

Cadogan sat on the bar stool sipping contentedly on his whisky. After the desperate effort he'd eventually put into his final speech, Farlow had obviously decided that it was time to revert to his normal sense of priorities. Feeding little Fiona Flibbertigibbet to the ageing Lothario had served its purpose well. All the pieces on the chessboard had been satisfactorily manoeuvred. Tomorrow marked the end game.

Chapter 46

Starting at ten o'clock sharp Cadogan had resumed his seat by a quarter to eleven. It was a tour de force. Forty-five minutes of undiluted, spell-binding brilliance. Both Naomi and Bellinger probably despised the Irish giant in equal measure, but neither could fail to recognise the power of his oratory, the grasp of detail, the withering annihilation of witnesses whose weaknesses he had exposed during the trial and his tactical appreciation of which points mattered and which did not. Unlike yesterday afternoon, there was not a yawn to be seen, not a sigh to be heard as twelve pairs of eyes were riveted upon the enormous figure who stood only half a dozen feet away from them and captivated them with that southern Irish lilt and, seemingly, undeniable logic. Hidalgo the drunk, Tisdale the thug, Daley the gangster's moll, were all tossed contemptuously into the forensic dustbin. The only witnesses who mattered in this case were his client and, even more importantly, Shrader Miskin.

"This," he told the jury, "is the case of The Blue Frog." Never would they forget the sight of those two amphibians hopping about in their cardboard box, a spectacle he reminded the jury, that perhaps "certain people were not keen for them to behold" and which meant that the Prosecution had been unable to prove that the body was Ray Millard. "Shrader Miskin's testimony destroys the Prosecution theory."

During this stunning performance Bellicose had been puffing and blowing, staring pointedly at the Courtroom clock, throwing his pencil down when he was brought personally into Cadogan's firing line and deploying any tactic to communicate to the jury his disdain for Cadogan's arguments. But, so engrossed had they been in the QC's analysis, that none of them had even noticed. However, Mr Justice

Bellinger was not to be under-estimated. He, too, was not without forensic skills. And he had two significant advantages over Cadogan. Firstly, the gravitas of his judicial office and, secondly, the fact that he had the last word.

Some Judges actually keep a tally of how many cases they preside over end up in convictions and how many in acquittals. There is a breed who view an acquittal in their Court as a mark of judicial weakness. A kind of perverse machismo drives them on. Image becomes everything. The Judge who always gets his man. Not only did Bellinger subscribe to this school of thought but he also excelled in achieving his objective. Regrettably, his tactics were remarkably successful. Juries tend to have an innate respect for the Judge in an ermine-trimmed robe and if he was telling them that the accused can be seen to be guilty, then he must be guilty. Bellinger deployed the authority and weight of his position to deadly effect.

Treating the fact that Vance was in truth Locke as so obvious as to warrant little consideration by the jury, he highlighted the intensity of Locke's burning desire to take revenge on Millard. The blood in the barn that matched Philip Vance's became a recurring refrain and he savaged him for his failure to give evidence. Sneering at Naomi Nicholas's submission that they may wish to consider manslaughter, he intimated that it represented little more than a last, desperate throw of the dice.

Fuelled by his own hatred of Cadogan, the Judge's attack on Susan Vance's defence was even more uncompromising. Saving his detailed references to the mutilation of the body until he reached his summary of the case against her, he asked the jury what they made of a woman who would stand by a man who had displayed such hideous brutality. Miskin's evidence, dealt with in thirty seconds flat, was dismissed as a Cadogan trick. Depicting Miskin as some under-world thug dredged up at the last minute when the net was about to close, simply called to offer contrived evidence founded on tabloid newspaper reports of the trial and a quick trip to the local pet shop.

With those blistering words ringing in his ears, he sent the jury out to consider their verdicts at five to twelve, whispering *sotto voce* to his clerk, but at a level designed to be heard by the jury, that he wouldn't be surprised to see them back before lunch.

Chapter 47

Jack Farnham had returned to London that morning to prepare for his live Saturday evening TV interview of the England Manager and so Naomi intended to ask Fiona out to lunch, assuming the jury were still out at one o' clock. She'd looked for the Junior before the Court sat that morning, but there had been no sign of her or of Luther Farlow. It was only at the very moment that the Judge had come into Court at ten o'clock that Fiona, looking rather dishevelled, had slipped into her seat, probably less than thirty seconds after Prosecuting Counsel had done likewise. At lunchtime they had both disappeared again and so she had had opted for a fruit juice in the crowded Courtroom coffee bar. Walking away from the cashier's till, the only spare seat she could see was at a corner table for two, where the sole occupant was Sergeant Rose. During the trial, Danny Rose's evidence had gone unchallenged and she had only been in the witness box for ten minutes, but Naomi, already impressed by the way she'd arrested Philip Vance and got the reluctant Alicia to Court, had been further impressed by her manner and general demeanour.

"Mind if I sit here? The place is packed," Naomi asked, looking down at the fresh, earnest face framed beneath the red curls.

"Not at all," came the immediate reply.

"You certainly had the Judge on your side," Naomi declared as she slipped into the uncomfortable seat.

"I thought the Judge behaved disgracefully," came the surprising response. "From beginning to end. Making you address the jury last night was completely unfair. And his summing-up was biased."

"My! You speak your mind, don't you?" Naomi retorted, warming even more to the girl."

"Don't you agree then?"

"Of course I agree. I'm just not used to Police Officers being so outspoken. Particularly when the unfairness is likely to work in their favour."

"Do you want the real truth then, Miss Nicholas?" Danny said quietly, now leaning across the red-topped table so that only the QC could hear."

"So long as neither of us is compromised by it," came the cautious reply.

"Well, if ever there was a re-trial then you should understand that I would deny that I'd ever said it," Danny answered.

"Go on, then," Naomi answered, now more intrigued than ever.

"I want your client to be acquitted," Danny breathed. "Millard was scum. They come no lower. Whether Miskin was telling the truth or not, we want to lose this case."

"We?" Naomi whispered back. "Surely you don't include Farlow in that?"

"No, I don't. I mean me. And Jake. Despite you trying to embarrass him over Tisdale."

"Why are you telling me this?"

"I'm not. I never said anything. I told you I'd deny it," she replied.

"No, you have a reason. Tell me," Naomi urged.

"Like I said, Millard was pond life. Pal lost fourteen of his best years for that bastard. And then he found Jenna. I've watched them in the dock. She could have blamed him and made things easier for herself. But they love each other. I can see it. I don't want Millard to be able to destroy that."

"A romantic copper? Isn't that a contradiction in terms?" Naomi asked.

"I'm a woman in case you haven't noticed, Miss Nicholas. And what you just said isn't particularly amusing, if you'll allow me to say so."

"You're right. I'm sorry. It was a cheap shot and I apologise,"

Naomi said anxiously, angry at herself for being so thoughtless. "In fact, I agree with everything you've said. And you have my word, I would never try to use it. I admire you for being so direct. It's just that you shocked me."

"Sometimes a shock is good for you. Anyway, I must go back to the Police Room," Danny said, leaning back in her chair and pushing her coffee cup away.

"Before you go, tell me something. Are you married?" Naomi asked.

"No, are you?"

"No. I live with a man. Jack. He was at Court yesterday. You probably saw him."

"I saw him. The ex-footballer. Does TV stuff. Why did you ask me if I was married?"

"Because your insight into the relationship between the two Defendants, whoever they really are, seemed so perceptive. I thought perhaps there was someone in your life who felt like that about you and you recognised it," Naomi replied.

"No," Danny answered sadly, getting up from her chair. "Perhaps the other way round," she enigmatically added, half under her breath, as she headed back to the smoky, grubby tabloid world of the Police Room, leaving Naomi alone to reflect on their bizarre exchange.

Finishing her insipid, warm fruit juice, Naomi returned to the Robing Room and found a quiet corner where she could start to read her next brief. Another murder. Manchester Crown Court. Her old university town. This time she was prosecuting and the Defence QC was someone she knew reasonably well, but all that really mattered to her was that it wasn't Ronan Cadogan. Spiller was sitting opposite her, nervously clutching a mobile phone. It transpired that the giant had retired to 'The Stinging Nettle' and Spiller had to phone him should the jury come back that afternoon and, Spiller had explained that Oliver Carne, Junior for the Prosecution, had been given the identical duty by Mr Farlow.

As the afternoon wore on, Naomi became resigned to another night in her uncomfortable hotel when, at just before four o'clock, the door flew open and Carne shouted the dreaded words across the Robing Room. "They're back," he cried and, in an instant, Spillers finger started punching numbers into his phone.

Naomi hated jury verdicts. Whichever side you were on, whatever the crime, the stakes were so high. The lives of the victim's families, the Defendants and their families were all changed in the space of one, or perhaps, two words from the Foreman of the jury. Always trying to keep sufficient emotional distance between her personal feelings and the case, Danny Rose's observations at lunchtime had made the task still harder.

Inside Court there wasn't a seat to be had. The public gallery had overflowed on to the Press benches and the ushers were trying to retain some kind of control over the crowds. Gerald was flapping around, like an officious car park attendant directing the drivers where to go. Walking quickly to her seat, Naomi kept her head down and waited for the hubbub to die down. Out of the corner of her eye she spotted Rose and Kempner, standing nervously against the wall, directly opposite the jury box, not looking at each other. After a moment or two she was aware of the other barristers taking their respective places, at which Gerald noisily demanded silence before setting off to collect the Judge from his chambers. A long couple of minutes passed before a heavy banging on the side door of the dais announced Bellinger's entrance and, white gloves in hand, he marched sombrely into Court, his presence producing total silence. Gesturing towards the dock, the Judge demanded that the prisoners should now take their places.

Mr Justice Bellinger: Before the jury return to Court I wish to make it clear that I require three Prison Officers around the male Defendant and one on each side of the female Defendant. When the verdicts are returned I demand total silence from the public gallery. Very well. Clerk of the Court, bring in the jury.

[The jury entered the jury box]

Clerk of the Court: Members of the jury, would your foreman please stand.

[Foreman; juror reference no. 369 Simon Tranter; university lecturer; stands]

Clerk of the Court: Mr Foreman, please answer my first question either 'yes' or 'no'. In the case of Philip Vance has the jury reached a verdict upon which all of you are agreed?

Foreman: We have.

Clerk of the Court: Upon the charge of murder do you find the Defendant Philip Vance guilty or not guilty of murder?

Foreman: Not Guilty.

Clerk of the Court: Mr Foreman, in the case of Susan Vance has the jury reached a verdict upon which all of you are agreed?

Foreman: We have.

Clerk of the Court: Upon the charge of murder do you find the Defendant Susan Vance guilty or not guilty of murder?

Foreman: Not Guilty.

Clerk of the Court: Thank you, Mr Foreman. Kindly be seated.

Nicholas: May my client be discharged from the dock, My Lord?

Cadogan: I make the same application.

Mr Justice Bellinger: No. I'm not satisfied as to their status in this country. Remarkably, the jury have seen fit to acquit them. I have grave misgivings about how they came into this country and their right to remain. I suspect that at least one of them, and maybe both, should be subject to a deportation order. Mr Farlow, I would assume that you would apply for a remand in custody while close investigations are carried out by the Home Office.

Farlow: In the light of their acquittals I'm not sure that Your Lordship has any such power. But, even if Your Lordship does have such power, I would like to take some instructions from Inspector Kempner first. It will only take a moment.

Mr Justice Bellinger: While you speak to the Inspector your Junior can check on my powers to remand in custody pending a Home Office investigation and possible deportation proceedings.

[Prosecution Counsel confers with Inspector J. Kempner]

Farlow: I have taken instructions.

Mr Justice Bellinger: Yes. A Home Office investigation and remands in custody I assume?

Farlow: No. Inspector Kempner believes that now they have both been acquitted the Home Office will have little interest in considering deportation. So long as the Defendants provide him with a means of contact, Inspector Kempner would not seek a remand in custody.

Mr Justice Bellinger: How generous. And, as to contact details, he's prepared to accept the word of a woman who, on her own confession, lied to the Police about who she was and where she came from, is he?

Farlow: Yes

Mr Justice Bellinger: And the word of man whose identity is still not properly established?

Farlow: Yes.

Mr Justice Bellinger: I'm appalled. The outcome of this trial is a matter of grave concern. It would seem that there's no more that I can do in this case to offer further protection to the citizens of our country. The Defendants will be discharged. These jurors will not sit on any other case. The Court is adjourned.

Chapter 48

Pal and Jenna did not leave the dock but asked if they might be taken down below and wait until the crowds had subsided and the frenzied aftermath had abated. The Senior Prison Officer, contrary to all rules and regulations, put them together in the same large cell at the far end of the cell passageway, away from all of the other prisoners. Telling them that the door was not locked and that they could leave as and when they chose, he walked off to complete his paperwork, noting the request made by Jenna that should either of their QC's ask to see them then the answer was 'no'.

"It's a bit ungrateful, Jenna. I actually liked Naomi in the end," Pal exclaimed.

"But you never met Cadogan. You never knew what he really wanted to do. I don't trust any of them. All that matters now is that we're free," she answered, as he hugged her close to him, trying to fight his way through the shell-shock that he was currently experiencing.

Sitting on the hard bench, holding hands, her head on his shoulder, there was little need for words. They'd make their plans another day. But, in both their minds, the same devil lurked. After all the effort and all the suffering, somehow, somewhere, the bastard must still be alive. The final chapter would still have to be written. Their thoughts were interrupted by the return of the Prison Officer, but this time he was accompanied by Kempner and Rose.

"I've come to take contact details," Kempner began, pushing open the grey steel door and walking in.

"Let's face it, Kempner, there's not much you can do about it if we simply make something up," Pal observed.

"I know all of that," Kempner replied. "I just need a means of contact to report to the Home Office. I really don't care if it's Mickey Mouse in Disneyland."

"I'll tell you what we'll do," Pal offered. "I'll give you a kosher way of getting in touch with me. But only if you promise me one thing."

"What?"

"If ever you hear where the bastard is then you let me know," Pal snapped.

"Do you want us to supply you with a loaded gun at the same time," Rose exclaimed. "We know what you'll do."

"I'm not making any promises. Just give me an address and we're out of here," Kempner added.

"How about an Email address. I've got an account. Paid twelve months in advance so it'll still be active. Will that do?" Pal asked.

"I told you. I don't really give a damn," Kempner retorted.

"OK. You won't need a pen. You'll remember this. It's 'Pal@tamazula.mex'

I'll check it regularly, I promise. So long," he announced, helping Jenna to her feet and walking past the Officers and out of the cell towards the door that led to freedom.

"That just leaves you and me then, Danny," said Kempner. "I'll give you a ride back to London."

"I'm not going back to London," she replied sharply. "I've given notice on my flat. My gear's already been shipped up to Leeds. Now the trial's over, I'm done with London. This is the end of the road."

Kempner stood in complete silence. As she had spoken his knees had felt weak and he'd sat down on the bench. Danny had remained standing, her face white and strained and he could see her fighting back the tears. He hadn't expected a farewell scene in the grey misery of a cell. Now that it was happening, it reminded him of a scene, long ago, by a bedside in a New York hospital where another desperate farewell had occurred.

"Danny, can't you . . . " he began, but she cut him off by placing a finger on his lips, before bending down, kissing him on the cheek and turning away. She didn't close the steel door behind her but he felt as if that was exactly what she had done. And then locked it and thrown away the key.

Chapter 49

On the Saturday night Jake Kempner was, yet again, alone in his flat with a glass of cheap wine. On Sunday he was due to meet Lauren and on Monday morning he had an eight o'clock appointment with his Chief Inspector at Bleak House where he would be introduced to his new Sergeant.

Lying on his sofa, he clicked the TV on to be confronted with a familiar face. Jack Farnham was interviewing the England Manager. It seemed to him that the old pro had picked up a few cross-examination tips from a tall blonde lady who'd just won a big case at Oxford Crown Court. The main theme of the questioning had been how many trophies, competitions or cups the England team had won under the new regime but, somehow or other, the guest succeeded in fumbling his way to the end of the interview without ever actually using the word 'none'.

Unsurprisingly, he drank too much of the two bucks booze, fell asleep on the sofa, woke at four in the morning and dragged himself off to bed. In the morning his head felt like Tisdale had wrapped one of his iron bars round it a few times and his spirits were somewhere south of his boots. Sunday mornings had always meant breakfast for two in the little deli over on Broadway and 11th. Street, picking their way through the New York Times, followed by a game of tennis in the park. Hell, he hadn't picked a tennis racket up since he'd arrived in London and, try as he may, the Sunday Times just wasn't the same as the telephone directories of the New York version. He'd grown up with the Yankees and the Mets not Middlesex and the MCC. Despite his half-English heritage, cricket and rugby did little for him. But, in his heart of hearts, he recognised that these were just the surface reasons and, just as he began letting self-pity take an even firmer grip, his phone rang. It was Lauren.

"I'm really sorry, Jake. I'm going to have to cry off. He's taken a turn for the worse. I've had to send for the Doctor. He'll be here any minute. I'm so sorry," she explained, her voice shaking.

"It's a put-on, Lauren. You've been running round after him for a couple of weeks now. He likes it," Jake had answered, sadness evident in his voice.

"You may be right. But I can't take the chance until after the Doctor's been. What if he just died?"

"Conscience? You'd have a conscience?" he asked.

"Look, we're just having a rough patch. The play finishing, the heart attack. It'll soon pass. Come and see me at the theatre tomorrow. Before the curtain goes up. I'll be in my room by six," she suggested.

"Can't make it. Got the new Sergeant starting. I won't be away before seven. You get through your crisis. Let's take stock when that's all over."

"I want to see you so badly but . . . oh, that's the front door bell. I'll have to go. I'll give you a call later in the day. Bye Jake."

"Whatever you say, Lauren. Whatever you say."

He shaved. Hot shower. Clean clothes. Walked to the pub. A pint of bitter. Walked back. It had started raining. Turned on the TV. Rugby or an absurd science fiction movie. Fell asleep on the sofa again. His phone rang. It was Shrader Miskin.

"How the hell did you get my number?"

"That doesn't matter. I know where he is."

"Where?"

"Italy. Otranto. Running with very big boys."

"It's out of my jurisdiction. I'd have to inform Interpol and the Italian Police."

"Better you just tell Pal. I try to find him. But no-one knows what happened to him or the American girl."

"I'll inform Interpol. Pal will kill him. I don't want to make myself a conspirator".

"Don't you want to see him dead? You think he can't handle the Italian cops? You tell, Pal. Else I take a trip down to Otranto myself."

"Keep your nose out of it, Miskin. I'll pass it on to the authorities."

The line went dead. He put the phone on the coffee table.

Of course the bastard was still alive. Dealing. Stealing. Cheating. Killing. Warming his body under the Italian sun. Eating at the best restaurants. With Alicia wrapped round him like a cobra. Picking up his phone again he dialled the number that had been going round in his head since he'd walked out of that cell in Oxford.

"It's Jake."

"I know. I haven't erased your number from my memory," the distant voice replied. "What do you want Jake? Not a post mortem. I haven't got the energy."

"No. I want advice. Miskin just called. Millard's been spotted in a place called Otranto in Italy. He wants me to tell Pal. I told him I'd tell Interpol," he explained.

"Pal will cross the world to kill him" she replied.

"I know. If I tell him, I'm making myself a party to it," he acknowledged.

"And you want me to make the decision for you, do you?" she asked sharply. "Make your own decisions."

"It's a big decision, I'd welcome your opinion, that's all. And I wanted to hear your voice," he added.

"I told you. No post mortems. You want my opinion. I'd go to an Internet café. I'd Email Pal. Off an anonymous address so it can't come back to you. One word. Otranto. After that it's up to him. But that's only what I'd do. The decision's yours. Try not to call me again, Jake. It just makes it tougher."

And then she was gone.

Chapter 50

Two days travelling South. Heading for the heel of Italy. Although the fiercest heat had now gone out of the sun as he embarked upon the last leg, it was still uncomfortably hot as the air-conditioning in the local train for the twenty-five mile journey from Brindisi to Lecca seemed to have given up the ghost. The Apulian coastline presented strange contrasts, starting with the abject poverty of the slums on the southern edge of Brindisi itself and progressing to glimpses of the caverns and grottoes at the bottoms of the cliffs overlooking the Adriatic. Suddenly, as the train rounded a bend, a forest of pines, junipers and enormous ancient carob trees would loom into view before giving way to vineyards and endless acres of olive groves. His travelling companions consisted of a smattering of poor Italian women, dressed all in black, old before their time, and surly young men who spoke in dialects that ranged from Kosovo to Tirana and beyond.

By the time the train finally arrived in Lecca it was dark and he took a cab from the station to the small bed and breakfast he had booked over the telephone. Wearing a maritime black cap, dark glasses and with three days stubble, he was unrecognisable. Tossing the canvas backpack that represented all of his luggage on to the hard single bed, he extracted the Spectre 4 still tightly wrapped in two T-shirts, placed it in the bottom drawer of the pine chest of drawers, pocketed the three magazines and walked straight back down the stairs and out into the balmy night air to grab a pepperoni and olive pizza chased down by a couple of bottles of the sharp local ale before hitting the sack.

Despite the hard mattress he slept until eight in the morning without stirring. Having showered but still not shaved, he set off for a strong cup of coffee and some acclimatisation. Starting in the Piazza

Sant' Oronzo, he strolled around the southern perimeter of the square which consisted of the excavation of a reasonably well-preserved Roman amphitheatre. The other side of the piazza was dominated by a tall Roman column which had apparently stood with an identical twin in Brindisi, marking the southern end of the Via Appia, the road that had run all the way from Rome. Somehow, the citizens of Lecca had purloined one of the columns, transported it here and stuck a statue of St Orontius, patron saint of Lecce, on top of the column.

Leaving the piazza, he came across dozens of baroque houses and churches constructed in a strain of fine-grained, yellow limestone. Most of the shops contained the same merchandise. Traditional wrought iron goods, ceramics and terracotta. Turning off down a narrow bustling alley, he found what he was looking for. A workshop no bigger than a single garage of an average house into which were crammed thirty or forty Italian motor scooters, some of which were awaiting repair and others of which were for hire. Selecting a non-descript, knocked-about four-stroke fifty cc Piaggio, which had a surprising volume of storage space under the double seat, he agreed a rate of twenty-five euros a day for at least three days. The problem arose when he explained, in faltering Italian, to the gruff, squat mechanic who ran the place, that he had no credit card, driving licence or ID.

Ten minutes of bad-tempered haggling and five hundred euros in the back pocket of the mechanic's oily overall secured him the hire of the wheels and the loan of a helmet.

Despite its low centre of gravity, riding it was easy enough. It had a handlebar twist-and-turn automatic gear change and enough power to chug along at the modest speed with which he felt comfortable. Avoiding other Lecce road users was another matter, as they cut each other up, tailgated and squeezed him to the sides of the rough roads.

Nevertheless, after a few minutes he began to get the hang of it and within another couple of miles he was out of the town and sailing along at what felt like eighty miles an hour but was in fact barely thirty.

Just a few miles to the South lay the village of Otranto. His information was that where the Lecce road hit the coast road, he would see a series of small coves, each with a strip of usable sand beach at low tide. Leading down to those beaches were wide dirt tracks easily covered by a four wheel drive vehicle. At some time after midnight, depending on the times of the tide, the speedboat which was kept in a secluded and inaccessible part of the Otranto harbour and operated by the heavy from the 'Sacra Corona Unita', would sweep up the coast and pull close alongside the selected beach where the two of them would be waiting to be taken on board. They would be dropped off at the same place before first light.

When he'd been in Bari before getting the train to Brindisi he'd gone over the tide tables for the stretch of coastline just south of Lecce and they'd worked out that the only night this week when the speedboat run could be made was Friday. As today was only Wednesday, he had ample time to check out Otranto tomorrow. Further north part of the coastline had been cliffs, some with fishermen's white painted houses glistening in the sun, but now the terrain was gently undulating. After five kilometres on the scooter's clock he came to the first track which cut off the road to the left and wound its way down to the shore. The earth was so hard baked that he rode the bike down for about a hundred yards before pulling over and walking the last stretch. There was a rocky cove and a couple of caves on the northern edge of the thin strip of beach but, to the south, it was clear. Wading out to the speedboat from here at the right tide time would be easy.

Returning to his room, he fetched the Spectre 4 from the drawer, unwrapped it and laid it out on the bed. He'd had no experience of handling a sub machine gun and the man in Bari had taken him out in to a field and shown him how to use it. The stock folded round when not in use so it would easily fit into the under-seat storage area of the Piaggio. Its rate of fire was a staggering eight hundred and fifty rounds per minute but the capacity of each of the three magazines supplied to him was thirty rounds. On the night, once he'd put the magazine in place, he would be carrying it with a loaded chamber and with the hammer down. There was no manual safety catch. As soon as he pulled the trigger it would discharge the entire magazine.

For most of Thursday he found himself kicking his heels as he did not want to get down to Otranto until late afternoon. Setting off at just after four he soon passed the tracks he had investigated yesterday and came quickly to an area of long white beaches and sandy dunes with thick pinewoods and flora crowding their way down to the shore.

On the train South he had noticed a number of '*i trulli*', white-washed cone-shaped buildings made of stones somehow held together without mortar, predominantly situated in wheat fields and olive groves and serving as barns, but on this stretch of the coastline some had been converted into homes. As the road curved round prior to the final descent into Otranto, he saw a side road leading inland and a cluster of '*i trulli*', nestling amongst some pines, which were clearly used as somebody's residence. Tucked away between a couple of the '*i trulli*' he spotted a black Mini Cooper S on British plates and right hand drive. It was on odds-on bet that this was connected with Millard, he reflected to himself as he continued to Otranto.

Occupying the site of Hydrus, a town of Greek origin, the ancient city centre seemed to remain untouched by the modern building around it. Parking the scooter by the Cathedral he ambled along the narrow, cobbled streets down towards the harbour.

The houses were a brilliant white with stucco walls and flowers and vines climbed up the stone work and across the terraces. One of the large ferries that plied its trade across the southern Adriatic and Ionian seas between Otranto and Greece sounded its horn as it set off on a journey that Greeks, Turks and Romans had been covering for the best part of two millenia.

The harbour was dominated by a Castle with great bastions looking out to sea. Paying little attention to the ferry terminals from which the Greece-bound ship had just sailed and from where other ferries ran to Corfu and Albania, he walked towards the dock area where small fishing vessels and rowing dinghies were moored and then to a small marina containing private boats and yachts.

A few people were on deck or busying themselves on the walkways, but by the time he reached the far end of the marina there was hardly anybody about. At this point a long narrow jetty led down to a small dock where about a dozen boats were moored, but access was barred by a tall, metal barrier which projected three or four feet each side of the jetty. Within the screen there was a padlocked door. Half of the moored craft were ordinary single-engined speedboats. Three or four were deep water charter fishing vessels but the only one he was interested in was a speedboat-cruiser hybrid whose name, etched in black lettering, he could just about make out on the white hull. '*Brucia dello Scorpione*'. Even his amateurish Italian understood that alright. 'The Scorpion Sting'.

There was no way of getting on board before nightfall and so he wandered slowly back towards the main harbour, picking up a couple of free brochures on the history of the town before locating a quiet trattoria on Corso Garibaldi where, over a plate of pasta strozzapreti he read that in 1480 a Turkish fleet had besieged the town, killing twelve thousand people before Otranto surrendered. Then the Turks had sawn the Bishop of Otranto in half before taking the eight hundred survivors up a hill where they beheaded them all. How appropriate, he had thought to himself, that his mission was going to end near to the site of mass decapitations.

Whiling away a few hours in a couple of bars he waited until his watch showed ten o'clock before returning to the area of the harbour where he'd seen the rowing dinghies. The sky was clear and the water was flat. Strains of incongruous heavy metal music floated through the air from some bar near the ferry terminal. This part of the dock was deserted and, having untied the mooring painter, he dropped silently into a small boat in the middle of the line and pushed off from the harbour wall. It was the work of less than ten minutes to row gently through the protected waters of the harbour and round to the '*Brucia dello Scorpione*'s mooring. Tying the dinghy up at the far end of the long pontoon, he ran his eyes along the line of vessels and saw no-one. In thirty seconds he was on deck.

It had obviously started life as a pure speedboat but various modifications had been made to fit it for its purpose when it was in mid-Adriatic. At least thirty five feet long and with a beam of a dozen feet it had a large platform protruding beyond the stern. Probably designed originally as a swimming platform it would hold three or four men comfortably. Jumping into the cockpit enabled him to see that there was a door forward of the helmsman which gave access to a small cabin but the door was locked. There was a bench seat aft and two raised helmsmen's seats behind the tall windscreen which had a bimini top attached to it covering the whole cockpit area but it could be dropped, like a car's convertible roof, by the press of a button.

Powered by a massive Volvo inboard engine it was obvious that it had the capacity to run the thirty or forty miles to a mid-Adriatic rendezvous in not much more than an hour on full throttle. A drag anchor sat on the starboard side of the forward deck. Near the bow a deep bait well had been constructed with a hinged hatch on top which opened so that, from within, the wheel and the helmsman would be clearly visible. It was already held open a few inches and, constantly checking that there was no-one about, he prised it fully open to reveal a couple of fenders, a tarpaulin and some ropes lying on the bottom. Dropping down into the well he brought the hatch back down to its original position so as to confirm that the viewpoint was as he had anticipated. Whilst there was sufficient room for him, he suspected that when the helmsman put the hammer down it was going to be a seriously bumpy ride. Moreover, with the Spectre 4 cocked ready for action there would be a significant risk of it being knocked and discharging accidentally. There was no way he could ride with the magazine in place. Climbing out of the well he repositioned the hatch and took one last look around before jumping back on to the pontoon and returning to the dinghy. Slipping quietly through the still waters he returned the fisherman's rowing boat to its rightful place and looked forward to borrowing it again tomorrow night. The only difference would be that the fisherman would have to go looking for it himself on Saturday morning.

Chapter 51

Although the average distance between the eastern Apulian coast and the western Albanian coast was less than a hundred kilometres the succession of Communist dictatorships had so controlled the movement of Albanians that the southern Italians knew next to nothing about their maritime neighbours. The Sacra Corona Unita, the Apulian branch of the Mafia went about their drug trading, prostitution and gun running unopposed by any other criminal faction. Then, at the beginnings of the 1990's, the Albanian Communist dictatorship collapsed and, almost overnight, Albanian gangs were able to construct a mafia of their own. Initially, they were small bands of hoodlums. Within a few years they had grown into organised, sophisticated crime syndicates. Completely ruthless, innately contemptuous of women, they moved into prostitution, gun running and drug and human trafficking. Apulia was their natural starting point and the Sacra Corona Unita recognised that, as tens of thousands of Albanians poured westwards, they had to learn to do business with the new order.

Even the overthrow of the Taliban worked in their favour. Afghan heroin was now travelling into Turkmenistan, across the Caspian Sea, on to Turkey and then into Albania. The final thrust was from the Albanian coast into the European mainland. Landed on the Apulia coast by dawn, heroin and cocaine was crossing the border into Austria by the evening of the same day.

It was hard for him to accept that, behind the serene façade of the seemingly tranquil and ordered society of this beautiful little corner of Italy, there was a monster spewing poison into the system which most of the ordinary people knew little about. Tonight he had no doubt that he would see its ugly face at first hand.

Dressed in dark, warm clothing, padded to withstand the jolting he expected at sea and with his face blacked by boot polish, he had crept into position at just after eleven. Surprisingly, there was a chill in the air, the breeze was freshening and the few clouds in the night sky were scudding across the face of the moon. Whilst still making sure that he could see through the aperture left by the open hatch, he had covered himself with the tarpaulin, securing the Spectre against the side of the well with its stock unfolded but the magazines in his pockets. By lying on his side with his knees curled up, he wriggled himself into a moderately comfortable position. Over the years he had developed a mental process whereby he lowered his level of consciousness so that he could hear and sense movement but his eyes were closed and his whole system was on hold, as if just on the edge of sleep. Maintaining this state he waited and rested.

The first development was a sound. In an instant he was completely alert. Squeaking wheels and footsteps along the pontoon. The noise stopped and the vessel rocked in the water with the weight of the arrival. He could hear someone straining to lift stuff on board but there was no talking, indicating that there was only one person. The cargo was dumped heavily in the cockpit and then feet appeared on the forward deck. Big feet in seamen's boots. Busying himself with some tackle which was out of view from within the well, he heard the man place something metallic right alongside the hatch and a gloved hand placed it down so close to the level of his eyes that he could have reached out and touched it. But he didn't need to touch it to know that he was staring at a fearsome Uzi Sub-machine gun.

After a few minutes the hand re-appeared to collect the Uzi and he saw the figure walk along the edge of the forward deck, round the bimini top and ease itself into the helmsman's seat. The figure just sat there, smoking one cigarette and then another, waiting until the timing was right. Suddenly there was a whirring sound as he activated the Volvo engine, a couple of rocks of the boat as he jumped off and on to release the mooring rope and then he manoeuvred the vessel gently away from the pontoon. Slowly meandering through the water towards the harbour exit he could feel the power of the engine straining to be unleashed. Even at a crawl the bow was pushing upwards, impatient to take off.

The change in motion came abruptly as the vessel moved beyond the sheltered harbour waters and nosed into open sea. Still holding her back, the helmsman eased her round the outer marker buoys and then pushed the throttle forward a few notches, taking her up to about fifteen knots and bringing the bow even further out of the water. Life inside the forward well had got increasingly uncomfortable but then, like a horse switching from an easy canter to a full-blooded gallop, he opened her up. Within seconds the bow was completely out of the water and the vessel began to plane, the engine driving her forward at over forty knots and the bottom slapping against the water with considerable violence. Bracing his elbows and knees against the bulwarks to minimise the movement of his body, he steeled himself for a desperate ride into the unknown, relieved that he'd had the foresight to pad out his clothing.

The first phase only lasted about ten minutes as the engine was suddenly cut so that, initially, there was complete silence except for the waves lapping against the vessel's sides. Then the sound of the waves changed and he could hear them breaking gently on a nearby shore. The man was moving about restlessly in the cockpit before abruptly returning to his seat, re-firing the engine and very cautiously easing her closer to the shore. Something knocked against the stern before the sensation of extra weight being taken on at the back transferred itself to the bow. That was when he heard the sound that sent a chill down his backbone. The voice was English. Ugly, clipped Essex accent. Short sharp half phrases barked out aggressively followed by another voice. English. Female. Surly. London. His heart was beating fast.

In an instant the helmsman was back in his seat and this time he made her fly. If the rendezvous was roughly equidistant from the Albanian and Italian shores, they had about forty miles to cover. Now the vessel had settled into a rhythm he realised that, uncomfortable though he felt, he could handle it. Closing his eyes he bounced across the wave tops of the Adriatic. The secret cargo of the Sacra Corona Unita and their latest English recruits.

After about an hour the engine noise receded and the bow dropped. Someone came forward on the starboard side and threw the drag anchor over the side. The earlier breeze had vanished and the sea was remarkably calm with hardly any swell at all and, after a moment, the engine was cut. He could hear the sounds of the two male voices but not clearly enough to follow the conversation. Bits of English and bits of Italian floated through the air but it wasn't possible to make sense of what was being said. A little later the female voice surfaced, obviously having emerged from the cabin to see if the Albanian boat had appeared. Slowly he noticed an edge creep into the tone of the voices. Impatience, anxiety, then, as the minutes passed, anger. Within the anger he identified a particular sound coming from the man with the Essex accent. A mix between a cold cruel laugh and the baying of a wild dog.

Then, from out of the blackness of the night, he heard the noise they had all been straining to pick up. The drone of a powerful engine in the distance but growing louder by the second. Instantly, the voices in the cockpit became animated and he risked moving, now actually kneeling with his eyes right up against the open hatch. One of the men must be standing on the platform at the stern because he could see a tall shape above the level of the windscreen and the bimini top had been taken down. Then the sound of the other engine came right alongside, faltered, before cutting out and the men began shouting to each other loudly enough for him to hear.

"Name?" demanded the Essex accent.

"Klodjan," came the Albanian response. "And you?"

"Ray."

"OK Ray. How you got the money?" Klodjan called.

"Three suitcases. All US Dollars. Fifty thousand in hundreds. Two hundred thousand in fifties," came the response.

"I come on board. Refiq has Uzi. Like you. He watch while I count," the Albanian directed.

"You bring the stuff on board with you, then," Ray countered. "It's meant to be forty percent pure. Marco will check it."

"No. Marco come here to check while I with you."

The voices went quiet and then he was aware of the two vessels bumping against each other and heavy footsteps moving backwards and forwards as the two men obviously crossed paths. After some more bumping and banging he saw again the figure of a man on the stern platform, struggling with something heavy, so it was obvious that the heroin was now coming on board and being stored on the platform at the back. This fitted exactly with his information which had specified that even if any attempt was made by the Police or Coastguard Patrol to intercept the boat at sea, the smugglers simply pressed a button on the dashboard which tilted the platform and the evidence disappeared forever into a hundred fathoms.

"We're ready for the girls now, Klodjan," the Essex accent shouted across.

"OK. We bring them up," the Albanian replied.

It had never occurred to him that the trafficking may not be confined to drugs, but may also include a human cargo and it concerned him that the small cabin and cockpit may get cramped, causing some to sit on the front deck, increasing the chance of discovery.

Albanian gangsters ran prostitute rings right across Europe and young girls out of Kosovo, Serbia and further east were bought, raped and subjugated and then shipped on to the mainland. Ever since he had heard the female voice on board he had tried to puzzle out why she had been brought along and now it became clear. When the bewildered human traffic came on board they wanted a female to take control of them.

Despite the risk, he pushed firmly on the edges of the hatch to force it up a couple more notches to get a better view of how many of these unfortunate women they were bringing on aboard. The hatch made a grinding noise as it moved and he held his breath for a second, but the men were obviously too pre-occupied to notice. The extra few inches gave him a clear view. The Albanian vessel stood higher in the water than the '*Brucia dello Scorpione*' and he was now able to see that it was pointing in the opposite direction so that the stern was closer to him, with one of the Albanians standing silently on the deck, sub-machine gun crooked in his arm.

With the bimini top on the Italian boat now down, he was able to pick out Marco in similar pose with his Uzi and, for the first time, he could actually see the man called Ray outlined on the stern platform, cradling a similar weapon. There was no sign of the girl. Straining his eyes to get a clearer view of Ray's face disclosed little detail of his features as he was wearing a dark woollen hat pulled down over his ears and low over his forehead, with a heavy three quarter length coat which had its wide collar turned up, making any attempt to pick out features impossible. There was still no sign of the girl as Klodjan appeared from below on the other boat and stood right against the handrail no more than twenty feet away from him. Even in the dark, illuminated by only the occasional shaft of moonlight, he could see the hard angles of the jaw, the white meanness of the face and the cruel shape of the mouth.

"There's three women," Klodjan shouted. "Schtie, Refiq."

In the instant that Klodjan uttered the command in Albanian the whole night was filled with the ear-splitting sound of bullets screaming through the air and the frenzied light flashing in the muzzle as Refiq responded to his cue and Klodjan started the engine of their vessel. For several seconds the shattering noise continued, unopposed by either of the men in the *Brucia dello Scorpione* who had been taken completely by surprise. The world order had changed. Where once the Sacra Corona Unita were the Masters, they were now being reduced to the ranks of the dispensable. In the space of a few seconds the Albanian had emptied his magazine and Ray lay slumped over the stern platform while the Italian was grotesquely draped over the helmsman's chair. From within the cabin the girl's screaming began, getting louder as she pushed open the door to discover what had happened.

He knew he only had a couple of seconds to react. There were no girls. The Albanians would quickly board the *Brucia dello Scorpione*, reclaim the heroin and, now that they were aware that there was a woman on board, they would kill her too, then him, before sinking the boat. It was kill or be killed.

Desperately feeling for the magazine in his pocket, he grabbed the Spectre 4, rammed the magazine hard inside and levered open the hatch. His body was stiff and it was awkward to pull himself out of the bait well quickly while at the same time swinging the Spectre into position to fire. The Albanian killer was actually on the point of jumping across to the forward deck of the *Brucia dello* Scorpione' when he saw the movement in the area of the hatch and immediately brought his weapon up to firing height. But, in the same way he hadn't given either the Italian or the Englishman a chance, the Albanian was ruthlessly gunned down in a hail of automatic fire and crashed headlong into the Adriatic as Klodjan, instead of firing back at the mystery man who'd appeared from nowhere, threw forward the power lever on the Albanian vessel and sent the craft screaming into the night, leaving behind a scene of complete carnage.

The waves lapped gently against the side of the boat while the girl could be heard whimpering in the stern and the body of the dead Albanian drifted slowly southwards with the current. He manoeuvred his way around the windscreen, the Spectre held straight out in front of him ready to shoot again if the girl made any attempt to get to the cockpit controls and activate the tilt on the stern platform but, as she came clearly into view, he could see that she was cradling the head of the Englishman in her lap, still whimpering. Keeping the muzzle trained on her, he placed a finger on the side of the Mario's neck to detect a pulse, but Refiq had done a good job on him. The Uzi still hung from the corpse's arm and, plucking it from him, he hurled it overboard.

"Ray's really dead this time, isn't he?" he said quietly.

"Are ya going to kill me as well?" she whispered.

"No, Alicia. There's been enough death," he answered.

"Who are ya? Your voice. I've heard it before," she declared, still gently stroking the head wearing the woollen cap.

"I want to see his face," the man responded.

"Kempner," she spat. "Under that black stuff you're fucking Kempner, ain't ya?"

"Pull his hat off. I want to see his face," the man insisted.

"How the fuck did you get here?" she screamed at him. "You're satisfied now, are ya?"

"I didn't come here to kill him, Alicia. I came to hand him over to the Italian Police. Together with his heroin. Before he had the chance to dump it in the sea. You should be grateful. If I hadn't been here you'd be floating in the Adriatic. Now, like I said, I want to see his face."

As he spoke he moved a step or two nearer the girl, watching her every move in case she, too, was armed but, when he came closer, she simply hugged the dead man tighter, her hands covered in blood from his wounds and tears streaming down her face. Kempner could see that she wore a jumper and tight jeans with no sign of any weapon. Still training the Spectre on her he reached out his hand and pulled the woollen cap off the head which lay in her lap. The right side of the head was uppermost and he winced as he saw the extent of the damage. The ear consisted only of a narrow, vertical welt of cartilage and flesh, about the thickness of a finger and there was an indented channel running across the temple.

"You bastard," she hissed as she looked up to see him staring at the damage Pal had done. "He's been to Milan three times for plastic surgery. Two more operations and he'd have looked alright."

"OK, I've seen enough," Kempner breathed, "we're heading back. The Bari cops have arranged a welcome committee on the Lecce road. When we get close to your beach I phone a number and they close in. But we had to get Ray with the drugs. Now it's all down to you. You'll take the rap. Let him go and get down below."

"I ain't moving from Ray," she answered defiantly, holding him even closer.

"You'll do as you're told, lady," he replied, reaching down to the deck where Millard's Uzi lay silent. Tossing it into the Adriatic, he grabbed her upper arm in a vice-like grip and pulled her away from the stern while she continued to writhe and protest. Keeping his body between her and the cockpit controls he wrenched open the half door which led to the small cabin and pushed her through. A dim light set in the bulkhead revealed that it was barely larger than a cupboard, with a narrow bunk on the port side, a few cans of Coke rolling about on the floor and a couple of boxes of tackle in the far corner. Satisfying himself that there were no other weapons down there, he threw her on to the bunk, directly beneath the light and stared at her as she looked up at him like a cornered rat. Her face was so contorted with hatred that all her physical attraction had vanished and Kempner realised that Millard had found his perfect match.

"You'll stay here. I'm going to start her up and head back. I reckon I should see lights in less than half an hour. When I do I'm dropping the anchor and coming down to get your answer," he declared, backing out of the cabin.

"To what fucking question?" she snarled.

"Either I hand you in with a quarter of a million dollars worth of heroin and two dead bodies and you get twenty years in an Italian gaol or you talk," he said.

"To who?"

"To me. Like you've always said, I'm a cop. Cops are curious. I've worked most of it out, but there are gaps. I want to know it all. I don't give a damn about you or what happens to you. You tell me the story and I'll toss the bodies and the drugs in the drink, call up and say wasted trip and let you go. But if you keep your secret then I'll turn you in. Twenty years of Albanian dykes in an Italian sewer and imagine what you'll look like. A withered hag," he shouted the last three words at her, before slamming the door and heading back up into open air.

Dragging the two bodies on to the cockpit floor, he hauled in the drag anchor and left it on the forward deck before hitting the starter, bringing the wheel round until the compass bearing was just south of west and opened her up.

Perched aloft on the tall, comfortable chair this baby was like driving a Cadillac to the liquor store. Instead of being bounced mercilessly around in his bait well, now he was riding like a child on a magic rocking horse as the 'Brucia dello Scorpione' headed for home. Millard was dead and, hell, he was even beginning to enjoy the ride.

Half an hour later he cut the engine. The Italian coastline looked like a necklace with beads of lights twinkling on the horizon. By his reckoning he was probably a dozen miles off shore and just north of Lecce. In the immediate area and to the south the sea was just a carpet of black. Dropping the anchor, he pushed his way back into the cabin where Alicia was lying on her back on the bunk. He could see the dried tears on her face and Millard's blood on her hands and clothing. His sympathy factor remained at a steady zero.

"Decision time, lady," he snapped.

"I'll talk," she muttered.

"And I'll know if you're lying or holding back," he retorted, moving inside the cabin and sitting on the floor with his back against the door. "One lie or half-truth and the Bari cops can have you. They only prosecute if they have the drugs and a live smuggler. With Ray dead they'll settle for you and the smack, so you're warned."

As she began talking in a cold, defeated voice, he could only see her in silhouette, but it was a clear enough view for him to realise that whenever she spoke of Ray her tone assumed a tone of reverence, never more so than when she related his use of violence on her. Within a minute, her chilling words had carried him away from the bilges of a boat bobbing about on the Adriatic to Nolan's Barn in a small English village in the days when he used to work with Danny Rose.

"Middle of the night he rings the bell down at the gate and tells me to drive down. Bring me the spare mobile and five grand cash out the safe. Sounded bloody awful. When I gets there he's lying on the grass, holding his jacket to the side of his head. I helped him into the car and he grabs the mobile. Calls this tame quack who looks after the boys and says to expect us in half an hour. On the way he tells me Pal done him in the barn. Bullet went through his ear so he played possum. But he reckoned he'd got Pal with his knife 'cos Pal was groaning and buggered off."

"Where was this Doctor's house?"

"Chiswick."

"The quack tells him he's been lucky and he ain't going to die but he needs a plastic," she continued. "Ray says he's got to patch him up and he'll get to a plastic in a couple of days in Milan. The quack says he'll call me with a name in Milan the next day. Three hours it lasted. Patching him up. Ray's as hard as nails. Never squealed once. Quack says his cheekbone's bust as well, but it'll mend. Gives him some painkillers. On the way home he decided it was all on top. He owed millions and these geezers he was dealing with from Turkmenistan had fucked up his cash flow. Ecklund was the main problem. Ray owed him big and he'd smelled trouble when he went to see him. Soon as he mentioned his name the idea hit him. Turn a disadvantage into an advantage, he said. We'll get Don over and he can 'ave me spot in the fucking barn. He was bloody clever, Ray was."

"How did you ever get Ecklund to come to Radford?" Kempner asked.

"Ray figured that for the toughest part. Getting Ecklund away from his minder. We gets home. Ray grabs some kip and rests up. Late morning he phones Don on the mobile, says he's at Heathrow on his way to Ankara and'll be away a week, but last night Turkmenistan's shown up with three hundred grand. He wants Don to have it now. Ray's being ripped off on the interest. Every day counts. Don says he'll send his man round to the drum"

"Presumably 'his man' meant Shrader Miskin?"

"Of course. Ray says I ain't having that animal in me pad with Alicia. So Don says he'll come himself, but he ain't getting out of the Cruiser and no dogs. Alicia can bring the readies out and put 'em in the back. If he sees a dog or anyone else, then he buggers straight off"

"What's the Cruiser?" enquired Kempner.

"Toyota Land Cruiser. Don always has a Cruiser."

"Are you telling me that while all this was going on you knew Ray was going to kill Don?" Kempner asked, finding it hard to accept that she'd gone along with everything without any kind of protest.

"You've got no idea, Kempner. What the fuck am I meant to do? Warn Don? Call your lot? Walk away? Ray'd have me done an'all. I owed Ray. Ray owned me."

"But you liked the fact that he was so ruthless, didn't you? His violence excited you. I can hear it in the way you're talking."

"You know what he done to me when I kicked up a stink after he tells me about chopping Don up? He bends me little finger back. The top joint. 'Til it breaks. And when I screams he puts his hand over me mouth until I passed out. Don't tell me it fucking excited me," she spat back at him.

"But you stayed with him. You took more. You expected it of him. That was his power. And his power turned you on," Kempner retorted.

"I had to go down to Newbury Hospital that evening. Get it seen to. You saw me finger when you come to the house. Anyway Don shows up late afternoon. I opens the gate. He drives to the front door. Puts his rear window down for the money. You ever carried three hundred grand? Ray knows how many grand to a suitcase. 'Cept these cases are full of books. I struggles down the steps with the first case, gets it to the back of the Cruiser and tells Don I can't lift it up into the back."

"Don checks around. Asks where's the dogs. I tell him locked up. He gets out, picks up the case and next minute Ray's got a gun pressed into his spine. You've been to our house. You seen that life-size statue of Hebe at the bottom of the steps. Ray's hid behind it when Don come up the drive."

"I remember. One on each side. Great chunks of marble."

"Right, well Don says what the fuck you up to? Ray tells him he'll put a bullet in him if he tries anything. Ray makes that sound. You never heard it. Does it when he's excited about summat. Like a laugh, 'cept it's really creepy. Like an animal. Don's shitting himself. Ray walks him to the garage."

"The garage where you took Danny and me?"

"Yea. You wasn't to know but there was a gap between the cars when you was there. Where the Mini should 'ave been. Ray pats Don down. He's got a gun in his pocket. Ray tells me to chuck it in the Cruiser. Orders Don to phone Miskin and give him the shit about driving to Singapore and all that crap. One word out of place he tells Don and I'll blow your fucking balls off."

"Were you in the garage while this was going on?"

"Yeh. 'Cept for the minute when I chucks Don's gun in the Cruiser. When I comes back Don's stark bollock naked. Ray had made him strip everything off. That's when we saw the frog. Ray says that's one of your fucking poison dart frogs right by your bollocks. You're a bloody kink, Don. Then he made Don put on clothes he'd already brought down from upstairs. Ray's own clothes. The stuff I said in Court was true. Harrods and the Armani gear an'all that."

"Did Don realise Ray was going to kill him?"

"I dunno. I'm not sure. But he knew if he didn't do what Ray said then he'd be shot for sure. The next bit I didn't see. This is what Ray told me after. They walked up to the old piggery. Them stalls up the back. Ray pops him in the back of the head. Don never saw it coming. Ray picks up the axe out there and does him, you know what I mean. The head and hands an' all that stuff. Puts the hose on him. Waits 'til the blood seems to stop coming out. Goes and gets the Cruiser and lays him out on his back in it. Lobs Don's clothing in there an'all. Puts the head and hands in some plastic bags and puts them in there. Then leaves the water running for hours out in the stalls so the blood goes down the drains. That's when he comes into the kitchen. I says you're soaked 'cos he's hosed himself down to get rid of the blood on him. Later he puts his own clothes into the Cruiser"

"When did he give you all this detail?" Kempner asked, still horrified at the matter of fact way in which the girl was recounting such a horror story.

"He told me he'd popped him when he comes in the kitchen. Then he lets out that he's chopped him and I played up."

"You mean that's when he broke your finger?

"Yeah. So I goes to the hospital. I'm gone nearly four hours. When I get back Ray tells me the rest of it."

"Where?"

"In bed."

"What exactly do you mean by that?"

"You know what I fucking mean. You want chapter and verse do ya? He gave me the rest of the detail while he was screwing me" she drilled back at him.

"With his face ripped open by a bullet and after killing a man, mutilating his body and breaking your finger, he wanted sex?" Kempner asked incredulously.

"You jealous, Kempner? Sex with me and you forget your fucking troubles."

"And you were turned on by what he was telling you?"

"You want more details about the sex or you want the end of the story?

"Go on."

"He's already phoned Billy out in Staines. Arranged to be at Billy's yard at five in the morning. It's a crushing yard. Over a hundred grand Billy paid for this crusher. Ray had helped him raise the cash so he owed Ray. We gets up at three. I drove the Cooper."

"OK, stop there, Alicia. I want to take a look and see there's no shipping close. I've been down here quite a while," he said, looking at his watch and getting up from the floor. "I'll be back in a minute."

"There ain't much more to tell," she grunted, swinging her legs round off the bunk. "Anyway, I want some fresh air. I'm coming up."

Leading the way, he went straight to the controls and put his right hand over the stern platform tilt button in case she tried anything on. His left hand had already picked up the Spectre 4 from where he'd left it on the deck between the corpses. Sending the girl on to the forward deck, where she didn't have to stare at the bodies, he scoured the horizon. A large cluster of lights had appeared to the south, signifying that the Otranto fishing fleet was now moving northwards and he didn't want to come too close to another boat. He reckoned that another ten minutes and they'd have to be on their way. Alicia had sat herself down with her legs crossed on top of the hatch which had successfully hidden him earlier and, working his way round to the forward deck, he lowered himself down opposite her and told her to finish her gruesome tale.

"Ray left just after three in the morning. Got this woollen hat over his dressing somehow. So he didn't look as bad as before. Put a bag with money, passport, clothes and so on in the Cooper. He drove the Cruiser. Told me to give him half an hour. Then to drive the Cooper down to Nolan's Barn. When I get there I can see the Cruiser backed up against the barn doors. A couple of minutes later Ray comes out. Drives into the road. Closes the gate and then leads the way to Billy's yard. Billy was waiting and him and Ray went off into the back. It's a massive place. I stays put. Twenty minutes later Ray walks out and gets in with me."

"Could you hear the machinery?"

"Just about. It's an industrial estate. Billy's got acres of these wrecks. Some are crushed and sent out for smelting, others are kept for parts. Ray says the crushed Cruiser'll be a set of scaffolding by dinner."

"Did he tell you what he'd done in the barn?"

"Yeh. Lifted Don flat in his arms. Ray's as strong as an ox. Only had a dozen paces to go from where he'd backed the Cruiser up to the doors. Laid Don out in the barn just where Pal had done him. And he'd put Don in the same position on the ground as he'd been in the Cruiser. So it don't show he's been moved, he says. Ray thought of everything. His worry was that there was a pool of his own blood there and he'd spent ages hosing and scrubbing away his blood. That's it. He drops me off and takes the Cooper. Channel Tunnel by eight. He's at the plastic's in Milan by the following morning. His contacts are down here. I gets my orders about the house and cars and all that by untraceable mobiles. The rest you know."

"Have you told me everything?

"Yeh. Everything I know."

"No lies?"

"Do you fancy I could have made that lot up then?"

"No. I don't."

"So what you going to do? Go back on your word or give me a break?"

"Go back down below Alicia. Unless you want to witness two burials at sea. The Albanians have turned these waters into a death zone. Drug runners, illegals and hookers being murdered on their way west. Washed up corpses are a penny a dozen round here. I've no interest in seeing you locked up for ever and a day. Millard's already destroyed you."

Ushering the girl back into the cockpit, he watched as she stepped over Ray's body to get back to the cabin door. This time she didn't even give her lover a second look. Alicia was already thinking of the future. As soon as she'd gone below Kempner lugged the heavy bodies to the guard rail and, one by one, levered them up and over the edge. The mobster first, then Millard. He stood and watched them float away into oblivion. It reminded him of watching bloated rats float down the East River when he was a boy in New York. Rancid detritus. Several buckets of sea water to get rid of the blood and a touch on the green button on the control panel to despatch a quarter of a million dollars worth of heroin to Davy Jones' locker.

Half an hour later later they were standing by the scooter in a quiet alley in the town. Pulling out his phone, he called the number he'd been given for the Italian Police who were waiting on the highway near the beach and told them it was a no-show and they'd returned empty-handed. The girl had watched him closely ever since they'd got back into harbour, waiting for the double-cross and showing surprise when he seemed to be honouring his word.

"You ain't going to get me banged up, are ya?" she observed.

"I'll give you a ride to those '*trullis*' where you're living. I suggest you pack your bags and move on in the next twenty-four hours. I never want to see you again after tonight," he replied sharply as he pushed his pack into the storage area, straddled the scooter and moved forwards in the saddle to make room for her.

Riding along the narrow streets of Otranto and out towards the coast road, the first hint of dawn appeared as a thin pink line on the eastern horizon. The wind in their faces was already warm and, when he opened the throttle to get some momentum up the hill, she held him tightly round the waist and he could feel her pressing herself against him. With the sea on their right when they reached the open road, she put her head on his shoulder and her hair, flying in the wind, kept brushing his neck as she continued to ensure he could feel her breasts thrusting against his back. Alicia Daley knew every trick in the book and, plainly, the horrendous events of the night were now receding in her mind. When he slowed up at the junction with the side road which led to the '*trullis*', she took her arms from around him and he came to a halt. Swinging herself off the scooter, she stood alongside him with a half-smile on her face, looking at his unshaven, polish-smeared face.

"OK, Kempner. You kept your word. I s'pose I owe ya. Ya wanna come up and take a look in the '*trulli*'? Life has to go on, doesn't it?"

Jake Kempner was a red-blooded male and Alicia Daley was as sexy a woman as he'd ever set eyes on. She was relaxing now that she knew that she was free and the earlier lines of anguish in her face were already evaporating. The eyes were wide and big and she knew that her sensual attraction was returning. The provocative angle of her legs and body as she stood at the side of the road reminded him of an old Edward Hopper painting where one pregnant moment became frozen in time. But Kempner knew who she really was and the evil bastard that she'd been bedding for the last few years. That was enough for him.

"Like I told you, Alicia. I never want to see you again after tonight. Go back where you belong," he answered cruelly.

"And where might that fucking be?" she replied, her manner changing in an instant.

"At the bottom of the pile, lady," he declared, turning the throttle in his right hand and pulling away into the Italian night, leaving her to remember how her lover with his Ferraris and statues of Bacchus and Hebe, ended up with a bellyful of bullets in a foreign sea.

Chapter 52

Although it was mid-winter instead of the end of summer, the sky reminded him of September 11th. The clarity and intensity of the blue were the same, lulling the millions of ants scurrying around on the earth's surface into the belief that nothing so evil or cataclysmic could actually happen. New York would never be the same for anyone who had beheld the wickedness of that awful day or tasted the ashes of the aftermath. But England had taught him that, for better or worse, this city was his home. He knew its rhythm, its heartbeat, its hostility and its embrace. The rattle of the subway, the smell of the hot dogs, the harsh edge of the voices, the bumping frenzy of a taxi ride and the seduction of the lonely, late-night diner.

After Otranto he'd taken a slow week getting back to London, the train and bus allowing him to think and, the day after his return, he'd handed in his badge and, bidding no farewells, turned away and headed home. Joe Kritzeck had put in a word and two weeks later he was back at the old desk, picking up the dead and bleeding, dodging the bullets and walking the walk. A studio apartment in a loft on Bleecker Street. The very name made the hairs on the back of his neck stand up. This was where Jack Kerouac had found his soul and where Dylan had shown the world the early glimpses of his genius.

In the four months that he'd been back in the NYPD he'd heard nothing from Lauren or Danny. Ironically, the only news he'd picked up had concerned Pal, Jenna and Alicia. Before he'd left Bari he'd visited an Internet Café and sent an Email to Pal, with a copy to Danny, which read: "*Dead. Definitely. JK.*" Although he'd never received any response, not even from Danny, a few weeks later he'd received a call at the precinct.

"Kempner. This is Jerome Zayer. I got a message for you from my daughter," he'd reported, not troubling with any of the niceties.

"You've kissed and made up, have you?" he'd replied.

"No. Just one phone call to say she'd been acquitted and another last week to say they're living near Kingman, Arizona. She's still with that no-hoper," he grunted charmlessly.

"So what's the message?"

"Some woman who was involved in all this. I've written the name down. Alicia Daley."

"Yeah."

"She's dead."

"How?"

"In a flashy car with a French playboy in Cannes. Went off the road. Both killed."

After he'd put the phone down Kempner had poured himself a generous glass of Californian Zinfandel and thought about that stunning body, those big eyes and the scooter ride back from Otranto. Her looks had attracted the kind of man who used her and, in return, she'd learned how to deliver the bill. If he'd turned her in, as he knew he really should have done, she'd still be alive, cursing him from the depths of some stinking Italian cell. Despite himself, he was saddened at the waste of a life. A beautiful creature, corrupted, abandoned and wasted.

Over the months, alone in his apartment, he'd tried to make some sense of it all. The events that had led him to London, his eventual disenchantment with Lauren for never really recognising the selfishness of what she'd done and how, because of his own selfishness, he'd let Danny slip through his fingers.

Now he missed her like hell and he knew it would hurt for a long time to come. Whenever he pictured her it wasn't when she put Tisdale on the ground or bowled up at Oxford Crown Court with

Alicia in a pincer grip or with her Inspector's pips in some Leeds Police Station. His memory was always of her in that tiny basement flat. Barefoot. On her own. Wanting him. But left alone and in pain.

Last night he'd taken a girl to dinner. Pretty, good company and they'd both tried hard. But it didn't work. He didn't know why it hadn't worked for her, but for him the answer was easy. She wasn't Danny.

Tonight a cold wind was blowing in from the Atlantic, whipping across the East River and funnelling between the tall buildings and along the New York streets. The temptation was to turn on the TV, open another bottle and watch the evening evaporate, indulging in all kinds of 'what may-have-beens.' But he'd already decided that he was going to wrap up warm, walk into the Village and visit one of the cafes where the lonely people go. Maybe hear the next Dylan or meet a budding Kerouac.

In the back of his wardrobe he'd got an old stevedore's jacket, just like the one Marlon Brando wore in 'On The Waterfront' and he slipped it on. With blue jeans, a Yankees cap and a pair of heavy duty gloves he was a New York boy again and, as he made his way down the four long flights of stairs, he tried to persuade himself that tonight just might be the night when everything changed.

Stepping through the door on to Bleecker Street the cold hit him straight between the eyes and he pulled the jacket tight across his chest. As he started to cross the street a yellow cab came round the corner and inconsiderately stopped right where he was standing, so he had to walk back a few paces to go round it and then wait for some more traffic to pass. He heard the back door of the cab open and shut, considered for a second whether to jump in it himself rather than walk in this vicious cold but, before he'd decided, the cab saw a gap and shot into the flow of traffic. Some unknown force made him turn his head. That's when he saw the small figure, bending down to read the nameplates in the entrance porch of his apartment block. It felt like a cannon had exploded in his chest. Wearing a green bobble hat so that all her red curls were tucked out of sight and sporting a very English three quarter length tweed coat with brown check trousers, he couldn't actually see her face, but every line of her body, every angle, every movement of her head, told him exactly who it was.

Walking back towards the entrance, he stopped a few paces behind her.

"It's the top button, lady," he called in his richest New York accent.

Unaware that anybody had been there, she jumped when he spoke and turned sharply to look at him. There, in Bleecker Street, New York City, was that lovely face that he'd been picturing alone in a tiny basement flat in London. The intelligent eyes were glistening, the cold was making the cheeks even rosier than normal and, when she realised who it was, that wonderful smile lit up her whole face.

"I called Joe," she said softly. "He told me you weren't really seeing anyone."

"How long are you here for?" he asked quietly.

"One week. But I'm open to persuasion," she continued, the smile broadening still further.

"Come here, Rose," he breathed, walking towards her as she came into his arms. As he kissed her and held her tightly to him, life changed. He bid farewell to the ghost of his wife, wished Lauren well but released her forever and looked at tomorrow, without forgetting that dreadful September day.

"We'll get your stuff from your hotel later," he whispered to her. "But first, we have a dinner date. At a restaurant right here in the middle of Greenwich Village. And you'll never guess what it's called."

"Go on, Kempner," she laughed. "Chocks away."

"The Blue Frog," he grinned. "I read a review. It'll be perfect."

Slipping his arm around her shoulders they strolled along Bleecker Street in the direction of 'The Blue Frog', oblivious to the cold East wind. For Jake Kempner and Danny Rose everything in the world was right.